Angel
of
Death

Angel

of

Death

Rochelle
Majer Krich

THE MYSTERIOUS PRESS

Published by Warner Books

A Time Warner Company

MYSTERIOUS PRESS EDITION

Copyright © 1994 by Rochelle Majer Krich
All rights reserved.

Cover design by Rachel McClain
Cover illustration by Marc Burckhardt

The Mysterious Press name and logo are registered trademarks of Warner Books, Inc.

 Mysterious Press Books are published by
Warner Books, Inc.
1271 Avenue of the Americas
New York, NY 10020

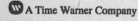 A Time Warner Company

Printed in the United States of America

Originally published in hardcover by The Mysterious Press.
First Printed in Paperback: January, 1996

10 9 8 7 6 5 4 3 2 1

For my beloved father, Abraham Majer,
and in memory of my beloved mother, Sabina
Tadanier Majer,
who survived to tell the story;

and in memory of the family I never knew
who perished with the six million:

My grandparents
Shlomo Chaim and Lana Majer-Mehler
Meshulam and Rochel Tadanier

and my aunts, uncles, and cousins

Tihiyena nafshoseyhem tzruros be'tzror hachayim.
"May their souls be bound in the Bond of Life."

"You want me to watch him?" Jesse wouldn't mind. She loved Matthew. She'd become close to him last summer, when he and Mom had stayed with Jesse for several months.

Acknowlegments

My thanks to the following individuals who were so generous with their time and knowledge: Det. Dan Andrews, Wilshire Division; Det. Paul Bishop, West L.A. Division; Byron Boeckman, Los Angeles Assistant City Attorney; Diana Casatro, Latent Prints, Los Angeles Police Department; Howard Gluck, Deputy City Attorney; Margo Gutstein, Assistant Librarian, Simon Wiesenthal Center for Holocaust Studies; attorney Mitchell Miller; Det. Dennis Payne, Robbery Homicide Division, Homicide Special Section.

Special thanks to my editor, Sara Ann Freed, for sharing my vision.

Finally, I'm indebted to my husband, Hershie, for giving me the seed of an idea that blossomed into *Angel of Death*.

RMK

Chapter One

In the glare of the headlights, the blood on the white door of the house glistened, slick and shiny.

It was *too* shiny, Detective Jessica Drake decided. She parked her Honda behind the black-and-white and hurried across a plush lawn carpeted with pale purple jacaranda blossoms to the uniformed policeman guarding the door.

The posts had been smeared dark red. In the same dark red, someone had painted a six-pointed Star of David in the upper part of the door; the star was centered around the peephole, an eye staring blankly at Jessie. Small globules had dripped from each of the points and coagulated, like droplets of blood.

A mean-spirited, day-late April Fools' joke? Jessie felt a twinge of revulsion at the hate that had inspired this act and shivered in her blazer.

She turned to the policeman. She hadn't recognized him, and he'd identified himself when she'd shown him her badge. Richard Garcia. He was in his early twenties, his clean-shaven face reddened with a few eruptions, leftovers of a stubbornly lingering adolescence, and stamped with the serious earnestness that labeled him a rookie.

"You answer the call, Garcia?" she asked, pocketing her badge.

1

"Yes, ma'am. Me an' my partner, Steve Kolakowski. He's inside with the Lewises now. I'm securing the crime scene."

Jessie nodded. She knew Kolakowski—he'd been with West L.A. for three years, and she'd seen him around the station. "What happened?"

Garcia read from a small spiral notebook. "The residents— Barry and Sheila Lewis—came home at ten-fifteen and found the door like this. The two daughters—ages seven and ten— were home with the housekeeper. Didn't hear or see a thing. A couple of TV reporters and a minicam van came but didn't stay. Lewis wouldn't talk to 'em."

Jessie didn't blame him. "What's the damage?"

Garcia shrugged. "No sign of forced entry. Nothing trashed inside. Just this door. I told the Lewises it was paint, not blood, but Mrs. Lewis couldn't stop shaking."

The wife's hysterical, the West L.A. dispatcher had told Jessie. Blood on the door. Possible vandalism inside. A death threat. Two units are there, but Lieutenant Espes wants you to check it out. So here she was—drama in Beverlywood on a Monday night. Except that the blood was paint, and there was no other vandalism. Probably no death threat, either. Even if there was, this should have been assigned to Crimes Against Persons (CAPS), not Homicide.

The wife probably *had* been hysterical, though—that would account for the lookers. Small clusters of women and men and two young children (what were children doing up past eleven o'clock, for God's sake?) had formed across the street and on the sidewalk several hundred feet to the right and left of the large, two-story house. Beverlywood was a quiet, upscale residential neighborhood; crime was no stranger here, but it wasn't as steady—or insistent—a visitor as it was in other parts of the city.

La Ciudad de la Reina de Los Angeles—Jessie's ninth-grade Spanish teacher had taught them the full name: City of the Queen of Angels. The queen and her angels were long gone; they'd probably moved to some small town in Oregon where the air was clean and the streets were safe. That's what everybody else in L.A. whom Jessie talked to was doing lately.

From the corner of her eye, she saw that the lookers to her right had stolen closer. She stared at them, watched them retreat. She was reminded of a game she and her younger sister Helen used to play with the neighborhood kids: *Mother, may I?*

She noticed a small puncture in the center of the door, below the star. "What's that?" she asked Garcia, pointing to the hole.

"There was a note tacked with a stick pin. Kolakowski has it."

The death threat? "You talk to the neighbors?"

Garcia nodded. "Nobody saw a thing."

Disappointing, but not unusual. Too bad the lookers weren't in force earlier. "I'll talk to the Lewises now," Jessie said.

"You'll want to use the back door, Detective. In case there's prints on the front doorknob."

Unlikely. Jessie would call downtown and have Scientific Investigation Division (SID) send out a photographer and a latent print expert to dust the knob and the surface of the door and doorjamb, but she doubted they'd find anything.

"You're right." She smiled at Garcia, remembering how much she'd appreciated approval when she'd been a twenty-one-year-old rookie. How much, almost fourteen years later, she still did.

She felt the lookers' stares as she walked toward the back, sensed their disappointment—in dark olive green wool gabardine slacks and a black blazer, with her long dark brown hair, tousled from lovemaking, brushed back hastily and held in place with a black velvet elasticized "scrunchy," she was hardly the quintessential cop. She resisted the urge to flip back her jacket and expose the 9mm Smith & Wesson sitting snugly in the shoulder harness she'd strapped on before she left her house.

And Detective Frank Pruitt. She wondered if he'd still be there, in her bed, when she returned, or whether he'd gone home. Probably the latter. His ex-wife, Rona, was in town with their two sons; Frank hadn't said, but Jessie sensed that he worried about his boys calling his apartment in the morning and not finding him in.

At the side of the house, she found a small gate. She opened it, stepped into the backyard, and pulled the gate shut behind her. Spotlights revealed redwood deck chairs and chaises around a large oval swimming pool in the center of a well-tended garden bordered with bushes and hedges. The air was filled with an almost cloying perfume of roses and jasmine.

Jessie walked to the back door and rang the bell. A moment later she heard heavy footsteps, then a male voice asking, "Yes?" She identified herself. The door opened. Kolakowski stepped outside and pulled the door half-shut. He was in his thirties, tall and muscular, with medium brown hair and a neat, clipped, reddish brown mustache.

"They're in the living room," he told Jessie. "She's calmer, almost like a zombie. He's pretty cool, considering. She's the one who called the station, by the way." Kolakowski squinted at her. "Jessie Drake, right? How come they sent you? You switch to CAPS?"

She shook her head. "The lieutenant wanted someone from Homicide." She felt a prickle of annoyance. Why had she been that "someone"? And why hadn't Espes ordered her partner Phil to come along? "Something about a death threat," she said. "I understand there's a note?"

"On the kitchen counter. Both Lewises touched it before we got here." He shook his head and rolled his eyes. "Shit, you'd think with all the cop shows on TV, people'd know better. And Lewis is an attorney, for Christ's sake." He snorted. "I asked them if they knew who could've done this. He said no."

Jessie asked Kolakowski to phone SID from his patrol car. She rubbed the soles of her flats along the concrete—jacaranda petals were beautiful but clinging—then entered the house and passed through a service porch to an enormous state-of-the-art kitchen. The cabinets and appliance panels were high-gloss white. The floor was white ceramic tiles with black-granite, diamond-shaped inserts. The same black granite, polished to a mirrorlike sheen, covered the counters. There wasn't a glass or plate or dish rack in view.

Just like *my* kitchen, Jessie thought, and smiled. She pictured the small rectangle and the rinsed and stacked—but not washed—dishes she'd used for the dinner she'd prepared for herself and Frank. Broiled lamb chops. Baked potatoes. A salad that, basically, had come preshredded in a bag from Pavilions supermarket. Judging from the thick butcher block square and the serious knives slotted at a rakish angle in a wooden stand on the center island, she doubted the Lewises ate salad that came from a supermarket bag.

A white slip of paper disturbed the sleek, uncluttered expanse of granite on the right counter. The note. It had been typed or printed via computer. Jessie leaned over and read it.

The Angel of Death spared your forefathers—will he spare you?

The Angel of Death.
"Blood" on the doorposts.
Jessie hadn't studied her Bible in years, but she'd seen Charlton Heston and Yul Brynner enough times in *The Ten Commandments* to understand the reference: After Yul Brynner—Pharaoh—had refused to let his Hebrew slaves leave with Moses, God cursed Egypt with ten plagues. Nine times Pharaoh relented. Nine times he recanted. "So it shall be written, so it shall be done," Brynner had intoned.

The final plague, the tenth one, was the most dire: God, through Moses, warned Pharaoh that all Egyptian firstborn males would die. The Israelites, following Moses's instruction, smeared blood on their doorposts so that the Angel of Death would know they were Hebrews and would pass over their homes. Their firstborn males were saved. Those of the Egyptians, including the son of Pharaoh, perished.

"So it shall be written, so it shall be done."

A grim ending for a ruler who reneged on his word one time too many and incurred the wrath of the God of the Hebrews.

But what did it have to do with Barry and Sheila Lewis?

Chapter Two

In the far corner of the large, step-down living room, a man was playing a one-note dirge on a black baby grand piano.

The room was permeated with the acrid odors of paint and lacquer. The bay window and two large mullioned side windows were draped in sheets; next to the windows, taped to the pristine pale gray walls, were swatches of material. There were more swatches on the square black marble-based glass table centered between two sofas upholstered in an abstract cotton print in pewter, black, and slate blue. Propped against the bottom left wall, their corners protected with padding, were framed lithographs that echoed the colors of the sofas. One of them would undoubtedly find a home above the mantel of the black marble fireplace.

"Mr. Lewis?" Jessie's voice echoed in the high-ceilinged room.

He turned sharply in her direction. "Yes."

"I'm Detective Drake." She saw his hazel eyes register first surprise, then a flicker of disappointment. Because I'm a woman, she knew. She wasn't surprised or particularly bothered.

He shut the piano lid, pushed back the black leather padded bench, and stood. The legs screeched on the bleached wood floor. Jessie winced, but Lewis didn't seem to notice the sound. He walked toward her. She met him halfway, almost sliding on the glasslike surface, and extended her hand.

"Barry Lewis." His grip was firm, but his palm was clammy.

He was in his early forties. About five feet nine inches, three inches taller than she was. He looked distinguished, if not handsome, in a black tuxedo that fit so well it had to be custom made. He'd undone the top onyx stud of his pleated shirt and the bow tie. Not a clip-on—she was impressed. His thinning dark brown hair was slicked back. His forehead was pronounced, as were his aquiline nose and round, elongated, Jay Leno chin.

"I'm terribly sorry about what happened," Jessie said. "I've talked with both officers, and I'd like to hear the details from you, and your wife." She looked around. Where *was* the wife?

"Sheila's resting. And I don't have any details to give you. You saw our front door, and the note. That's all I know."

"I understand," she said, responding not only to his statement, but to the weariness and impatience in his voice. She smiled. "But I *do* have a few questions. Can we sit down?"

"Of course." The diamond in his cuff link winked as he gestured toward the sofas and sat down.

Jessie sat down opposite him. "First, I'd like to know—"

"Barry, I checked on the girls again and—Oh, I'm sorry."

Jessie turned toward the woman standing in the entrance.

"My wife, Sheila." He introduced Jessie, then said, "Detective Drake needs to ask some questions, honey, but I told her you're drained. You don't have to stay."

"I don't mind." Her tone was listless, and she seemed to be half sleepwalking as she made her way, barefoot, down the three steps and over to her husband. When she sat down near him, the crinoline-lined skirt of her cobalt-blue taffeta gown popped up. She smoothed it down and played with the fabric.

She was several years younger than her husband and had pretty, though not exceptional, features. Her face was streaked with mascara, her blue eyes reddened and puffy.

She'd bitten off her lipstick, and the remaining maroon liner accentuated her pallor. Strands of tawny blond hair had escaped from her French twist. Cinderella after the ball.

Jessie took a notebook and pen from her purse. "What time did you leave the house, Mr. Lewis?"

"Six o'clock. We attended an AIDS benefit at the Beverly Wilshire. My firm—I'm an attorney with Haus, Berkman, Lowell, and Lowell—has been active in raising funds for AIDS research."

Jessie had heard of Haus, Berkman, Lowell, and Lowell. She nodded to show she appreciated the philanthropic efforts of Barry Lewis and his prestigious downtown firm. "Officer Garcia says your two daughters were home with the housekeeper. They didn't hear anything? See anyone approach the house?"

"Thank God!" Sheila whispered. "I can't bear to think the girls were home when this happened!"

"But they're all right, Sheila." Barry's voice was a gentle caress. He put his hand on hers. "Nothing happened."

"Something *could* have happened! Thank God Angelina didn't open the door! Those monsters could have pushed their way in, they could have . . ." She shut her eyes briefly and clutched a diamond-encircled oval sapphire suspended from a diamond necklace.

"Who is 'they,' Mrs. Lewis?" Jessie asked.

"My wife just meant whoever did this," Lewis said. "We have no idea who. I told that to the other officers."

"I see," Jessie said, wondering why Lewis was speaking for his wife. "Both the star on the door and the Angel of Death mentioned in the note have Jewish references. Do you have any idea why someone would vandalize your door in that way?"

"I *know* why," Sheila said. "Angel of Death refers to Passover. Passover begins Saturday night. They're warning Barry to drop the case."

"You can't *know*, Sheila. You can only surmise. This could be an unrelated, racist act."

Sheila looked at him a moment. "You're right. I can't

know." Her hand abandoned the pendant and kneaded another section of taffeta.

"What case is your wife referring to?" Jessie asked. And why was Lewis being so insistent about nothing?

Lewis cleared his throat. "I'm involved in a dispute with some members of the Los Angeles Jewish community. It concerns a client—actually, a group—whose civil rights I'm defending."

"Who's the client?"

"Hitler," Sheila Lewis said quietly. The word detonated in the room. "That's what some of the letters said."

Jessie stared at her, then looked at Lewis.

Color had flooded his face, but when he spoke his voice was inflectionless. "I'm representing the White Alliance, a group that has petitioned the court to parade in the Pico and Beverly-Fairfax neighborhoods on April twentieth to celebrate Hitler's birthday."

Neo-Nazis. Skinheads. There were pockets of them in L.A. County. Jessie had come across them from time to time, especially when she'd worked Juvenile. It was disheartening, and frightening, to hear impressionable adolescents mouthing hate-filled platitudes to justify the violent acts they committed against the "non-Aryan" enemy: Jews, Asians, Hispanics, African Americans, homosexuals.

"Those neighborhoods are predominantly Jewish," Barry said. "The residents are naturally upset about the parade. I sympathize with their feelings—I really do, especially since my wife and I are Jewish. I assume you figured that out from the note?"

In her mind Jessie saw again the somber message—"The Angel of Death spared your forefathers . . ." She nodded.

"But the First Amendment guarantees my client a right to conduct that parade," he continued, "and I'm committed to seeing that those rights aren't violated. Sometimes you have to defend your enemy to ultimately protect yourself."

Truth, justice, and the American way. Sounds like a rehearsed speech, Jessie thought. Which didn't mean that Lewis wasn't sincere—only that he'd delivered the speech numerous times. She wondered how many times. And to whom. And why *would* a Jewish lawyer be defending the rights of Nazis?

"Many of the residents are Holocaust survivors," Sheila added. "April twentieth is also Yom HaShoah. I think the detective should know that, Barry."

"What's Yom HaShoah?" Jessie asked Sheila, wondering if she was pronouncing the words correctly.

"Holocaust Remembrance Day. Our rabbi explained that it's always held on the twenty-seventh day of the Hebrew month of Nisan. This year that falls on April twentieth."

Jessie noted the information. "Did you ask your clients to change the parade date, Mr. Lewis?"

He nodded. "They claim it would be senseless to celebrate Hitler's birthday on any other day."

"How is it they came to retain you as their attorney?"

"They didn't. Rita Warrens—she's director of the American Civil Liberties Union L.A. chapter—asked me to take the case."

"Even though you're Jewish?"

"*Because* he's Jewish," Sheila said.

"We don't *know* that, Sheila." It was obvious from the note of long-suffering patience in his voice, almost a sigh, that this was well-traveled ground.

Jessie recognized that note—it had underscored many of her final conversations with her ex-husband, Gary. "Mr. Lewis, your wife mentioned letters referring to Hitler. Who sent them?"

He shrugged. "Most were anonymous. Some were from organizations. I've received flak from tons of people in the Jewish community. Hate mail, phone calls."

"Did you notify the police?"

"No. I didn't think it was serious." He lifted the stapled swatches and fanned through oblongs of nubby raw silk in deepening shades of gray and slate blue.

"Did you keep any of these letters?"

He shook his head. "Again, I didn't think they were significant. Frankly, I wasn't surprised to receive them. And as I said, I'm sympathetic to the feelings of the other side."

Not very lawyerly, throwing out papers. Neither was getting fingerprints on the note. "When did you receive the first letter?"

"Five weeks ago, as soon as I filed for my client."

"Where did the letters come? Here or to your office?"

"The office, mostly. A few here. Some to the ACLU office."

"And the calls?"

"The same. Our home number's unlisted, but when you're part of the Jewish community, your address and phone number get on lists. We give to the United Jewish Appeal and Jewish National Fund. We buy Israel bonds." He tossed the swatches onto the table.

Philanthropy, Jessie guessed, wouldn't win points for Lewis with the Jewish community now. "Has a court date been set?"

Lewis nodded. "This Wednesday, April fourth."

Just two days away. No wonder the "persuasion" had escalated. "We'll check the door and note for prints, but anything we find will be helpful only if we have other prints to match them against." Jessie sensed Lewis's hesitation. "I'll need the names of people you think may have done this, so that I can pursue this investigation." Or preferably hand it over to someone else.

Barry leaned forward, his elbows on his knees. "I don't see the point. You'll never find out who did this. Look, I'm angry and shaken up, but there's no serious damage. We'll have the door painted. Compared to other stuff I hear about, this is minor."

"What if they bring a gun next time?" Sheila's shrillness pierced the room. "You have to drop the case! We need protection, Barry. The girls . . ." Her eyes filled with tears.

"I won't be intimidated." Lewis's tone had a steely edge.

"Then give Detective Drake the names." Her voice quavered.

He moved closer to his wife. "They're venting their frustrations, honey," he said gently. "I don't want to exacerbate their anger by going after them." He rested his hand on the nape of her neck. "And I don't want to make this an ongoing media event. That's what they want, don't you see? I'm sure they're the ones who called the TV stations. You want to expose the girls to more of that?"

Silence. Jessie waited a moment, then said, "If you want to think about this, I can—"

"Talk to Joel Ben-Natan," Sheila said, turning to Jessie.

"Christ!" Barry muttered, then sighed. He removed his hand from his wife's shoulder and ran it through his hair.

Finally, Jessie thought. "Who's Ben-Natan? A rabbi?"

Sheila shook her head. "He's the leader of the Shield of Jewish Protectors. They were located in the Fairfax area, but I heard they moved."

"Are they part of the JDL?" Jessie had never encountered anyone from the Jewish Defense League, but she knew of the organization and its militant position against anti-Semitism.

"No. The Shield is a separate group."

"They're thugs," Barry said. "Hardheaded punks looking for a fight. Jews don't need their kind of protection."

"Not everyone agrees with you." To Jessie, Sheila said, "Ben-Natan's made threatening calls to Barry, here and at the office."

"What kinds of threats?" Jessie looked at Lewis.

"Like if I don't drop my client, I'll get mine. God'll get me. Stuff like that." He flicked lint off his trousers.

"That doesn't scare you?"

"Ben-Natan's full of shit. As far as God is concerned, I go with Sheila and the girls to temple on the High Holidays and a couple of other times during the year, but I'm not religious. Still, I think He'd approve. *I* know I'm doing the right thing."

Assurance or bravado? "How old is Ben-Natan?"

"In his mid- to late thirties. Why?"

I'm asking the questions, Jessie felt like telling him. "It could help us locate him," she said with practiced politeness. "Who else wrote you?"

"The Anti-Defamation League," Sheila said when her husband didn't answer. She kept her eyes on Jessie. "The Organization of Jewish Associations sent a letter signed by other Jewish agencies and most of the rabbis in the city." She waited for Jessie to write down the information. "The Simon Wiesenthal Center sent a letter, too—and the director called."

The Wiesenthal Center was in West L.A.'s jurisdiction. Jessie drove by it frequently. It was named, she knew, for the man who had survived the Holocaust and dedicated his life to hunting Nazi war criminals and bringing them to justice. Obviously, the center would have contacted Lewis. "Anyone else?"

"An Ezra Nathanson sent several letters, saying he wants to meet with Barry. His letterhead was from a school." Sheila frowned in concentration, then said, "Ohr Torah." She spelled the name for Jessie. "Strangers have written us. Neighbors have stopped us. It's been awful." She bit her lip.

Were those neighbors among the lookers outside? Was one of them admiring his or her handiwork? "That's it?" Jessie asked.

Sheila hesitated. Lewis was staring intently at his wife. "That's all I can think of," she finally said.

Jessie turned to Barry. "Can you add anything?"

"My wife's list is pretty thorough. I'm sure she'll call you if she thinks of anyone else."

Jessie found his snide tone annoying. "Your wife's doing the right thing, Mr. Lewis. You could be in serious danger."

"I doubt it." Barry Lewis stood. "Thanks for coming, Detective. I think we've taken enough of your time."

Jessie stood, too. "I'll be in touch. If you get any more letters or calls, let me know. Handle the letters as little as possible." She waited until he nodded curtly, then said, "And please save them, Mr. Lewis. Let *us* decide their significance."

Lewis pursed his lips and turned toward the fireplace.

Barry Lewis was probably right, Jessie thought as she walked out of the room—in all likelihood, the Star of David was theatrical more than threatening. Then again, she sensed that Barry Lewis probably *always* believed he was right.

She felt sorry for his wife.

Chapter Three

Yaffa Aloni was half-asleep when she heard the front door being opened. She rolled to the edge of the bed and slipped her hand between the mattress and box spring.

"Yoel? Is that you?" Her hand was on the gun. "Joel?" she called again, using his American name.

"Yeah."

She glanced at the digital alarm clock on the nightstand: 11:10. She got out of bed and padded to the kitchen. He was standing at the counter, pouring Heineken from a can into a glass.

"What took you so long?" she asked, her words swallowed in a yawn. Goose bumps appeared on her skin. She hugged herself.

"I had to stop at the office." He glanced at her. "You look tired. Go back to bed." He let the foam build, then topped off the glass and carried it and the can into the living room.

She followed him and watched as he placed the can on the rectangular wood table in front of the brown Naugahyde sofa. It was his table, and there were other rings from other beer cans; still, she wished he would use a coaster or a napkin. But she didn't want to start a fight. He had been distant lately and tense—because of the parade, she knew—and she sensed he would ask her to leave at the slightest provocation. She didn't want to leave him, even though sometimes, like tonight, she didn't know why she wanted to stay.

He sat on the sofa and took a swig of beer. With his free hand he picked up the remote control from the table and clicked on the TV. He selected channel two.

She sat down next to him, her legs tucked beneath her. "Is everything all right?"

He didn't answer her. He switched to channel four, then seven, then back to four. Nothing.

"Yoel?" She leaned against him and ran her fingers through his thick, curly dark brown hair. "Talk to me."

"Everything's fine." He drained the glass of beer, then refilled it. "Sorry. I have a lot on my mind."

Yaffa's lips were grazing the nape of his neck. She had pressed herself against him, and he could feel her unspoken longing through the thin ivory silk camisole. He knew he'd been neglecting her lately. Turning, he traced her lips with his finger. He held her face in his hands and kissed her mouth. When he heard "Coming next, an update on plans for a controversial parade," he pulled away and looked at the screen. A swastika and Star of David appeared over the anchorwoman's head.

His stomach twisted. "Wait," he said. He stroked her arm absentmindedly during the commercial break but said nothing. When the anchorwoman reappeared, Joel hunched forward. He rested his arms on his thighs and brought his clasped hands beneath his chin.

". . . defaced the home of Sheila and Barry Lewis of Beverlywood." A shot of the white door with the blood-red star flashed on the screen.

Joel grinned. "Nice. Very nice."

Yaffa inhaled sharply. "Did you do that, Yoel?"

". . . Mr. Lewis has declined to be interviewed," the anchor continued, "but Channel Four News has learned that the vandalism is probably connected with the parade planned by a group of neo-Nazis for April twentieth. Mr. Lewis, an attorney with Haus, Berkman, Lowell, and Lowell, is representing the ACLU. . . ."

"Mamzerim," he said in Hebrew. "All of them, bastards."

"More to come," the anchorwoman said. "Tomorrow night, part two in a five-part series. . . ."

"Did you?" Yaffa asked again.

"More to come, Mr. Lewis," Joel promised, and saluted the television screen with his glass of beer.

Chapter Four

"We decided we wouldn't name names."

They were lying in the dark. It was the first time Barry had spoken since the detective had left over an hour ago. Sheila had gone upstairs to check on the girls again, and when she'd entered the master bedroom, the lights were off and he was in bed, his arms folded behind his head, his eyes locked on the ceiling. She'd changed into a nightgown, leaving her gown a stiff, semicollapsed tent of blue taffeta on the carpeted floor, and slipped between the cold sheets on her side of the king-size bed. She'd found the silence oppressive but had learned from experience that trying to break it would just extend her punishment.

"I want you to drop the case," she said, drawing strength from the darkness. "These neo-Nazis *hate* you. They hate me, the girls. If they had their way, we'd all be in concentration camps."

"You think I don't know that?" He propped himself on his elbow. "I hate my client, Sheila. I hate the idea that they're going to parade in Jewish neighborhoods. My parents are survivors, for God's sake! But if we limit the rights of one group, who's to say whose rights will be limited next? Blacks'? Jews'?" The filtered moonlight coming through the window cast his face in shadow and darkened the familiar, resolute set of his jaw.

"There are other lawyers, Barry. Let one of them handle this case."

"I can't do that. I *won't* do that."

She was silent, listening to the *whoosh* of the warm air entering through the central heating vents. "What if you're wrong, Barry?" she finally said. "What if your First Amendment doesn't apply here? I've talked to some people. They think—"

"Since when are you an expert on constitutional law?" He lay down with an abrupt movement that jounced the mattress.

She was startled by the intensity of the anger that coursed through her. He was so stubbornly righteous, so smug in his conviction, that she wanted to shake him. She clenched her hands. Her nails dug into her palms. "You have the ACLU line down pat, don't you?"

"It's not a line, goddammit! I can't think of anything more important than the First Amendment."

"Not even your family?"

"Get off it, Sheila! I don't need this crap from you, too."

"You volunteered to take this case, didn't you? Did you want to please Haus, Berkman, Lowell, and Lowell, the WASP partners in your very WASP firm? Did you want to prove that being a Jew won't keep you from being a team player? They're all ACLU members, aren't they?"

"Yes, they are." He leaned over her. "I'm committed to protecting constitutional rights, Sheila. And I'm committed to showing my loyalty to the firm. Haus, Berkman, Lowell, and Lowell pay our bills," he whispered, his breath fanning her face with his anger. "They pay for the girls' tuition at Crossroads. They paid for your Lexus and your jewelry." He fingered her diamond tennis bracelet. "They paid for the baby grand and the new kitchen and the decorator who brings you swatches so your drapes will match your ten-thousand-dollar sofas."

"I don't need all this. Not at the expense of our safety."

"Don't you?" He paused. "Well, in any case, it's too late to give it all back, isn't it?"

She hated him for being right, hated herself. "What if . . . what if they harm the girls?"

"They won't." He drew her closer. "I need to know you're on my side, Sheila."

He was always so sure of himself. Always right. "Of course I'm on your side, Barry." She knew she should say "I love you," but she wasn't sure she did, not anymore. She was too consumed with anger and fear. He was placing them all in terrible danger.

He kissed the hollow of her throat, then her mouth. She put her arms around his neck and felt his hands caress her and decided that if anything happened to the girls, she would kill him.

Chapter Five

"Have a seat, Drake," Lieutenant Karl Espes said without looking up from the mound of papers on his desk.

"Thank you." Jessie sat on a beige vinyl padded chair and waited for Espes to finish riffling through the papers.

It was still strange seeing Espes behind the desk that, until less than a month ago, had belonged to Lieutenant Jack Kalish. Kalish had taken an indefinite leave to nurse his wife, who had suffered a mild stroke. Everyone at West L.A.— Jessie included—had expected Bernard Morales from their division to fill Kalish's spot, but the powers above had appointed Espes from Foothill.

Physically, the two lieutenants were strikingly different. Kalish was tall and angular with intelligent brown eyes and graying dark hair. Espes was broader but shorter—about five feet ten inches—with light brown, close-cropped hair. He had small brown eyes and sharp, pointed teeth that reminded Jessie of a rodent. She'd said so to her partner, Phil Okum; he'd told her she just didn't like change and should give Espes a chance. Phil was probably right.

Espes neatened a stack of papers and weighted them with a stapler. "Tell me about the Lewises."

Jessie described the interview with Barry and Sheila Lewis. The front door. The note. "That's basically it," she finished.

"What's your take?" He picked up a pencil and rolled it between his palms.

"Lewis may be right—the note and the paint are dramatic, maybe overly dramatic. The note's sinister, but it's in the form of a question—'*Will* he spare you'—not 'He *won't* spare you.' Still, I think CAPS should follow up on Ben-Natan and the others."

Espes shook his head. "It's your case. You follow up."

She hesitated, then said, "It's not a homicide, Lieutenant."

The rolling of the pencil stopped. His eyes narrowed. "So?"

She chose her words carefully. "I could be of more use on a homicide. We're overloaded with old cases, plus we have three new deaths this week. And it's only Tuesday."

Espes was studying her face. "I'm fully aware of what our caseload is, Detective, and I know the day of the week."

"Of course. I'm sorry." Her face reddened.

He nodded, then started rolling the pencil again. "I've heard good things about you. You helped catch that psycho serial killer half a year ago. Got a commendation from Chief Hanson and a certificate from the mayor." He smiled. "You miss being on Task?"

She shook her head. "Not really." It had been exciting working downtown at Parker Center, the LAPD administrative headquarters, and there had been perks—a car at her disposal; no nagging need to call in every few hours; immediate, easy access to files and information. And after an initial rough start, she'd enjoyed working with Detective Frank Pruitt. But she'd missed being with Phil and the others at West L.A.

"The press liked you. Couldn't tear their cameras away from your face. Nice." He nodded. "This a comedown for you? A little boring? You miss the limelight?"

Her palms were suddenly sweaty. "No, sir."

He dropped the pencil onto his desk. "The Lewis case may not seem like much to you, but these people deserve our help. The Jewish angle's gotten media attention. The story made the eleven o'clock news. There's a blurb in today's *Metro*. Which means I need someone in charge who can handle the press. Someone like you." He paused. "That's a compliment, Detective."

Was it? "Thank you."

"The threat in the note may be real. I want you to talk to Ben-Natan and Nathanson and the rabbis. Is that all right with you, Detective?"

He was baiting her. Why? "It's fine, sir. Will I be working on this with Detective Okum?"

Espes cocked his head. "A detective of your caliber can easily handle a case like this solo. And as you pointed out, Homicide is swamped. Have a problem with any of this?"

"No problem, sir." What the hell was *Espes's* problem?

"You write everything up, Drake?"

"Not yet." It had been one A.M. when she'd returned home. It was ten after eight in the morning now. Unlike Espes, she hadn't had time to read the papers or watch TV. "I'll do that now."

"Good." Espes smiled again. "Keep me posted?"

She stood up. "Absolutely, sir."

Definitely a rodent, she thought as she crossed the large, partitionless room to the Homicide table. She felt like slamming her purse on her desk, but the miniblinds to Espes's office were open, and she sensed he'd be watching her with his beady eyes.

Her partner was standing in front of a bank of green file cabinets at the opposite end of the room, talking to two detectives from Burglary. At six feet two inches, Phil Okum was a large, well-proportioned man with a walrus mustache, a ruddy complexion, and protruding ears—"Your personal teddy bear," he had told Jessie more than once.

She needed a teddy bear now. "Hey, Phil," she called softly.

He turned and smiled at her. In one hand he was holding his omnipresent coffee mug, in the other a "blue book"—one of the loose-leaf binders that contained reports and photos related to a homicide. He saluted her with the mug, then walked toward her.

"Spilled some," he announced cheerfully when he was at Jessie's side. "I always fill it too high."

"No one'll notice." The industrial brown-gold carpet camouflaged most stains. "I just talked to Espes." She slumped down on her chair.

"Cold this morning. Radio said fifty percent chance of rain." He placed the blue book on his desk and drank from the mug. "So what's wrong?"

"My new case. A Beverlywood couple called the station last night. Espes sent me over to see what happened. Their front door was defaced with a Star of David, and—"

"Heard about it on the radio." Phil frowned. "But it's not a homicide."

"Tell me about it." Jessie repeated what had transpired in Espes's office. "I don't know why he's badgering me."

"Fight with his girlfriend? Bad hair day?" He shrugged.

"Thanks, Phil." She pulled over a sheet of paper to begin writing up her report. There were now two PCs in the room, but she rarely used them. Phil depended on them—his handwriting was barely legible.

"Coffee?" He held the mug in her direction. "It's half-decent today. Might perk you up." He grinned at his pun.

"Ha, ha." She grimaced, then smiled. "You know I don't drink coffee." Sometimes she felt as if she were the only person in Los Angeles who *didn't* drink coffee. Her parents did. Her sister Helen did. Her ex-husband, the crime reporter did—she'd given Gary custody of the Mr. Coffee machine they'd received as a wedding gift.

Frank Pruitt liked coffee, too, but she wasn't ready to invest in a coffee machine until she knew where their relationship was heading. Last night he hadn't been there when she'd come home—she'd expected as much but had been disappointed nevertheless. And he hadn't called this morning.

"Maybe Espes envies your success." Phil took another sip.

She swiveled toward him and frowned. "Why?"

"Ever since you were on the task force, people know who you are. Downtown people, too—like Chief Hanson. Maybe

Espes thought you were pushing your weight around 'cause you're a celebrity."

"I wasn't! This should be handled by CAPS, Phil. Espes knows that. He gave me a line about how my former relationship with the press will be helpful!" She paused. "I've been friendly since he arrived. I haven't asked for favors."

Phil held up his hand. "Don't preach to the choir, Jess. I'm just telling you what Espes may be thinking. Look, I'm sure this is just temporary. You do things his way—no fuss—he'll relax."

"Maybe." She wasn't about to hold her breath. "You ever hear of a group called the Shield of Jewish Protectors?"

"Nope. Must be new. Are they bugging Lewis?"

"Yeah." Jessie told Phil what Sheila Lewis had said about the group. "She gave me some other names, too."

"Why do you think Lewis doesn't want you to go after the guys who decorated his door?"

She shrugged. "He said something about not wanting media attention and not wanting to exacerbate the situation."

"He use that word, did he? *Exacerbate?* Must be a top-notch lawyer." Phil smiled.

"Top-notch firm." Jessie smiled, too. "Maybe Lewis is feeling guilty. A Jew defending neo-Nazis."

"He seem guilty?"

She thought for a moment, then said, "Not really. But he may not have wanted to show it. Or he may be repressing his feelings." She knew about repressing feelings. She'd done it throughout her childhood and later, during her three-year marriage to Gary. It was one of the reasons, she'd come to realize, that the marriage had failed. It was something she was trying not to repeat in her relationship with Frank.

"This psychological stuff's too deep for me," Phil said. "I'll leave that to you and the wife. Maureen's *always* talking psychology to me and the boys. We love her anyway." He smiled and drained the contents of his mug. "I have to go downstairs to Records. Behave yourself around Espes till I'm back."

She watched him pass through the double doors, the coffee mug in his hand, then dated the blank sheet of paper and began writing. After a few minutes she picked up the phone and punched the numbers she had come to know so well.

"Robbery Homicide, Special Crimes Section. Yaeger speaking."

"Frank Pruitt, please."

"Pruitt's off today. Do you want to leave a message?"

"No. No message, thanks." Jessie hung up. Frank hadn't mentioned having the day off. He was probably taking the boys somewhere. With or without Rona? she wondered suddenly.

She phoned Central Division to air her complaints about Espes to her friend Brenda Royes but learned she was out in the field. Jessie left a message, then went back to writing up the report. When she was done, she flexed her cramped fingers and stretched her arms above her head. Then she sat back and read the four-page report, checking it against the notes she'd written at the Lewis home. She nodded, pleased with her work. It was concise, thorough, accurate. Espes, no doubt, would find something wrong with it.

Don't get defensive, she told herself. Maybe the bit about the press connection is true. She read the entire report one more time, recalled the tension in the house, Sheila Lewis's urgency, her husband's arrogant nonchalance. Typical of an attorney.

Jessie wondered again why Lewis had been careless about protecting the hate note from fingerprints, why he hadn't retained the letters he'd received from those protesting his support of Hitler's birthday parade, why he'd been so irritated with his wife when she'd given Jessie a list of names to pursue.

She hadn't given Jessie *all* the names—Jessie had noticed the woman's hesitation and Lewis's silent direction.

She wondered what names Sheila Lewis had omitted.

Chapter Six

The Shield of Jewish Protectors was out of business—according to the phone company, at least. An electronic message informed Jessie that the number she'd called had been disconnected and that there was no new listing.

From directory assistance, she learned that there were no listings for Joel or J. Ben-Natan in Los Angeles County. Ben-Natan had probably unlisted his number. More and more people were doing that. In Ben-Natan's case, considering his high profile and controversial activities, it would be prudent.

Jessie walked over to the desks on the wall opposite the bank of lockers and sat down in front of one of the two computers used for networking with other government systems. From what Barry Lewis had said, it was likely Ben-Natan would pop up somewhere on criminal records; the problem was, Jessie couldn't search for him unless she had a birth date. She had only an approximate age—Lewis had said Ben-Natan was in his mid- to late thirties.

This was the tedious part of detecting, the part they never showed on *Hill Street Blues*. Silently thanking Lieutenant Espes, Jessie accessed the Department of Motor Vehicles automated name index and CALOP (California Operators License) files, entered "Joel Ben-Natan, thirty-five years old," and waited.

Ben-Natan was an unusual name. Still, she was prepared for the computer to rebuke her with a "too many probables" message. So she was pleasantly surprised when, seconds later, the screen presented her with only eight names and their cities of residence. She repeated the search, listing Ben-Natan's age first as thirty, then forty (CALOP scanned for names within a five-year range of the age entered) to make certain she wasn't losing him in the overlap. When she was done, she'd added fourteen names to her list.

She was damn lucky, she saw immediately—she could eliminate seventeen of the men. They lived well outside of Los Angeles County, several north of San Francisco. Of the remaining five Ben-Natans, one lived in Santa Monica. One in Beverly Hills. One in West L.A. The fourth in North Hollywood, the fifth in Van Nuys. Sheila Lewis had mentioned a Fairfax location for the Shield of Jewish Protectors, but she hadn't been certain that the organization—or Ben-Natan—was still there.

Still accessing the DMV system, Jessie switched to DLF (Driver's License Files) format. DLF provided a replica of the front of a driver's license, minus the photo. It also listed traffic tickets and accidents and relevant information, including the date of the offense, the license number of the automobile involved, and the court date, if any.

She fed in the first of the five names and areas of residence and printed out a copy of the file. She repeated the process for the second and third names. The third Joel Ben-Natan, the one who lived in Santa Monica, had a history of moving violations and parking tickets. Maybe that was her man. Or was she stereotyping, assuming that someone who had made vocal threats against Barry Lewis would be reckless in other ways, too?

She typed in the fourth name and residence.

"Phone for you, Jess," Phil called from across the room.

The data appeared on the screen. "Who?" she answered without turning. Phil didn't answer. She swiveled around, saw Espes standing in his doorway, and understood. A personal call—Phil didn't want Espes to know.

Frank? "Be right there." She activated the printer, cleared the screen, typed in the last entry, and printed out the information. Holding the five sheets, she returned to her desk, forcing herself to smile at Espes on the way, and picked up the phone. "Detective Drake."

"Hi, Jess."

Disappointment flashed through her. "Hi, Helen," she said to her sister. "What's up?" She sandwiched the receiver between her shoulder and ear and scanned the top paper in her hand.

"I just called to say hello. But you sound busy. Maybe I should call you at home, tonight." Her voice quivered with hurt.

You are too damn sensitive, Helen, Jessie said to herself, but she *had* been abrupt. Because Espes was watching? Or because Helen wasn't Frank Pruitt? "I'm a little busy, but I have a minute. Everything okay?" She hoped there wasn't a crisis. With Helen there was frequently some minor crisis.

"Everything's fine. Neil has an engineering conference in Tucson this weekend. He'd like me to come down Saturday."

"Sounds like a good idea to me." It was a positive sign. There had been a point several months ago when Jessie had worried that Neil would leave Helen and move back to Winnetka, Illinois. And take their eight-year-old son Matthew with him. The family counseling was obviously helping. Thank God. Unconsciously, Jessie rapped her knuckles on her desk.

"The thing is, I don't know where to leave Matthew, Jess. The sitter he likes, Corinne, isn't available. She has a friend she says is reliable, but Matthew's never met her, and I don't know . . ." Helen's voice trailed off.

"You want me to watch him?" Jessie wouldn't mind. She loved Matthew. She'd become close to him last summer, when he and Helen had stayed with Jessie for several months.

The closeness had deepened after Helen and Neil had moved to Los Angeles three months ago.

"I don't want to impose."

Then why are you calling? Jessie shook her head and smiled. Why couldn't Helen be direct? "I'd love to do it. It'll be fun." Frank probably had weekend plans with his boys. Maybe they could all get together. Or was it too soon?

"You won't have to go to the station on the weekend?"

"Unlikely." Not as long as she was stuck baby-sitting Barry and Sheila Lewis. "If something comes up, I can take him to Paige's." Paige, Jessie's neighbor, had a son Matthew's age; the two boys got along well together.

"Thanks, Jess. We'll be back late Sunday evening."

"No problem." Espes, she knew without turning, was looking at her. She could feel his eyes boring into her back. "I have to go, Helen. We'll talk details later. Give Matthew a hug for me."

She placed the receiver in the cradle, thought about Helen and Neil and Matthew, then shook her head to clear her thoughts. Focus on Joel Ben-Natan, she told herself. She studied the five sheets. She was drawn to the Santa Monica Ben-Natan, the one with the parking and traffic violations. She returned to the computer, accessed County Criminal Records, entered his name and birth date, and waited.

The screen remained blank, then reported, "Cannot locate." So much for stereotypes; she smiled, then entered the next two names and birth dates. Nothing. She entered the data for the fourth Ben-Natan and was rewarded with a screen full of information.

Joel Ben-Natan of North Hollywood, age thirty-six, had an interesting history. Over a period of five years, he'd been arrested numerous times, primarily for failure to disperse, disturbing the peace, unlawful assembly. All misdemeanors. Mickey Mouse stuff. For the first offense he'd received a slap on the wrist and probation. For the next one, sixteen months later, two nights in a local jail and a three-hundred-dollar fine. The most recent arrest had been a year ago for unlawful assembly and disturbing the peace. The judge had set bail at five hundred dollars, ordered Ben-Natan to perform twelve hundred hours of community service, and sentenced him to four months of weekends in jail.

If Ben-Natan was responsible for the Star of David on the Lewises' door, he hadn't taken his punishment all that seriously.

Or maybe he considered what he was doing community service.

Jessie phoned Records and Identification. From the booking slip package, she verified that this was indeed the Joel Ben-Natan affiliated with the Shield. She asked R&I to fax her a copy of Ben-Natan's mug shot. A minute later she held it in her hands. The facsimile was faint, but she was able to make out dark, curly hair, a square chin, large eyes that stared almost defiantly at her. All in all a handsome face and not a bad photo, if you ignored the strip underneath the chin with the booking number.

From R&I Jessie also learned Ben-Natan's phone number. She couldn't be certain the number was current, but the prefix—818—fit North Hollywood. If it wasn't, and if his number was unlisted, OCID (Organized Crime Intelligence Division) at Parker Center could help her—although that could take days, she knew from experience.

She leaned against her desk and, studying the photo, tried the phone number she'd been given for Ben-Natan. After three rings a woman answered.

"Is Joel Ben-Natan there?" Jessie asked.

"No. He is out of town until tomorrow. Who is calling?"

At least it was the right number. "A friend." The woman sounded sleepy and had an accent Jessie couldn't identify. Mideastern or European, she decided.

"What friend?" The voice was suddenly sharp, slicing through the sleepiness and an aborted yawn. "Who is this?"

Was she exhibiting caution or suspicion—because another woman was calling Joel? The 5.10 form from R&I hadn't mentioned a wife. Was she his girlfriend? Sister? Colleague?

"I'll call back," Jessie promised.

Or maybe she'd just drop by. The surprise would shock Ben-Natan into confessing to painting the Star of David and writing the note. She'd lead him off in handcuffs to West L.A. and hand him over to Espes, who would smile at her with his beady little eyes and commend her on finding the guilty party and let her get back to solving homicides.

Yeah, sure. Jessie smiled and hung up the phone.

Chapter Seven

"I'm going," Morris Lewis said. "My lunch is ready?"

"It's in the refrigerator." Rose placed the two cereal bowls on the white drainboard and shut the faucet. Wiping her hands, she saw from the corner of her eye that her husband was checking the contents of his brown lunch bag. She smiled.

"No cake?" he asked.

"You had this morning."

He shrugged. "A thin slice."

She shrugged back.

"I'm living in a jail," he grumbled good-naturedly. He re-folded the bag and put it on the counter. "I look all right?"

It was the same question he'd asked for most of the forty-eight years they were married. Though he prided himself on his strength, he had long ago lost the firm, muscular tone of his youth. His shoulders were sloped, his belly rounded. His remaining hair, once brown, was now almost white. She gave him the answer she always gave, the one that, to her, was still true.

"Like a million dollars." Rose smiled again, deepening the lines around her warm brown eyes and mouth.

She adjusted the knot on his tie and smoothed the shoulders

of his charcoal-gray tweed sports jacket. He always wore a jacket and hat to work; the minute he arrived at the building supply business they owned, he stored them in a closet in the back office. The tie always stayed on. Rose kissed his cheek.

"You smell nice," Morris said. "Something new?"

She nodded. "Calyx. By Prescriptives."

"It's a perfume or a pill?" His eyebrows rose to an exaggerated height.

They both grinned. She hesitated, then said, "Sheila gave it to me for my birthday."

"Very nice." The grin had disappeared. "What time will you be back from the Hadassah meeting?"

"I told Molly I can't make it."

Morris frowned. "You don't feel good?" He touched her face.

She put her hand over his. "I'm fine. It's just . . ." She dropped her hand. "They showed the house again, on the news this morning." She saw Morris's lips straighten into a grim line. "I'm not in the mood for people's questions."

His face and the scalp on the top of his head were blotched with sudden anger. "Who said they'll ask questions?"

"On the phone, Molly said, 'So how's Barry?' She wanted to let me know *she* knew."

"Go to the meeting. They have questions, let them ask me."

She shook her head. "After." The word had taken on monumental significance in their home: After the court hearing was over. After the parade date came and went. After the notoriety died down. After their lives were back to normal. If ever.

The court hearing was tomorrow. Maybe there would be no parade, she thought, but the twisting of her stomach muscles told her otherwise. "Go to work," Rose said, giving Morris a gentle shove. She tried a smile. "I'll be fine."

Morris left the kitchen to get his hat from the hallway closet. Rose dried the breakfast dishes and put them back in the cabinet. Then she took the filled trash bag outside to the narrow paved strip behind the garage where the barrels were stored.

She opened the lid of the nearest barrel and was surprised to see a pair of black shoes. She lifted out the shoes, put the bag of trash into the barrel, and closed the lid. As she entered the house, Morris was returning to the kitchen. He was carrying his worn brown leather briefcase and a gray felt hat.

"You threw these out?" Rose showed him the shoes.

"The heels are almost gone, and there's a big hole in the right sole. It doesn't pay to have them fixed." He placed the briefcase and hat on the counter and held out his hands. "Give me the shoes. I'll take them back outside."

"You bought these not three months ago. Already they're ruined?" She turned over the shoes. Stuck to the soles were pale purple petals. She took the shoes to the sink and brushed the petals into the sink.

"I can afford, thank God, new shoes. I can afford twenty pairs of new shoes." His voice carried a hint of impatience.

It was a statement, she knew, not of boasting, but of proud accomplishment. She had come to this country almost fifty years ago as Morris Levitsky's bride. She and Morris had been penniless, beaten. Orphaned. Haunted by the shadow of Europe. But Morris had been determined to escape the past. He had changed their name to Lewis. He had worked hard as an employee in a dry goods store and saved his money to buy the building supply business and eventually move from a small apartment to this house on Martel Avenue. And he had provided their two children with everything, including a Harvard Law School education for their oldest son.

Rose sighed. "So buy twenty pairs. But since when are you such a waster?" She studied the soles. "The hole's not so bad. I'll take these to the man on Ogden. He'll fix the sole and put on new heels." She turned the shoes back over. "What's this?" she said, pointing to the toe of the right shoe.

"What?"

She scraped at the leather with the nail of her index finger. "It won't come off." She looked up at him. "It's paint." Red paint. She flashed to the Star of David on the house in Beverlywood. Their son's front door. She felt sick, weak-kneed.

Morris frowned. "Let me see." He took the shoe and peered at the toe. "Paint," he agreed. "Last night while you were playing cards by Bernice, I finished the chimney on the doll house. I must have dripped paint on my shoe. Sloppy." He looked at Rose.

She nodded. "It's almost finished, the doll house?"

"Almost. A couple of weeks, it'll be done."

"And then we'll take it over to the girls?" she asked softly.

He was silent for a moment. Then he said, "I miss them. It's not their fault, is it, that our son is friends with Nazis?"

She shook her head. Her eyes welled with tears.

"Maybe after." He handed her the shoe, then put on his hat and picked up his briefcase.

"Like Cary Grant," she said. Her voice was thick.

"Yah." He sighed and pecked her cheek.

After Morris left, she took the shoes and went into the workroom he had partitioned from the two-car garage. The doll house was there, sitting on a tarp-covered worktable. The chimneys were slick red. Feeling disloyal, but unable to stop herself, she touched one of them with the tip of her finger. The paint was dry, not at all sticky. But why would it be sticky?

She studied the paint on the shoe. To her eye, the shade of red seemed to match the red of the chimneys. She found a rag, soaked a section in turpentine, and rubbed the toe of the Rockport until the stain had disappeared.

Then she threw both shoes into the trash.

Chapter Eight

"Making progress?" Espes asked, approaching Jessie's desk.

"I'm going to the Wiesenthal, then to Nathanson. Everyone else I called—Lesley Wittiger of the Anti-Defamation League, Mark Pell of the Organization of Jewish Associations, and Rita Warrens of the ACLU—is out. So is Ben-Natan. I'll check back with them."

Espes nodded. "Let's wrap this up. And Drake, make sure you handle this with kid gloves. These people are sensitive. I don't need any complaints that we're stepping on rabbis' toes."

She contemplated asking him why he'd saddled her with a job she didn't want if he wasn't confident she could handle it. Phil's eyes silenced her. "I'll be extremely diplomatic," she told Espes.

Her Honda was in the police lot on Butler. She exited the lot, turned right to Olympic, then east. As she passed Beverly Glen, she watched the towers of Century City rise to meet her, like the pages in a pop-up children's book. Twenty-six years ago, when she was an eight-year-old living in Los Angeles with her parents and sister, Century City had barely existed.

She parked on Pico. Dark gray clouds blanketed the sky and eclipsed the sun. A fine mist greeted her as she got out of

the car. Phil's weather report had been right—too bad she
hadn't turned on her radio this morning. Or borrowed his um-
brella. She hoped her new black suede flats wouldn't get ruined.

As she neared Roxbury and Pico, she was startled by the
street sign. It was silly, really—she knew that the city had
named the southeast corner of the intersection Wiesenthal
Square. She'd been in the area on the day the sign had been
erected.

The mist had turned into a drizzle. Jessie pulled up the collar of her black-wool jacket and quickened her pace. It had
been raining that day, too, she recalled. She and Phil had
questioned a witness to an armed robbery at a grocery market
that had left the Iranian proprietor dead. Walking along Roxbury to Phil's car, they'd passed a large square courtyard
filled with rows of unoccupied, waterlogged chairs. Around
the perimeter of the square, people of various ages had stood
unprotected in the blustery rain that, abetted by the wind, was
pelting them and whipping their umbrellas inside out. And
soaking the Marine Corps band that had remained erect, resolute, unsmiling.

Why are they standing in the rain? she'd wondered. And
why the Marine Corps? Then she'd remembered: this was the
opening of the Museum of Tolerance, a fifty-million-dollar
educational complex that offered a unique collection of exhibits and high-tech facilities. Jessie had read about it in the
L.A. Times.

The eight-story building was impressive, she thought
again—three graduated tiers of green glass bordered on either
side by walls of staggered dark salmon granite blocks. An imposing structure in a neighborhood of shops, delis, groceries,
and businesses. She hurried along Pico to the smaller, original
Wiesenthal, still its administrative headquarters, and, crossing
a courtyard, opened a wide glass door and stepped into a narrow lobby. She put down the collar of her jacket and ran her
fingers through her long hair, which had been flattened by the
rain.

Behind a desk to the right sat a swarthy guard with sleepy, heavy-lidded eyes that had watched her entrance. Jessie approached him, took out her badge, and held it open.

"I'm Detective Drake, LAPD. I'd like to see the director."

"I need to see your badge better." His hand was on his gun. His biceps bulged under his short-sleeved knit shirt.

She handed him her badge. His eyes flicked over her, then the badge, then studied her again. "I have to phone your station." He put her badge on the desk and picked up the receiver.

He had the same accent as the woman who'd answered Ben-Natan's phone. Israeli? Jessie gave him the number to West L.A. and told herself not to be annoyed—he was being conscientious and understandably wary, if abrupt. The center had a high profile. There had been bomb threats. Anyone could masquerade as a cop.

To her left was a gate; above it was the second floor, exposed except for a protective balustrade. Jessie could see people walking along the hall, some to the left, some to the right.

The guard hung up the phone and returned her badge. "You have an appointment, Detective Drake?"

"No. But it's important that I speak to the director."

"He's called dean, not director. He's probably busy."

"Maybe he's not." Jessie smiled. Now she *was* annoyed. "Why don't you check." She pointed to the phone on the desk.

The man debated a moment, raised the receiver to his mouth, punched three buttons, and turned his back to her before he spoke. Then he replaced the receiver and faced her.

"The dean is busy." He sounded smug. "His assistant will see you." He jerked his thumb in the direction of a foyer on the other side of the gate. "You can wait there."

"Thanks." A buzz released the gate. She opened it and walked toward a bench at the far left of the foyer. The wall above the bench was filled with brass plaques. One of them bore the likeness of Simon Wiesenthal. Others were covered with etched inscriptions. She leaned closer to read them.

"Detective Drake?"

Jessie turned toward a thin, harried-looking woman in her late twenties. She was wearing a cream-colored sweater over a brown leather skirt and had dark brown suede boots. Nice boots. Jessie wondered if they were waterproof.

"I'm Adina Raskin. How can I help you?" She had a young, high voice that held curiosity and wariness.

Jessie was used to eliciting that reaction in people. She smiled. "I'm investigating the vandalism of the Lewis home." She saw recognition flash across the woman's face. "I need to speak to Rabbi Korbin about it."

"He's very busy right now. Perhaps I can help you?"

"I'm afraid not."

The woman tucked a strand of straight blond hair behind her ear, then turned to the guard. "Boaz, please enter Detective Drake's name in the log. She'll be with me."

A grunt from Boaz. Jessie followed Adina up a wide, brown-carpeted staircase to the second floor, then continued left to an open door halfway along the hall.

Adina ushered Jessie into an office. "Please wait here." She pointed to a chair in front of a desk, then left the room.

There was a calendar on the desk. Jessie turned it toward her. Over today's appointments, which had been crossed out, someone had written in large red letters "ADL/OJA. STAT." ADL was obvious. So was OJA—the Organization of Jewish Associations. She returned the calendar to its original position. God, what luck! She'd save herself two trips. Save time, too. Wouldn't Espes be pleased.

A moment later Adina Raskin reentered the room, accompanied by a thin, wiry man in his fifties with a graying goatee. It was Korbin. Jessie recognized him from his numerous media appearances. "I'm Sheldon Korbin, the center's dean," he said, a half question in his gravelly Brooklyn-accented voice. His brown eyes looked serious behind tortoise-tone metal frames.

"Jessie Drake." She extended her hand. After a hesitation so brief she wondered if she'd imagined it, he shook her hand

and quickly released it. Maybe it was a religious thing. "I know you're busy, Rabbi. This probably won't take long."

"I'm involved in an important meeting, Detective, but I'd be happy to take a few minutes to answer your questions. We can talk here."

"Your office would be better. I'd planned to meet with the ADL and OJA people, too." She saw his startled expression. "Miss Raskin didn't reveal anything."

"Then how . . . ?" His eyes went to his assistant, then to the calendar on her desk. He turned to Jessie and smiled good-naturedly. "A little detecting?"

"That's what the city pays me for." She smiled, too.

"As a citizen, I'm glad we're getting our money's worth. But I should probably warn my colleagues that we'll have to watch our steps while we talk to you."

"Only if one of you has something to hide, Rabbi."

"Nothing to hide, Detective. And nothing to worry about."

Korbin's office was spacious and the furniture impressive—rosewood bookcases, a credenza with carved panels, and a large rosewood desk cluttered with papers. The walls were covered with framed photos of Korbin posing with various national and local political figures, including former Los Angeles mayor Tom Bradley. Former president Reagan. Bush. Clinton.

Pell and Wittiger were sitting in front of the desk. They exchanged quick glances of surprise when they saw Jessie—obviously, they'd expected Korbin to deal with the police quickly, and alone. Korbin performed the introductions.

Lesley Wittiger was in her forties with chin-length, dark brown hair and piercing blue eyes. Mark Pell was taller than Korbin and older—in his late sixties or early seventies, Jessie guessed—with still thick gray-white hair and a slight paunch. Lesley Wittiger's gray wool suit looked like a feminine version of the suits the men were wearing. Their shirts were pale blue; her blouse was white. They all wore identical, somber expressions.

"I'll be direct," Jessie said. "Sheila Lewis says all three of your organizations sent her husband letters protesting his representing the group petitioning to parade on April twentieth. Last night someone painted a Star of David on the Lewises' door."

"I hope you're not suggesting one of us is responsible!" Pell exclaimed with a mild European accent.

It was a day for accents, Jessie thought. The woman who'd answered Ben-Natan's phone, Boaz the guard, Korbin—if you counted Brooklynese. Now Pell.

"Detective Drake hasn't suggested anything, Mark." Korbin smiled. "She's stating a fact, being direct, as she promised."

The consummate diplomat. Jessie had watched him several times on *Nightline*. "Any idea who *is* responsible?" she asked him.

"We spent years raising funds to build *Beit Hashoah*, the Museum of Tolerance. It would be a travesty if we encouraged—or condoned—any act that smacks of intolerance."

"The ADL would *never* condone an act of hate against anyone, Jew or non-Jew." With her hand, Lesley tossed back her hair and the suggestion.

"You're not upset about Lewis's actions?"

"I'm infuriated." Korbin leaned across his desk. His eyes flashed. "I think what Lewis is doing is reprehensible. I indicated that in my letter. I would say so to his face."

Nods of agreement from Wittiger and Pell.

Jessie deliberated before she spoke. Kid gloves, Espes had said. "Lewis says he's defending the group's constitutional right to voice their opinions. Their civil liberties."

"What about *our* civil liberties?" Pell's accent was more pronounced. A vein pulsed on his forehead. "My wife and I lost our families in the Holocaust, Detective. We came to this country because it promised us freedom and protection from persecution. Where is our protection now, can you tell me?"

Jessie didn't know how to respond. In investigating the in-

creasingly violent crimes that were becoming epidemic in the
city, she'd met victims who were Holocaust survivors. But
she'd never discussed their experiences with any of them.

Korbin said, "The men who drafted the Constitution didn't
intend to sanction the dissemination of hate and the incitement of violence. This group wants to intimidate, to cause
grievous pain to the Jewish community, especially to those
who escaped Hitler."

"Yemach sh'mo ve'zichro," Pell whispered hoarsely.

" 'May his name and memory be obliterated,' " Korbin
translated. "What they're doing is vile. What Lewis is doing,
betraying his own people, is unforgivable." He shook his
head. "But painting a *Mogen Dovid* on a door accomplishes
nothing."

"Mogen Dovid?" Jessie repeated, puzzled.

"The Star of David. Actually, *mogen* in Hebrew means
'shield' or 'protection.' "

Hardly a symbol of protection for Lewis, Jessie thought.
"Someone vandalized Lewis's door. You're important members of the Jewish community. You're in a position to know
things, hear things." She looked at Lesley Wittiger. The
woman shook her head. So did Korbin and Pell. A triumvirate
of silence.

"Whoever painted the star also left a threatening note,"
Jessie said, studying the three faces. "I'm pretty sure it refers
to the tenth plague: 'The Angel of Death spared your forefathers—will he spare you?' "

"Mengele!" Pell whispered. His face had paled.

"Josef Mengele, the infamous doctor who performed inhu-
mane experiments on the inmates of the death camps, was
also called the Angel of Death," Korbin said, his voice grave.
"But I think Detective Drake is right, Mark. This reference is
to the tenth plague, not Mengele." He stroked his goatee. "It
doesn't sound like a threat. More like a moral warning. A reminder that God can exact vengeance."

"But it *could* be a threat," Jessie said, and waited. No answer. "What's your next step, Rabbi, regarding Lewis?"

"I'll call him again today. I'll try to nudge any conscience the man may have buried inside him. But I don't plan anything violent, I can assure you."

Affirming nods again from Wittiger and Pell. Jessie was reminded of the miniature puppies people kept on the dashboards of their cars. A little push, and their heads bobbed for minutes. "Tell me about the White Alliance."

"They're a relatively new group," Lesley said, "organized by a man named Roy Benning. We don't know much about them yet. We're sure other neo-Nazi groups will join them, by the way."

"Like who?"

She shrugged. "There are over two hundred and fifty hate groups in the country, over forty thousand skinheads. Quite a few groups are here in Southern California. Take your pick."

"Insanity," Pell muttered, and Jessie had to agree that two hundred and fifty hate groups bordered on the insane. "I told you, Sheldon. We have to be ready. We have to be vigilant."

"We *are* vigilant, Ira." Korbin's voice held a shade of irritation. "We've been monitoring their actions. So has the ADL."

"Do you expect the White Alliance to win the petition?" Jessie asked.

"In 1977 Frank Collins won a petition to hold a neo-Nazi demonstration in Skokie, Illinois," Lesley said. "Skokie has a large Jewish survivor population. The ACLU lawyer who represented Collins was Jewish. Like Barry Lewis." She spit the name. "In the end, Collins decided not to come. After all that."

"But they were going to demonstrate in front of Skokie Village Hall," Korbin said. "The White Alliance plans to parade through Jewish neighborhoods. They distributed leaflets warning that they're coming in storm trooper uniforms with swastikas. We can argue 'incitement to riot,' 'fighting words.' "

Pell shook his head. "In Skokie the Nazis warned they were

coming with swastikas, too. The lawyers argued the same things. Lewis will scream First Amendment. There's going to be a parade." He turned to Jessie. "The Jews of Los Angeles are angry. I hope the city plans to have extra police at both parade routes."

"I'm sure we'll be notified," Jessie said, aware of the repressed fury in his voice. "Are you planning an official presence?"

"Nothing's been decided," Korbin said. "On one hand, the less attention we give the parade, the better. They're doing this to get media attention and gain credibility. On the other hand—"

"So we let the sons of bitches march near our homes?" Pell exclaimed. "Why are we afraid to stand up for ourselves? Six million people were murdered, and we learned *nothing?*"

"We haven't ruled out a counterrally, Mark," Korbin said in a soothing voice. "Here, in front of the Wiesenthal."

"Not good enough! In Canada this wouldn't happen. They know how to deal with hate crimes in Canada. We have to meet these Nazis"—Pell banged his fist on Korbin's desk—"and show them they can't get away with this. Not again."

"I think you're overestimating how many of these neo-Nazis will show up, Ira," Lesley said. "They'll have their parade. They'll go home. It'll be over."

"Hitler started with seven people," Pell said. "Seven." He held up seven fingers to illustrate his point.

Lesley sighed. "You're overreacting, Mark."

"Don't tell me I'm overreacting!" The vein in Pell's forehead was throbbing madly. "You weren't there! You can't know what it was like to see storm troopers breaking down our doors. Killing parents, sisters, brothers. Now they're coming again."

No nodding puppies now. The tension in the room was electric. "Some individuals have contacted the Lewises," Jessie said. "Ezra Nathanson, for one. Do you know him?"

Korbin shook his head. The other two followed suit.

"What about Ohr Torah? Nathanson teaches there."

"Ohr Torah is an outreach program," Korbin said. "It means 'the Light of Torah,' or Bible. The school provides classes for men and women of all ages and levels of knowledge about Judaism."

She noted the information. "What about Joel Ben-Natan?" All three faces were suddenly wary. "Could he be behind all this?"

"Ben-Natan's a wild card," Lesley said. "He wanted to work for us a while back. We turned him down."

"I admire his commitment to protecting Jews," Korbin added. "But I can't condone his methods. Violence breeds violence."

It sure as hell does. Pell, Jessie noted, had been silent on the subject of Ben-Natan. She stood. "Thanks for your time. And your candor." Korbin, she noticed, suppressed a smile. "By the way, I'll need a copy of the letter each of your organizations sent Mr. Lewis. You can fax it to the number on my card." She handed cards to Pell, Korbin, and Wittiger.

Pell stared at the card, then at Jessie. "Why?"

So I can learn which rabbis signed their names to the OJA letter. Aloud, she said, "I want to compare them with the letters Lewis received and make sure someone unauthorized didn't use your stationery to send his or her own letter."

Pell looked at Korbin. Korbin nodded. "I'll fax you a copy right away, Detective," Pell said. He sounded unhappy.

Korbin rose and escorted Jessie into the hall.

"Still think you're getting your money's worth?" she asked.

He smiled. "Absolutely." In a serious tone he said, "You think we're in collusion to keep you in the dark. I saw it in your eyes." He shook his head. "I don't like what Lewis is doing, but I like even less what happened to him. The idea of Jews fighting with Jews saddens me. It makes our enemies glad. If it's true."

Jessie nodded but said nothing.

"By the way, Detective, while you're here, why not tour the museum? It'll help you understand our antipathy to groups like the White Alliance and what they stand for. And to people like Lewis, who help them spread their hate."

"Sorry. I have to see Ezra Nathanson. Another time."

She walked along the hall and down the staircase, wondering if he'd noticed the blush that belied her words. It was true she had to meet with Nathanson, but she'd shied away from touring the museum, seeing the grim exhibits it had to offer. Exhibits of man's atrocities against man. It wasn't that she was squeamish—as a homicide detective, she'd seen her share of atrocities.

Enough is enough.

The phrase popped into her head. It was the phrase her mother uttered every time she saw a reference to a feature film or television movie or magazine or newspaper article that dealt with the Holocaust. "Enough is enough," Frances Claypool would say to her two daughters and husband, even though she herself had some distant Jewish relatives. "How many times do they have to go over this? Can't they forget about it already?"

Had her attitude rooted itself in Jessie?

Maybe I *will* tour the museum, Jessie thought. In the lobby, she signed the guard's log. She looked up toward the second floor. Korbin was leaning over the balustrade, watching her.

Chapter Nine

"... still no suspects. And the controversy about the upcoming parade continues. For more on that story and others, tune in at four. ..."

Emery Kraft shut off the television with his remote control. "Jews fighting Jews," he said aloud in the large, empty room. "Terrible." He shook his head. He reached for the telephone on the lamp table to his left and picked up the receiver. In a Rolodex on the mahogany butler's tray in front of him, he found the number he wanted, then placed the call.

"Barry Lewis, please," he said when the receptionist answered.

"I'll see if Mr. Lewis is available. Who's calling, please?"

"Emery Kraft."

"Will he know what this is regarding?"

"I don't think so, madam."

There was a slight hesitation. Then, "Please hold on."

A moment later a male voice came on the line. "Mr. Kraft? Barry Lewis. How can I help you?"

"I saw on television what happened to your home, Mr. Lewis. I feel terrible about it. I wanted to tell you that."

"Thank you. I appreciate your concern."

"I also wanted to say that I know how difficult this must be for you, taking a position that is unpopular with your people.

That takes courage, Mr. Lewis. I admire courage. It's a rare commodity in our nation."

"I'm simply doing what I think is right." Lewis paused. "May I ask what your connection is to this case?"

"No connection, Mr. Lewis. I'm a citizen concerned with protecting the rights of individuals to express themselves. Just as you are. I support your every move and wish you good luck tomorrow."

"Thank you. I have another call, Mr. Kraft. If you'll excuse me?"

Kraft smiled, deepening the lines in his face. "Of course. You're a busy man, I know. I'll be saying a special prayer for you, Mr. Lewis."

Kraft placed the receiver in its cradle. Then he pushed himself off the overly plump black leather sofa cushion and walked to a bank of mahogany cabinets built into the opposite wall. He opened a cabinet and was about to activate the button that would retract the theater-size screen. Instead he selected a VCR cartridge, inserted it into the videotape player, and resumed his seat on the sofa.

A moment later the screen was filled with newsreel images of Adolf Hitler in uniform, standing in a jeep surrounded by stone-faced marching Nazi infantry. Kraft relaxed against the leather.

The door opened. A large German shepherd poked his head into the room.

"Come here, boy," Kraft called. He slapped the sofa cushion twice.

The dog approached quickly, detouring around the expensive Oriental rug he had been trained to avoid. His paws clicked against the peg and grooved dark wood floor.

"Watch the movie," Kraft said. "These are the good guys. They are much maligned." He directed the dog's head toward the wall.

The dog glanced briefly at the soldiers, then turned back to Kraft and nuzzled his hand. The soldiers marched off the screen. They were replaced by a succession of black-and-white grainy photos of unsmiling women and children and bearded men wearing skullcaps, all staring straight ahead at no one.

"These are the liars," Kraft said softly. "See their eyes?" He yanked the dog's collar to get his attention.

The dog yelped, then bared his teeth and growled.

"Patience, boy." Kraft buried his fingers in the dog's coarse black-and-tan coat. "All in good time."

Chapter Ten

Rain stung Jessie's face as she exited the Wiesenthal lobby and hurried to her car. The sky, ominously gray, promised no relief. It was eleven-twenty; Ezra Nathanson wouldn't be available until ten after twelve. Jessie decided to have an early lunch at a neighborhood deli.

The deli, long and narrow, was filled almost to capacity. With the exception of two men, each sitting alone at a small table, and a woman accompanied by three blond children, Jessie saw pairs—pairs of women, pairs of men, several pairs of mixed-gender couples. She thought of Noah's Ark and wondered why—she rarely made biblical associations. Must be the investigation.

Jessie came to the deli often, most of the time with Phil—the place made terrific pastrami burgers. The sign in the window said the food was kosher, and though she'd never paid close attention to the people around her, she'd noticed before that many of the men who frequented the deli wore skullcaps; it was the same today. Pell didn't wear a skullcap; Korbin did, but he was a rabbi. Some of the women in the deli wore berets or colored scarves on their hair. Others were bareheaded. A mixed bag.

Jessie knew very little about Judaism. Years ago, rummaging through boxes for a baby picture for her senior yearbook, she'd found an aged, sepia-toned photo of a family—parents, grandparents, children. The men were bearded; the women wore wigs. There was something exotic about their dress, and Jessie had asked her mother about them. They were Jews, Frances had explained, distant relatives. Jessie had pressed for details, but Frances had had none to give her.

In high school and in college, Jessie had been friendly with Jewish students, but the topic of religion had never come up. Nor had it come up with Manny Freiberg, the LAPD psychologist to whom Jessie had turned for professional and personal help during the past few years. Manny made numerous references to his Jewish heritage, but they were always light, bantering. She wondered suddenly what he was thinking about the planned neo-Nazi parade.

Jessie's ex-in-laws were Jewish, too, but neither they nor Gary had expressed any interest in their religion or its rituals. When Jessie had asked Gary if he wanted a rabbi to perform their wedding ceremony, he'd declined. Frances, relieved, had arranged for a nondenominational judge to officiate.

Jessie paid for the burger, told the proprietor it was delicious as always, and used the pay phone to call Phil.

"Arrest anyone?" he asked when he came on the line.

"Hardly." She described the interview she'd conducted. "Any calls for me?" She didn't mention Frank's name, although it was no secret to Phil that she and Frank were seeing each other.

"Two. Brenda returned your call and said she'd phone you tomorrow. Sheila Lewis wants to know did you find out anything. A frightened lady, Mrs. Lewis. I told her you'd call her back."

"I will, later. I'm going to see Nathanson." She felt a twinge of disappointment that Frank hadn't called after their night together, then reminded herself that he was busy with the boys.

"Happy hunting," Phil said. "Espes sends his love."

"Kiss him for me, will you?" Jessie smiled and hung up.

*   *   *

Ohr Torah was on Pico near Livonia, across the street from Dunkin' Donuts. It was a small, pale yellow stucco storefront sandwiched between a dry cleaners and a dress shop that labeled itself a boutique but, judging from the tired-looking merchandise in the display windows, wasn't. On the front windows of Ohr Torah, curtained with a simple beige fabric, black stenciled letters spelled the name of the school in English and in Hebrew.

There was no canopy, and it was raining harder. The door was locked. It was sad how conscious schools had become about security, almost paranoid. As a cop Jessie could hardly blame them. It was sadder, too, and terribly frightening that in a growing number of junior high and high schools, the danger was often not from the outside, but from within. Kids bringing loaded weapons to school. Killing other students. She thought about her nephew and thanked God Matthew was only almost nine. Maybe by the time he was in junior high things would be better.

Probably not.

She rang the bell. Its strident *brrring* was muffled by the staccato *plink*ing of the rain against a metal gutter.

"Can I help you?" a woman's cheerful, static-laced voice asked from a speaker to Jessie's right.

You can get me in out of the rain. "Detective Jessie Drake," she announced into the speaker. "LAPD."

A pause. Then the woman said, "Just a minute, please." Her voice had traded cheer for caution.

A few seconds later Jessie heard approaching footsteps.

"I'll need to see some identification," the woman said.

So sad. "Of course," Jessie said. The door opened an inch, secured on top by a chain. She held her opened badge to the space. She knew the woman was studying the badge, comparing Jessie to her photo; she seemed to be taking an interminably long time.

I was years younger when that picture was taken, Jessie wanted to tell her. My hair was shorter then, fuller, not plastered by the rain. I had fewer lines around my eyes. I am who

I say I am. She wanted to be annoyed with this woman who was making her stand outside, shivering, but she understood her caution, even applauded it. Too many unsuspecting people became victims like those Jessie had seen when she was on Robbery, Sex Crimes, CAPS, Burglary. And, for the past four years, Homicide.

Finally the woman said, "Thank you." She shut the door. Jessie heard the chain being released. Then the door opened wide.

"Please come in," said the woman. "I'm Shulamit Cohn." She was in her twenties—pretty, with shoulder-length, medium brown, wavy hair. She was wearing an oversize burgundy sweater with a cable pattern and a long, straight denim skirt.

And boots. Everyone, it seemed, had known it was going to rain today except Jessie. Her shoes made squishy sounds as she walked on the pebbled gray-and-white linoleum.

"You're soaked!" the woman exclaimed. "I'm so sorry I kept you waiting outside."

"No problem. Can I freshen up somewhere?"

"Of course." She pointed to a door down the hall. "You can put your jacket here," she said, indicating a coat tree.

Inside the bathroom, a cubicle decorated in pale-gray-striped wallpaper, Jessie studied her bedraggled reflection in a small mirror. She took paper towels from the dispenser attached to the opposite wall and blotted her hair; then, using a scrunchy she found in her purse, she secured the still damp strands and twisted them into a knot. Not great, but presentable.

Shulamit was hovering when Jessie exited the bathroom. "I don't know where to reach the school's director. If you could tell me what this is about?" She was almost breathless with anxiety.

"I'm here to see Mr. Nathanson."

"Ezra?" She paled. "Is—is something wrong?" Suddenly, she pointed a finger at Jessie. "You're the one who called earlier!"

Jessie nodded. "Where is Mr. Nathanson's classroom?"

"He'll be finished in ten minutes. Can't you wait, please? He's one of our most popular teachers," she added.

It was a little premature for character references. Jessie smiled. "I won't interrupt the class. I'd just like to watch."

Shulamit hesitated, then pointed to the back. "The room to the left."

Jessie walked down the hallway and looked through the rectangular window on the door to the classroom. She counted sixteen people—more women than men, she noted— seated in a semicircle around the tall, rangy man in the camel sports jacket who she assumed was Ezra Nathanson. There was no apparent dress code. Two of the other men were also wearing sports jackets; three wore jeans and knit shirts. All except one had a skullcap. Some of the women wore jeans, too; others wore long skirts and, like the women in the deli, covered their heads with colorful scarves.

There was a desk in the center of the circle, but Nathanson was standing. He was gesticulating with one hand; the other was hidden in the front pocket of his brown slacks.

Jessie inched the door open as circumspectly as she could and took a seat at the back of the room.

". . . review the rituals of the seder, the special Passover home service we'll be conducting Saturday and Sunday nights, as we read the Haggadah, the story of our exodus from Egypt, the redemption of our people, the birth of a nation."

Several people twisted their heads to see who had entered, then returned their attention to Nathanson. He smiled at Jessie. He had a nice smile, she thought. Warm, sincere. But she had known criminals with warm, sincere smiles. Killers, too.

"Any of you have any special memories about the seder when you were kids?" Nathanson asked.

"Drinking four glasses of wine," one man said. "After two glasses, I'm asleep."

"Drink wine for the first, grape juice for the rest," Nathanson advised. "Or mix the wine with the grape juice."

"Eating matzoh," another man said. "Why do we do that?"

"Matzoh—flat, unleavened bread—symbolizes the haste in which the Israelites fled Egypt. There was no time for the bread they baked to rise. So on the eight days of Passover, we don't eat *chometz*—leavened or fermented grains. Instead, we eat matzoh."

Jessie liked matzoh—she found the crispy, large-squared crackers tasty—and though she realized it was connected with Passover, she hadn't known why. She listened intently.

"I remember hiding the *afikomen*," said a young woman with a paisley scarf. "My father could never find it." She smiled.

"Ruth is referring to the matzoh we eat at the conclusion of the seder," Nathanson said. "It's taken from the middle of the three matzohs each adult male has in front of him. The *afikomen* symbolizes the *korban pesach,* the sacrificial paschal lamb. In Egypt we were commanded to smear its blood on our doorposts so the Angel of Death would pass over our homes."

The Angel of Death again, Jessie thought. She shifted on her seat.

"I remember hiding the *afikomen,* too, but I never knew why we do it," said a woman with close-cropped gray hair.

"To motivate kids to stay up for the entire service. During the seder kids 'steal' the *afikomen* and hide it, then 'sell' it back. They're encouraged to participate in the seder. The youngest kids ask the four *Mah Nishtanah* questions—'Why is this night of Pesach different from other nights of the year?' "

"What's the going price for this *afikomen*?" asked a middle-aged man in jeans and a plaid shirt. "I want to know what I'm getting into."

"Depends on how savvy a businessman your son or daughter is, Marty." Nathanson smiled. "My nephew and niece ask for a board game or a trip to Universal Studios."

"My daughter always asks for a new outfit," Ruth said.

"Another Nintendo cartridge," said another woman.

"My kid would probably hold out for an Isuzu Trooper," Marty said. "What do I do, Ezra?"

"Your choice, but don't stick me with the bill." He grinned. Friendly laughter tinkled through the room. Jessie smiled.

"You know what I remember?" said another woman with streaked blond hair. "Opening the door for Elijah the Prophet. Does he really take a sip of wine from his cup in every home he visits?"

"Absolutely. Please don't disillusion me if you know better, okay?" Nathanson feigned dismay, then smiled.

"So why *do* we read the Haggadah?" Marty asked. "I mean, it's the same story year after year. What's the point?"

"To remember that God redeemed us from slavery." Nathanson's tone was serious. "We don't want to be complacent about our freedom. Complacency is dangerous. Look what happened in Nazi Germany. Look what's happening today, in our city."

There was a moment of silence as heads nodded in solemn affirmation. Jessie found herself nodding, too.

A thin, gangly young man with long brown hair raised his hand. "Ezra, last month we learned about the holiday of Purim and how Haman tried to destroy us. Would you say that Haman and Pharaoh are equally villainous?"

"Excellent question, Paul. No, Haman is far worse. Pharaoh killed our firstborn males because his advisers warned that his Hebrew slaves would revolt and overthrow him. Haman wanted to annihilate us for absolutely no reason. Haman is descended from Amalek. And we're commanded to blot out Amalek. *Yemach sh'mo ve'zichro.* May his name and memory be obliterated."

May his name and memory be obliterated—that's what Mark Pell had said about Hitler, Jessie remembered.

"That's why on Purim, every time Haman is mentioned in Megillat Esther, the Scroll of Esther, we use noisemakers called *graggers* to blot out his name," Nathanson added.

"Who's Amalek?" asked Marty. "I missed that lesson."

"Our archenemy, and, ironically, a grandson of Esau, the

twin brother of our forefather Jacob. Esau commanded his son and his grandson, Amalek, to destroy Jacob and his descendants. Amalek, on his deathbed, commanded his children to continue the crusade to the end of the generations."

"Talk about family feuds." Marty shook his head.

Nathanson nodded. "During our forty years of wandering through the desert after the Exodus, one nation after another attacked us. But the enemy that attacked us not for gain or retribution or out of fear, but out of malice, is Amalek. 'Remember what Amalek did unto thee by the way as ye came forth out of Egypt . . . and he feared not God. Therefore . . . thou shalt blot out the remembrance of Amalek.' "

"You used the verb 'is,' " said a ponytailed woman in jeans. "But Amalek has been dead for thousands of years."

Nathanson shook his head. "Amalek lives, Ellen. It's the personification of evil. In the fourth century before the common era, in what we now call Iraq but was Persia, Amalek was Haman, a direct descendant of King Agag of Amalek. In the 1940s in Europe, we believe it was Hitler—not because we have geneaological proof, but because of his all-consuming, baseless hatred of our people. That hatred is the banner of Amalek."

There was another moment of silence. Then Marty said, "The three faces of eve-il," and another wave of subdued laughter made its way around the semicircle.

Nathanson joined in, then said, "More or less."

"Who is Amalek today?" someone asked.

"The neo-Nazis and skinheads," Marty said. "The ones planning that damn parade. Too bad we can't blot *them* out with *graggers*."

A wave of murmuring assent. Jessie watched Nathanson.

"I don't know if they're Amalek." His tone was somber. "We can't jump to conclusions. At the same time, we have to be vigilant. That's what our history teaches us."

Mark Pell had talked about vigilance, Jessie recalled. *We have to be ready.* Did vigilance include painting a Star of David on the enemy's door?

"Not a great history," another man said.

"But it *is* a great history. It's a heritage of survival." Nathanson was gesturing with both hands. "Pharaoh and his soldiers drowned in the same Red Sea that opened to let the Israelites cross to the other side. Haman was hanged on the very tree on which he'd planned to hang Mordechai, Queen Esther's uncle. The king issued a new decree permitting the Jews to defend themselves. The Jews defeated their enemies." He paused. "I guess you could call it 'reversal of fortune,' Marty. Unfortunately for Haman, he didn't have Alan Dershowitz for legal counsel." Nathanson grinned.

Marty gave him a thumbs-up. "Good one, Ezra. Pretty cool."

More laughter. Jessie could see why the students liked Nathanson. He had an easy style that invited participation.

"That's it for today. Let Shulamit know soon if you'd like an invitation for one seder or two, so she can make arrangements. And if you're interested in watching how the special hand-baked matzohs are made, sign up. Tomorrow we'll talk about the symbolism of the foods on the seder plate. And I'll explain about *bedikat chometz,* the search for products containing fermented grains."

Most of the class filed out of the room. Jessie waited while the few remaining men and women talked to Nathanson. When they, too, had left, she approached him. He was very attractive and somehow familiar looking. She wondered if she'd seen him on the news. Facing him, she saw his black suede skullcap. From the back of the room, it hadn't been visible against his thick, curly, dark brown hair.

"Hi." Nathanson smiled at Jessie. "Something I can answer?"

"Why does Elijah the Prophet come to every home?" It had nothing to do with why she was here, but she was curious. Later Nathanson would hardly be in a chatty mood.

"During Passover we thank God for redeeming us from slavery in Egypt and pray for the future redemption that will accompany the coming of the Messiah. Elijah—or Eliyahu—

will herald that coming. So we set aside a special cup for him in every home, welcoming him and, hopefully, the Messiah."

"And does he really take a sip from every cup?"

"As a kid, I'd stare at Eliyahu's cup after we'd open the door to welcome him. I always saw the bubbles he made from taking a sip. Who knows?" Nathanson smiled again. "I haven't seen you around. What's your name?"

"Jessie Drake." She extended her hand; he shook it briefly but firmly. Then she said, "*Detective* Jessie Drake, LAPD."

He stared at her, then grinned. "You're kidding, right?"

She took out her badge, opened it, and showed it to him.

He studied it a moment, then said, "What are you going to do, Detective, arrest me for my poor attempt at humor?" His tone was light, but his hazel eyes were intense, and his body had stiffened.

"Can we sit down, Mr. Nathanson?"

"Your wish is my command, isn't it?" He pulled a chair around so that the back was facing her and straddled the seat, effectively setting up a barrier between them. "What's going on?"

She sat on one of the chairs in the semicircle. "Sheila Lewis told me you sent her husband several letters about the parade."

"Is that what this is about?" Relief flooded his face with color. "Yes, I sent the letters. That's not a crime, is it?"

Was the relief genuine? "Vandalizing property is."

"The Star of David?" Nathanson shook his head. "I didn't do it." The suede elbow patches of his jacket rested on the top of the chair. His hands were clasped, propping up his chin.

"Can you prove that?"

He raised his head off his hands. "What happened to 'innocent until proven guilty'?" He wasn't smiling now. "I was on a date last night. We went out for a late snack and coffee. I got home around eleven." The knuckles on both hands were white.

"What's your friend's name?"

"I don't want to implicate her."

"Implicate her in what?"

Nathanson was silent. Finally he said, "Eileen Pasternak." He told Jessie the woman's phone number. "It was a blind date. If you call her, who knows what she'll think?"

"I'm sorry."

"I'll bet. All in a day's work, huh?"

She was accustomed to sarcasm from the people she questioned. Generally, it masked fear. Generally, it didn't bother her. Now it did. That bothered her, too. "How many letters did you send?"

"Two. I sent them to him care of the ACLU office."

Maybe the ACLU had kept a copy. She would check. "When did you send the last one?"

"About a week ago. Why?" He stood abruptly, walked to his desk, and leaned against it, his arms folded across his chest.

Me teacher, you student? She ignored the question. "What did the letters say?"

"Why not ask Lewis? I'm sure he kept them. He must have quite a collection, I'd think."

"I'd like to hear your version."

He looked at her a moment, then smiled. "Lewis didn't keep the letters, huh? Probably made him feel guilty."

She reciprocated with a noncommittal smile. "What did the letters say?"

He shrugged. "Nothing threatening. I offered to meet with Lewis, to present my point of view."

"Why?"

"Because what Lewis is doing is vile. And because I think somewhere down the road he'll regret selling out his people."

"What if he thinks he's doing the right thing? Protecting the civil liberties of Americans?" She still wasn't clear about Lewis's motivation. Commitment to a political ideal, yes. But there was something stubborn about that commitment. And arrogant.

"I know the rhetoric—'We Jews should be the most vigilant about protecting the rights of others in order to ultimately protect ourselves.'" Nathanson shook his head. "Look, I respect the ACLU and their determination to protect our civil liberties. They're looking at this from a rigid, the-First-Amendment-rules-above-all-else position. Procedure is everything. Content and substance don't count. I disagree with that, but I respect their right to their opinion. What I can't respect, what I can't condone, is a Jewish lawyer helping Nazis spread their hate."

"What about the rights of the neo-Nazis?"

Nathanson gripped the edge of the desk. He leaned forward. "What about the agony of the survivors, Detective? What about *their* rights? Why should they be forced to relive the terror that haunted them for years? To see the military uniforms and the swastikas that will always be in their nightmares?"

Jessie didn't answer. In the sudden stillness she could hear the rain slapping the windowpane. She thought about Mark Pell and the family he'd lost. "You sound very angry. In your lecture you talked about Amalek, about evil personified. Do you think Barry Lewis is evil personified?"

He folded his arms against his chest again. "I am *very* angry. But I don't think Lewis is evil. I think he's misguided. And I didn't vandalize his door." He paused. "Other people are angry, too. I'm sure I'm not the only one who sent Lewis letters."

"Anyone specific in mind?"

"That's your job, isn't it? We have a precept in Judaism called *lashon hara*—literally, the 'evil tongue.' It's a prohibition against spreading harmful gossip or talking badly about someone."

"Even if someone's life is at stake? There's been a threat against Barry Lewis."

"Maybe it's just an empty threat."

"Maybe it isn't." Again she found herself suggesting something she didn't believe. She wondered idly whether constantly mentioning that Lewis was in mortal danger would make it come true.

Nathanson shook his head. "Sorry. I can't help you."

Can't or won't? "Do you know Joel Ben-Natan?"

Nathanson stared at her, then smiled. "Yes. I'm quite familiar with him."

"Do you think he could be responsible for all this?"

"*Lashon hara*, Detective."

There was an odd expression in his eyes. Jessie sensed he was playing with her. "What do you know about Ben-Natan?"

"Everything, and nothing." He was gazing somewhere beyond Jessie's head.

"Is this a riddle, Mr. Nathanson?" She didn't hide her anger.

"It's the truth." He looked at her. "Joel Ben-Natan is my twin brother. 'Ben' means 'son' in Hebrew. 'Natan' is 'Nathan.' Son of Nathan, Ben-Natan."

That was why Nathanson had looked so familiar! Jessie had taken the facsimile of Ben-Natan's mug shot with her. She'd looked at it again in the Honda after she'd left the Wiesenthal Center.

"I know Joel's history, of course. It's my history, too. And I know everything about him. His favorite foods, his favorite colors—they're my favorites as well. What kinds of TV shows and clothing and women he likes. There we differ." Nathanson smiled. "But to tell you the truth, Detective, I don't have the slightest clue as to who my brother has become."

"Is he close to your parents?"

"My parents have been dead for over five years."

"I'm sorry," she said softly, not knowing how to respond to the quiet pain in his voice. She confronted death almost every day, yet she always felt inadequate in offering comfort to the loved ones the deceased left behind.

Nathanson nodded. "Thank you."

"You mentioned a niece and nephew."

"You're a good listener." He smiled. "My sister Dafna's kids. They live in West L.A. My sister and I are close."

"Where do you live?"

He frowned. "Why?"

"I may have more questions and may need to contact you at home."

He gave her an address on Reeves and watched as she wrote it down.

"What about your brother?" Jessie asked. "Are you close with him?"

Nathanson shook his head. "We talk once in a while. Dafna gets us together for the holidays. Usually, there are arguments."

"Why?"

"I thrive on instilling the love of Judaism into people who thirst for it. My brother, on the other hand, thrives on hate. He sees himself in a world where almost everyone hates Jews."

"What do you see?"

"I see people, Detective, who are innocent until proven guilty." He paused. "I see senseless violence and wonder where it will end." Again he stared at the wall.

"Unless, of course, the violence is directed against Amalek. Then it's not senseless, is it?"

He turned, startled, and faced Jessie. A smile tugged at his lips. "You're a good student, Detective."

"You're a good teacher."

Chapter Eleven

"Mark Pell of the Organization of Jewish Associations is on the line, Mr. Lewis," his secretary informed him.

"Tell him I'm not available."

"And Rabbi Korbin of the—"

"Tell him the same thing," Lewis snapped. "Can't you handle this without bothering me? You know I'm busy!"

"I'm sorry, sir."

He could hear the hurt in her voice. He sighed. "*I'm* sorry, Joanne. This situation has made me tense. I hope you understand."

"Of course, sir."

She was still upset. Join the crowd, he felt like telling her. He hung up the phone and stared at the legal pad in front of him. With an abrupt movement, he pushed himself away from his desk and walked from his office into the main room.

"I'm going to lunch," he told his secretary.

She looked up at him. "Where can you be reached?" She picked up a pencil and held it, poised, over a steno pad.

"I don't know. I'll call you."

His black BMW was on the second level of the underground parking structure. He deactivated the alarm, opened the door, and got in. It was then that he noticed the windshield. Written in broad red strokes on the outside was a message. Below it was a Star of David.

He sat on the tan leather seat, staring at the backward letters. His cheek twitched, and his hands were gripping the steering wheel so hard that his knuckles ached.

A moment later he was standing in front of the car.

PHARAOH HARDENED HIS HEART AND DIED

MUST YOU HARDEN YOUR HEART, TOO?

He gritted his teeth, then touched one of the letters. It was wet and smeared easily. He sniffed his finger and smelled what he thought was water-based paint.

Tucked low behind one of the wipers was a five-by-five-inch white square. He lifted the square and read the handwritten note:

TOO YOUNG TO BE ORPHANS!

With shaking hands, he turned the square over and saw the smiling faces of his blond-haired daughters playing on a seesaw in the yard of their private school. His heart felt leadlike in his chest.

Back inside the car, he switched on the windshield washer, again and again, and watched the letters wobble and turn into bloody rivulets. He wiped the residue with a rag from the trunk.

He questioned the parking attendant, but the man had seen no one near Barry's car.

He decided he would call Detective Drake. He went back upstairs and was crossing the large reception room to his office when he heard his name being called. He turned to face Walter Haus, the firm's managing partner.

"All set for tomorrow?" Haus asked.

Barry hesitated a fraction of a second, then nodded.

"I'll bet you'll be happy when this is over." Haus smiled, placed his hand on Lewis's shoulder, and squeezed. "Proud of you."

"Thank you, sir."

Seated at his desk, he lifted the receiver, then put it down. They were just trying to scare him; he knew that, and it angered him. He ripped the photo into small pieces which he tossed into the wastebasket under his desk and thanked God the picture hadn't arrived at the house, where Sheila would have found it.

He drew his legal pad toward him and began writing.

Chapter Twelve

"Yo, Gene! See your face at the meet with Dorsey?"

Eugene Oppman shut his locker and turned around. He smiled. "Can't tonight, Cal. Too much homework. My folks are cracking the whip." He shrugged.

"Thought for sure you'd be there, wishin' me luck."

"Wish I could. Anyway, you don't need luck. You're our star sprinter. Everyone knows that."

Cal grinned. "Next time, huh?" He extended his hand, palm up.

"Count on it." Gene slapped him five, then walked down the long corridor. On the way out of the building, he stopped in a restroom and washed his hands. He probably could have waited until he got home, but this was better. Less risk.

On the bus he found two empty adjoining seats. He took the aisle seat and placed his book bag on the other one. From the bag he took a paperback copy of *An American Tragedy* and found the dog-eared page that marked where he'd left off. He'd found Dreiser rough going at first, but now he was involved in Clyde Griffiths's life and troubles.

Griffiths was getting a raw deal. Tight-assed Salvation Army parents making him crazy. One career disappointment after another. Clyde Griffiths was trying hard to get someplace, but someone or something was always messing things up for him.

That was how Gene felt much of the time—frustrated, angry. Of course, Dreiser was making it sound like it was Clyde who had the wrong ideas, wanted the wrong things. Wanted what he couldn't have. That was the American tragedy, Dreiser was saying, according to Gene's English teacher, Mrs. Rosenthal.

Dreiser was wrong. That wasn't the American tragedy. It was something else, something that gnawed at Gene every day. But at least he was doing something about it.

The bus came to a stop. Gene continued reading. A minute later he felt a lurching motion as the bus began moving again.

"Can I get in, please?" asked a woman with a Hispanic accent.

Gene looked up. The woman was short and wide, with light brown skin and curly black hair. Smiling, he picked up his bag, stood up, and waited in the aisle until she had seated herself. He glanced around the bus. There were no other empty seats. He placed his bag under his seat, sat down again, and tried to resume his reading, but he couldn't concentrate. Even with his eyes focused on the pages in front of him, he could see the woman's wide hips spreading on the seat toward him. Almost touching him. The rank smell of her wool coat, wet from the rain, and her flowery perfume overpowered the exhaust fumes from the bus. He felt nauseated.

He wondered if she knew how much he hated her. He wondered if anyone at school knew how he really felt. Mrs. Rosenthal, who was so proud of his essays and was continually encouraging him to apply to one of the Ivy Leagues, try for a scholarship. Calvin Donnert, the African American track star of Long Beach High, Gene's classmate of three years. All the others who didn't belong. He smiled at all of them, laughed at their jokes, helped them with their homework.

Everybody liked Eugene Oppman.

He hated them all.

The woman shifted on her seat. The sleeve of her coat

brushed against him. Gene cringed. He drew away and imagined he was encased in a protective, transparent bubble. He did that often—in class, at gym, in the market, at the movies. Whenever he was surrounded by *them.*

They were ruining his life. This woman and her hundreds of relatives and friends—illegal aliens, most of them—who were draining the government's resources. The slanty-eyed man and his two children sitting two rows up. Mrs. Rosenthal, who was laughing at him behind his back, encouraging him to waste his money on college applications when she knew damn well he'd never get in, never get a scholarship, because the Jews and the Asians were smarter than he was, and the Jews were all rich so they could buy their way in, too. The Blacks and Hispanics weren't smarter than he was, but they got more chances because they were minorities.

They got more summer jobs, too, for the same reason. Last summer he'd tried real hard to get a job. He'd talked to managers at a number of stores that had put Help Wanted posters in their front windows. McDonald's. The Foot Locker. Ralphs supermarket. The Warehouse. He knew he'd made a good impression—he was tall, slim, neatly dressed, intelligent. But every damn time he'd been told the same thing: "The position's been filled. Please try us again."

Well, he knew damn well who'd filled the positions.

Minorities.

This year he had no intention of applying for a summer job. He didn't feel like making a fool of himself again.

Dreiser had it all wrong. The real American tragedy was what was happening right now in this country. Real Americans being outnumbered and outmaneuvered more and more, every day, by foreigners who didn't belong here. Jews, Blacks, Koreans, Hispanics, Arabs, Chinese—his high school was full of them.

We're the minority now, Gene said to himself.

He hadn't always known what the problem was. His parents talked constantly about "hard times" and "the recession," but he knew now they were just repeating what they heard on the media. And the media was controlled by the Jews. Of course, before Gene had joined the group, he hadn't known that, either, but then he'd seen the facts and statistics, and it was true. All of it was true. And unless somebody did something, *they* would take over the whole damn country.

Gene had tried once to explain the truth to his parents. "How could you say something like that?" they'd cried. "Where on earth did you get these ideas? We've always taught you that you shouldn't judge a person because of his religion or race or the color of his skin. Don't you see . . ." He hadn't tried explaining anything again. Deep down, he sensed, his parents knew he was right. They were just too afraid to admit it. Gene had been afraid, too, at first, to admit his resentment, but when he finally had, he'd felt cleansed, almost reborn. Free.

The bus was approaching his stop. He pulled the cord above his head and activated the bell, then picked up his bag and walked to the side doors. The bus driver—a Black— swerved and brought the bus to an abrupt stop, causing Gene to stumble down the stairs. The bastard had done it on purpose. The hydraulic doors hissed open. Gene stepped off the bus and walked the three blocks to his house.

"Is that you, Gene?" his mother called from the kitchen when he opened the front door.

"Yeah." He walked down the narrow hallway to his room, tossed his schoolbag onto his bed, then went to the bathroom and washed his hands again. He didn't really believe he could pick up a disease from touching Cal; he was just being careful.

Back in his bedroom he shut his door. From his closet he took out a pair of dark brown military boots Roy Benning had given him. They were spotless and shiny, but he took a soft cloth and buffed them again.

A moment later his mother knocked. "Gene? May I come in?"

"Sure." He put the boots back in the closet. When his mother entered the room, he was sitting on his bed.

"School okay?" She kept her eyes on him.

He knew she was trying to avoid looking at the poster of Adolf Hitler and the swastika on the wall above his bed. In a way, he enjoyed her discomfiture. When he had first put up the poster and swastika, his parents had asked him to take them down. "It isn't right," they'd said. "We don't want that kind of thing in our house." He'd told them it was his room, and wasn't he entitled to his privacy? And his schoolteacher mother had frowned and his psychologist father had said, "Well, I think you should think this over," and Gene had known then it would be all right.

At night he'd overheard his parents talking. His mother wanted to make Gene take the poster and swastika down. His father had said it was just a phase, and if they forced him to capitulate now, he'd just resent them and repress his feelings. At least he's not shaving his head like those skinheads, his father said.

The poster and swastika had stayed up. He'd added two felt number eights—eight stood for the letter *H*; two eights was "Heil Hitler." And Gene had known that his father, even more than his mother, was secretly proud of what he was doing.

"School's fine," he told his mother.

"What's new and exciting?"

It was a line from a Melanie Griffith movie called *A Stranger Among Us*. It was about Hasidic Jews; his parents had rented the video and practically forced him to see it with them. He cringed inwardly, partly because he was sickened by the image of swarms of Hasidic Jews with their filthy earlocks and their strange black attire; partly because he hated the fact that his mother had appropriated the line and used it to pretend that they had a close relationship and that she loved him as much as she loved his kid brother John.

What was new and exciting? Tomorrow, he wanted to tell his mother, when they got permission to have the parade, there would be something new and exciting. Gene couldn't be at the court hearing—he couldn't cut school for that—but Mr. Benning had assured him the White Alliance would win.

Gene would be at the parade even if he got expelled. No way would he miss that.

"Nothing's new," he told his mother. "Same old stuff."

"There's a track meet tonight, isn't there? Are you going?"

"I have other plans."

"It's that group, isn't it?" She pursed her lips. "Gene—" She broke off, then said, "Don't be out too late, okay?" and left the room, pulling the door shut behind her.

Chapter Thirteen

"My money's on Ben-Natan," Espes said. "He's got a history of militant protest. You haven't talked to him yet, huh?"

"He's out of town for the day." She'd made that clear in her report. Couldn't Espes read?

"What about the twin brother? You check out his alibi?"

"I called Eileen Pasternak, the woman he claims he was with that night. No one answered. I'll try again before I leave."

Espes scanned the report again, then looked up. "Good work, Drake. Thorough. Handwriting's actually legible, not like your partner's." He smiled. "Any more people to question?"

Jessie recrossed her legs, noting again the water stains on the hem of her taupe slacks. Slacks she'd just taken out of the cleaners. "Rita Warrens of the ACLU may have some leads. I called her office a number of times, but she's never in. Mark Pell, the Jewish Associations guy, still hasn't faxed me a copy of the letter he sent Lewis. Most of the rabbis in L.A. signed it." She had the feeling Pell might "forget" his promise—he probably didn't want to implicate any of the rabbis. She'd call him.

"I can interview the rabbis." She didn't relish the prospect—it could take days. "I also figured I'd run their names past Rita

Warrens. Maybe one or more of them contacted the ACLU, as well as Lewis. That could narrow the field."

"Good idea." Espes dropped the report onto his desk and leaned back in his chair. "You think this is a waste of time, huh?" He studied Jessie's face.

Had he picked up on her reluctance? Or was he baiting her again? "Almost anyone could have vandalized the Lewises' door. It may be impossible to find out who."

Espes thought a moment, then nodded. "Get the fax, but hold off contacting the rabbis. I want you at the courthouse tomorrow morning. And see if you can make Warrens available sooner."

"I'll try."

"Do more than try. Get it done, Drake, so you can get back to Homicide. That's what you want, isn't it?" He swiveled sideways and picked up his phone, anchoring it between his shoulder and ear.

Of course it was what she wanted, Jessie told herself as she left Espes's office. Still, now that she'd spent all day investigating the Lewis case, she was more than a little curious to find out who had painted the star.

"The *Mogen Dovid*," she said aloud as she neared her desk. *Mogen Dovid, lashon harah, afikomen, yemach sh'mo ve'zichro*, Amalek. Quite a bit of Jewish education in one day. She entertained the idea of phoning Manny Freiberg at Parker Center and impressing the LAPD psychologist with her new-found knowledge. She smiled at the thought.

She phoned the ACLU office and was told again that Ms. Warrens was unavailable. She punched the numbers for Eileen Pasternak and let the phone ring twelve times before she gave up. She wondered suddenly whether Ezra Nathanson was out with Ms. Pasternak again, cementing his alibi.

Damn.

Her new suede shoes were definitely ruined. Jessie kicked them off as soon as she stepped into the service porch through the side door to her house. The toes of her panty hose were soaked and blackened from the shoes. She took off her slacks, peeled off her hose, and dropped both on top of the washing machine. Then she went to the living room to check the mail chute and slid on the hardwood floor. The wet hardwood floor.

She looked up and cursed softly. Directly over her, the ceiling, newly painted, was stained with a large, ugly, blistering patch of muddy ocher. Beads of water had formed along a crack in the center of the patch. Jessie watched, fascinated, as the beads became larger and clung tenaciously to the crack, first-time divers afraid to let go and plummet to the shallow pool below.

One drop plopped onto her forehead. Another landed on the floor beside her. It was lucky, she thought, that Gary had taken the living room furniture as part of their settlement; at least there was nothing to ruin. When it stopped raining, she'd go up on the roof and repair the leak. Soon after she and Gary had moved into the house, they'd bought *Reader's Digest* "how to" home repair guides and patched the roof, afterward they'd showered together and made love on the new carpet in the master bedroom. She found herself smiling and, feeling vaguely disloyal to Frank, shook her head to unseat the memory.

She went back to the service porch for a towel and for the small mustard-colored basin that was a souvenir of her miscarriage two years ago. It was no small victory that she could regard the basin as just that—a molded piece of plastic. The nurse had placed it on Jessie's lap and wheeled her out of the hospital to Gary's car; Jessie had cradled it on the silent drive home. She'd intended to throw it into the trash along with the beauty care samples the hospital had given her, but she'd kept the basin and forced herself to use the Keri lotion and the other items to prove to herself that she was all right.

As she lifted the basin down from a shelf and returned to the living room, she felt a twinge of sadness, but not the searing, knifelike pain that had sliced through her for months. She spread the towel on the floor and stepped on it, blotting the water with her feet, then placed the basin on the towel. A *plink* told her she'd positioned it perfectly.

There wasn't much mail. A few bills. Some junk. Ed McMahon was smiling at her, promising her untold millions. "Jessica Drake! You are a winner! . . ." She would love untold millions but would settle for thousands, especially if she needed a new roof.

She was in the shower, shampooing her rain-battered hair, when she heard the doorbell. Again and again and again. Her first inclination was to ignore the ringing—probably somebody selling cookies or gift wrap or household cleaning products—but then she wondered if it was Helen and whether there was some new crisis.

Jessie shut the faucets, stepped out of the shower, and wrapped herself in a white terry robe. "Coming!" she yelled as she hurried down the long hallway. At the front door she looked through the peephole, then opened the door.

"I saw your Honda in the driveway, so I knew you were home," Frank Pruitt said as he stepped into the entry hall.

"Still raining?" she asked as she locked the door. She was happy to see him but annoyed that he hadn't called and was taking for granted the fact that she'd be here, waiting for him.

"Drizzling. I rang the bell about a hundred times." He opened the entry closet and hung up his raincoat. "I got scared for a minute. I thought you might've hurt yourself."

"I was in the shower."

"So I gather." He grinned, then put his arm around her waist and drew her toward him. Bending his head, he kissed her.

She was passive at first, punishing him for not calling her all day, then realized she was punishing herself, too. She relaxed and returned his embrace and opened her mouth under his. She liked the light musk of his after-shave, the familiar strength of his muscular arms, the pressure of his torso against hers.

"I called you at Parker Center," she said a moment later, smoothing his damp, dark brown wavy hair with her fingers. The gray was becoming more pronounced, and she remembered Helen's recent comment—"Frank's forty-six. Neil's forty-four. Looks like we both like older men, huh, Jess?"

"I was out all day with the boys," he said. "We were going to try Magic Mountain, but the radio said rain, so I took them to the Hollywood Wax Museum, then showed them around the academy. Negative on the museum. They had a blast at the academy. Especially in the gift shop." He grinned woefully.

"Did Rona go along?" She immediately regretted the question. She didn't want to sound jealous, proprietary.

"Yeah. The boys asked if she could come. I couldn't say no." He shrugged, then met her eyes. "It wasn't a big deal, Jess."

"I know." She smiled to show she meant it. "I just wondered."

"I thought we'd go out for dinner. The boys are eating with Rona at her parents'."

"Dinner sounds nice. Maybe a movie afterward? There's a new Mel Gibson film in Century City."

He hesitated, then said, "I promised the boys they could sleep at my place tonight." He put his hand on her shoulder. "It's important for me to spend time with them, Jess. I see them only a couple of times a year."

"Of course. You don't have to explain, Frank."

"I get the feeling I do," he said quietly.

She shook her head. "I'm just disappointed. I'm being unreasonable, and silly. Sorry." Maybe it was the weather, she thought, but she knew it wasn't.

"You're not being silly. I'm disappointed, too, sweetheart. Rona and the boys will be here only another week or so. Think we can last?" He kissed her again and slipped his hand inside her robe.

After eight months she was still almost unbearably excited whenever he touched her, and she knew she excited him, too. She worried sometimes that the sex was all there was between them—they made love every time they saw each other, and sometimes there wasn't much conversation; unlike Gary, Frank rarely talked about himself.

But of course there was more to their relationship than sex. They were both cops. They were both divorced. They had a lot in common. In time he would open up to her. She moved out of his arms. "Give me fifteen minutes to dry my hair and get dressed."

"No real rush, is there?" He nuzzled her neck and untied the belt of her robe and pulled her close.

She thought about resisting, to prove something to herself, but she wanted him with an intensity that embarrassed her. "Not really."

In the end, they didn't go out. Jessie defrosted two salmon steaks and prepared them for the broiler—a dab of margarine, a sprinkling of lemon juice, garlic powder, and paprika. Microwaved baked potatoes. A salad. Haute cuisine à la Drake.

She had put on a dark green sweater, khaki slacks, and warm socks. No shoes. Her long hair had dried naturally and was curlier and messier than she liked. She brushed it back and held it in place with a scrunchy, but Frank slipped the scrunchy off and fanned her hair with his hands.

"I like it this way," he told her.

Men had a thing about women's hair. Gary had liked her hair loose and curly, too. And long. She wondered suddenly why she was thinking about her ex-husband. Probably because Rona was in town.

Over dinner she listened while Frank talked about his sons. Christopher was nine, a little older than Jessie's nephew, Matthew. Andy was almost twelve. She took mental notes while Frank talked, trying to store for future recall everything he told her.

"I wish you could meet them," he said.

It seemed like the perfect opening. "How about this weekend?" she suggested. "Helen and Neil are going to Tucson. Matthew will be with me. It'll be fun, Frank." She smiled.

"It *would* be fun, but Rona's folks invited the whole family to come celebrate Andy's birthday on Saturday. I thought I told you." He looked at her.

She shook her head and took a sip of water.

"Guess I forgot. And I promised I'd take them to Disneyland Sunday." He paused. "Rona's coming along. I'm sorry, Jess."

Isn't this where I came in? she thought wryly. "No problem. Matthew and I will find things to do. Have more salad," she said, moving the glass bowl toward him. They ate silently for a few minutes. She'd never realized how noisy forks and knives could be.

Finally Frank said, "So how's murder in West L.A.?"

"I wouldn't know." She told him about the Lewis case. "The court hearing's tomorrow. If Lewis wins the petition, which seems likely, whoever vandalized his door may try something else."

"But not necessarily murder, huh?" He ate a few bites of salmon. "You think Espes is riding you?"

"Kind of. Well, maybe not." She sighed. "I just don't see why he doesn't give this to CAPS."

"Pressure from downtown. They have a lot of influence, you know. With the department, with the mayor's office, city council."

She frowned. "Who?"

"Jews. In this case, Lewis. I'll bet if Lewis weren't Jewish, Espes wouldn't have put you on this."

Jessie shook her head. "Lewis didn't demand special attention, Frank. He didn't even want me to pursue this. Actually, he was upset when his wife named people who were harassing him."

"Well, the rabbis, then." He speared a cucumber slice.

"I don't think so. Espes said he put me on the case because it was getting media attention and he knew I had experience with the media. Phil thinks Espes may be telling the truth."

"Maybe." He told her about the case he was working—a series of drive-home muggings apparently perpetrated by the same suspect or suspects. When he'd finished the last of the salmon on his plate, he leaned back and sighed.

"Great meal, Jess. Next time, though, I'm taking you out to dinner. Pick a fancy place."

"Chasen's?" She smiled.

"Not *that* fancy." He laughed, then checked his watch. "I'd better go."

She felt a stab of disappointment. It seemed as if he'd just arrived. "No dessert?"

"Already had it, sweetheart." He smiled and caressed her hand with his thumb.

Another time his comment would have amused her. Now it annoyed her. She felt used somehow, cheap. She knew it was her fault, not his, and forced herself to laugh. "I meant apple pie."

"Wish I could. I told the boys I'd be home by eight-thirty. I'll call you tomorrow. Maybe tonight, after the boys are asleep."

After Frank left, Jessie went into her den and, sitting on the black leather sofa, picked up the receiver and called Brenda Royes. They spoke for a while—Jessie talked about the Lewis case and listened while Brenda discussed a homicide she was investigating. Jessie was tempted to tell her friend about her evening with Frank but decided to sort things out for herself first. Brenda still resented him for the shabby way he'd initially treated Jessie when she'd joined the task force at Parker Center.

"Talk to you soon," Jessie told Brenda fifteen minutes later. She hung up, turned on the television with the remote control, and, on an impulse, picked up the receiver again and phoned her parents. They lived a hundred miles south of Los Angeles in La Jolla, a beach resort just north of San Diego.

Arthur Claypool answered the phone. "Jessie! How nice! Everything okay?" he added quickly.

"Everything's fine, Dad. How about you?"

"Fine, fine. No special reason for the call?"

"Nope. Is Mom there? I wanted to ask her something."

"Sure. Hold on while I get her." Her father's voice held a blend of caution and surprise.

She wished that her calling wasn't such an event, but her communications with her parents—especially with her mother—were infrequent. Jessie had left her parents' home when she was seventeen and had lived on her own, first in La Jolla, then in San Diego. Two years later she'd moved to Los Angeles, and after getting a degree in political science from Cal State Northridge, she'd enrolled in the police academy. Her career move had worried her father and displeased her mother.

But then, almost everything she did displeased her mother. Jessie had come to terms with that fact. Using the remote control, she switched from channel to channel and had settled on a sitcom when her mother came on the line.

"Jessica? What's wrong?"

"Nothing's wrong, Mom. I just felt like calling."

"Is someone there with you? I hear people talking."

"It's the TV, Mom."

"Well, it sounds like people," Frances Claypool said.

"No people, Mom." Jessie lowered the volume. "How are you?"

"Fine." Frances's tone was guarded. "This isn't about Helen, is it? Neil isn't leaving her, is he?"

Jessie sighed. "Helen and Neil are fine. In fact . . ." She was about to say they were going to Arizona for the weekend and leaving Matthew with her, but she realized her mistake in time. Frances would be upset that Helen hadn't told her parents about her weekend plans and hadn't asked them to watch Matthew.

" 'In fact' what?" Frances asked.

Her mother was always sharp. "In fact, Helen and Neil are getting along really well. I think the therapy is helping."

"Therapy is idiocy. An expensive waste of time. Helen and Neil need to work things out on their own."

"Therapy can help, Mom." It had helped Jessie resolve some of the anger she'd felt for years against her beautiful, well-mannered, abusive mother and against her father, who had stood silently by, not wanting to see. She hoped it was helping Helen deal with her own legacy of pain and abuse.

"It didn't keep you and Gary together, did it?" Frances said.

"No, it didn't," Jessie answered pleasantly, forcing herself not to react to her mother's smug tone. She dug her nails into the leather of the sofa. I shouldn't have called, she told herself.

"Helen put you up to this, didn't she? She's been after me to participate in some of her sessions, but I have no intention of doing that, and you can tell her so for me."

"Mom, Helen didn't ask me to call."

"Don't lie to me! I know what's going on. You think her problems are all my fault. Is that what you told her therapist?"

Count to ten. "Mom, I haven't talked to Helen's therapist. Honest. And I didn't call to talk about Helen. I'm sorry if I upset you." She paused. "Okay?" Silence. "The thing is, Mom, I wanted to ask you something." Still no response. She continued anyway. "I'm investigating a case where someone painted a Star of David on the front door of a Jewish lawyer who—"

"I saw that on the news this evening. They didn't mention your name. At least I don't think so. I'll ask your father."

"Mom—"

"Just a minute. Arthur, did they mention Jessica's name on the news report about the Star of David thing?" A moment later Frances said to Jessie, "Your father didn't hear your name, either. Maybe it'll be on the eleven o'clock news."

"I'm not concerned about being mentioned, Mom. I wondered what you thought about the parade the neo-Nazis are planning."

"I think it's terrible, of course. So does your father. Why?"

"I was thinking about the case, and the people I interviewed today. All of them are Jewish, Mom, and I thought about your Jewish relatives and—"

"What on earth does that have to do with anything, Jessica?"

"I thought you might be more upset about the parade because of that connection."

"Your father and I are concerned about this neo-Nazi thing because it's racism, and racism is dangerous to everyone living in this country. It has nothing to do with me personally."

"Don't you think about them? Wonder how they must feel?"

"They're not alive, Jessica. I never knew them. To tell you the truth, I'm sorry I ever mentioned them to you."

"How do you know their children aren't alive? Who were they, Mom? What were their names?"

"Jessica, I will say this one final time. I vaguely remember overhearing my parents discussing some Jewish relatives. They showed me the photo. I forgot about it until you found it. That's all I know about these people. You're obsessing about them, although I can't imagine why, unless you have such an empty life that you have to fill it with other people's problems."

Jessie ignored the barb. "Mom, do you think the neo-Nazis should be stopped?"

"Honest to God, Jessica! You don't call for months, and now that you do, you bother me with irrelevant nonsense and hypothetical questions about long-lost relatives and Nazis!"

"I needed to talk to you, Mom. You're always saying you want us to talk more. *Do* you think they should be stopped?"

Frances sighed. "In my opinion, those rabbis are making too much of this thing. Let these Nazi animals have their little parade and be done with it."

"What if they decided to march in La Jolla, Mom?"

"Good night, Jessica."

"Mom—"

"Give Helen my regards. You might tell her it would be nice if she gave her parents a call now and then, too. Unless, of course, her therapist advises against it."

The blare of the dial tone sounded in Jessie's ear.

Frances one, Jessie zero. She hung up the phone.

Chapter Fourteen

Department 85 of the Los Angeles County Superior Court was packed. Jessie arrived twenty minutes early, but there were only a few empty seats on either side of the spectator's gallery when she entered the eighth-floor courtroom at ten after eight on Wednesday morning.

She spotted familiar faces in the right gallery: Korbin, Pell (she was still awaiting his fax), Wittiger. Myron Perkins, the Los Angeles city councilman for the affected district. Jeffrey Beal, the assistant city attorney, a handsome man with thick, prematurely white hair. Jessie had often seen Beal at Parker Center, and he'd been in the mayor's office when she'd received her commendation seven months ago.

Ben-Natan was there, too—even from a distance, Jessie recognized him from his mug shot. He was talking with a familiar-looking man whom Jessie finally identified as the leader of the Jewish Defense League. She couldn't remember his name.

Across the aisle were the petitioners—more men than women. Some had the trademark shaved scalp of the skinheads. A handful of teens had shown up, too—they should be in school, Jessie thought, but truancy was hardly the problem. A tall, broad-chested, brown-haired man in a gray suit was circulating, keeping order. Probably Roy Benning, the leader.

Behind the group were average-looking people—supporters or disinterested parties who had come to view the courtroom event. Jessie hoped it was the latter—it was troubling to think that the group's platform of racism and hate had found popularity among Mr. and Mrs. America.

And, of course, there was the press—newspaper reporters with their telltale notepads; a courtroom sketch artist; television field reporters and their cameramen, positioned at the sides and back of the courtroom, ready to catch the action. Having been the object of the press's intense scrutiny as department spokesperson, Jessie was more than happy not to be in the limelight now. She would leave that to Jeffrey Beal and Barry Lewis.

There was no sign of Lewis. He was probably waiting outside the courtroom until it was time for the hearing to begin. She wondered if Rita Warrens would be attending.

The high-ceilinged room hummed with conversation. Every once in a while excited voices rose and quickly subsided, Fourth of July firecrackers hissing to their deaths. From the back, Jessie could see the Shield and the White Alliance telegraphing hostility and defiance, but no verbal exchanges crossed the aisle. She wondered how long the restraint would last.

Only a handful of seats remained, all in the left gallery. Jessie sat down next to an elderly, spectacled woman with short, frizzed gray hair who was reading a paperback novel. Every few seconds the woman clacked her tongue against her palate.

Jessie's grandfather, William Claypool, had made that same sound, that same motion, to push his dentures into place; his wife, Louise, had chided him about it. Jessie felt wistfulness tug at her heart. Whenever she thought about her grandparents, she felt a fresh sense of loss. She'd never met her mother's parents—they had died before Jessie was born—and Frances never talked about them. Too painful, Arthur Claypool had explained to his daughters.

Sighing, Jessie turned toward the front of the courtroom

and locked eyes with Korbin. He glanced at the White Alliance, then at her. She flushed. She'd taken an empty seat, not chosen sides.

"Quite a turnout, huh? Looks like I got here just in time."

Jessie turned to her right and looked up into the smiling face of Ezra Nathanson. "Cutting class?"

He sat down next to her. "My first class today is at ten-fifteen. I figure this should be over pretty quickly, don't you?"

"Depends on the day's calendar and the order in which the cases were filed. Usually, it's first filed, first heard, unless there's a priority. The Lewis case may not be heard until this afternoon." She saw Nathanson's frown. "You teach afternoons?"

"Afternoons I study the Talmud." He scanned the rows in front of him and to the right, then looked behind him.

"Not a bad life if you can afford it."

"My inheritance from my parents helps. I used it to make some sound investments. And no, it isn't a bad life. I feel quite fortunate." He leaned closer. "Did you speak to Eileen Pasternak?"

He sounded anxious. Or maybe his half whisper was creating that effect. The whisper wasn't necessary—with all the noise in the room, their conversation was quite private.

"She confirmed the date." Last night, after talking with Frances, Jessie had finally reached the Pasternak woman. "She wasn't surprised by my call."

Nathanson colored and adjusted his tie. "I didn't want her to be upset that I gave you her number. I told her to tell you the absolute truth." He darted a glance at the woman to Jessie's left.

"Nice of you." Jessie looked, too. The woman was reading her book, oblivious of the various conversations around her. Clack, clack. "Ms. Pasternak said you arrived late—nine-ten—and took her home an hour later. Not a great date, huh?"

"I had a flat tire on the way there. Didn't she tell you?"

"Did you call the auto club?"

He shook his head. "I put on the spare. I got grease on my slacks and had to change into another pair."

So no witness. "I hope the stain comes out." She heard a hiss spreading, wavelike, from the front of the right gallery. Turning, she saw that Lewis had entered, accompanied by a short, thin blonde wearing glasses. Rita Warrens? Lewis and the woman crossed to the left gallery and were approached by the brown-haired man who had been shepherding the White Alliance. The hiss died down.

Jessie looked for Sheila Lewis, but Sheila wasn't standing by her man—or sitting near him. No surprise. Jessie couldn't envision Sheila sitting in the left gallery, amid the White Alliance. And she couldn't very well sit on the right.

Jessie turned to Nathanson. "Yesterday you didn't mention you were late for your date."

"It didn't seem important."

"It was important enough to review with Ms. Pasternak."

"I didn't *review* it." His face and voice betrayed annoyance.

"All rise for the Honorable Judge Phoebe Williams."

The silence was sudden and absolute. Jessie stood and watched the judge ascend the steps to the bench. She was a statuesque woman, about five feet ten inches, and walked with a regal gait. Her hair was drawn back from her face, dramatizing high cheekbones and sculpted lips. Jessie had never sat in her courtroom, but she'd heard a great deal about the forty-seven-year-old African American from South Central Los Angeles who had escaped a life of poverty and violence and made her mark as a highly successful prosecutor, then as a justice of the superior court.

"Good morning," Phoebe Williams said after she was seated. Her low, husky voice resonated in the room. "My court calendar tells me it's going to be a long, *long* day"—she drawled the second "long"—"so, Counsel, I'd like you to state the name of the party you represent and give me time estimates." She put on half-glasses and read from a paper she was holding. *"Angelo* versus *the State of California."* She glanced up.

A man in the front left gallery stood. "Representing Vincent Angelo, Your Honor. Five minutes." He sat down.

"Representing the State of California, Your Honor," said another man from the right gallery. "Five minutes."

"Connelly versus *Meyers,"* Judge Williams read.

"Representing Andrew Connelly, Your Honor. Five minutes."

"Representing . . ."

"Five minutes?" Nathanson whispered to Jessie. "Obviously, these guys aren't Jewish." He smiled.

"The judge hears from twenty-eight to thirty cases a day," Jessie whispered back. "Anyone who gives a longer time estimate is scheduled at the end of the session."

"Representing . . ."

In rapid sequence attorneys announced their time estimates. Finally it was Lewis's turn. "Representing the White Alliance, Your Honor. Five minutes or less."

Show-off, Jessie thought.

"Then by all means try to make it less, Counselor."

Jeffrey Beal stood. "Representing the City Council of the County of Los Angeles, Your Honor. Five minutes."

Two more cases were announced. Then Judge Williams asked, "Any priority matters this court should hear?"

Beal stood again. "I'm due in another court at nine this morning, Your Honor."

"In that case, I'll hear from you now, Mr. Beal."

"You're in luck," Jessie whispered to Nathanson.

He nodded, unsmiling, and looked straight ahead.

Beal approached the counsel table on the right. Lewis sat at the table on the left. Jessie noted that the woman next to her hadn't closed her book. Probably a veteran member of the courtroom audience, familiar with the tedium that often marked the hearings.

"Mr. Beal," Judge Williams said, "I've studied the points and authorities of the papers submitted. I've read the declarations, affidavits, and the administrative record. I'm aware that the police commission approved this parade, that the city council exercised its right and voted to review the commission's decision, and subsequently denied the petitioner's request. Frankly, Mr. Beal, I fail to see the merit behind the city council's action. Perhaps you can explain to me what I'm not seeing?"

"Your Honor, this parade would cause egregious harm to the citizens of Los Angeles, in particular to the residents of Beverly-Fairfax and Pico-Robertson, the two routes indicated in the petition. Many of these residents are Holocaust survivors. The city council finds this parade a deliberate attempt to intimidate and harass the Jewish population of Los Angeles, to inflict trauma, and to incite religious and racial hatred. This is especially striking since the planned date of the parade, April twentieth, is the birthday of Adolf Hitler. The public—"

"*Yemach sh'mo!*" exclaimed a male voice from across the aisle.

Jessie turned quickly to her right, then looked at the bench. Judge Williams was frowning.

"The public display of the swastika in connection with this proposed parade," Beal continued, "constitutes a symbolic assault on a large number of the residents of Los Angeles and is a clear incitation to violence and retaliation. Further—"

"We are ready!" cried a voice from the back.

Jessie couldn't tell whether it was the same man or another. She looked at Ezra Nathanson but could read neither approval nor disapproval on his face.

"Ladies and gentlemen." Phoebe Williams's voice was stern with quiet authority. "I realize emotions are running high, and I am highly sensitive to the feelings of all concerned. I want to warn you, however, that I will not tolerate any disrespect to this Court or any further interruption of these proceedings." Her eyes made a survey of the room. "Please continue, Mr. Beal."

Beal cleared his throat. "Furthermore, this parade and the

display of the swastika will engender a hostile crowd reaction and create danger for the petitioners and innocent bystanders. In fact, the presence of the petitioners in full military uniform and swastika will constitute 'fighting words.' As so defined in *Chaplinsky* versus *New Hampshire*, 1942, this demonstration and this message are not protected by the First Amendment.

"Your Honor, the petitioners have advertised their parade by circulating flyers in the Beverly-Fairfax and Pico-Robertson areas. These flyers and the message of hate and violence against the Jewish people that they proclaim constitute group defamation. Libelous speech has never been protected by the First Amendment.

"Finally, Your Honor, the City submits that there is a significant distinction between unpopular speech and assaultive speech. The First Amendment protects the first. It should have no bearing on the latter. The Jewish residents of Beverly-Fairfax and Pico-Robertson are a targeted audience for this assaultive speech. We ask the Court to uphold the constitutional rights of these residents and deny the petition. Thank you, Your Honor."

Beal sat down.

"Mr. Lewis," Judge Williams said.

Barry Lewis stood. "Your Honor, my client is petitioning the Court for a writ of mandate that will order the city council to issue the permit granted by the police commission to allow my client to parade peaceably on April twentieth. My client—"

"Traitor! You should have died in the ovens!"

Judge Williams rapped the gavel sharply. Jessie couldn't see Lewis's face. What he was feeling? Anger? Fear? Ezra Nathanson sighed and shook his head.

"You, sir, in the second to last row, three seats in from the aisle," Judge Williams said. "Stand, please."

A red-faced man in his sixties stood up hesitantly. He was wearing a skullcap.

"What is your name?"

"Samuel Hochburg."

"Do you understand English, Mr. Hochburg?"

"Of course, Your Honor."

"Well, then, Mr. Hochburg, I find it hard to understand your outburst after my warning."

"This is a free country, isn't it, Your Honor? A Nazi can come into a Jewish neighborhood, so a man can say what he thinks."

"This is a free country, Mr. Hochburg, and you are entitled to voice your nonlibelous opinions about Mr. Lewis and his actions. But not in my courtroom. Not without my permission. Is that understood?"

Hochburg nodded.

"You may sit down. Another comment, and I'll have you cited for contempt. If there are any other outbursts, I'll have this courtroom cleared." She paused, then said, "Proceed, Mr. Lewis."

"Your Honor, re the swastika as 'fighting words,' Mr. Beal cited *Chaplinsky* versus *New Hampshire*, 1942, but that case did not involve prior restraint, which Mr. Beal would have this court authorize in regard to my client. As to incitement to riot, this argument presents a hypothetical possibility and as such is another attempt to mandate unconstitutional prior restraint. Mr. Beal contends that my client may be subject to physical harm as a result of the proposed parade. This 'heckler's veto' is also an unconstitutional application of prior restraint. Mr. Beal himself mentioned that my client has advertised his impending parade and his message. Thus my client will not have compelled a confrontation with anyone who voluntarily listens." Lewis paused.

The courtroom was still. Nathanson, Jessie saw, was staring intently at the ACLU attorney. His hands were fists.

"Your Honor, Mr. Beal spoke about the trauma to the residents of the neighborhoods where my client plans to conduct its parade. I do not argue this trauma, nor do I mean to minimize it, but the First Amendment gives my client the constitutional right to parade and to express views that may be abhorrent to most of us in this courtroom today. They are, in fact, abhorrent to me. But more abhorrent, and far more frightening, is the possibility that my client's constitutional rights may be violated. Justice Oliver Wendell Holmes stated this most eloquently: 'If there is any principle of the Constitution that more imperatively calls for attachment than any other, it is the principle of free thought—not free thought for those who agree with us, but freedom for the thought we hate.' Thank you, Your Honor." Lewis took his seat.

Phoebe Williams clasped her hands and rested them on the desk. "Mr. Beal, I wish I could say I need time to reflect on the merits of your arguments. While your words were eloquent and emotionally convincing, the fact remains that this Court must ignore emotion and concentrate on the law. And the law in this case is clear. Precedent, as you well know, was set in the case of the *Village of Skokie* versus *Frank Collins*. This Court reluctantly concurs with the decision of the Illinois Supreme Court: 'that the display of the swastika cannot be enjoined under the fighting words exception to free speech, nor can anticipation of a hostile audience justify prior restraint.' This Court is well aware that the swastika is an abhorrent symbol to the Jewish citizens of Los Angeles and that they, in particular those who survived the Nazi death camps, have strong feelings regarding its display. This factor, however, does not justify enjoining the petitioner's speech. The Court finds, reluctantly, in favor of the petitioner."

There was polite applause from the left gallery.

"Two 'reluctantly's," Nathanson said. His tone was ironic.

"Nazi lover!" someone whispered from the back of the right gallery. Was the reference to the judge, Jessie wondered, or to Lewis? Had the judge heard it?

Judge Williams rapped her gavel. "Mr. Lewis, please have your client refrain from any exhibition of this nature. I find nothing to applaud here this morning."

"Yes, Your Honor. I apologize for my client." Lewis collected his papers.

"Surprised by the decision?" Jessie asked Ezra.

He shook his head. "No, but I'm disappointed anyway.

Silly, isn't it?" He checked his watch. "I'd better go. I don't want to be late for my class." He stood and left the courtroom.

The man in the gray suit rose. As if on cue, the White Alliance stood en masse. Jessie wondered for a moment whether they were going to salute the man or Lewis and proclaim "Heil Hitler," but of course they didn't. They began filing out of their rows in an orderly fashion, as if someone had orchestrated their exit. Someone probably had. It made sense to have them counteract with ultracivil behavior the innate uncivilness of their beliefs and proposed actions.

They were nearing the back rows. Jessie made a quick exit and found the press in the hall, lying in wait. Several reporters, microphones in hand, gave her a quick "are-you-someone-important?" stare, then shifted their attention to the people thronging behind her through the wide doorway. Jessie crossed the hall and watched.

Within minutes the hall was filled with bodies and noise. The lines of demarcation were still there—as in the courtroom, the White Alliance had grouped to the left of a narrow aisle; the Shield and the other Jewish citizens, to the right. It must be hell for the press, Jessie thought not very sympathetically. They don't know whom to approach first.

". . . Roy Benning," the man in the gray suit was saying to reporters who had swarmed around him. ". . . great day for democracy and the White people of America." He was beaming, his face flushed with sweat and triumph. Around him, members of the White Alliance were grinning, their arms extended in the Nazi salute.

". . . a tragedy not only for Jews, but for all the people of Los Angeles," Rabbi Korbin told a woman reporter. "While I respect Judge Williams's decision, I'm gravely disappointed by it."

"I don't respect it!" shouted a man near Korbin. Jessie recognized him as the person Phoebe Williams had chastised.

"You feel there was bias?" The reporter turned toward him.

"Absolutely. She didn't pay attention to one thing the city attorney said. She made up her mind before. She—"

"Thank you." The reporter turned away, looking around her. "Councilman Perkins," she yelled above the din as she pushed her way toward him. "Councilman, does the City plan to appeal?"

"They have to appeal!" another man exclaimed. "This parade is an outrage, a violation of our rights!"

It was Mark Pell; Jessie recognized his voice.

"Councilman?" the reporter prompted.

"I can't tell you at this time," Perkins said.

"But do you think—" The reporter broke off and swiveled abruptly toward the open doorway to the courtroom.

Jessie did likewise and saw Barry Lewis exiting the courtroom; at his side was the woman Jessie assumed was Rita Warrens. Seconds later they were surrounded.

"Nazi lover!"

"Mr. Lewis! How do you feel—"

"No comment." His face was white.

"Never again!" someone yelled, his fist raised.

"Ms. Warrens, are you pleased with today's decision?"

"Never again!" another person echoed.

"Mr. Lewis, in view of the fact that you're Jewish—"

"No comment." Using his briefcase as a shield, he made his way past reporters and almost collided with Joel Ben-Natan.

"Had your day in court, did you, Mister ACLU Attorney? The First Amendment *über alles,* huh?"

Lewis stepped to his left. Ben-Natan blocked him.

"Move out of my way." Lewis's voice seemed abnormally loud in the sudden quiet.

"What will you do if I don't, Lewis? Have one of your Nazi playmates beat me up?"

Jessie darted a glance at the White Alliance. Benning was standing in front of the group, his legs apart, his hands forming a wide V in a silent order for control.

"Why don't you grow up, Ben-Natan?"

"Why don't you drop dead and make the world a better place?"

"Is that a threat?"

"It's a prayer. And God's on my side."

Barry Lewis elbowed Ben-Natan aside. Ben-Natan grabbed the offending arm and twisted it. Lewis swung his briefcase into the side of Ben-Natan's head. Ben-Natan dropped Lewis's arm and staggered backward.

"Yoel!" a woman screamed.

Lewis pushed through a knot of people and disappeared. A moment later Jessie heard a cry, then a thud. An opening formed in the crowd, and she saw Lewis sprawled facedown on the floor.

Christ! Jessie's hand went to her weapon. She looked around. Weren't there any uniforms? She reached Lewis just as Rita Warrens did. Rita bent down and helped him to his feet.

"Someone pushed me." He recognized Jessie. "Someone pushed me, Detective!" he repeated in a now angry tone.

"Who?" Jessie asked.

"I don't have eyes in the back of my head!"

"Barry," Rita said, "the detective is trying to help."

"I know. I'm sorry." He brushed himself off and straightened his jacket. "Ask them," he told Jessie, pointing behind her.

She turned and saw a wall of masklike faces. She noticed Ezra Nathanson standing toward the back. Their eyes met. He turned quickly and walked toward the elevators.

It was definitely time to talk to Ben-Natan—before he left town again. "Wait here, please," Jessie told Lewis and Rita Warrens, then worked through the crowd, looking for Ben-Natan.

He'd disappeared.

Where the hell had he gone?

Chapter Fifteen

"I don't know what I can tell you that you don't already know," Rita Warrens said to Jessie.

The two women were in a booth in a restaurant near the courthouse. An hour had passed since the confrontation between Lewis and Ben-Natan. Jessie had told Rita she wanted to talk to her. Rita had suggested that they meet later that day, or the next day, at the ACLU office. Jessie had politely insisted that now was better—while Rita was "available." It was bad enough that Jessie had lost Ben-Natan; she was still steamed about that. Rita had waited with foot-tapping impatience while Jessie combed the crowd for a witness who had seen Barry Lewis pushed. And found no one.

Naturally.

As they waited for their orders, Jessie sized Rita up and wondered if Rita was doing the same. The ACLU director was in her late thirties, judging from the faint lines around her eyes and mouth, but she looked like a Kewpie doll. She had brown, saucerlike eyes with long lashes that threatened to brush against her red-framed eyeglasses. Her mouth was small and pouty; her short, blond-streaked hair was layered and brushed back from her face. She was wearing a tailored taupe wool suit with an ivory silk camisole and gold circle pin on her lapel. No earrings.

The waitress brought their orders—a blueberry muffin and red zinger tea for Jessie, a cup of coffee for Rita. No wonder the ACLU woman was so thin.

"Mr. Lewis said several of the letters and calls he received protesting his representation of the White Alliance came to the ACLU office." Jessie broke off a piece of muffin and ate it.

"That's correct." Rita held her coffee cup with both hands and took a tentative sip. Her fingernails were short and lacquered with clear polish. She wore a silver ring with a turquoise stone.

"Do you have the letters?"

"Barry took them. We couldn't tape the calls, of course. It's illegal." She emptied a packet of Sweet'n Low into her cup, then stirred the coffee with her spoon.

"Did you see the letters yourself?"

Rita nodded. "Some were vile, I can tell you. Hateful." She shuddered and brought the cup to her mouth again, inhaling the coffee aroma but not drinking. "Others were angry but civilized."

"Do you remember any of the senders' names?"

She shook her head. "Sorry. And I didn't answer any of Barry's calls. I *did* get a few letters and calls myself. But I assume Barry told you that." She took another, less tentative sip.

Rule number one: Never assume. "From whom?"

"Most of the letters were from people quitting the ACLU because of the parade. A couple were from Jewish organizations. The ADL. The Wiesenthal. One was signed by a list of rabbis."

"Was that sent by the Organization of Jewish Associations?" Maybe Jessie wouldn't need Mark Pell's cooperation after all.

"That sounds right. I can check my files and fax you copies. I kept all the letters."

Unlike Lewis. Jessie felt like hugging the woman. "That

would be great. Does the name Ezra Nathanson sound familiar?"

Rita frowned in concentration, then shook her head. "Sorry."

"What about Ben-Natan and the Shield? Has he contacted you?"

"He and his pals have been camping out in our lobby and outer office. Now that the judge has ordered the permit, I hope we've seen the last of them."

Maybe, maybe not. "What about the callers? Organizations or individuals?"

"Individuals. They didn't identify themselves."

"What did they say?" Jessie ate another section of the muffin. It wasn't fresh, but she was hungry. All she'd had for breakfast was a glass of nonfat milk and a handful of Cheerios.

"More or less what they told Barry. I was a horrible person. God would punish me. My life was over if I didn't convince Barry and the ACLU to drop the case." She shrugged. "Lovely, isn't it?" The sober expression in her eyes belied her flip tone.

"Did it scare you?"

"Sure it scared me! I've had angry calls before. They kind of go with the territory, you know? But not like these. Not this . . . ugly. To tell you the truth, when I heard what happened to Barry, I felt like going to my ranch and staying there forever. At least with my horses, I know where I stand. Do you ride?"

"Not anymore. My dad used to take my sister and me to the pony rides in Griffith Park on Sundays, and when we vacationed in Lake Arrowhead, he took us horseback riding in Blue Jay." Frances had rarely accompanied them. "It was fun. Where's your ranch?"

"Near Palmdale. It was my parents'. They divorced, and my mom didn't want it. She wasn't exactly the rustic, I-love-nature type." Rita smiled for the first time. "So my dad left it to me. I go there every weekend and whenever I get a chance and ride in the canyons. I love it there."

"Obviously, you decided not to go to the ranch."

"No." She sighed. "But I had an alarm company wire my condo. I guess I'm being silly." She looked at Jessie questioningly.

"It's probably not a bad idea in general." It wasn't foolproof. Bars on windows and doors and burglar alarms with posted signs discouraged pranksters and encouraged professional thieves to practice their craft on less protected homes. But nothing prevented someone persistent—or desperate—from breaking in.

"Looking back, are you sorry you took the White Alliance case?" Jessie asked. "I'm just curious."

"Absolutely not. What Barry said in court, that he hates what the White Alliance stands for? I feel the same way. Yet we both know that if you limit one person's civil rights, you're chipping away at democracy." She paused. "I can't tell you how my skin crawled talking to Benning and his punks. They *know* we think they're scum, but that we had to take their goddamn case." She drained her cup and set the cup down a little too hard on its saucer. "They loved every minute."

"Why didn't you give this to someone who isn't Jewish? You had to know the Jewish community would be upset by this."

"Barry insisted on taking the case, even though he knew he'd be getting all this flak. We talked about it. But I don't think either of us realized how heavy it would be." She sounded glum. "God, I can't wait for this to be over!"

"You were in the courtroom today. Did you recognize the voices of any of the people who called out?"

Rita shook her head.

"Was there anything distinguishable about the voices of the people who called you? A cadence or style of speaking? An accent?"

"Several of them had accents. That's hardly surprising,

considering that many of the people upset with Barry and me and our office are European Jews who survived the Holocaust."

"Did the callers seem equally angry with you and Mr. Lewis?"

"Most of them were angrier with Barry, because he's Jewish." She paused. "Actually, one man accused me of 'forcing' Barry into this situation. That isn't true, you know. Barry volunteered."

That was interesting. Jessie was pretty sure Lewis had said that Rita had approached him. Not that it made much difference. "But you don't know who that caller was, huh?"

Rita hesitated. "I don't know if I should be telling you this." She ran her finger around the rim of the coffee cup. Finally she said, "It was Mr. Lewis. Morris Lewis, I mean."

Jessie's eyebrows rose. "Barry Lewis's father?"

Rita nodded. "He's not speaking to Barry. Neither is Mrs. Lewis. They're both Holocaust survivors, by the way. Barry doesn't say, but I know he's terribly upset by all this, and hurt."

Obviously, this was the name Sheila hadn't revealed to Jessie. Were the senior Lewises responsible for the Star of David and the attached note? Was that why Barry Lewis had handled the note and disposed of the letters—to eliminate any evidence that would point to his father or mother?

"Do you think the parents could have vandalized his door?"

Rita's face was tinged with pink. "To be honest, it's occurred to me. Maybe they did it to scare Barry into dropping this because they're afraid someone else might try to hurt him."

"Maybe." Or maybe they felt incensed by their son's actions. More than incensed—betrayed. "Did you see Mr. or Mrs. Lewis in the courtroom today?"

"I've never met them. Barry didn't mention seeing them. But then, we didn't really have a chance to talk after the hearing, not with all the commotion." She picked up her cup, then remembered that it was empty. She put it back down.

"More coffee?"

"No thanks." Rita checked her watch. "God, it's late! I'll miss my next appointment if I don't leave now." She opened her purse and took out her wallet. "Two dollars okay?"

"Don't be silly. My treat." Jessie smiled.

"Thanks." Rita returned the smile and snapped her purse shut. She slid off the bench and was several steps away from the booth when she turned around. "Detective Drake, you don't think Barry and I are really in danger, do you? I mean, now that the judge has made her decision, what would be the point, right?" She looked at Jessie for confirmation.

"Probably not. But it's always a good idea to be careful."

"Maybe I should arrange to spend some time at my ranch, huh?"

Chapter Sixteen

The house on Emelita was a moderate-size, one-story structure surrounded by a black wrought-iron fence that made it look more like a fortress than a home. Ben-Natan was evidently a cautious man.

A black Ford Explorer sat in the driveway. Jessie walked to the gate and peered between the bars of the fence. The house was white stucco, its complexion marred by last night's rain with dark, uneven blotches and pink-red streaks that descended from the painted Spanish roof tiles like broken capillaries. The lawn needed trimming; the flower beds showed the leggy leftovers of multicolored pansies that had surrendered to the weather.

Someone hadn't pulled the gate completely shut. Not much of a fortress after all, Jessie thought as she pushed it open and stepped onto the water-beaded lawn. She shut the gate and turned around. Within an instant she heard ferocious barking, then the muffled sound of legs pounding the still wet grass.

She saw a blur of twin movement bounding toward her.

Seconds later she was facing two enormous black Doberman pinschers.

They had stopped less than ten feet away from her and were still barking, their cacophonous duet made more terrifying by the sharp, glistening fangs visible in their gaping jaws and the predatory, feral gleam of their eyes. Their bodies were poised, taut, quivering with anticipation.

Jessie stood, frozen, her heart lurching wildly in her chest. The muffin she'd eaten threatened to come up.

Her gun was under her jacket. She raised her hand and quickly dropped it as the dogs moved menacingly toward her, snarling their protest. She waited a moment, then took a cautious step backward.

The dogs advanced. They were panting now, exhaling and inhaling their hostility in short, rapid-fire breaths.

She retreated another foot.

The dogs moved closer.

She reached slowly behind her and groped for the knob to the gate. Why had she closed it?

"What the hell are you doing on my property?"

The man's voice came from behind, but she didn't dare make a sudden movement or take her eyes off the beasts glaring at her.

"Detective Jessie Drake, LAPD." She was amazed her vocal chords worked. "Call off your dogs." She'd tried to strike a note of polite authority but didn't think she'd succeeded.

"How do I know you're police?"

"Call them off, and I'll show you my badge."

"Show me your badge, and I'll call them off."

She couldn't tell if he was playing with her or if he was wary. "The dogs won't attack if I take my badge out of my pocket?"

"Only if I give them the signal."

She heard the click as the gate was opened, another click as it was shut. She reached slowly into her jacket pocket, took out her badge, flipped it open, and held it to her side.

There was a long silence. Then he was in her line of vision, walking toward the dogs. Joel Ben-Natan. Up close, the resemblance to his twin brother was even more striking. Same curly, dark brown hair. No skullcap. Jeans and a gray sweatshirt with a UCLA Bruins logo instead of a sports jacket and slacks. A swollen, split lip and an angry bruise that was darkening the left side of his face.

Careful not to make an abrupt motion, she put away her badge. Her hand was shaking.

Ben-Natan stooped down. The dogs leaped at him and licked his face. He ruffled their sleek coats, then stood up. "Go," he told them.

They obeyed instantly, moving with a casual, leisurely pace now that they had been transformed from beasts into pets.

"Beautiful, aren't they?" Ben-Natan watched as they trotted to the side of the house and disappeared. He turned to Jessie. "Sorry if they scared you. They're trained to keep strangers out."

Her heartbeat was still accelerated. Her face was flushed with a trace of lingering fear and fresh anger. "You should have a sign warning people about the dogs!"

"People shouldn't come onto my property uninvited."

"Your gate wasn't locked."

"It wasn't?" He frowned. "I'm not usually careless. Anyway, no harm done. Why are you here?"

"I'm investigating the vandalizing of the Lewis home."

"I repeat, why are you here?"

Pretty cool attitude. And no sign of nervousness. Maybe he wasn't responsible for the vandalism. Or maybe he'd been prepared for a visit from the police. "Can we go inside? It's chilly."

He studied her for a moment, then said, "Sure."

She followed him across the lawn to the front entrance. It, too, was barricaded with a wrought-iron, mesh-screened gate in front of a wooden door. He unlocked the gate and door, stepped aside, and ushered Jessie in with a flamboyant wave of his arm.

"My castle," he said.

He led her to a living room furnished with a brown Naugahyde sofa, an undistinguished coffee table, and a low stand that housed a TV and a VCR. On the table were an empty beer can, a glass, and a stack of stationery.

Ben-Natan gestured to the sofa with exaggerated chivalry and waited until she sat down. Then he sat at the other end. His hazel eyes were large and expressive—like his brother's. But harder.

Jessie said, "Mr. Lewis told me you threatened him several times because he's representing the White Alliance."

"I *suggested* he drop the case." Ben-Natan's smile tugged at the split on his lip. He winced. "I never threatened him."

She took out her notebook. "This is Mr. Lewis's statement: 'If I don't drop the case, he'—meaning you—'he said I'll get mine. God will get me.'" She looked up at Ben-Natan.

"I said that. So what?" He shrugged. "Lewis *will* get his. It's the truth, not a threat."

"And you don't plan to implement the truth?"

"Last I heard, assault is illegal."

"What would you call your fight at the courthouse?"

"Lewis was walking away. I wanted his attention. *I'm* the one who got hurt, if you haven't noticed." He touched his jaw gingerly, then squinted at her. "You look familiar. Have we met?"

"Where were you Monday night between six and ten?"

"Home." He shifted on the sofa.

Had there been a beat of hesitation? "Two witnesses saw a man of your description in front of the Lewis home that night."

She said this with a straight face and without a twinge of guilt. Police can lie in pursuit of the truth. She'd been disconcerted to learn that precept in the academy and hadn't appreciated the irony—then. Working in the field had quickly taught her the necessity of using all legal means to pry the truth out of people reluctant to part with it.

"There are thousands of men in this city who look like me," Ben-Natan said. "My face isn't all that unique."

"I showed them your mug shot. They're pretty sure it's you."

"Nice photo, isn't it?" His red face belied his nonchalance. "It wasn't me. I wasn't anywhere near Lewis's home Monday night."

"Is that where you sent the letters? To Mr. Lewis's home?"

"I didn't send any letters. I called Lewis a couple of times. No letters," he repeated.

"Where'd you call him?"

"At his place of work."

"Never at his home?"

Ben-Natan hesitated, then said, "I might've called him at his home once. I don't remember."

He's wondering what Barry and Sheila Lewis told me, Jessie realized. He doesn't want to be caught in a lie. She said, "The Lewises' home phone number is unlisted. How did you get it?"

"I made a few calls to some people. It wasn't too hard."

Lewis had mentioned that his address and phone number were on several lists generated by Jewish organizations. "Tell me about the Shield of Jewish Protectors."

"The name explains who we are."

"Explain it to *me.*"

He sighed to indicate boredom with the question and her attitude. "We fight anti-Semitism. We stage protests. We make noise when Jewish homes and synagogues and property are defaced or torched. That's what we are. That's what we do."

"By any means?"

"By any *legal* means." He recrossed his legs.

"You've been arrested for some of your activities."

"Gandhi was arrested. Martin Luther King was arrested. I'd say I was in pretty good company."

"Gandhi and King were opposed to violence."

"I'm opposed to violence, too. Violence against Jews."

Pretty quick. "There's no directory listing for your organization. Why is that?"

"We relocated to a small office on Chandler."

"And you don't have a phone?" Her tone and her raised eyebrows expressed her skepticism.

"Temporarily, it's listed under one of our member's names."

"Then how can people find you?"

"Word of mouth. And we don't want everyone to find us."

"Hiding, Mr. Ben-Natan?"

"Keeping a low profile, Detective." He smiled. "We have our detractors. Some of them are Jews, I'm sorry to say."

Thugs, Barry Lewis had called the Shield. "Like the ADL? I understand they turned down your offer to work for them."

"Probably didn't like my wardrobe." Ben-Natan glanced down at his sweatshirt, then looked up at Jessie and grinned stiffly. He draped his arm on top of the sofa. "A lot of Jewish organizations like to bad-mouth us. The truth is, they're glad we exist. We make them look good. We get all the negative press. At the same time, we get media attention for the issues that need it."

"Does the Shield pay you a salary?"

He shook his head. "It's all volunteer."

"How do you support yourself?"

He frowned. "I don't see what that has to do with Lewis."

"It doesn't. You don't have to answer if you don't want to."

"Sure. If I don't, you'll think I'm into drug trafficking." He paused. "I made some real estate investments with an inheritance years ago, when real estate was alive and well."

Nathanson had referred to the same inheritance. "You say you were home all Monday night?" That was another thing she'd learned—mix up the questions. Keep the suspect on his toes.

He removed his arm from the top of the sofa. "All night. My girlfriend Yaffa can verify that. She was with me the entire time. She's out shopping for groceries, but I'll have her call you."

After he coached her. Just as Nathanson had coached the Pasternak woman? Twin brothers—twin stories? "I'll wait for her."

He shrugged. "Suit yourself. Yaffa won't be back for quite a while. I'm going to get a beer. Want one?"

Jessie shook her head.

"Can't drink on duty, right?" He smiled, then left the room. When he returned he was carrying a beer can and a bag of potato chips. He put the can on the table and ripped open the bag of chips. "No salt, low fat, nonalcoholic. No taste. Yaffa likes them. She's watching my health." He extended the bag to Jessie.

"No thanks. Mr. Ben-Natan—"

"TV!" he exclaimed. "*That's* where I saw you! You're the cop who nabbed the serial killer last year. Am I right?"

"Right. Mr. Ben-Natan—"

"So why are you on *this* case? I thought you were with Homicide. Nobody's been killed."

Call Espes, Jessie felt like telling him. Maybe the citizens of Los Angeles could draft a petition and send it to him: "Help put Detective Jessie Drake back on Homicide where she belongs."

"Let's talk about your relationship with Mr. Lewis," she said.

"We have no relationship. I hate what he's doing. I hope he burns in hell." He glanced at Jessie to see her reaction.

"But you didn't paint the Star of David?"

"Asked and answered, Detective. I'll tell you one thing—I salute whoever did it. Wish I could've seen Lewis's face when he came home." Ben-Natan maneuvered a chip into his mouth, careful to avoid the split, and crunched.

"Okay if I look around your property?"

"Hell, no! Why would I let you do that?"

"What do you have to hide?"

"Nothing. I'm just protecting my civil liberties." He grinned. "If you want to look around, come back with a warrant. I know my rights."

"I guess you've been through the system enough times, huh?"

"Hitting below the belt." He shook his head. "Not nice."

"Your brother said you're a very angry man, that you see the world filled with people who hate Jews."

Ben-Natan's eyebrows rose. "You met Ezra? Nice guy. He's the Jacob in the family." He saw Jessie's puzzled expression. "You know—Jacob and Esau from the Bible? Isaac's twin sons?"

Jessie nodded. It was a good thing she'd sat in on Nathanson's class yesterday.

"Ezra's the good twin. Everybody loves him."

Poor baby. "Nobody loves you?"

He smiled. "I wouldn't say that. Everyone respects Ezra 'cause he's a scholar, just like Jacob was. Bible commentators say that when Rebecca was pregnant with her twins, Jacob would kick whenever she passed by a house of study. That's Ezra to a tee."

"What was Esau?"

"A hunter." Ben-Natan crunched on another chip.

"Is that what you are?"

"I love animals, Detective Drake. There's no bullshit about them. They're your friend, or your enemy. I'd never hunt animals."

What about people? She picked up a sheet of the letterhead on the coffee table. Printed in red ink in the center of the page were the words *THE SHIELD OF JEWISH PROTECTORS*.

"Nice logo." She pointed to the embossed red Star of David at the upper left corner.

"We like it." His tone was guarded.

"That's called a *Mogen Dovid*, isn't it? And *mogen* means shield, right? I hope I'm pronouncing it correctly."

"Your pronunciation is perfect. Who taught you? Ezra?"

"Kind of interesting that your logo is a *Mogen Dovid*, and that someone painted a *Mogen Dovid* on Lewis's door." She smiled.

"Everybody knows that's the Shield's logo." He was clearly irritated now. "Anybody could've painted the *Mogen Dovid* on Lewis's door, hoping to implicate me. So I'd be pretty stupid to paint a *Mogen Dovid*, wouldn't I? Leave a calling card?"

Or smart. Do something that draws attention to you, then claim you'd be stupid to do it. "Will you be at the parade?"

He stared at her. "Is that a serious question? Of *course* I'll be there. The Shield will be there, in numbers."

"You could be arrested."

He shrugged. "As you know, I've been arrested before."

"You've gotten off with light penalties. Next time you might not be so lucky."

"Thanks for the warning. Maybe you'll come visit me."

She frowned. "You're treating this very lightly."

"I'm dead serious about this. It's pretty simple. The Nazis plan to march in Jewish neighborhoods. My people and I don't plan to sit by and let them do it without a protest."

"And if people get hurt?"

"We'll take measures to ensure the safety of our Jewish brethren, Detective. As for the other side, I don't give a shit what happens to them. They come into our Jewish neighborhoods, they do it at their own risk." He chomped on another chip as if to emphasize his point.

Lots of bravado, very little common sense. There was no predicting the direction a protest could take. More often than not, innocent people were injured. She thought about telling Ben-Natan that but decided he wouldn't be interested in her opinion.

She heard a burst of loud barking and reminded herself she was indoors, safe. "Just a few more questions. Do you think—"

"Yoel?" a woman's voice called. "Are you here?"

"Coming! Yaffa's here," he told Jessie as he got up. "I have to help her with the grocery bags. Be right back."

"Yoel"—it rhymed with Noelle—must be Hebrew for Joel. Jessie stood. "I think it would be better if you waited here."

"Not better for me. Yaffa will be cranky." He grinned. "She'll get over it."

He placed his hand on his chest. "You don't trust me?" Jessie smiled.

"Who are you talking with, Yoel?" the woman called

again. A moment later she was standing in the entrance to the room.

She was beautiful. She had smooth, olive-toned skin, high cheekbones, and coal-black eyes fringed with thick black lashes. Her black hair was braided into one long plait. No makeup except for clear lip gloss. No jewelry. She was wearing an oversize, off-white fisherman's sweater over tight jeans and dark brown boots. She was pencil slim.

She took a few steps into the room, moving with the willowy elegance of a dancer. "You have company, Yoel?" She stared at Jessie, then at Ben-Natan. Her eyes and the rigid set of her shapely mouth demanded an explanation.

Ben-Natan was right, Jessie decided—Yaffa *was* cranky.

"This is Detective Drake. Detective, Yaffa Aloni."

Yaffa inhaled sharply, deepening the indentations on her nostrils. "There is a problem?"

"No problem. The detective wants to know—"

"Miss Aloni, where were you Monday night?" Jessie positioned herself so that she was standing between the woman and Ben-Natan.

"Here. All night, I am here. There is something wrong?"

"What time did Mr. Ben-Natan come home Monday night?"

"Monday night?" Yaffa frowned. "Yoel was here the whole time with me Monday night. We were watching television."

The woman was lying, Jessie knew; Ben-Natan had silently telegraphed the right answer. There had been a time when she and Gary had shared that magical ability to communicate without words, to know what the other was thinking, what the other needed. She missed it and the feeling of oneness that accompanied it. She wondered if she'd ever experience that closeness again.

"What show did you watch?" Jessie asked, realizing she could prove nothing.

"Not a show. A video. What was it, Yoel?" Yaffa turned to him. He was standing next to her. *"Dancing Dirty?"*

"Dirty Dancing," Yoel/Joel answered. He grinned and put his arm around Yaffa's shoulder. "Any more questions, Detective? If not, I have some stuff to do."

"No more questions right now. I may want to talk to you again." She hesitated, then said, "Would you walk me out, please? I'm nervous about your dogs."

"My pleasure. Be right back," he said to Yaffa, and followed Jessie out of the room.

As she stepped past the front door, she looked around her. The dogs were nowhere in sight, but she sensed they were nearby, lurking. It was drizzling again.

"See you at the scene of the crime?" he said when they were standing in front of the gate.

Jessie frowned. "What?"

"The parade, Detective. You'll be there, won't you?"

"Probably." Espes, no doubt, would insist.

"You know, it's kind of funny. The media and the government keep talking about the rise of the extreme Right in Germany. The fact is, in Germany these neo-Nazis and skinheads would never be permitted to run this parade. Matter of fact, they'd be arrested."

He opened the gate. "Makes you wonder, doesn't it?"

Chapter Seventeen

"I *think* I remembered everything." Helen turned to Matthew, who was sitting cross-legged on the white linoleum in Jessie's sparc room. "I gave you today's vitamin, didn't I, hon?"

"Uh-huh," he said without looking up from his pocket-size electronic game.

Helen turned back to Jessie. "He has handwriting exercises and a spelling lesson to do. You'll find his workbook in his backpack. Make sure to do the challenge words, Matthew." When he didn't respond, she said his name again.

He looked up at his mother. "Mrs. Kalb told us we don't have to if we don't want to."

"Well, at least *try* them."

"But I don't *have* to, right?"

"Well, no, you don't *have* to." Helen smiled. "But it would make Mommy happy if you did. You should always do your very best."

Shades of Frances, Jessie thought. Although with their mother, the sisters had learned, it was impossible to do the best. Jessie and Helen had vowed to be different. "When we have children . . ." they'd said so many times about so many things. They would be less critical, less rigid. They would be wiser, more relaxed, more accepting of failure and near success. Happier.

Jessie wondered how many people honored similar promises made with similar solemnity. Judging from Helen, not too many. She wondered, too, whether she would be any different with her own child if she had one, someday.

"So you'll do the challenge words, Matthew?"

" 'Kay, Mommy. Bye."

Jessie hid her smile with her hand and pretended to cough.

"Well, he seems eager to get rid of me, doesn't he?" Helen's laugh was self-conscious. She checked her watch. "I'd better go. I have to park in the airport lot and take a shuttle to the terminal." From her purse she took out a typed list and handed it to Jessie. "Here's the hotel number. I also wrote the name and number for the pediatrician, in case Matthew gets sick."

"I won't get sick," Matthew said. "I have vitamins."

Jessie covered her grin. "Did you pack a bathing suit, Helen?" According to the morning paper, Tucson's weather was in the high eighties. L.A. was in the sixties, but at least it wasn't raining.

Helen nodded. "And a tennis racket." She leaned closer to Jessie and whispered, "And a new negligee." She smiled, then bent down to Matthew. "I'm going to miss you so much, honey. Are you going to miss Mommy?" She combed his hair with her fingers.

"Uh-huh." He kissed her cheek and allowed her to hug him.

Jessie walked Helen to the front door. "He's grown since I saw him three weeks ago. I bet he'll be as tall as Neil." And as lanky. With his almost black straight hair and coal-gray eyes, Matthew looked like a younger version of his father.

"Thank God. Imagine if he had *my* genes."

Like Frances, Helen was petite, only five feet two inches, four inches shorter than Jessie. Helen had also inherited their mother's coloring—blond hair, green eyes—and, unfortunately for Helen and sometimes for those around her, Frances's migraines. And temperament. Ergo the therapy.

"He's looking much better, don't you think?" Helen whispered, as if echoing Jessie's thoughts. "More relaxed?"

"Definitely. So are you." Jessie had noticed a perceptible softening in her sister over the past few months. The tightness around her mouth seemed less pronounced, too.

"I've been working on it. I guess Dr. Rossman's techniques are helping."

Jessie grinned. " 'Working at relaxing'? Talk about oxymorons."

" 'Second best.' "

" 'Student teacher.' "

" 'Civil unrest,' " Helen smiled. "You're right. It *is* funny. We should call Mom. Think she still has that notebook?"

"Probably." Frances found oxymorons entertaining and wrote them down in a leather-bound journal. Arthur and Jessie and Helen had added to her collection. Frances had appreciated their contributions, although when Gary had offered "holy shit," she hadn't been amused. Arthur had. Jessie smiled at the memory.

"Speaking of Mom, Helen, I called her last night. She's hurt that you haven't phoned her in a while."

"You called her?" Helen's eyebrows rose to dramatic heights.

Jessie smiled and shook her head. "I can hardly believe it myself. You know the parade this neo-Nazi group is planning?" When Helen looked blank, Jessie said, "Someone painted a Jewish star on their lawyer's door? You must've heard it on the news, Helen."

"Oh, that. What about it?"

Jessie explained her connection to the case and described her conversation with Frances. "Don't you wonder what your reaction would be to this parade if you were Jewish?"

"Not at all. Why would I do that?" Helen stood on tiptoe and kissed her sister. "Thanks for having Matthew, Jess."

"My pleasure. Just have fun. That's an order."

"You sound like Dr. Rossman. She said Neil and I should spend time together, without Matthew, and 'focus on enjoying each other physically, emotionally, and spiritually.'" Helen paused. "I guess I'll have to *work* at it. I think I'll start with 'physically.'" She grinned. "Look at me. I made a joke."

Jessie and Matthew spent the day at the downtown Children's Museum. It was located on Main Street, a block north of City Hall and just blocks from the Los Angeles County Courthouse. Driving back to the station after her meeting with Rita Warrens, Jessie had noticed banners advertising the museum. She'd asked Phil whether Matthew would enjoy it. Definitely, he told her. His two sons had liked going there when they were younger.

They glanced at children's artwork. They viewed underground pipes in "City Streets." At the fire station, Matthew, wearing a firefighter's coat, boots, and hat, "fought a fire" with a real hose. They visited "the Cave," where he explored his own "secret cave" and discovered dinosaur footprints, bones, and holograms.

"Neat," he told Jessie.

At the "Face Paints" site on the lower level of the museum, he was hesitant about smearing the paint on himself even though Jessie assured him it was washable—Helen, she knew, had instilled in her son an almost neurotic fastidiousness. But he giggled when Jessie transformed herself into a monster, giggled again uncontrollably after he'd made himself into a monster, too.

She loved watching him. She felt an intense, aching joy at seeing his freckled face, so often in shadows, shine with carefree pleasure. Was this what motherhood was like?

They sat on one of the benches in the museum's courtyard and ate the tuna-filled pita bread sandwiches Jessie had prepared. Matthew was methodical, allowing himself a potato chip after every two bites of tuna and pita as he observed two young boys playing tag on the other side of the courtyard.

"I think they're brothers," he told Jessie. "They're wearing the exact same shirts." He resumed watching the boys.

"Mommy said maybe someday I'll have a baby brother or sister. It takes nine months to make a baby." He looked at Jessie again.

Jessie smiled. "Would you like to have a brother or sister?"

"Sure. I'd teach it things and share my toys, too. But not my Lego, 'cause a baby could choke on a tile and die." He chewed another bite of pita. "Do you want to have a baby, Aunt Jessie?"

She felt a pang. "Someday."

"If you married Detective Pruitt, you could."

"I don't know if I'm going to marry Detective Pruitt. Right now we're just good friends." Good friends with separate lives. She hadn't seen Frank since Tuesday, had spoken to him only once, when he'd called Friday night. She pictured him at his former in-laws', standing with his ex-wife, helping their son unwrap his birthday gifts.

"Mommy says he's nice, but she likes Uncle Gary better."

Helen had always liked Gary; she'd been distressed by the divorce. "Gary is very nice, too," Jessie said, wondering why her sister was discussing her social life with her eight-year-old son. Or maybe Matthew had overheard Helen talking with Neil.

"You still like him, right? Even though you're not married."

"Right."

He chomped on a chip. "If you had a baby, who would watch it while you're at work?"

"I'd probably hire a baby-sitter from a reliable agency."

"But you wouldn't stop being a detective?"

Gary had wanted her to quit. Her refusal had been the source of much of the friction between them. Then she'd lost the baby, and although the obstetrician had told Gary that her being knocked to the ground by a suspect she was chasing hadn't necessarily caused the miscarriage, the rift between them deepened.

"I don't *think* I'd stop being a detective," she told Matthew. "I don't know for sure."

He nodded, satisfied by her answer. "So what case are you working on now, Aunt Jessie?"

"A couple of things."

She'd spent most of Thursday checking out the people who had written to Rita Warrens at the ACLU; Rita had faxed Jessie copies of the letters late Wednesday. Many of the individuals who had written to inform the ACLU of their resignation weren't California residents. Jessie had phoned the seven local members—five men, two women—but had ruled them out. They were angry with the organization, not with Lewis.

She *did* have a copy of the OJA letter and the names of the rabbis who'd signed it (actually, she had *two* copies—Pell's fax had arrived almost immediately after Rita's, naturally), but Espes had told her to hold off contacting the rabbis. Lots of sensitive toes. On Friday, with Espes's okay, she'd helped Phil follow up leads on a nineteen-year-old call girl found in her Westwood condominium with her throat slashed.

"I'm working a new case with my partner, Phil," she told Matthew. No need to go into the gruesome details. She hesitated, then said, "Plus I'm working another case that isn't a homicide." She explained about the vandalized door and the note, about the neo-Nazis and the parade. She told him, in simple terms, about the Holocaust, watched his face cloud, wondered what was the right age to teach a child that although the bogeyman was fiction, there was real, senseless, violent hate in the world.

"That's why the Jewish people here in Los Angeles are so upset about the parade, Matthew."

"But how come these people hate Jews?"

"They hate lots of people, not just Jews. They hate Blacks and Latinos and Asians. Anybody different from them. These are angry, unhappy people. I guess they need someone to blame for their unhappiness."

"So if I was Jewish, they'd hate me, too?" His eyes were wide with incredulity. "Even though I never *did* anything to them? Even though they never *met* me?"

"No one could hate you, Matthew," she said lightly.

He was quiet while he finished his lunch, subdued, and she regretted having told him anything about the neo-Nazis. But a short while later, as they watched a live production in the museum's Louis B. Mayer Theater, he was cheerful and buoyant again and enjoyed the other exhibits they visited. They stayed until five o'clock, closing time for the museum.

All in all, a very nice day; she'd have to tell Phil. They stopped at a pizza place for supper, then the video rental store. Then home. Helen and Neil had left a message on Jessie's answering machine. Jessie called the hotel, was connected with her sister, and, after speaking to her briefly, handed Matthew the phone.

"A fantabulous time!" she heard him say as she walked to the kitchen. "The best!"

She smiled. It would've been nice to meet Frank's sons, but she was glad she'd spent the day just with her nephew.

Matthew took a bath. Afterward they played several rounds of casino, then sat in the den and watched *Aladdin* and munched on microwave popcorn. Later, after she had tucked him into bed and listened to his prayers, she called her friend Brenda and spoke to her a while. Then she went to her room, changed into a nightshirt, and decided to read.

The king-size bed seemed larger somehow, emptier. She reached for the phone receiver on her nightstand to call Frank but changed her mind. He was busy with his boys.

On Sunday they were going boating in Marina del Rey. Jessie had worried about the weather, but the sky was a cloudless, azure sheet, and the *Times* promised temperatures in the seventies.

At the beach it would be at least ten degrees colder. Jessie reminded Matthew to take his windbreaker. She was heading for the hall closet to get hers when the front doorbell rang. She thought fleetingly that it might be Frank, then remembered that he was taking his sons to Disneyland, with Rona.

At the front door, she looked out the privacy window and was startled to see her ex-husband standing in the walkway. His back was toward her, but she would recognize his dark blond, curly hair and broad shoulders anywhere.

She opened the door. "Hi, Gary. What's up?"

He turned and walked with a loping gait until he was inside the house. "Hi, yourself." Smiling, he leaned forward and kissed her cheek.

It was a friendly kiss, but it compounded the confusion she felt whenever she saw him. It would have been so much easier, she often thought, if their marriage had been a battleground of screaming arguments and mutual loathing. But there had been no screaming, no loathing, simply the painful realization that they wanted and needed different things. Now that they were apart and there was no tension between them, she remembered mostly the happiness they'd shared and found herself missing him more often than she cared to admit.

"Matthew's with me for the weekend. We're on our way out."

"To the marina," he said. "Helen told me. She thought it'd be nice if I came along to keep you and Matt company."

What the hell was her sister doing—playing matchmaker? "Helen shouldn't have said that. She should've checked with me."

"I thought she *did* check." He shrugged. "I figured it would give me a chance to see Matthew. The last time I saw him was a month ago. I finally kept my promise and showed him around the *Times.*"

Helen had mentioned that to Jessie. "That was nice of you."

"He's a good kid. So what do you say? Can I tag along?" He smiled again.

He was dressed for the marina—jeans, white deck shoes, a midnight-blue crew-neck cotton sweater the color of his eyes. She had bought him that sweater two years ago, for his thirty-fifth birthday. She hesitated.

"If it's no, I'll understand, Jess. I don't want to make you uncomfortable."

What was the big deal, anyway? "You can come. Matthew will love having you."

"And you?"

"Don't press your luck, Gary." She smiled, too.

He followed her into the kitchen and leaned against the counter while she made two extra roast beef sandwiches. The others were already in the picnic basket, along with fruit, cookies, and four small bottles of Snapple.

"Don't skimp on the mayo, Jess."

"You don't need it."

He reached for a slice of beef. She slapped his hand away.

"Just like old times, huh?" He grinned and took the slice of beef anyway.

They decided to go in his Audi. The last time she'd been in the car had been months ago. She'd called him and told him she needed to clear up some unresolved issues.

"Closure time?" he'd quipped, but she'd heard the nervousness in his voice. At a coffee shop the following evening, he'd listened while she talked about Frances, about the myriad punishments Jessie and Helen had been subjected to over the years, about its psychological effects on both sisters. About Jessie's fear that, like Frances, she would be an abusive parent.

"I never guessed," Gary said. "Your mom seems so nice, so . . ."

"Refined. Beautiful. Sophisticated. I know." Everyone thought Frances Claypool was nice.

"You should've told me, Jess." His voice resonated with mournful accusation. "We were married, for Christ's sake! You should've told me everything."

"I know," she said again, not knowing what else to say.

On the drive back, Gary was silent, and she wondered if she'd made a mistake telling him the truth. So much for closure, she thought, but when he parked in front of the house, he turned suddenly and, drawing close to her, put his arm on her shoulder and stroked her hair.

"You'll make a great mother, Jess," he whispered. "Don't doubt it for a minute."

"Maybe."

"No 'maybe.' " He paused. "I'm glad you told me. I just wish it had been sooner."

He called a few days later and asked her out. She turned him down. "I'm seeing Frank Pruitt," she told him.

"Is it serious?" he asked, and she told him she didn't know, but that maybe it could be.

That was the last time she'd talked to him. Until this morning.

Matthew was clearly delighted that Gary was coming along. He expressed no surprise, and Jessie wondered whether he'd known that Gary would show up and was an accomplice to Helen's matchmaking conspiracy. At the marina the wind was brisk, raising tiny peaks on the water and whipping their hair around their faces. Jessie loved it. They rented a motorboat, and Matthew sat at the helm, helping Gary steer. Every once in a while he turned his head back toward Jessie to throw her a quick, exhilarated, "look-at-me!" grin.

After they returned the boat, they spread the blanket Jessie had brought along on the sand and ate lunch. A while later a boy came over and asked Matthew to join him in a game of Frisbee.

"Can I, Aunt Jessie?" His eyes were bright with eagerness.

"Sure. Have fun. Just stay in sight, and don't go wandering." She sat, hugging her knees, and watched him as he ran across the sand with the boy to a cluster of children.

"So how's L.A.'s number one homicide detective?" Gary asked. He was lying on his side on the blanket.

"Okay. I'm handling another case, too. The neo-Nazi parade?"

He nodded. "But—"

"I know. It's not a homicide. My new boss gave me the assignment. Don't ask, okay?"

"Okay. Any idea who painted the Star of David on the lawyer's door?"

"Nope. It's called a *Mogen Dovid,* by the way."

He whistled. "Pretty good for a shiksa. Where'd you pick that up?"

She smiled. "In court on Wednesday the judge said that the police commission approved the parade, but that the city council reviewed the decision and went against it. Do you know anything about that?"

He nodded. "It was in the papers a couple of weeks ago."

She frowned. "I didn't see anything."

"It didn't get much play. The commission knew they couldn't block the parade because of the First Amendment. The city council knew it, too, but they used Prop Five to over-rule the commission."

"Even though they knew they'd lose? Why waste the time?"

"Councilman Perkins called in his favors. A lot of people in his district are Jewish. Can you imagine how many calls he got when they heard about the parade? He couldn't *not* protest the commission's decision, not if he wants to get reelected."

"So it's all politics?"

"Not *all.* The council's taking a moral stand, too." He sifted sand with his fingers. "As a reporter, I get damn nervous when anyone tries to abridge someone else's right to say what he wants. But these creeps scare the hell out of me. Right now they're a small group of fringe fanatics. But the economy stinks, people are unemployed, uninsured. Who knows how many people will listen to this group's warped message and say, 'Hey, these guys are right on the mark. Let's get rid of all the Jews, Blacks, Hispanics, and Asians and get this country working again.' "

A Frisbee landed a few feet from the blanket. Matthew raced over to retrieve it, waved at Jessie and Gary, then ran back.

"He looks great, doesn't he, Gary?"

"He's a changed kid. I'm glad for his sake that Helen and Neil are working things out. For their sakes, too," he added. "A good marriage is worth saving, Jessie." He reached for her hand.

She moved it away. "Don't." They were having such a nice afternoon. Why did he have to ruin it?

"You still seeing the detective?"

She tensed. "Yes."

"Any chance you'll go out with me?"

"It would be too complicated, Gary, too confusing."

"So what's happening between you two? Do you love him, Jess?"

"I don't know."

"You've been seeing him for months. You said you knew you loved me after our third date, remember?"

She remembered. They'd spent a Sunday doing silly stuff—miniature golfing, bumper cars, video games. They had giggled like kids. That night he'd surprised her with tickets to an Elton John concert in the Forum in Inglewood—she'd told him on their previous date how much she loved the singer's music. Afterward they'd spent the evening drinking espresso and talking in the cocktail lounge of the Beverly Wilshire Hotel. By the time he brought her to her apartment, it was three in the morning. She'd known then that she could see herself spending the rest of her life with him, and she had wanted so badly to share that knowledge with someone. She couldn't call Brenda—it was too late. She'd lain in bed until five, unable to sleep, then had called her sister two time zones away in Winnetka, Illinois. She hadn't told her mother until much later.

"I don't want to discuss this, okay?" Jessie reached into the picnic basket, found a Granny Smith apple, and took a bite.

"Helen said his wife's in town with their boys and you're feeling kind of left out."

Damn Helen! Jessie would know better than to confide in her sister again. "Helen has a big mouth! And it's his *ex*-wife."

Gary smiled. "So why not go out with me while Pruitt's not available? He's busy with his ex. You can be busy with yours."

"It's not a good idea."

"Why? You're not engaged to the guy or something, are you?"

"I'm sleeping with him, Gary. Is that what you wanted to know?" She blushed. "I'm surprised Helen didn't tell you."

His face reddened. He looked away.

Damn. She hadn't wanted to hurt him. "You asked, Gary."

"Yeah, I did, didn't I?" He pushed himself up, brushed the sand off his jeans, and loped over to Matthew.

Chapter Eighteen

"Sheila?" Barry called from the hall. "It's late."

"I said I was coming." Looking in the mirror, she adjusted the veil on her white felt hat. Several strands of blond hair trailed down her neck. She was tucking them into her French twist with a hairpin when she heard his approaching footsteps.

"You're the one who has to say *yizkor* for your father," he said, entering the bedroom. *Yizkor,* a memorial prayer for deceased parents and close relatives, is recited four days a year—on the last day of the holidays of Passover, Shavuot, and Sukkot, and on Yom Kippur. "If you want to miss it—"

She jabbed the pin into her scalp and winced. "I'm not going to miss it! Please don't rush me. You're making me nervous."

"When *aren't* you nervous lately?"

And whose fault was that? She glared at his reflection in the mirror. "You don't have to go with me. I told you that yesterday."

"And the day before, and the day before that. I can take a hint."

She turned to face him. "The truth? I dread going altogether, seeing everyone stare at me and the girls. Your being there will make it worse." She paused. "We could go to another temple."

126

"I'm not hiding like some criminal, Sheila. I haven't done anything wrong."

You never do, she thought. She turned back to the mirror and picked up another pin.

Rose leaned closer to her husband. "Sheila and Barry are here," she whispered. "And the girls."

"So?" He looked at the stage, where the rabbi was sitting in conversation with the cantor. "Why don't they start already?"

He'd been edgy from the moment they'd arrived, expecting people's stares, comments. There had been none. "I think we should say hello, Morris. We haven't seen them in six weeks."

"You want to say hello, say hello." His mouth was a grim line. His hands gripped his knees.

Rose sighed. She stood and edged out of the row. Turning, she spotted her two blond, ponytailed granddaughters at the same time they saw her. "Grandma!" she heard ten-year-old Jennifer say.

Rose broke into a smile. "Morris," she called.

He turned and watched his granddaughters run down the aisle. A moment later Rose was bending down, clasping both girls to her chest. Tears stung her eyes.

"Say hello to Grandpa." Rose pointed to Morris.

The girls sidled into the row and hugged him, then returned to their grandmother.

"We missed you, Grandma!" seven-year-old Monique exclaimed. "How come you didn't come to our seder?"

Rose wiped the tears from under her eyes with her fingers. "Grandpa Morris wasn't feeling so good, *sheifeleh*. Next year, God willing, we'll come. You said the *Mah Nishtanah?*"

Monique nodded. Her ponytail bobbed. "I said it by heart, all four questions. I didn't make one mistake. Want to hear me do it?"

"That's only for the seder, Monique," her ten-year-old sister said. "You can't do it over. That's silly."

"Jenny wanted to say it, too, Grandma. Mommy said she could, but Daddy said only the youngest gets to say it."

"Next year Grandpa and I will hear you say the *Mah Nishtanah,* Monique. You, too, Jennifer." Rose patted her older granddaughter's head. "I'm sure you *both* know it perfect. So it was a nice seder?" She and Morris had been invited to a friend's seder, but Morris hadn't wanted to go. Instead they'd spent a miserable evening alone. Rose had cried herself to sleep.

"Daddy was rushing 'cause he had a headache," Jennifer said. "Mommy wouldn't let me open the door for Eliyahu. She was scared, 'cause of what happened last week." She spoke with an air of importance and looked at her grandmother.

Monique said, "Daddy said she was silly, and he went to the door and *pulled* it open and said, 'See, Sheila, there's nothing to worry about.' "

"Don't call Mommy by her name," Jennifer said.

Monique pouted. "I'm just telling what Daddy said."

"Who got the *afikomen?*" Out of the corner of her eye, Rose saw Sheila coming down the aisle. She glanced at Morris. He had seen, too; he turned his head abruptly toward the front.

"I got it the first night," Jennifer said.

"I got it the second, but it wasn't so fun 'cause Grandpa hides it better. Daddy didn't even *try* to hide it. He let me take it from under his matzoh cover when he was *looking!*" She giggled and saw Sheila. "I told Grandma about the *afikomen,* Mommy!"

Sheila's smile was strained. "How are you, Mom?"

"Fine. You look pretty. A new hat?" The veil obscured the expression in her daughter-in-law's eyes.

Sheila nodded, then turned to the girls. "The rabbi's going to speak now. Why don't you play in the lobby."

Monique planted a good-bye kiss on her grandmother. So

did Jennifer. Both girls raced up the aisle and out of the sanctuary.

Rose leaned closer and put her hand on Sheila's arm. "I'm sorry what happened to your door. Did they find out who did it?"

Sheila shook her head. "The police are working on it. Barry's here," she added in a low voice. "Won't you come talk to him?"

"A son should come to his mother, I think," she said quietly.

"Dad hung up on him the last time Barry called. Barry thinks you and Dad hate him."

Rose cast a look in Morris's direction. "We don't hate him, God forbid. We hate what he's doing."

"Rose," Morris called without turning, "they're starting."

She glanced at the stage and saw that the rabbi had approached the lectern. "I have to go, Sheila." She kissed her daughter-in-law's cheek and returned to her seat.

"Today, on the eighth day of Passover . . . ," the rabbi began.

Rose only half listened. The rabbi, an earnest man in his mid-thirties with a resonant voice, would explain the importance of giving charity in memory of loved ones to elevate their souls and bring them closer to God. When he was done, all those present whose parents were alive would leave the sanctuary, and the *yizkor* service could begin.

Half a century ago, when Rose was a young child in a different continent and a different world, she had been curious about the *yizkor* service, had wondered why she and the other children and many of the adults would be shooed outdoors. What secrets did the service hold? What mystic brotherhood united those who stayed? One time she'd hidden behind a bench in the women's section while her mother led her sisters and baby brother outside. An elderly, toothless woman had found her. "Get out, get out!" she'd squawked like a flustered hen. "Do you want to bring the evil eye on you and your family, God forbid?" Later, when Rose and her family had been taken to the camps, she had often remembered that day.

From her purse Rose took a list with the Hebrew names of the family members she would be remembering today. Her father. Her mother. Her grandparents on both sides. Her three sisters, four brothers. Nieces, nephews. Aunts, uncles, cousins. All gone.

". . . will be saying a memorial prayer first for our parents," the rabbi was saying, "then for our extended family, for the United States of America, for the state of Israel and its soldiers, and for Jewish martyrs. The liturgy mentions those martyrs who 'were killed, murdered, slaughtered, burned, drowned, and strangled for the sanctification of the Name' and adds, parenthetically, 'through the hands of the German oppressors, may their name and memory be obliterated.' And I can't help but wonder, my friends, what is our responsibility to these martyrs today in the face of the heinous action that will take place on April twentieth, Yom HaShoah?"

Rose stifled her gasp with her hand. She bit her palm. She turned to Morris. His face paled, then became flooded with color. She reached for his hand. He jerked it away.

". . . . an action that was eloquently and persuasively argued before the court not by a stranger, but by Barry Lewis— a Jew, one of our own. I grieve for Barry Lewis and pray that he will seek atonement for the harm he has done to the entire community. I grieve for his parents—good people, committed Jews—and pray that God will give them strength to bear this tragedy, as they have borne so many others throughout their lives. I grieve for the martyrs of the Holocaust and urge all of you to join your Jewish brethren on April twentieth at a memorial service in the courtyard of *Beit Hashoah* in a dignified demonstration of solidarity and strength against the new breed of oppressors who would, if they had their way, add fresh names to the lists of martyrs for whom we pray. We cannot, we *will* not, allow that to happen."

The rabbi stepped away from the lectern. The cantor took his place. *"Yizkor,"* he chanted.

There was a rustle of clothes, the squeak of seats springing up, as all around Rose congregants stood. Morris was standing, too, tears streaming down his face. Holding on to the back of the pew in front of her, Rose pulled herself up, opened her prayer book, and, with trembling lips, began.

"Yizkor elokim es nishmas ovi, mori, Menachem ben Yosef, sh'holach l'olamo. . . . " May God remember the soul of my father, my teacher, Menachem the son of Yosef, who has gone on to his world. . . .

"Yizkor elokim os nishmas imi, morasi, Mulka bas Shimon, sh'holchoh l'olama. . . . " May God remember the soul of my mother, my teacher, Malka the daughter of Shimon, who has gone on to her world. . . .

"Yizkor elokim . . .

"Yizkor . . .

"Yizkor . . . "

Chapter Nineteen

It was a perfect day for a parade.

Floating in the sky were gauzy clouds that veiled the sun and tempered its rays. The morning air was invigorating, cool and crisp, and redolent with the perfume of spring flowers and freshly mowed lawns.

On Beverly Drive a mile south of Pico, three blocks past the "Welcome to Beverlywood" sign posted on Monte Mar Drive, Beverly temporarily widens to accommodate a circular minipark at the center of a six-spoked "wheel." It was on this island of green that the White Alliance and about eighty supporters, most of them in military gear and swastika, assembled at a quarter to nine on Friday, April 20.

Standing several hundred feet away on the curved sidewalk between Sawyer and Bolton, the two streets radiating east from the "wheel," Jessie wondered whether the neo-Nazi group had chosen this spot arbitrarily or intentionally, as an in-your-face sneer at Barry Lewis, the Jewish lawyer who'd successfully defended their constitutional rights. Lewis lived only blocks away.

Lewis, of course, wasn't here this morning to appreciate the irony. In fact, hardly anyone was here. Two jeans-clad young mothers, pushing toddlers in strollers, had paused briefly to eye the uniformed congregants on the center island,

132

then hurried away when they were accosted by a handful of bored reporters and a minicam operator, all waiting for something to happen. One reporter, with the minicam operator at his heels, had approached Jessie. She'd flashed her badge. The reporter had spun away, clearly annoyed, and searched for fresh prey.

The press had already interviewed and filmed the paraders, some of whom had grinned into the camera. They'd also interviewed the protesters, a dozen restless members of the Jewish Defense League and twenty-five members of the Shield, all standing in a loose confederacy on the sidewalk directly across the circle from Jessie. Ben-Natan had arrived early with Yaffa and his two dogs. He'd said something to Yaffa and waved at Jessie. She'd smiled back, trying not to stare at the dogs. To the average person they probably seemed friendly enough, but Jessie knew better and was relieved to see they were leashed.

The absence of a turnout was no surprise. Rabbi Korbin had promised as much. Earlier in the week Jessie had contacted him and learned that there would be no official Jewish community presence—not here, at the designated start point of the parade; not along the court-sanctioned route down Beverly Drive to Roxbury via Cashio, north to Pico, then east on Pico to La Cienega; not along the second part of the parade that would originate, close to noon, at Beverly Boulevard and Fairfax Avenue and continue along Beverly to June Street. Instead, the Wiesenthal, in conjunction with the OJA (was Pell satisfied? Jessie wondered) and the ADL, had arranged for a memorial Yom HaShoah service to take place in the courtyard of the Museum of Tolerance. They had advertised the service in the community newspapers and asked rabbis to announce it in their weekly Sabbath sermons. The Jewish people of Los Angeles, Korbin had assured Jessie, would follow their leadership.

Jessie had been relieved. So had Espes, to whom she'd relayed the message, and, in turn, Chief Hanson and the mayor—controlling large crowds of protesters would have been difficult and the possibility of someone being injured almost inevitable. Still, the city had prepared for an unofficial response. Working in conjunction with the LAPD Special Events Planning Unit and the Los Angeles Department of Transportation, Wilshire and West L.A. divisions had stationed detectives and uniformed police along the Beverly Drive–Pico route; Wilshire and Hollywood divisions would do the same for the second route. Beverly Drive from the circle to Pico had been closed to traffic until nine-thirty. Traffic going east on Pico Boulevard from Rancho Park until Highland had been reduced to one lane until the parade was concluded. Similar restrictions would be in effect along the Beverly Boulevard route.

The paraders, Jessie and the others had learned in a briefing with Espes, had parked their vehicles near La Cienaga and Pico, the terminal point of the first segment of the parade. They would then drive to the Beverly-Fairfax assembly point. Police were also prepared to provide them with an escort in case trouble erupted.

At precisely nine o'clock a voice from the minipark came through a bullhorn. Ben-Natan's dogs yelped at the sudden sound.

"We're here this morning to celebrate the birthday of Adolf Hitler," a man said. "We're here this morning as proud Americans to march for the rights of the White citizens of this country and reclaim what is ours. No longer will we tolerate . . ."

It was Roy Benning, dressed in a storm trooper's uniform, a swastika prominently displayed on his arm. Jessie only half listened to him, focusing her attention instead on the JDL and the Shield, many of whom had raised their voices and fists in the direction of the neo-Nazis as soon as Benning had begun speaking. Ben-Natan's dogs were howling. Perfect copy for the seven o'clock news. The minicam operator finally had something to film.

The bullhorn was suddenly quiet. The dogs' cries became whimpers, then stopped altogether. The neo-Nazis formed a line and, three abreast, marched in orderly fashion off the circle of lawn and down Beverly Drive. Some carried posters with Hitler's photo; others, posters that demanded WHITE POWER NOW! The JDL—sporadically yelling, "Never again!"—and the Shield followed on the sidewalk, monitored by uniformed police with their hands on their batons. The press scurried to keep up.

Fifteen minutes later the paraders were nearing the corner of Pico and Roxbury. From across the street, Jessie could see the museum's courtyard. It was a sea of people—men, women, teenagers; an overflow wave had spilled onto the sidewalk on Roxbury and rounded the corner onto Pico. There were a large number of African Americans in the crowd. Jessie had read in the *Times* that two churches and several other Christian organizations had planned to support the Jewish community by attending the memorial service. Uniformed, helmeted police were positioned along the curb, one every fifteen feet. Jessie recognized Kolakowski and other officers from West L.A., some from Wilshire. There were more reporters, more photographers, more minicams.

Someone was singing a mournful tune into a microphone. Jessie crossed Roxbury and, walking along the edge of the crowd, heard a whispered, "They're here!" The whisper rolled through the crowd, but as if by prearranged agreement, no one turned to acknowledge the slim phalanx of approaching neo-Nazis.

Now Korbin was speaking; Jessie recognized his gravelly voice. ". . . ask for silence as Cantor Russell begins to read off the names those of you who are here today have written down and given us, names of a minuscule number of our six million brethren who perished in the Holocaust. Cantor?"

There was a moment of amplified static, then the cantor began. "Hindl *bas* Yonah, Treblinka. Meyer *ben* Chaim, Dachau. Yisroel *ben* Noam, Auschwitz. Yonasan *ben* Sholom, Buchenwald. Faige *bas* Menachem Mendl, Majdanek. Mordechai *ben* Sholom, Teriesen—"

"The Holocaust never happened!" Benning boomed through the bullhorn.

There was a second of silence. Jessie turned sharply in Benning's direction. He was marching across Roxbury, leading the others. She heard a collective gasp behind her. Turning back, she saw bodies swivel, almost in unison, to face the enemy.

"Mordechai *ben*—" the cantor tried again. His voice shook.

"The Holocaust is a sham!" another man yelled. "It's a Zionist lie!"

The minicams and cameras jerked wildly from the crowd to the paraders. Jessie saw Ben-Natan hand the dogs' leashes to Yaffa. Then he and the others were running toward Benning and the neo-Nazis. The uniformed officers who had been monitoring the JDL and the Shield sprinted in front of the protesters and forced them back. Ben-Natan's face was livid with helplessness and fury.

"The Holocaust never happened!" Benning repeated through the bullhorn. He and the other neo-Nazis were now within arm's distance of the crowd that lined Pico.

". . . never happened!"

"Liars!" Ben-Natan yelled. "How can you say it never happened? Goddamn liars!"

"The Holocaust never happened!"

"Never happened! Never happened! Never happened! Never happened! Never . . . !" The words became a loud chant.

A man at the front of the crowd lunged toward a neo-Nazi. A policeman blocked him. Seconds later, in an undulating motion, several other men and women lunged toward the paraders.

Shit! "Detective Drake here," she said into her radio. "We have trouble on the corner of Pico and Roxbury!"

Kolakowski and three other uniforms were running toward the corner, their batons raised. The cameras devoured everything.

". . . never happened!" Benning was yelling through the

bullhorn. He had stepped back several feet from the curb. His face was flushed, his eyes feverish with excitement.

Kolakowski and the other officers had formed a human barricade in front of the surging crowd. "Everyone stay in place!" Kolakowski ordered. "Stay back!"

Fifty feet away a man broke through and punched a skinhead on the jaw. The skinhead kicked him viciously with his Doc Martens boot. Jessie ran over as the man raised his hand to strike again. He looked vaguely familiar. Where had she seen him?

"Police!" She grabbed the attacker's arm and twisted it behind him. "You're under arrest!"

"*Me* you're arresting? What about those Nazi murderers, they should burn in hell!" He struggled to get free.

It was the same man, she realized, whom Judge Williams had rebuked. Jessie forced him to his knees. She took handcuffs from her jacket pocket, pulled his other arm behind him, and snapped the cuffs onto his wrists. Out of the corner of her eye, she saw reporters and cameramen advancing.

"Sit here!" she ordered the attacker, pointing to the curb. "Don't move an inch." She looked at the skinhead. He was grinning, rubbing his jaw. She turned to Benning; the White Alliance leader had stayed a safe distance away and seemed to be in a trance.

"Move your people!" she called. "Now!"

"Murderers!" screamed a short, brown-haired woman. "My whole family I lost in the camps, and now you try to kill my Shmuel!" She had slipped past the police. Before Jessie could stop her, the woman ran toward Benning.

"Ma, don't!" The man Jessie had arrested had gotten to his feet and started to run after her. Kolakowski's arm stopped him.

"Liar!" The woman grabbed at the bullhorn.

Benning yanked it out of her reach. She raised her fists toward his chest. He pushed her away. She staggered and fell backward to the ground. Her head hit the asphalt.

"Ma! Oh, God, Mama!"

Jessie raced to her side. The woman's light brown wig had fallen half-off, revealing white hair. She was gasping for breath, clutching at her throat. Her eyes, wild with fear, stared at Jessie, then rolled upward.

"I need a paramedic!" Jessie barked into her radio. She took the woman's wrist. There was a pulse. She slipped out of her jacket, folded it, gently lifted the woman's head, and cushioned it with her jacket. She adjusted the wig.

"Is she going to die?" asked a reporter standing ten feet away. He extended his microphone toward Jessie. She ignored him.

"That's my mother! I have to go to her!" The arrested man strained against Kolakowski's arm. "Please, I beg you."

Kolakowski looked behind him at the woman lying in the street, then at Jessie. She nodded. Kolakowski released the man. With his arms cuffed behind him, he ran to his mother clumsily, as if he were in a bizarre relay race, and knelt at her side.

"She's dead!" he exclaimed. "She's not breathing!"

"Nazi murderers!" a voice yelled.

"She's not dead," Jessie assured him. "She's unconscious. Paramedics are on their way."

"She's dead!" someone else yelled. "They killed her!"

"They killed her?"

"Stand back!" Kolakowski commanded.

"Someone killed the woman! Nazi murderers!"

"The Holocaust never happened!"

There was a roar of anger. Jessie looked up at the crowd. One man broke through the barricade, then another. Within seconds, tens of protesters, men and women, were in the street, fighting with the neo-Nazis. Jessie stood and tried to create a pocket of safety around the woman.

Someone pushed her and elbowed her aside to get through to the woman. Jessie stumbled but quickly regained her footing and whirled around. It was the reporter.

"Detective, can you tell us—"

"This woman needs air!" Jessie yelled, infuriated. "Get the hell out of here!"

The reporter retreated. She turned back to the woman. Again Jessie was shoved, and again. If the paramedics didn't arrive soon, she thought, the woman and her son would be trampled to death. So much for Ben-Natan and his "precautions."

The man was stroking his mother's hand, oblivious of the melee around him. "Look what they did, Mama!" he cried, his voice breaking. "*Gottenyu*, look what they did to you!"

"Murderers!" someone yelled again, and then the piercing sound of a siren drowned out everything else.

Chapter Twenty

    At ten after one on Friday afternoon, after waiting forty minutes in the elegantly decorated anteroom of Haus, Berkman, Lowell, and Lowell, attorneys at law, Emery Kraft entered the spacious office of Walter Haus.

    Haus was standing behind an oversize high-gloss, black walnut desk. He was a tall, distinguished-looking man in his mid-fifties with expertly groomed, thick, graying black hair, a square jaw, and intense brown eyes. Standing in front of the desk on what Kraft recognized to be an Aubusson rug was Barry Lewis, looking solemn and uncomfortable.

    Walter Haus performed the introductions. Then he said, "I understand that you and Mr. Lewis have spoken previously."

    Kraft nodded. "On the phone, once." He turned to Lewis. "It's a pleasure to make your acquaintance." He shook Lewis's hand.

    Haus seated himself behind his desk. Kraft sat down on one of the black leather armchairs in front of the desk. Lewis sat on the other and avoided looking at Kraft.

    "I appreciate your seeing me on such short notice," Kraft said.

    "I'm pleased that we were able to accommodate such a good friend of Ronald Macklin." Haus's smile, polite but not warm, indicated that he wasn't all that pleased. "You explained on the phone that you wish to retain Mr. Lewis to represent Roy Benning. May I ask why you chose this firm? And why Mr. Lewis?"

Kraft smiled and adjusted the monogrammed cuffs of his white-on-white custom-made shirt. "As to your first question, your firm's reputation for excellence speaks for itself. Ron Macklin has often expressed his satisfaction with your firm's services."

Haus nodded his acknowledgment of the compliment. "There are other excellent firms, other excellent attorneys."

"I feel strongly that it would be in Mr. Benning's best interests if Mr. Lewis represented him." Kraft smiled at Lewis, but the attorney stared, unsmiling, at his superior.

"Has Benning been charged?" Haus asked. "I haven't heard."

"Not yet. There is no word yet as to the injured woman's condition or prognosis. But various *individuals*"—he stressed the word—"and *organizations* are exerting strong pressure on the police department and the mayor to arrest Mr. Benning."

"Why not wait and see what happens?"

"Roy Benning *will* be charged. That is a given. And though he will be prosecuted ostensibly because he *allegedly* pushed a woman who subsequently *fell* to the ground and suffered yet-to-be-determined injuries, the real, though unspoken, issue will revolve around his constitutional right to express his opinions and beliefs—in this case, his skepticism about the veracity of the Holocaust." Kraft turned to Lewis. "More than anyone else in this city, you, Mr. Lewis, are prepared to safeguard that right. That is not flattery, sir. It is fact."

"I appreciate your confidence, Mr. Kraft." Lewis's smile was a thin line. "But I represented the White Alliance, of which Mr. Benning is a founding member, and there may be a conflict of interest in my representing him if he's charged with assault."

"I admire your ethics and your foresight—just two of the attributes that attest to your character and professional excellence." Kraft smiled again. "Rest assured, the White Alliance is more than willing to sign the usual waivers."

"That's good," Lewis said. "Still, I think you should know that if the firm decides to represent Mr. Benning, it will assign the case to the most suitable and most available litigator. That may not be me."

"I want *you,* Mr. Lewis." Kraft pointed at Lewis. "You may find Mr. Benning's position repugnant. By now, you are no doubt aware that as the founder of History Is Truth, I, too, endorse those views. But I am not your enemy. I take no pleasure in pitting you against your own. I am not an anti-Semite. I am not a neo-Nazi, though some of our views coincide. I am not a violent racist. I am a credentialed historian who has presented a highly controversial reexamination of an episode of twentieth-century history. And I hope that your personal feelings won't dissuade you from taking the case."

Haus said, "I can assure you, Mr. Kraft, that if we decide to represent Mr. Benning, Mr. Lewis, like every other attorney connected with this firm, will have no problem in arguing the case effectively." He laced his hands and studied Kraft.

Kraft nodded. "This case is important not only to Mr. Benning and to me, but to the freedom of expression which History Is Truth supports. I know this isn't the type of case your firm normally handles. I'm prepared to pay your usual retainer for a minor criminal matter, which I understand from Ron Macklin is seventy-five thousand dollars." From his inside breast pocket, Kraft withdrew a check and placed it near the edge of Haus's desk.

Haus slid the check toward him and centered it on the polished black walnut surface, as if it were a work of art. "We'll certainly consider the case, Mr. Kraft. And if Mr. Lewis is the most suitable and most available, we'll assign him to the matter."

"I'm gratified to hear that." Kraft turned to Lewis. "When we last spoke, I commended you on your courage in taking a position that was unpopular with your people. Yet you seem reluctant to accept a similarly unpopular case." He tapped his index finger against his upper lip. "Perhaps you regret having represented the White Alliance. You received threats. Your home was vandalized. I can understand your hesitancy in putting yourself or your family at risk again."

"My hesitation has nothing to do with regret or with fear of reprisal." Sudden color tinted Lewis's face. "The issues here are entirely different from those related to the parade."

Kraft leaned toward Lewis. "The issues are entirely the same. The White Alliance wanted to express its views. Mr. Benning chose to express his."

"Mr. Benning knocked a seventy-nine-year-old woman to the ground and put her in a hospital." His tone was heavy with irony.

"*She* assaulted *him*. He was defending himself." Kraft turned to Haus. "While both Mr. Benning and I regret what happened, it's important to get the facts straight."

"Mr. Kraft's point is well taken, Barry," Haus said.

Lewis didn't answer.

"Did you see what actually happened?" Kraft asked Lewis.

"No."

"Perhaps you should." Kraft reached for the burgundy alligator briefcase at his feet, opened it, and removed a video cassette. "I took the liberty of bringing a tape of this morning's unfortunate incident. Will you take a few minutes to view it?"

"An excellent idea." Haus took the cassette and walked to a black walnut armoire on the left side of the room. Behind the doors of the armoire was a television screen. He inserted the cassette in the VCR, pressed play, and resumed his seat.

The screen was suddenly filled with scenes from the parade. The gathering in the museum courtyard. The marching phalanx of paraders, most of them in military uniform. Then Benning's voice was heard—"The Holocaust never happened!" The camera flashed from Benning to the Wiesenthal crowd struggling to attack him and the other neo-Nazis. Finally, there was a shot of the elderly woman running toward him.

"Watch." Kraft watched, too, as the woman grabbed at the

bullhorn. "See that?" he said as the woman raised her hands toward Benning's chest. "She's about to strike him. He pushes her in self-defense. She falls and strikes her head on the ground. Tell me, should Mr. Benning be arrested for trying to protect himself?"

"She's a short, elderly woman, for God's sake!" Lewis exclaimed. "Benning is over six feet tall and built like a truck."

"She was irrationally angry. Could Benning be certain that she wouldn't harm him? That she wouldn't try to gouge out his eyes?" A click indicated that the tape had finished. "Would you like to see it again, Mr. Lewis?"

Lewis shook his head.

Kraft removed his tape and faced Lewis. "You may hate me for my views on the Holocaust. I understand that, and I can respect your position and accept it. But do not allow your emotions to interfere with your judgment. If you are truly committed to protecting the First Amendment, as I believe you are, you have no choice but to represent Roy Benning if he is charged. You were, after all, instrumental in obtaining permission for the parade. Your persuasive argument in court made it possible for Benning to say what he did with impunity. Abandoning him would undermine the integrity of your actions."

Kraft paused. "Unless, of course, as I suggested before, you fear reprisals from your people? I can understand that, too."

"I'm not afraid."

"Excellent." Kraft turned to Haus. "When can I expect to hear your decision?"

"By five o'clock today."

Kraft nodded. "I look forward to your call."

"I can't represent Roy Benning," Barry Lewis told Haus after Kraft had left the room.

"Everyone is entitled to a defense, Barry." Haus's tented hands rested inches from the check on his desk. "We can't be the guardians of our clients' morals. You showed that when you fought to protect the constitutional rights of the White Alliance."

"Kraft doesn't want me to represent Benning because of my expertise with constitutional law! He wants me because I'm a Jew."

"Possibly." Haus swiveled on his chair. "If you examine Kraft's thinking logically and try not to react emotionally, you have to admit that there's great sense behind his strategy."

"Great sense, and a little twisted pleasure, too. 'See the Jew boy help the Nazis. Round two.' " Lewis shook his head. "Not this time. I won't do it."

Haus sighed. "Ron Macklin sent him to us, Barry. Macklin, as you know, is a valued client who generates a great deal of business for this firm. It would be awkward and uncomfortable, to say the least, if we were to embarrass Macklin by turning down Kraft."

Lewis leaned forward and grabbed the edge of the desk. "My parents survived the Holocaust that Kraft says never happened! They almost died in the concentration camps that he and Benning and his organization claim didn't exist!" In a calmer voice he said, "I don't see how I can zealously defend Benning and do his case justice."

"Of course you can, Barry," Haus said softly. "You're a superb litigator. And though you and I despise Kraft and Benning and everything they stand for, we can't ignore the very important fact that Benning was acting in self-defense. You saw the tape."

Lewis remained silent.

"You should watch it again." Haus paused. "You've impressed me and the other partners with your dedication and loyalty to the firm, Barry. That's why you have a great future with us." He smiled. "I'm sure you wouldn't do anything to disappoint us or to jeopardize the best interests of the firm."

Lewis removed his hands from the desk and sat back on his chair. "No. No, of course not."

"Of course, I wouldn't ask you to do anything that you

found morally abhorrent. But I think that after examining the tape again, and evaluating all the factors, you'll be able to make the right choice." Haus stood. "I'll discuss this with the committee and let you know our decision."

Lewis nodded.

Chapter Twenty-one

Standing in front of the sterling-silver candelabra on the dining room table, Rose lifted her hands and made three slow, overlapping circles above the Sabbath candles she had just lit. As she completed each circle, she brought her hands toward her chest, as if she were embracing the candles. When Rose was a child, her mother, Malka, had explained that Jewish women all over the world welcomed the Sabbath queen into their homes in just this way.

Since their liberation from the concentration camps, Rose and Morris—she had been eighteen; he, twenty—had not practiced the Orthodox Judaism of their childhood homes, but Morris had bought her a pair of simple chrome candlesticks a few days before they had married, six months after meeting in a DP camp near Munich. She had lit the Sabbath candles the first Friday night of their marriage and every Friday night after that. When Barry had been born, Morris had bought the silver, five-armed candelabra, and Rose had begun lighting a third candle. With the birth of their daughter, Janice, the candles had numbered four. Janice lit Sabbath candles in her home in Chicago. So did Sheila.

Rose placed her hands over her eyes and recited the blessing over the candles: *"Baruch atah hashem . . ."* When she was done, she rocked softly on her heels and, with her eyes

still covered, prayed in Yiddish for the welfare of her husband
and children and grandchildren and added a fervent plea for
the swift recovery of Lola Hochburg, the first casualty of the
parade.

"Morris, supper's ready," she called, and waited a moment.
"Morris?" When he didn't respond, she walked to the den and
found him on the brown plaid couch, his eyes on the television screen.

". . . fifty-three persons arrested and twenty-four injured,
seven in serious condition," the anchorman reported. "And
Lola Hochburg remains in critical condition. We take you live
now to Cedars-Sinai Medical Center and Connie Alvarez.
Connie?"

A slim, petite reporter appeared on the screen.

Rose sat down next to her husband. "Morris, why don't you
turn that off? It's just upsetting you."

"*Shah,*" he said, not unkindly.

The reporter was speaking. "Peter, I'm standing in front of
the North Tower of Cedars-Sinai. Things are not looking
good for Lola Hochburg, who suffered a stroke and is on a
respirator."

"Her son was booked and released, is that right?"

There was honking in the background. The reporter cupped
her ear. "What's that?"

The anchor repeated his question.

"That's right, Peter. Samuel Hochburg was booked this
morning for assaulting one of the paraders, but was released
almost immediately and came directly here to the hospital. He
hasn't left his mother's bedside. The man Hochburg struck
wasn't injured in any way. I think that helped speed Hochburg's release."

"Connie, have you been able to talk to Mr. Hochburg?"

Vultures, Rose thought. Jackals. Morris, she saw, had
pulled himself forward and was hunched on the edge of the
sofa cushion.

"Briefly, Peter. He's devastated and angry at Roy Benning,
the man who pushed his mother. He blames Judge Williams

for permitting the parade. He also blames Barry Lewis, the lawyer who argued the case for the White Alliance, and the ACLU. Mr. Hochburg is an only child, by the way. His mother is a widow. Emotions are clearly running high." The reporter flashed a sympathetic smile.

"Have you been able to contact Barry Lewis?"

Another smile. "He and Rita Warrens, the local ACLU head, have been unavailable. And Judge Williams is in Palm Springs for a long overdue vacation. In the meantime, people in the community are tense, praying for Lola Hochburg, waiting to see what will happen. This is Connie Alvarez, reporting live from Cedars-Sinai."

Morris turned to Rose. "What did I do wrong? Tell me, what did I do so bad that this is happening to us?"

"Don't." Rose took her husband's hand. It was trembling.

"Thank you, Connie. We'll check back with you later." The anchorman reappeared in Morris and Rose's den. "In a related story, Roy Benning has been arrested and charged with assault. Benning is the leader of the White Alliance and is involved with HIT—History Is Truth—a group that denies that the Holocaust took place. We're going to show you some clips now from this morning's events and hear some comments about what happened."

Rose turned away as the screen was filled with the brutal images of the parade. She had seen them earlier this afternoon, on the special report. She didn't need to see them again.

". . . pretty obvious that the judge made a terrible decision," someone was saying. "Look at the results."

Rose looked at the screen and recognized Joel Ben-Natan, the leader of the Shield of Jewish Protectors.

"Are you saying the judge should have violated legal precedent and the Constitution?" the reporter asked.

"I'm saying someone should have used common sense. I'm saying Mrs. Hochburg shouldn't be in a hospital, near death. I hope Barry Lewis and the ACLU are happy with their constitutional victory."

"He's right," Morris said. "God should help me, he's right."

"In a recent development," the anchorman continued, "Eye Witness News has learned that Barry Lewis has agreed to represent Roy Benning. Mr. Lewis . . . "

"No!" Morris stared at the television screen, then turned to his wife. "What did he say, Ruzha?"

She cleared her throat. "He said Barry is going to be this Benning's lawyer."

Morris sat for a moment, then stood up abruptly and left the room. Rose hurried after him to the kitchen.

"Where are you going?" she asked anxiously as he removed his car keys from a cup inside the cupboard. "Morris, answer me!"

"Ge'neeg schoin," he said in Yiddish. Enough already. He headed for the side door off the service porch.

Sheila answered the door. "Hi, Mom. Hi, Dad. This is a nice surprise." Her smile and her voice betrayed her anxiety.

Her daughter-in-law looked terrible, Rose thought, standing with Morris in the entry hall. Haggard, pale. Her eyes rimmed in red. She looks how I feel, Rose said to herself.

"Where is he?" Morris asked.

"What's wrong, Dad? You don't look well."

"I have to talk to Barry. Where is he?" Morris repeated.

Sheila had turned bright red. "In his office."

With Rose and Sheila behind him, Morris left the marble-floored entry and walked down a wide hall to his son's office. He opened the door without knocking and took a few steps into the paneled room. Rose followed him inside. Sheila stayed in the hall and pulled the door closed behind them.

Barry looked up at his father's entrance and stiffened. "Hello, Dad." He stood. "Hi, Mom."

"It's true what they're saying?" Morris demanded. "I heard on the news that you're going to defend this animal, this liar, but I couldn't believe it. I said, '*This* Barry wouldn't do.' So?"

Barry walked around his desk and stood several feet away from his father. "I was going to call you, Dad. I want to explain."

"What's to explain? You are or you're not?"

Barry sighed and ran his fingers through his hair. "Look, can we sit down and talk about this calmly?"

"*Calmly,* you want to talk? When a house is burning, does a person stay *calm?*" Morris's voice was rising.

"You don't understand. This is complicated, Pa. There are—"

"Don't 'Pa' me! Don't tell me I don't understand, like I'm a stupid *greeneh* off the boat!" He was yelling now. His face was red with anger. "You think you're smarter than me because I never went to high school? Big-shot lawyer! Big university degree! Your mother and I saved and sacrificed for years so you and your sister should have the best education. What good is an education if you don't know what it is to be a decent human being, a good Jew?"

"You *wanted* me to be a good lawyer. You *and* Mom. Make us proud, you said. Do the right thing." His hands were clenched. "I did what I thought was right about the parade. I know you didn't agree, and I know I've hurt you, and I'm sorry about that, but I *have* to represent Benning. It's the firm's decision, not mine."

"What, they'll fire you if you don't take the case?"

"Maybe."

"So let them fire you. You'll get another job. A better one."

"It's not just that. It's—" Barry shook his head. "I don't have a choice, Pa."

"*Everybody* has a choice! Everybody!" Morris extended his hands upward, in supplication to heaven. "*Riboinoi shel oylam,* what kind of Jew makes friends with Nazi murderers, *yemach sh'mom,* can you tell me? What kind of Jew takes for a client an animal who says the lawyer's grandparents and his wife's grandparents and uncles and cousins didn't die in the gas chambers?"

Barry was silent.

Morris stepped closer to his son. Barry flinched.

"You think I'm going to hit you?" Morris shook his head. "I'm not going to hit you. When did I ever hit you?" He paused, and when he spoke again, it was in an almost inaudible whisper. "You spit on my parents' graves. You spit on your mother's parents' graves. When you help spread lies like this, you spit on the graves of six million people. So now I spit on you."

He spat at his son, then grabbed the collar of his own shirt with both hands and yanked at the fabric until it ripped.

"Morris, don't!"

"Now you can do what you want," Morris said. "Now I have no son. Finished. To me, you are dead."

"Morris!" Rose wailed and put her hands on her ears. *"Chas ve'sholom!* God forbid! Don't say what you don't mean."

Barry stood frozen in place. He made no move to wipe the spittle off his face. His father spun around, walked to the door, yanked it open, and left the room.

Rose looked at her son, then followed her husband.

Chapter Twenty-two

"God, it's awful, isn't it, Frank?" Jessie sighed and shut off the eleven o'clock news with the remote control. "Twenty-four people injured."

"Not a pretty picture." He pulled her closer to him on the den sofa and massaged her shoulders.

She tucked her legs under her and relaxed against his chest. It was so nice, now that Rona and the boys were back in Arizona, to have his full attention. She'd felt so insecure when they were here, so threatened. Now she felt silly for having worried; she was happy she hadn't said anything to Brenda or Helen. She sighed again and laced her fingers through his.

"Rough day, huh?" he asked.

She realized that he thought she was sighing about the parade. She didn't correct him. He lifted her hair and kissed the nape of her neck. A tingling warmth coursed through her. He pulled her blouse out of her jeans. His fingers were hot against her skin as he unhooked her bra, and her breath quickened.

"Let's go into the bedroom," she whispered. It was where they always made love in her house, on the king-size mattress she'd bought after Gary had moved out with their black lacquer bedroom furniture.

She pulled herself up. Frank pressed down on her shoulders

and lowered her to the couch. His mouth was still on hers and her heart was racing and she tried not to think about the fact that she and Gary had made love here countless times. It wasn't as if the black leather cushions had retained the indentations of their bodies or the heat of their passion.

She moved her head up abruptly and hit the arm of the couch. She drew in a whistlelike breath.

"Sorry," Frank said. "You okay?"

His face was an inch from hers, and she could see the etched lines around his dark brown eyes and mouth. "I just thought about Mrs. Hochburg," she lied. "I keep hearing the sound of her head cracking against the asphalt." She pictured the woman falling and winced, and now she wasn't lying.

"Never should've happened. What did the old lady think she was doing, charging Benning?" He bent his head to kiss her again.

"Frank, she *survived* the concentration camps. Can you imagine what she felt when she heard him saying the Holocaust never happened? I think Benning and HIT are despicable."

"Maybe." His hands slid down to her jeans. "I've been thinking about you, and us, all day. God, I've missed you, Jess!" he whispered. He pulled at her zipper.

She stopped his hands. "What do you mean, 'maybe'?"

"Shit, Jessie. You sure as hell know how to ruin a mood."

She pushed him away so that she could see his face clearly. "What do you mean, 'maybe'?"

He sighed. "If they're lying, they're despicable. What if they think they're telling the truth?"

Jessie frowned and sat up. "This isn't funny, Frank."

"I'm serious, Jess. How do we know there really *was* a Holocaust? I mean, okay, there was a war, and Jews died. So did lots of other people. That's what happens in wars. But six million Jews?" He shook his head. "Sounds exaggerated to me."

She felt a rush of impatience. "Frank, the history books give those figures. Documentaries corroborate them."

"Yeah, but where do they *get* those figures, huh? Probably from Jewish sources. Hardly unbiased, are they?"

"That's not true. American soldiers liberated the camps, Frank. They *saw* what was going on."

"They saw prisoners of war, sweetheart. They didn't see gas chambers or any of the other horrors that were supposed to have happened."

Her impatience turned to exasperation. She tried to filter it from her voice. "Why would anyone make this up, Frank?"

"To gain world sympathy, for one thing. To lay a guilt trip on us goyim because we didn't rush in to save them. I think that's how they get Congress to give so much money to Israel, you know."

"That's ridiculous! Do you realize *how* ridiculous it is?" In a calmer voice she said, "Frank, Israel is the only democracy in the Middle East. Of *course* the United States has to support it. Who told you all this?"

"I read stuff. What's the difference?" He shrugged. "I'm just saying what a lot of people are thinking. Don't get mad at me."

"I'm not mad. I'm upset that you'd believe HIT's lies. It's garbage, Frank, anti-Semitic garbage. Can't you see that?"

She realized suddenly that though she was intimately familiar with his body, she knew little about him aside from the fact that he was a respected veteran cop with an ex-wife and two sons; that he had enemies who resented his politically incorrect bluntness, friends who admired it. Manny Freiberg, who was a psychologist, an expert on people, had told her Frank Pruitt was a nice guy. Get to know him, Manny had said, and she thought she had.

"What I *see*," Frank said slowly, not bothering to hide his anger, "is that we're having a difference of opinion, and you're doing your goddamn best to ruin a nice evening. I don't know why you're making such a big deal about this. It's not like you're Jewish and I'm offending you."

"That isn't the point." She contemplated telling him about her mother's Jewish relatives—over the past few weeks, ever since she'd started investigating the Lewis case, she'd thought about doing so. Somehow she hadn't, and now wasn't the right time; Frank would feel embarrassed, guilty. Or was she rationalizing?

She slipped off the couch, wanting him gone so that she could be by herself and think. She tucked her blouse into her jeans. "It's late, Frank. Let's call it a night. Thanks for dinner," she added to soften the abruptness of her tone. "I really *am* tired. The parade and everything." She blushed as she piled lie upon lie.

"You *are* mad, aren't you?" He stood up. "Lately, every time we're on the phone or together, we end up talking about Jews and you get all serious." Irritation flickered in his eyes.

"That's not true."

"Yeah, it is, sweetheart. You just don't see it."

"Sorry I'm late," Manny Freiberg said when he joined Jessie at the table. "I got a ticket for a rolling stop. On a Sunday, for crying out loud! Can you believe that?" He took a sip of water.

"I'm sorry, Manny." She felt guilty—he was here because she'd called him at home and told him she needed to talk. He'd suggested that they meet at the kosher deli on Pico.

"Why? The ticket wasn't your fault. It wasn't mine, either, but go argue with a traffic cop." His Adam's apple, always pronounced, strained against his throat. "They are so goddamn rigid and tight-assed. Talk about pathology. They probably all need shrinks." He picked up the menu. "Did you order?"

"Not yet." She'd never seen Manny irritated; she found it somewhat amusing and wonderfully human. She was used to seeing the psychologist behind his desk at Parker Center in a suit, not in jeans and a crew-neck red sweater that emphasized his tall, lanky frame and made him look younger than his forty-six years. On top of curly, light brown hair that was receding at the temples lay a small, crocheted skullcap. That was surprising, too.

The waitress came over. Jessie ordered a tuna sandwich; Manny ordered pastrami and corned beef.

"It isn't just the money," Manny said after the waitress left. "I'll have to go to traffic school to keep the points off my record. Those classes are terminally boring."

"Gary once went to the Improv Comedy Traffic School. He said the instructors were very funny."

"Comedy traffic school. Only in Hollywood." Manny shook his head and grinned. "Yeah, maybe I'll try that. So how *is* Gary?"

"Okay."

"I sense hesitation in your voice."

"Very astute, Herr Doctor." She smiled. "I saw him last week." She told him about the day at the marina. "I hurt his feelings, and that bothers me."

"Why?" Behind his tortoise-shell framed glasses, his warm brown eyes studied her.

"What do you mean, 'Why?' 'Cause I'm a nice person, and he's a nice guy."

"You don't want to resume your relationship with him?"

"I'm seeing Frank. I can't be involved with two men at the same time."

"Not really an answer. Why did you let Gary come along?"

"It wasn't a big deal, Manny. I wasn't leading him on. Are you saying people who divorce can't have friendly relations?"

"I'm saying it's hard to pretend the marriage never happened. Are you still attracted to him?"

She hesitated, then said, "Yes. But why wouldn't I be? He looks the same as he did a year ago." Better, actually. "Anyway, Gary isn't my problem. Frank is."

The waitress arrived with their orders, placed them on the table, and left.

"Be right back," Manny said.

Before Jessie could wonder where he'd gone, he was seated

again and, lifting the sandwich to his mouth, silently uttered what she decided must be a benediction.

"Terrible for the body, but damn, this is good!" he said after tasting the pastrami and corned beef. "Okay. Talk to me." He tried a forkful of coleslaw, then took another bite of his sandwich.

She told him about her involvement with the Lewis case, about the people she'd interviewed. "I'm sure you saw on TV what happened at the parade. The demonstrators from HIT?"

" 'Shit' is more like it," he said through clenched teeth. He leaned forward. "Why don't they ask my folks whether the Holocaust happened? My folks will show them the numbers tattooed on their arms. So will their friends." He moved back and in a calmer voice said, "Basically, HIT's message is anti-Semitism dressed up in a suit instead of an SS uniform and a swastika. Scary as hell, 'cause it can take in a lot of uneducated people." He chomped on his sandwich. "So what does this have to do with Frank?"

Jessie hadn't known about Manny's parents. Now she felt awkward telling him. She hesitated then said, "Frank more or less agrees with HIT."

Manny's eyes narrowed. He put down his sandwich. "Explain."

She repeated their conversation of the night before. "At first I thought he was joking. But he's serious, Manny, and I suddenly realized how little I know about him. I can't tell if he's misguided or racist. Have you ever heard him make any anti-Semitic remarks?"

"Hey, I'm the last person he'd do that to. 'Manny Freiberg' kind of gives me away, don't you think?" He took off his glasses and rubbed the bridge of his nose. "Frank seems like a nice guy. He's a good cop, but he doesn't always say the politically correct thing. That's why he hasn't advanced in the department. But is he racist or anti-Semitic?" Manny shrugged. "Did you call him on it?"

"I told him I'm upset by his views. He can't understand why." She ate a bite of her tuna sandwich. Then she said, "I didn't tell him my mother's part Jewish. I told you that, remember?" It had come up during one of their conversations.

Manny nodded. "So why *didn't* you tell Frank?"

Since last night the question had been on her mind. "I thought he'd be embarrassed, after what he'd just said about the Holocaust. And it's not as if I'm hiding who I am. I've never considered myself Jewish. I still don't. It's just that lately, with the Lewis case, I've been thinking about it more."

"Makes sense." Manny nodded. "Are you worried how Frank would react if he knew you were part Jewish?"

She thought for a moment. "Maybe. I don't even know how *I* feel about it." She picked up her goblet and took a sip of water.

"Does it bother you, being part Jewish?"

She stared at him. "No! Of course not."

"Just asking." He smiled. "You think of yourself one way your entire life, and all of a sudden you're forced to reexamine who you are. It can be confusing and unsettling."

"Actually, I'm intrigued by the idea of having Jewish relatives. My mom doesn't know much about them, and she gets irritated whenever I bring up the subject." Jessie paused, then said, "She's also irritated whenever there's an article or program about the Holocaust. I can't understand that."

"You feel your mother doesn't like Jews or having Jewish relatives?" Manny asked quietly.

"Sometimes," Jessie admitted. She flushed.

"And that embarrasses you?"

"Yes. Other times, though, I'm not sure what she's thinking."

Manny drummed his fork against the table. "Sounds like you want to resolve this on two levels, Jessie. First, as far as your mother's concerned, there *are* Jews who don't like Jews—it's not unheard of. But I'd think you'd want to talk to her and get a clear answer before you jump to conclusions. That's only fair."

"I've tried. You know we don't get along. She hung up on me the last time I brought it up."

"Try harder. And not over the phone. Face to face."

"She's coming in this Friday with my dad. We're all having dinner at my sister's. It's Matthew's birthday. I guess I could talk to her sometime that night."

"Wait until after dessert." Manny smiled. "About Frank—"

"Maybe he *is* just misinformed. I'll get material on the Holocaust and let him read the truth. And I *will* tell him I'm part Jewish. I'm sure it won't make a difference to him." She paused. "What do you think?"

Manny drew circles in the coleslaw with the tines of his fork. "What I think is, you really want this relationship to work."

Chapter Twenty-three

At ten forty-five on Sunday evening, a lone television reporter noticed nurses and doctors running in and out of Lola Hochburg's hospital room and notified his news station.

An hour later the reporter was waiting, a cameraman at his side, when Samuel Hochburg emerged from the room, flanked on one side by Rabbi Sheldon Korbin and on the other by another rabbi with a gray beard.

"Mr. Hochburg," the reporter began, "is there any—"

"Please," Korbin rasped. "Show some decency."

"They killed her," Hochburg said in a low voice. His deep-set eyes were glazed.

"Who is 'they'?" the reporter asked, stepping aside so that the cameraman could get a tighter shot of Hochburg's tear-streaked face.

"They killed her," Hochburg repeated.

Chapter Twenty-four

When Rose came into the bedroom Monday morning after preparing breakfast, she found Morris lying in bed, fully clothed, except for his shoes.

"You don't feel good?" she asked.

"I feel all right."

"You're not going to work?"

"Not today."

He hadn't gone to the building supply store on Saturday, either. At another time she would have called the doctor. In the forty-eight years of their marriage, her Morris had rarely missed a day of work. Part of it, she knew, was his burning drive to succeed and provide for his wife and children; part of it was the work ethic ingrained in him from childhood and hardened in the work camps.

Now, though Rose was worried, she wasn't surprised. Since the Friday night confrontation with Barry, Morris had been unusually quiet and preoccupied, and she had done little to coax him out of his mood. She understood his anger. She shared it, and the pain of betrayal, and carried her half of the burden of shame and failure.

Still, Barry was their son. In the car on the way home, she had said only one thing: "To me, he's not dead." Morris hadn't answered, but he hadn't performed any of the rituals of mourning that she dreaded: the covering of mirrors; the inverting of photographs of the deceased; the recital of the *kaddish*, the mourner's prayer. So she had said little, not wanting to provoke and cement his resolve, and waited for her husband to calm down.

And then last night Lola Hochburg had died. Throughout the weekend Morris had sat in front of the television for hours at a time, listening for news updates: Mrs. Hochburg has suffered another stroke. Mrs. Hochburg is in a coma. Mrs. Hochburg is on life support. For Rose, it had almost been a relief when the woman's death had been announced and the television had finally been silenced.

"Now Barry will drop the case," Rose had said. "You'll see."

"Who is Barry?" Morris had asked. "I don't know a Barry."

Still, the mirrors had remained undraped, the *kaddish* unsaid.

"Come eat breakfast," Rose said now. "I made oatmeal with cinnamon, the way you like it."

"I'm not hungry." With an abrupt movement he sat up, swung his legs off the bed, and stood. "You eat."

She followed him into the den, puzzled, concerned, and watched as he searched among the volumes in a bookcase until he found the book he wanted and put it on the coffee table. At first she thought it was a *siddur*, a book of daily prayer, and her heart stopped—he was going to say *kaddish* after all. But then she saw that it was a leather-bound *machzor*, a prayer book for Yom Kippur, the holiest day of the Jewish year.

She was almost giddy with relief. Then she frowned. "Why do you need that, Morris? Yom Kippur is not for six months."

"*Vi iz mein kittel?*" he asked in Yiddish. Since Friday night he had been speaking more in the language of his youth than in English, the language he had fought so hard to master.

"I don't know where your *kittel* is."

He was referring to a white, robelike cotton garment that Orthodox Jewish males wear under the wedding canopy, during the seder on Passover, and in the synagogue on Yom Kippur. Morris had bought a *kittel* when he and Rose had first come to America and attended an Orthodox synagogue for a while; he had wanted to fit in with the other congregants on Yom Kippur. After two years he and Rose had joined a Conservative synagogue. She hadn't seen the *kittel* in years. Who knew if it was in the house or if it had been given away when they had moved here from the apartment?

"Someplace in this house it has to be," he said in Yiddish.

She helped him look for it. Finally, she found it at the back of a deep linen closet, folded neatly in a plastic bag. It was slightly musty and yellowed with age.

Morris slipped it on and tied the accompanying white cotton belt loosely around his hips. Next he went to a hall closet and took down a blue velvet bag in which he kept his *tallis*, a cream-colored fringed prayer shawl with black stripes.

"What are you doing?" Rose felt a spasm of fear. This was not her Morris.

He wrapped the *tallis* around him, kissed the fringes, then adjusted it so that it was resting on his balding head. He bent down and picked up the *machzor* from the coffee table.

"Morris? Please, you're making me nervous."

"Zet zein git," he told her. Everything will be all right. He opened the prayer book and thumbed through the pages. Then he began chanting.

"Ohshamnu bohgadnu . . ." "We have become guilty, we have betrayed . . . we have caused wickedness. . . ." With each word he beat the left side of his breast with his right fist, as he had learned to do as a child in Poland.

Rose's eyes filled with tears. He was reciting the Yom Kippur liturgy of confession. Now she understood.

"Al chait sh'chotonu lefonecha be'ohness oove'ratzon. . . ." "For the sin that we have sinned before You under duress and willingly; and for the sin that we have sinned before You through hardness of the heart. . . ."

"Morris," she whispered. "Morris, it's not your fault."

"Al chait . . ." "For the sin that we have sinned before You

without knowledge; and for the sin that we have sinned before You with the utterance of the lips. . . ."

"*Al chait* . . ."

With each verse he beat his breast, as he had learned to do when still a child in Poland. At the end of the first section, he recited the imploring refrain: "For all these, O God of forgiveness, forgive us, pardon us, atone for us." With each request, he again beat his breast.

There were four major sections. He recited the last specific verse of confession—"And for the sins for which we incur the four death penalties of the human court: stoning, burning, beheading, and strangling." Then he completed the prayer and shut the book. He turned to Rose.

"*Zet zein git, Ruzha,*" he repeated. "*Zet zein git.*"

Chapter Twenty-five

Sheila Lewis looked as if she'd aged ten years, Jessie thought as she steered her past reception into the large detectives' room and to her desk.

"Can I get you some coffee, Mrs. Lewis?"

"No, thank you." Her lips quivered. She sat down and pressed her hand against them to quiet them. "I'm sorry. I can't seem to stop crying. I'm so scared."

"What happened?" Jessie asked, sitting down.

"You know that Mrs. Hochburg died last night?"

Jessie nodded. It had been on all the channels.

"The hate calls started almost immediately. I took the phone off the hook for a while, but at two in the morning, when I finally went to sleep, I worried that someone with an important message might try to call, so I put the receiver back on the hook, and the calls started again. They just won't stop!"

"You can put a trap on your phone. Basically, you notify the phone company. They notify the switching control people—they handle computer input on the line—to store every call and the time it's made. Every time you get a harassing call, you note the time the call came in. You give phone security the times. Then they locate a trunk identification number.

If the routing isn't complicated, they can tell us where the calls originated."

Jessie waited for Sheila's nod of understanding, then continued. "You can also attach a recording machine to your line and turn it on whenever you get a harassing call. That's easier than trying to write down what the caller said. Could you tell if the calls were made by one person or different people?"

"Mostly different callers. Some kids, too."

Not so good. "It's easiest to trace a group of calls made by the same person. Still, I think the trap's worth a shot. Did you recognize any of the voices?"

Sheila shook her head.

"What did the callers say?"

"The kinder ones said we should move out of town. The others were more direct." She looked down at her hands. "They said that Barry will die. That I'll die, too, and the girls. One man . . . one man mentioned the girls by name," she whispered. "Please, I don't know what to do." She began crying.

Jessie handed her a tissue. "I think we should try the phone trap, Mrs. Lewis."

Sheila dabbed at her eyes, then wiped her nose. "I don't know if Barry will agree to do that. He's frightened, but he won't admit it. And it isn't just the calls. This morning I found a paper under the front door. It said, 'The Day of Judgment is coming. Prepare for the Angel of Death.' "

The message sounded more grim this time. Jessie felt a flutter of unease. "Did you keep the letter?"

Sheila opened her purse and handed a plastic bag to Jessie. Inside was a folded sheet of paper. "I tried not to touch it."

"That's good." Luckily Sheila Lewis, and not her husband, had found the letter. "We'll see if we can raise prints. There were prints on the first note, but we weren't able to identify them." They didn't belong to Ben-Natan; Jessie had asked SID to check. "Can you move in with a friend until things calm down?"

"We have almost no friends, not anymore. We're like lepers. I thought about staying at a hotel, but I'm afraid people would find out where we are. The press are living on our doorstep."

Typical of the press. "What about family out of town?"

"My mother lives in New Jersey. She's a widow. I could take the girls there, but they'll miss school, and their friends. . . ."

"You should strongly consider going to your mother's," Jessie said gently. "In the meantime, talk to your husband about the trap. You can set up a recorder yourself—you can get a connector from Radio Shack. Or we can do it for you."

"I'll talk to Barry." Sheila stood. "You really think we could be in danger, don't you?" Her voice was small, like a child's. "I was hoping you'd tell me that I'm overreacting, that all of this would go away." Her tone was wistful. "I guess not."

"Barry won't do the phone trap," Sheila told Jessie an hour later. "He said it's pointless. The girls and I are moving in with a friend. Nancy Reiss." She gave Jessie the friend's phone number. "Barry's staying home. He thinks my moving out will just encourage whoever's doing this to continue."

"I think you're doing the right thing, Mrs. Lewis."

"Maybe. All I know is that I can't go on living this way."

Jessie hung up the phone and wondered again why Lewis, whose wife was terrified and whose parents were Holocaust survivors, was defending Benning, a man who claimed the Holocaust hadn't happened. Had he been pressured by his firm to take the case? Had he worried about losing his job and the luxurious lifestyle it provided if he refused? Did he believe that Benning had acted in self-defense and therefore deserved his help? Or maybe he'd worried that a refusal to represent Benning would have been an admission that he should never have represented the White Alliance.

Late Tuesday afternoon Barry Lewis informed Jessie that he was willing to try the phone trap.

"I'd like to get this over with and get Sheila and the girls back home. When can you set it up with the phone company?"

"First thing tomorrow morning. It's after business hours now. You can do it yourself, really. You'll need to keep a log of the exact times of each phone call you want checked out, and—"

"My wife explained all this," he interupted in a "my-time-is-valuable" voice.

Tough shit. "That's good," Jessie said pleasantly. Sheila Lewis, she decided, would probably enjoy a few days away from her husband. "Do you want us to hook up a recording machine to your phone, or would you prefer to do it yourself?"

"I don't have a recording machine. I'd like *you* to do it, tonight. Unless it's after business hours for the police, too?"

His attitude was really annoying her. She was beginning to sympathize with the people who were making the harassing calls. "I can have someone at your home sometime this evening. What time would be convenient?"

"Nine o'clock is okay. I have an important brief to finish before I leave my office."

"Indicate on your phone log which calls are made by the same person. That's important, especially if the calls originate from outside the Beverlywood area."

"Fine."

"Also, if you get a few calls from the same person, immediately report the exact times to the phone company. That way, if the call originates from a different routing station—like L.A. Central, for instance, or Pasadena—they'll be able to put another trap on that station before the next group of calls."

"I understand. When will you pick up the recorder?"

"First you have to get some calls."

"Oh, I will. My fans won't disappoint me."

At ten-thirty on Thursday night the West L.A. dispatcher phoned Jessie at home. Lewis wanted the recording machine and his phone log picked up as soon as possible. Jessie had no intention of rushing to Beverlywood. There was no urgency. Lewis was probably accustomed to having people jump to do his bidding, but she wasn't his lackey. And she was in the middle of *When Harry Met Sally* and wanted to return the video to The Wherehouse before midnight so that she wouldn't be charged for another day.

She phoned Lewis and told him she'd be at his house Friday morning. Lewis and Jessie agreed on eight forty-five. He had to leave for work, and the housekeeper wouldn't be there—Sheila had given her the rest of the week off.

At eight forty-four Jessie rang Barry Lewis's bell. The front door was white. There was no trace of the blood-red paint or Star of David.

Lewis opened the door but didn't welcome her into the house.

"Thanks for coming." He handed her the recording machine and a notepad. "Sorry if I'm abrupt, but I'm in a rush."

"No problem."

"I'm pretty sure Ben-Natan called. I wrote down his name and the name of one caller who identified himself. Also, some kid phoned a few times Wednesday night and two times Thursday. I gave the phone company the exact times for the Wednesday calls." He picked up a black lizard briefcase. "When do you think you'll have some information for me?"

She counted twelve entries on Lewis's log. "I'll phone these times in as soon as I get back to the station, but it may take a while to trace the calls. Some we may not be able to trace."

"Why?"

"As I explained to your wife, single, isolated calls that originate outside your area are almost impossible to trace. That's why I'd suggest that you continue to keep a log and—"

"No thanks. I've had it with all this shit. Frankly, I don't think you'll learn anything other than the fact that I'm not too popular right now. Hardly earth-shattering news, is it?" He stepped outside and pulled the door shut. "After you."

She felt an unexpected tug of sympathy for Lewis as she walked ahead of him down the flagstone walkway and crossed the street to her Honda. She placed the recording machine and phone log in her trunk and looked at him. He was opening the door to the black BMW in his driveway. Gary's dream car.

She shut the trunk and was reaching for the handle on her car door when she heard a loud explosion. As she turned toward the sound, she was knocked down by a cannonball of air. Her body was jarred by the impact. She pushed herself up quickly and ran toward the Lewis driveway.

There was a second explosion. Then a *whoosh.*

A few seconds later Gary's dream car was engulfed in flames.

Chapter Twenty-six

The explosion had shattered the Honda's windshield and left side windows, creating gaping holes in the now crisscrossed glass. Another patch of glass broke off from the driver's window and tinkled to the ground as Jessie opened the door wide. Careful to avoid the confettilike crystals sprinkled all over the interior of the car, she reached under the driver's seat for the cellular phone her father (bless him!) had insisted she accept for a Christmas gift. She called 911, then West L.A. dispatch.

Blistering air seared her lungs, and she was overcome with a paroxysm of coughing. Her throat was raw. Her eyes were burning. Pulling her jacket over her nose and mouth, she watched, helpless, as the flames divided and multiplied and leaped, higher and higher, toward the blackening sky as they consumed the car in a frenzied, sacrificial dance. She tried not to visualize Barry Lewis, trapped inside the inferno. She hoped he had died quickly.

She was overwhelmed suddenly by the knowledge that had she been closer to Lewis's car, she would have been killed, too. She started shaking uncontrollably. Two patrol cars, each with two units, arrived within five minutes of Jessie's call. She heard the screaming sirens first, then saw the flashing red lights. The bomb squad responded three minutes later, a fire engine six minutes after that. She was still shaking but forced herself to say she was fine, partly out of a professional pride that she recognized as stupid, partly out of a worry that everyone on the scene—all males—would attribute her vulnerability to her being a woman.

Keeping busy helped. Along with the patrolmen, Jessie vacated and secured a three-hundred-foot perimeter around the site of the explosion. She explained patiently to the impatient drivers of approaching cars why they couldn't enter the area, not even to pick up children for preschool carpool; had the explosion occurred around eight, she realized with sharp suddenness, there would have been more cars in the area—and more children, unattended, on the streets.

She talked with the bomb squad captain. She talked with neighbors farther up the block who had ventured outside to see what had happened. No, they all told her, they hadn't seen anyone this morning or last night near Lewis's car. Nothing suspicious.

"If you think of anything   " Jessie told each one, and handed out her cards.

There were more neighbors. She saw some peering out at the carnage from behind the safety of draped windows. Others, she supposed, were still sleeping, although how anyone could have slept through the two deafening explosions was beyond her. She would have to talk to all of them. It was a tedious, though necessary, process, and she knew it would probably be futile.

Fifty minutes after the explosion, three male detectives from Criminal Conspiracy Section arrived. On their heels was Lieutenant Horner, the watch commander of West L.A. Horner and CCS talked. Then, while CCS viewed the fiery scene and talked to the bomb squad captain, Jessie described to Horner what she'd witnessed.

"You have the recording machine and the log?" Horner asked.

"In my trunk."

"CCS will want them, plus a copy of your reports to date."

She hesitated, then said, "I'd like to handle the case, Lieutenant Horner." She rarely had contact with her station's silver-haired watch commander; she knew little about him or how he would respond to her request. She had heard that, unlike some officers and detectives at West L.A. who were sexist—she'd had her run-ins with a few—Horner wasn't.

Horner frowned. "This belongs to CCS. You know that, Drake."

She also knew that it wasn't unheard of for CCS to relinquish a case. "I've been investigating the vandalism. I know the people involved. I'd really like to pursue this, sir." She didn't add that the explosion could have killed her, too; that she needed to find out who was responsible.

He squinted at her. "Is that bruise on your face from the explosion?"

Her cheek had scraped against the ground when she'd fallen. She'd forgotten about it; now she felt it throb and resisted the urge to touch it. "I was knocked down by the explosion. I'm fine now," she said for the same reasons she'd insisted she was fine earlier.

"Close call, huh? Probably scared the shit out of you. Scared the shit out of me when I was almost blown up fourteen years ago. You don't forget something like that." He studied her appraisingly. "Is that why you want to get the guy who did this?"

"Maybe." Horner was a smart man. Or was she transparent?

He nodded. "You feel responsible for what happened to Lewis?"

The question had burned in her mind. "Even if I'd picked up the recording machine and phone log last night, the phone company wouldn't have traced the calls until sometime today."

"You're right. Don't forget that. Be back in a minute," he said.

He walked across the lawn to the detectives from CCS. Jessie watched the backs of their heads and their hands, trying to read their body language, but soon gave up. A few minutes later Horner returned to her side.

"It's yours," he said. "The guys from CCS grumbled, but they weren't unhappy. They've got enough on their plate as it is." No smile, just the same appraising look. Even after she thanked him.

Four more patrol cars and the medical examiner's van had arrived. Television reporters had parked their van up the block and penetrated the secured area. Jessie escorted them back outside the three-hundred-foot perimeter, where they joined the other lookers—older men and women, probably retired; young mothers and housekeepers, several of them holding the small, chubby hands of heavy-lidded toddlers sucking intently on bottles or pacifiers.

Déjà vu. Jessie wondered why anyone would voluntarily inhale noxious air, wondered even more why any mother would expose her child to it. Her eyes were still tearing from the smoke and the acrid odor of burning rubber and scorched metal. She turned from the lookers to see what they found so fascinating.

The charred remains of Barry Lewis's black BMW smoldered in the driveway. The trunk and roof and all the windows were gone. The hood was buckled, and the front was misshapen but recognizable. From where she was standing, Jessie couldn't see the interior; five minutes ago, someone from the coroner's office had removed Barry Lewis's body—or what was left of it—and bagged it. A few minutes before that, she had declined the medical examiner's invitation to view Lewis. She'd wondered if the ME had been testing her. If so, she'd failed. She could live with that.

Bright yellow police tape, fluttering gently in the morning breeze where it hadn't been pulled taut enough, cordoned off an area that included Lewis's lawn and driveway and the adjacent lawns. Members of the bomb squad, their hands gloved, were sifting through the debris on both lawns. Also sifting through the debris were men whose uniform jackets identified them as coroner's staff. Jessie hated to think what they were searching for.

She saw Phil pulling up in his green Cutlass. She walked over and waited while he parked his car.

"Pretty goddamn awful," he said when he was standing next to her. "What the hell happened to your face?"

With forced nonchalance, she told him about her fall.

"You could've been killed," he said quietly. After a moment he added, "They gave you the case, huh? How'd you wangle that?"

"My charm."

"Lots of that." Phil smiled. "Espes didn't seem too pleased."

She frowned. "Oh? Why not?"

Phil shrugged. "I can't figure him out. Does Sheila Lewis know about her husband?"

"Not yet. I figured I'd call her at her friend's after the bomb squad and the coroner's people finish."

"Good idea. You talk with the guys from the bomb squad?"

"They're saying a pipe bomb with gunpowder, probably a mercury switch. They won't know for sure till they find all the pieces. The bomb was attached to the gas tank." That accounted for the heavier damage to the rear of the car.

"We're sure it's Lewis?"

"I saw him get into the car."

"What about the house next door? Was anybody hurt?"

"Vacant. It's for sale by owner."

"Lucky for the owner," Phil said. "Do you think—"

"Barry!" a woman screamed. "Ohgodohgodohgod!"

Jessie turned and saw Sheila Lewis at the north end of the cordoned-off area. She was kneeling on the sidewalk, clutching the yellow police tape. In her gray sweats, she looked like a marathon runner trying desperately to finish the race, knowing she won't.

"You go talk to her," Phil said to Jessie. "You two have a rapport. I'll stay out here and keep an eye on what's happening."

Mentally bracing herself, Jessie hurried toward Sheila. "Mrs. Lewis, I'm so sorry," she said when she reached her. Standing beside Sheila was a short woman with curly, reddish brown hair. The friend. The woman helped Sheila to her feet.

"I can't believe this happened!" Sheila whispered. Her eyes were rimmed in red. Her face was almost the same shade as her sweats. "Maybe it isn't Barry?" She looked at Jessie imploringly.

"I'm sorry."

Sheila darted a look at the driveway. She swallowed. "Is he . . . ?"

She tried to soften with her voice the brutality of her words. "They took the body away, Mrs. Lewis. I think it would be better if we talked inside. Do you have the keys to your house?"

"I brought her purse," the friend said. "I'm Nancy Reiss."

Jessie lifted the police tape until Sheila and Nancy passed under it. The two friends walked ahead, Sheila leaning against Nancy. Jessie followed.

The Lewises' lawn was littered with scraps of metal and glass that glinted in the sunlight. Several panes of the mullioned front windows had been blown out by the explosion. The fresh white paint of the front door had been dulled by a film of soot. Even the transom above it had been blown out.

Nancy rummaged through Sheila's purse and found the keys. She unlocked the door, and all three women stepped inside. Shards of glass from the transom were on the entry floor. Nancy tried to steer Sheila around the shards, but Sheila, oblivious, walked straight ahead; the rubber soles of her running shoes crushed some fragments of glass and pulled one along, etching it into the black marble with a thin, eerie screech that made Jessie wince.

Nancy led Sheila to a large family room off the hall. She helped Sheila onto a gray, L-shaped leather sofa and sat next to her. Sheila started to weep quietly. Nancy stroked her hair.

Jessie sat down on the other section of the L, hating the pain she was about to inflict on the newly widowed woman.

She waited a few minutes, then said, "I'm terribly sorry, Mrs. Lewis." The words seemed empty, lame. "I know this isn't a good time, but I have to ask you some questions so that we can try to find out who killed your husband."

"I can't believe Barry's dead." Sheila's gaze was focused on the floor. She had picked up a navy blue fringed throw pillow and was holding it to her chest. "I told him to be careful." Her voice was almost a whisper. "I told him, but he didn't listen, and now he's dead, and I don't know how I'm going to tell the girls."

"She shouldn't be answering questions," the woman said to Jessie, her voice crisp with disapproval. "She needs a doctor." Her hand was gripping Sheila's knee like a tourniquet.

"I don't need a doctor. I want to get this over with." Sheila turned to Jessie. "I don't know anything more than what I heard on the radio at Nancy's. I was straightening out the beds, and I heard them say a bomb exploded in Beverlywood, and I just knew. I just *knew*." A sob escaped her lips. "Oh, God! How can this be happening?" She buried her face in the pillow.

Jessie took out her notepad and pen. "Did you speak to your husband this morning, Mrs. Lewis?"

Sheila nodded. "He called before I took the girls to school. He sent them kisses over the phone."

"What time was that?"

"I don't remember exactly."

"It was seven-fifteen," Nancy offered.

"Did he drive to your friend's last night?" It was most likely that whoever had placed the bomb under the gas tank had done so under the cover of night or predawn.

"No. He called to say good night to the girls, of course. That was around nine o'clock. Later, he called me." Sheila frowned. "It was a little after eleven. I was watching the news."

"Did he leave the house after he spoke to you?"

"I don't know."

"What about earlier in the evening?"

"I don't know."

"Did he do any errands, Mrs. Lewis? Did he go to the market, for instance? Or out to eat?"

"I don't *know!* I'm trying to remember, but I can't think straight!" She pressed her hands against her temples.

"Is this really necessary?" Nancy asked.

Jessie was annoyed by the interference; at the same time, she understood and admired the friend's protectiveness. "I'm trying to establish the last time Mr. Lewis drove his car." She faced Sheila again. "Try to remember, Mrs. Lewis. Take your time."

Sheila frowned in concentration. "He told me he stopped for milk on his way home from work. He called me when he got home. That was around eight-thirty. He usually comes home late. Eight-thirty or nine. Sometimes later. Never earlier."

"That's good." Smiling, Jessie leaned over and patted Sheila's hand. "Very good. Anything else? Did he eat out?"

Again Sheila concentrated. Finally she shook her head. "He had a lot of work to do, and he didn't want to waste time going out. He fixed himself an omelet. He works very hard," she added.

"So as far as you know, your husband didn't drive the car after he came home." Jessie would check with the neighbors to see if anyone had noticed Lewis driving away during the evening. "Does your husband leave for work the same time every day?"

She nodded. "Ten to nine. He likes to be in his office by nine-fifteen. He rarely comes home before eight-thirty. Usually later. Did I tell you that? I can't think clearly."

"You're doing fine." Jessie smiled again. "Did your husband discuss any of the calls he received during the past few days?"

Sheila shook her head. "I wanted him to come with us to Nancy's, but he said he had too much work, and he needed his books and his office. I told him not to stay here. I *begged* him." Tears streamed down her face. She wiped them with the back of her hand and licked her lips. "Did you find out who wrote the second note?"

"Unfortunately, no. We were able to raise only a smudged partial print, not enough for identification purposes."

The prints on the second note didn't match those on the first note. Jessie decided not to share that information with Sheila Lewis. The knowledge that two people, not one, had sent threats would hardly be comforting.

"Mrs. Lewis, we have to inform your in-laws what's happened. Could you give me their phone number and address?"

Sheila's hand flew to her mouth. "This will kill them!" she whispered. Her voice shook as she dictated the home and business phone numbers and addresses. "It's Morris and Rose Lewis," she added.

"Was your husband their only child?"

"They have a daughter in Chicago. Janice."

"They must have been very close to their son, then, since the daughter's so far away." She watched Sheila carefully.

There was a beat of hesitation. Sheila nodded. "Very close."

Now was not the time, Jessie decided, to question Barry Lewis's widow about what Rita Warrens had told her, that the senior Lewises were furious with their son. It was probably unnecessary, too—Jessie couldn't imagine parents attaching a pipe bomb to the gas tank of their son's car, no matter how angry they felt. And the Lewises would've known that they could be risking the lives of their daughter-in-law and granddaughters, too.

Then again, Sheila Lewis and her daughters hadn't been at home this morning. Had her in-laws known that?

"Did you talk to your in-laws last night?" Jessie asked.

Sheila shook her head. "Could you excuse me, please? I think I'm going to be sick." She dropped the pillow and stood up shakily, then hurried out of the room. Nancy Reiss threw Jessie an accusing look and followed her friend.

Jessie jotted notes in her pad while she waited. A few minutes passed with no sign of the women. Maybe Sheila had gone upstairs to lie down. Who could blame her?

Jessie was heading for the front door when she heard sounds from the back of the house. She walked down the hall to the kitchen and found Sheila standing in the breakfast area in front of a glass-topped round table. On top of the table was a magnificent three-story painted wooden doll house, the kind Jessie had dreamed of having when she was a little girl.

"I'll be leaving now, Mrs. Lewis," Jessie said. "I may have to call you and ask some additional questions."

"It's beautiful, isn't it?" Sheila fingered one of the tiny red shutters on the front windows of the doll house.

"It's very beautiful," Jessie agreed. "Again, I'm terribly sorry about your husband's death, and I want to assure you we'll do everything we can to find the person responsible."

She nodded. "My father-in-law made this for the girls. He must've brought it by last night." She turned to Jessie. "How will I tell them about Barry?"

Chapter Twenty-seven

The crowd of onlookers had grown, and two more television vans and additional reporters had arrived. Jessie walked over to Phil.

"Learn anything?" he asked.

"Lewis came home last night from work around eight-thirty—that's when he called his wife at the friend's. She doesn't think he left the house after he came home—he had a lot of work to do, she says. We'll have to talk to the neighbors."

"No shortage of neighbors." Phil smiled.

"Hardly. But I've already talked to most of them. They'll be sick of me before the day's out." She smiled back. "Lewis usually comes home late, according to his wife. No set pattern there. But he does leave for work the same time every day—eight-fifty."

"So what? The person who set the bomb probably did it at night. Less risk of being spotted."

"Or very early in the morning. And maybe the bomber studied Lewis's routine and factored in that there wouldn't be a whole lot of kids around at a quarter to nine in the morning."

"Good point." Phil nodded. "You have someone in mind?"

She shook her head. "Someone who wanted only Lewis dead."

"Bring me up to date on the people involved. Ben-Natan I know about. You said he's got a rap sheet. Could he have done this?"

"He's been in for petty stuff. Disturbing the peace. Failure to disperse. That's a far cry from blowing a guy up in his car."

"Push the right buttons. . . . Who else?"

"Samuel Hochburg. He's the one whose mother had a stroke after she was shoved during the parade. She died Sunday night. There's Ezra Nathanson, too. I have the recording machine we set up Tuesday night for the phone trap, and the log. Maybe we'll—"

"Tell me later." Phil was looking at something behind Jessie.

She turned and saw Gary standing five feet behind her. She wasn't surprised that he was here—he was a crime reporter—but she hadn't talked to him since their afternoon at the marina, and she wished the *Times* had sent anyone but him.

"What happened to your face?" Gary reached for her cheek.

She pulled away. "I fell. No big deal."

"She almost got blown up with Lewis," Phil said.

"That's 'no big deal'?" Gary had paled. " 'A day in the life of a cop,' huh?"

"Thanks, Phil." She couldn't tell if Gary's voice had held more anger or concern. He'd wanted her to quit her job all along because it was too dangerous.

"Sorry," from Phil. "Missed you last week, Gary."

When Jessie and Gary were married, they had doubled once in a while with Phil and Maureen, and Phil had invited Gary to join his weekly poker group. The poker night had survived the divorce, although Phil was careful never to talk about Gary to Jessie.

"I had a last minute date," Gary said. "Who won?"

"Battaglia. He pulled straight flushes all night."

Who was the date? Jessie wondered, and quickly reminded herself that Gary's personal life was none of her business.

"Glad I missed it, then." To Jessie, Gary said, "So your vandalizing turned into a homicide, huh? Tough luck."

Was he blaming her? "Stuff it, Gary."

He frowned. "What did I say?" He turned to Phil. "Did I say something wrong?"

He sounded sincere. She flushed. "Sorry. I'm tense."

"So who done it? Ben-Natan? Hochburg? The JDL? One of the rabbis? Good thing I've been following this on the news. At least I know the cast of characters." His hands were in his pockets.

Jessie shrugged. "Too many possibilities."

"You know, but you're not saying, huh?"

"We *don't* know," she said, bristling.

"And if we did, we *still* wouldn't be saying." Phil smiled.

Gary grinned. Why was it so easy for them? she wondered, annoyed with them and with herself. She was sick and tired of male bonding.

"What's this about a tape?" Gary asked.

Shit, Jessie thought.

"What tape?" Phil's eyebrows rose to an exaggerated height.

"Come on. I heard Jessie say something about a tape."

"I don't know anything about a tape," Phil said. "Do you know anything about a tape, Jess?"

"Just promise you'll tell me before the other papers scoop it up. Deal?" When Phil nodded, Gary said, "Is Mrs. Lewis inside?"

"Christ, Gary, you're not going to try to talk to her now, are you?" Jessie said. "Her husband's just been killed!"

"*You* talked to her already, didn't you?"

"That's totally different!"

"How is it different? You're trying to get at the truth. So am I."

"Goddammit, Gary!" They had argued this point to death when they were married. She had no intention of rehashing it now. She started crossing the street.

"See you tonight," he called after her.

She stopped and turned around. "What are you talking about?"

"Matthew invited me to his party. Helen said she told you."

Helen *had* mentioned that Matthew wanted "Uncle" Gary to come; she hadn't said she'd actually invited him. "She did. I forgot."

"Want me to pick you up?"

When hell freezes. "No thanks."

"Jess, you can't drive your car, not the way it is," Phil reminded her. He was smiling.

"My mechanic usually has a loaner," she lied, and walked away.

The yard of Lewis Lumber and Hardware was a square lined with racks of various kinds of wood. At the far end, a large, burly man in a plaid shirt and jeans was standing, his hands on his hips, talking to a short, balding man in his early seventies wearing gray slacks and a white shirt and tie.

As Jessie and Phil crossed the yard, the balding man strode to one of the racks, lifted a sheet of wood as if it were a pillow, and brought it to the other man.

". . . nothing wrong with this ash," the short man said. "This is the same like what I gave you."

"Well, the grain isn't the same in the veneers I got, is what I'm saying, Morris. And my people aren't going to be happy with the cabinets if the grain isn't the same."

"That's Lewis?" Phil whispered to Jessie. "Not bad for a guy his age."

"You want to exchange the panels?" Lewis said. "Exchange them. I shouldn't let you do it, because it's already six weeks since you took them. But fine, exchange them."

"Thanks, Morris. I'll unload them from my pickup."

The tall man left. Morris Lewis returned the sheet of wood to the rack.

Jessie followed him. "Mr. Lewis?"

He turned around. "I'm Morris Lewis, yes."

He was staring at her face, and she wondered why, then re-membered her cheek. She must look a fright. "Detective Drake, LAPD." She showed him her badge.

He frowned. "Something's wrong?"

God, she hated this. "Do you have an office where we can talk?" She and Phil had stopped at the senior Lewises' Martel Avenue residence first, but no one had been home.

"It's Barry?" Sighing, he slumped his shoulders, as if the weight of what he was about to hear were already pressing on him. "What happened? Another *Mogen Dovid* they painted on his door?"

"I think it would be better if we went inside."

Lewis paled. He started to say something, nodded instead, and led the detectives across the wide yard into the store. They walked single file in a silent pilgrimage down an aisle crowded with hinges, doorknobs, handles, and other assorted hardware, then turned left to a small office.

A woman in her early seventies with stiffly teased and lac-quered reddish brown hair was sitting on a beige tweed couch. She stood and looked questioningly at Jessie and Phil when they entered behind Morris.

"Rose, these are detectives. They're here about Barry."

"Barry?" The word was strangled. She turned to Jessie and Phil. "What happened? An accident?" Her hand went to her throat.

Jessie exchanged a swift glance with Phil, then said gently, "I'm terribly sorry, Mr. and Mrs. Lewis. Your son is dead."

Rose sagged against her husband and stuffed a fist into her mouth. He eased her onto the sofa and sat next to her.

"How?" Morris's face was ashen. "When?"

"Someone put a bomb under his car this morning," Phil said.

"Barry!" Rose screamed. "Oh, my God, Barry!"

Morris shut his eyes. "Sheila and the girls?" he whispered.

"They were at a friend's," Jessie said. "Your daughter-in-law is all right. Her friend Nancy is with her." As all right as you could be when you've just lost your husband and the father of your children. She waited a moment, wishing she didn't have to subject them to more grief. Then she said, "I know this isn't a good time, but we have to ask you some questions. If you prefer, we can come back later."

"Makes no difference," Morris said. "Now or later."

"When was the last time you spoke to or saw your son?"

"Last night, we saw him. Ten o'clock, I think it was. Right, Rose?" His voice was hoarse.

Rose sobbed quietly against his shoulder.

"Is that when you brought over the doll house?"

"Yah. The doll house." His eyes welled with tears. "My God, what if the girls were in the car with him, or Sheila? What kind of monsters could do such a thing, can you tell me?"

She wondered again why he'd brought the doll house so late at night, when he knew his granddaughters would be asleep. "Did you notice anyone around your son's car when you were arriving or leaving?" Jessie asked.

Morris shook his head. "It was dark. We stayed awhile, then went home."

"When you were at your son's house last night, did he mention anyone specific that he was afraid of? We know that a lot of people were angry at him because of the parade and because he was defending Mr. Benning."

Morris shook his head. "He mentioned no one." He stared somewhere beyond Jessie's head, then said, "The Star of David I could understand. People were angry. I was angry, too. It's no secret." He looked at her. "You want to know the truth? I hoped it would change his mind. But not Barry. Once Barry made up his mind, you couldn't change it." Tears were streaming down his face. "To paint a star is one thing. But to kill someone?"

Phil drove Jessie back to the station. Her Honda had been towed to her mechanic's; he'd promised that her windshield and windows would be replaced by Saturday afternoon. Phil had offered to take her home after work today, and she had no plans for the weekend, other than going to Helen's tonight. She would ask her brother-in-law, Neil, to pick her up.

In the ground-floor restroom, she was startled by the wild-haired chimney sweep staring at her from the mirror above the sink. She washed her hands and the sooty patches off her face and grimaced from time to time as she worked gingerly on her scraped cheek with a wad of wet toilet paper until she'd removed all the crusted blood. She brushed her hair, put on lipstick, and, feeling more human, walked upstairs.

Espes was standing in front of his door when she entered the detectives' room. "Drake! Right now!" He beckoned sharply to her and disappeared into his office.

She saw some of the other detectives glancing at her as she walked to her desk. Her face was hot with embarrassment.

Phil frowned at her. "You should put on some Neosporin so your cheek won't get infected. Maureen uses it on the boys."

"I will, when I get home." She put down the recording machine and phone log and slammed down her purse. "What's up *his* ass?"

Phil shrugged. "Make nice." He touched her arm.

Espes was leaning against his desk when she entered. "Had a busy morning, did you? Find the killer yet?"

If Espes was in a foul mood, that was his problem. She wasn't buying into it. She described what had happened. "We've spoken to all the available neighbors. We still have to contact those who weren't home. Phil—Detective Okum and I spoke to the parents. We'll question everyone whose name has come up in connection with the vandalization. I have the recording machine and Lewis's phone log. I called phone security from the field and gave them the times he listed. They said they'd trace the calls immediately."

Espes folded his arms against his chest. "Well, you are just hopping, aren't you? Looks like you got your homicide after all, Detective Drake. I guess good things come to those who wait."

She stared at him. Was the man crazy? "I'm hardly happy

Lewis is dead!" Calm down, she told herself. This man is your superior. He can have you fired for insubordination.

"You certainly jumped right in there and asked to work the case, didn't you? What did you say to Horner, Drake? 'Pretty please?' Did you show a little leg?"

Had she angered Espes by speaking to Horner? Was that the problem? "I explained that since I'm familiar with the vandalizing, it made sense that I investigate Lewis's murder. I resent the implication that I did anything irregular. Sir." She was shaking and pressed her clenched hands against her sides.

"Well, I resent the hell out of the fact that you've been griping to everyone in town about your assignment!" His eyes narrowed. "Your boyfriend's been checking me out, as if you didn't know." Espes smiled grimly at the startled expression on her face. "Peter Corcoran heard about it and called me last night. Peter and I go back a long ways."

Shit, Jessie thought, her face suddenly hot with humiliation and anger. Corcoran was Frank's nemesis and, as officer in charge at Parker Center, his superior. When Jessie had been on the task force, she'd witnessed the hostility between the two men. She'd also witnessed Corcoran's egoism and male chauvinism. Corcoran wasn't a nice guy, but what the hell had Frank thought he was doing, asking around about Espes? She didn't need a man coming to her rescue, thank you very much. She'd tell him so the next time she saw him, although she didn't know when that would be. He'd called her several times since last Friday night, and their conversations had been pleasant, if light, but he hadn't asked her out. In a way, she'd been relieved; she'd told Manny she would tell Frank how she felt, but she didn't relish the prospect.

"I had no idea Detective Pruitt was sharing my professional concerns with anyone. I was sharing with him my frustration with the Lewis case, saying that it seemed to have reached a dead end. I suppose he took my frustration for dissatisfaction. I apologize if his questions embarrassed or upset you."

Espes was studying her. "I'm pissed off, Drake, not embarrassed. I thought you and I squared all this away when I first assigned you to the Lewis case. You wanted CAPS to handle it. I explained why I wanted you in charge."

"I understood perfectly, sir, and while I didn't agree with your decision, I've done everything I can to find out who was responsible for vandalizing the Lewises' door."

"*Have* you, Detective? I understand from dispatch that Lewis wanted you to pick up the recording machine and the log last night. But I guess you were having too good a time getting it on with your boyfriend." Espes unfolded his arms and walked around his desk. "Maybe if you'd taken this case *seriously* and spent more time working it than bitching about it, bits and pieces of Barry Lewis wouldn't be all over Monte Mar Drive."

Chapter Twenty-eight

"What an effing jerk," Phil muttered.

"Espes or Frank?" Jessie saw his startled expression. "I didn't ask for Frank's help. I'm all grown up, Phil. Frank made me look like an idiot. He—" She broke off. "Enough of this shit." She reached under her desk and plugged in the tape recorder.

"He called while you were with Espes. Heard about the explosion and that you were there. He sounded upset. I said you'd call back."

"I will. Later." Maybe.

She rewound the tape that was in the machine and pressed play. She heard a series of squeaks and the *swoosh*ing, slithery sound of blank lead tape, then voices against a static background.

CALLER NO. 1:	. . . bad enough the parade took place, but now you're defending a murderer?
LEWIS:	Who is this?
CALLER:	You can live with yourself, Lewis? You're proud of yourself that a lady, she didn't harm anybody in her life, is dead? Your parents are proud? They're survivors, too, I hear.

| LEWIS: | I'm doing what I believe is right. |
| CALLER: | Nothing good comes to a person who goes against his own. Nothing. |

"One down." Phil pressed the stop button. "Recognize the caller?"

"I'm not sure." Jessie frowned. "The tape isn't clear, but the caller is someone European, judging from his accent."

"Let's run it again." He rewound the tape and pressed play, then picked up his coffee mug.

"It sounds like Mark Pell," she said after she'd listened to the call again. "He's the director of the OJA," she reminded Phil. "We'll have confirmation when phone security traces the calls."

"You think it's suspicious that Pell called?"

"Not really. He was upset with Lewis even *before* the parade. But I find it odd that he didn't identify himself."

"Maybe he wants to be careful not to involve the OJA."

"Maybe." Next to the first listing on Lewis's log, she wrote "Pell—?" and a brief summary of the call. Then she pressed play.

CALLER NO. 2:	. . . this the Nazi-loving Jew who sold his soul to the devil?
LEWIS:	Who's calling?
CALLER:	Your conscience, Barry Lewis. I'm not surprised you don't recognize me. We haven't been in touch for quite some time, judging from your recent activities."
LEWIS:	Hello, Ben-Natan. I'd be happy to get in touch with you. Where would you like to meet?
CALLER:	Nowhere. I couldn't stomach seeing you. Drop Benning, Lewis. You're making a big mistake.

LEWIS:	You said that about the parade.
CALLER:	I was right, wasn't I? The whole thing blew up in your face. I hope you're proud of yourself.

Phil stopped the machine. "*Is* it Ben-Natan, Jess? That's what Lewis wrote down."

She nodded. She pressed rewind, then play, and listened to the second call again.

"What are you listening for?"

"Ben-Natan said, 'The whole thing blew up in your face.' "

"So?" Phil opened a small bag of Oreo cookies. "Want one?"

"No thanks. Could he have been warning Lewis about a bomb?"

"You feel guilty because of what Espes said. I told you, Jess, he's a jerk. It's risky reading something sinister into everything someone says. You know that."

"But—"

"Next."

Calls three and four were made by the same adolescent male. No distinguishing accent. Next to the corresponding times listed on her paper, she wrote down the unoriginal obscenities he'd screamed at Lewis before slamming down the receiver.

"You shouldn't be writing words like that." Phil shook his head and smiled. "What would your momma say?"

"That you shouldn't be reading them." She grinned, feeling a rush of affection for her partner, then pressed play. Caller number five was Nathanson. He identified himself.

NATHANSON:	. . . disagreed with you vehemently about your representing the White Alliance, Mr. Lewis, but that, at least, involved a constitutional issue. Roy Benning's case has no such issue.

LEWIS:	Thanks for your opinion, Nathanson. I didn't know you were an attorney.
NATHANSON:	I don't think you've considered what an explosive situation you're creating by defending Benning. What if—
LEWIS:	Good night, Nathanson.

"Lewis is pretty cool, don't you think?" Phil said.

"*Was.* I don't think he took the threats seriously." Neither did I, she told herself. Not seriously enough. "Did you notice Nathanson used the word *explosive?*"

"I was waiting for you to mention that." He took another sip of coffee. "Lemme ask you something. If you'd heard the tape last night, would the words *blow up* or *explosive* have made you think someone was going to attach a pipe bomb to Lewis's car?"

"I guess not."

"Damn straight. There's nothing on this tape that constitutes a clear threat or hints at what was gonna happen to him."

Phil made sense. Still, she wished she'd picked up the tape last night.

There were several more callers she couldn't identify. All except one were male. Ben-Natan called again—on Thursday night, according to Lewis's phone log. He said nothing revealing.

"Last call," Phil said. "Last cookie, too. You missed your chance." He crumpled the cellophane wrapper and tossed it into the trash can under his desk.

| CALLER NO. 12: | Hey, Mr. I-know-the-Constitution lawyer, not too popular these days, are you? |
| LEWIS: | Oh, it's the kid with the foul mouth. It's past your bedtime, isn't it? How old are you—fifteen? sixteen? |

CALLER: Old enough to know you're in deep
                 shit. The Jew boys hate you. The
                 White Alliance hates you, too. Plus
                 they think you're a wimp for selling
                 out your own people. Any way you
                 look at it, you are dead, man. D-e-a-d.
LEWIS: Do your parents— Hello? Hello?

"The kid hung up," Phil said. "That's it. Want to rewind
or—"

LEWIS: Hello?
CALLER NO. 13:   Hi, hon. It's me. I just called to say
                 good night.

Phil stopped the tape. "Lewis didn't realize he left the
recorder on. Should we fast-forward?"

"Maybe he said something revealing."

"Admit it, you're just nosy."

"I learned it from living with Gary." Jessie smiled and
pressed play.

LEWIS: I was going to call you to tell you I'll take the
          girls to school tomorrow.
SHEILA: Don't do that. You'll be late for work.
LEWIS: Let me worry about it. What time should I be
          at Nancy's?
SHEILA: Barry, they like going in Nancy's van. And I
          don't want their schedule disrupted any more
          than it has to be. Leave it alone, okay?
LEWIS: I miss them, Sheila. I miss you, too, baby. I
          want you to come home.
SHEILA: I will, as soon as the police find out who's ha-
          rassing us. I wish you were here with us.
LEWIS: I could come over now.
SHEILA: It's late. Nancy and the kids are all asleep.

LEWIS: All the better. We'll have some privacy.
SHEILA: I'm sharing a room with the girls. I'll come to
          the house. But I can't spend the night.

"Heard enough?" Phil asked.
"Shh!"
"Voyeur."

SHEILA: . . . have to be here when the girls wake up.
LEWIS: Fine. I'll pick you up. It'll be like a date.
SHEILA: No. I'll drive over. That way, if there's an-
          other call, you'll be there to record it. I want
          this over with, Barry.
LEWIS: Me, too. When are you coming?
SHEILA: It's eleven-thirty. Give me half an hour.
LEWIS: I'll be waiting.

"Yawn, yawn," Phil said when the tape ended. "Not exactly
an X-rated conversation, if that's what you were hoping for."

"Pretty interesting, though. Number one, Sheila Lewis
didn't tell me she went to her house last night."

"Maybe she didn't end up going." He raised his mug to his
mouth. "Number two?"

"Sounds to me like she didn't want her husband to drive his
car—last night or this morning."

"The carpool bit, you mean."

"Yeah."

Phil swiveled back and forth on his chair. "Yeah."

Chapter Twenty-nine

The yellow police tape was still in place in front of Barry Lewis's home, but there were no lookers. The show was over. Across the street, Jessie rang the neighbor's bell, then identified herself and Phil to the woman who came to the door.

"You gave me your card this morning," Cynthia Fishburn told Jessie as she opened the door. She was in her mid-thirties, petite, overweight, with chin-length blond hair. She was wearing a blue sweater and too-tight jeans. "I haven't remembered anything, or I would've called." Her tone and the fact that she made no move to invite them inside conveyed annoyance and a little apprehension.

Jessie smiled. "We have just a few questions."

"All right." Her tone was grudging. She moved aside to let Jessie and Phil enter and led them to an all-white living room with overstuffed sofas. Jessie felt as though she'd stepped onto a cloud bank.

When everyone was seated, Jessie said, "This morning you told me you didn't see anyone suspicious near the Lewis home last night or today. Did you see *anyone?* Mrs. Lewis, for example? We're just trying to find witnesses," she added vaguely.

"Well, Sheila was here. But I guess you know that."

Jessie nodded. "What time was that?"

"Around midnight. I'd baked a cheesecake and was waiting for it to cool so I could put it in the fridge. David Letterman was on, and I kept going back and forth from the family room to the kitchen to check on the cake. That's when I saw Sheila leaving. You *do* know they moved to a friend's house earlier in the week?"

"Mrs. Lewis told us. Did you see her arrive?"

The woman shook her head. "Barry's parents were here, too. They used to come all the time, before . . . well, you know." She tucked a strand of hair behind her ear. "I didn't mention it this morning because I didn't think you meant Barry's family."

"I understand." Jessie smiled. "What time were they here?"

"Around ten o'clock. Barry's father parked behind Barry's BMW. He took this huge doll house from the trunk and handed it to his wife. She took it into the house. Sheila told me her father-in-law loves making doll houses," she added.

"The father didn't go inside?"

"No. He stayed in the car."

Not exactly what Morris Lewis had implied. "How long did Mrs. Lewis stay in the house?"

"About fifteen minutes. That's how much time passed before I heard Barry's father honking. A few minutes later the car was gone. But I don't understand why you're asking these questions."

"The senior Lewises may have noticed something that could be important to our investigation," Phil said. "You understand."

"Of course." She nodded. "I feel terrible for Sheila. She and I are friends. We go shopping together. Our kids attend the same school. I want to go over, but now's too soon, don't you think?"

"I'd wait a while," Jessie agreed. "It must have been awkward for you lately, with everything that's been going on."

"Well, yes." The woman plucked at an invisible thread on her sweater. "I liked Barry, but I *do* feel he was wrong in taking these cases." She glanced at the detectives. "Not just because of the issues involved, which I think are very, very important, but also because of the effect on his family."

"You mean the harassing phone calls?"

"Yes." She sighed. "Sheila told me she was terrified something terrible would happen. I guess she was right."

"Is that why you waited until Thursday night to call Barry Lewis and tell him you thought he was"—Jessie stopped and read from her notepad—" 'a despicable human being and a traitor to his people and religion who would probably burn in hell'?" Her eyes were locked on the woman sitting across from her.

Cynthia Fishburn had turned white. "Where did you . . ." Her voice trailed off. Tiny beads of sweat dotted her upper lip. "I don't know where you got the idea that I said anything like that to Barry. It's ridiculous. These people are my friends."

"Mr. Lewis taped the calls he received Wednesday and Thursday nights. Detective Okum and I just listened to the tape. We heard your call. I wrote down your words verbatim."

"Well, there's a terrible mistake here." She squared her shoulders with indignation. "Obviously, you heard a woman's voice on the tape, but it wasn't me."

"The phone company traced the call—it was made at ten forty-seven on Thursday night—to your phone."

Seven of the twelve calls had been traced: the first had been traced to Mark Pell; the third and fourth to Robert Oppman in Long Beach; the fifth, Nathanson; the sixth, Lola Hochburg (obviously, someone else had used the dead woman's phone); the ninth, Oppman again; the tenth, Paul Fishburn; the last, Oppman yet again.

When Cynthia Fishburn finally spoke, her voice was almost inaudible. "You may not believe me, but I was trying to help Sheila. I thought if Barry got enough calls, he'd drop the Benning case, and Sheila and the girls could come home. And to be honest, I was furious with him for endangering the entire neighborhood. I was terrified for my family—obviously, with good reason. It's a miracle no one else was hurt this morning!"

"How furious were you, Mrs. Fishburn?" Jessie asked.

She frowned. "Excuse me?"

"Was there someone at home with you last night?" Phil asked.

"Why do you—" She stared at him, her mouth agape. "Oh, my God! You think I killed Barry?" Her hand flew to her mouth.

"You harassed Mr. Lewis. You had access to his car."

"But I *told* you why I called him!" She turned to Jessie. "Please, you can't possibly think . . ." She twisted her hands, then shrieked, "My husband! My *husband* was with me!"

"Where can we reach him?" Jessie asked.

"You're going to call him?" Her eyes were wide with fright.

"Are you afraid he won't verify your story?"

"It's not that! He doesn't know I made that call to Barry. Please, do you have to tell him?"

Jessie glanced at Phil. In the car, they'd decided to play good-cop-bad-cop to teach the woman a lesson. To Jessie it seemed as though the woman already regretted her action.

"Maybe we can ask him to corroborate what he saw or didn't see last night without mentioning the phone call," Jessie said to Phil. "What do you think?"

"Could you?" Cynthia whispered. "I would be so grateful!"

"Making hate calls is ugly, Mrs. Fishburn," Phil said.

"I know that now. I swear I'll never do anything like that again." She paused. "Does Sheila know what I did?"

"Not yet," Jessie said.

"Do you—" She cleared her throat and tried again. "Do you have to tell her? It would just hurt her so."

That was something Cynthia Fishburn should have thought about before.

*   *   *

Sheila Lewis was resting upstairs, her friend Nancy told Jessie and Phil. She stood, wardenlike, in the entry hall.

"Would you please tell her we need to see her?" Jessie said. "It's important, or we wouldn't be disturbing her," she added, seeing the irritation in the woman's eyes.

Nancy hesitated. "I'll see if she's asleep. You can wait in the family room."

Jessie led Phil to the family room. A few minutes later Sheila Lewis appeared, alone. She was still wearing her gray sweats. Her hair was disheveled. Her eyes were puffy.

Jessie introduced Phil, then said, "We're sorry to bother you, Mrs. Lewis, but—"

"Did you find out who killed Barry?"

"Not yet." Jessie waited until Sheila sat down on the sofa. "You didn't tell me you were at the house last night." She spoke gently, careful not to let accusation creep into her voice.

Sheila looked at Jessie, bewilderment creasing her forehead. "Last night? I don't—"

"We listened to your husband's tape of his incoming calls. Apparently, he didn't realize he was taping your call, too."

Sheila's face, so pale a moment before, was flooded with color. "That was a personal call," she said, her voice tight with annoyance. She kept her eyes on Jessie. "It has nothing to do with the investigation, and your listening to the tape is an invasion of my privacy."

"In a murder investigation, everything about the victim is relevant. And we can't always honor a person's privacy."

"What time did you get here?" Phil asked.

"A little before midnight."

"You weren't afraid to drive here that time of night?"

"Not really. There's a Beverlywood patrol. And I called Barry before I left Nancy's. He was waiting outside when I pulled up, and he saw me to the car after we . . . when I left. I don't understand why you're asking me these questions!"

"We just want to get a clear idea of your husband's activities that night," Jessie said.

"I see," Sheila said, but it was clear from her tone that she didn't. "Did you recognize any voices on the tapes?"

"We're working on that now. One other thing that made me curious, Mrs. Lewis. On the tape you told your husband that your daughters were going with your friend Nancy's carpool to school."

She nodded. "That's right."

"But this morning you told me you'd just returned from taking the girls to school when you heard the radio report of your husband's death. I'm a little confused." Jessie smiled.

"I just changed my mind." She shifted on the sofa.

"I got the feeling that you didn't want your husband to pick them up. Why is that?"

Sheila didn't answer.

"Mrs. Lewis?" Jessie prompted.

"You don't know how frightened I was! You're right—I *didn't* want Barry to pick up the girls. I didn't want him *near* them until this was over! I was afraid someone would follow him to Nancy's. That's why I didn't want him to pick me up last night, either."

"But you weren't afraid to drive to your house last night? Weren't you concerned about the possible danger here?"

"Of *course* I was concerned! But I missed him, I really did," she said in a low, mournful voice. "And things have been strained between us because of the parade and Mrs. Hochburg's death, and I just needed to be with him." She wiped her eyes. "I'm so glad I saw him."

"Mrs. Lewis, did your husband mention that his father was bringing over the doll house I saw this morning?"

She shook her head. "I was surprised to see it. I thought Dad would bring it over when the girls were home."

That would have made more sense. "Did he know you and the girls were at your friend's?"

"Yes. The girls spoke to them on Wednesday."

When Jessie had questioned Lewis, he'd implied that he hadn't known where his daughter-in-law and granddaughters were that Friday morning. Had he thought Sheila and the girls had returned early in the morning? Or had he been agitated and confused?

"Where are your daughters now?" Jessie asked.

"Upstairs. Nancy picked them up from school. I told them about Barry, but I don't think they understand he's never coming back." She sighed. "Detective Drake, can I ask you something? One of the policemen told me you were the last one to see Barry alive. Did he say anything special? Anything . . . I don't know . . . something I should know?"

Jessie had been expecting—and dreading—this question and others. "We talked about the tape. He was eager to have this over so you and the girls could come home." No need to mention that the conversation had bordered on the snide.

"Did you see it happen?" she whispered.

"Yes." Again, Jessie heard the explosion, saw the ball of fire. She felt the heat that had seared her lungs and the helplessness that had flooded through her as she had stood, watching, knowing that she had almost been killed, too.

"Do you think he suffered long?"

"It was quick. I'm sure he died instantly." She wasn't sure of any such thing, but what was the harm in telling the woman what would give her the most comfort?

"Did you . . . did you see him after?" She clutched the edges of the sofa cushions.

Jessie reached over and took the woman's hand. "Mrs. Lewis, I understand your need to know what happened to your husband, but I think a few days from now would be a better time, don't you?"

"I don't think there's ever going to be a better time."

Probably not, Jessie thought. She released Sheila's hand.

Chapter Thirty

Rush hour traffic had clotted the southbound San Diego Freeway. Even the "diamond" carpool lane was sluggish—probably, Jessie decided, because it was filled with passengerless cars driven by people who, like the man in the Ford Taurus in front of Phil, risked paying the $271 fine if they were caught by the highway patrol. (Where on earth did the state come up with that fine, anyway? Why not $270 or $275?) By the time she and Phil had driven the thirty-some miles to Long Beach, it was ten after four.

Robert Oppman lived in a middle-income, racially mixed neighborhood typical of Long Beach. The homes—mostly one-story ranches—were attractive but not extravagant. The Oppman house had been recently painted a creamy beige. A well-tended front garden was blooming with multicolored impatiens and hot pink azaleas.

"Shasta white," Phil said as they walked to the front door.

Jessie frowned. "What?"

"The house color. We're having ours painted this summer. Maureen's been bringing home color charts. That's Shasta."

"Nice." Jessie's house was pale blue—Gary's choice. She hated the color but didn't have money to repaint and had turned down her father's recent offer to pay for it. Helen had no problem accepting gifts from their parents. "You're cutting off your nose to spite your face," she'd told Jessie, and Jessie wondered sometimes whether she was protecting her painfully earned independence or punishing her parents (her mother, for years of abuse; her father, for allowing it to happen) by depriving them of the satisfaction of helping her. Independence was expensive.

"Maureen's undecided." Phil rang the doorbell. "It's Shasta or Pueblo Peach."

A moment later a woman said, "Yes?"

"Mrs. Oppman? LAPD." He held his open badge to the peephole.

The door was opened by a waiflike, not unpretty woman in her late thirties with short, layered light brown hair and anxious brown eyes. "Is something wrong?" She stared at Jessie's cheek, then looked at Phil.

"We'd like to speak to your son," Phil asked.

"Gene, you mean. He's doing his homework. Can you tell me what this is about?"

The quaver in her voice told Jessie that the woman had expected a visit from the police for some time.

"It's better if we talk to your son, ma'am," Jessie said.

"Should I call my husband? He's still at work—he's a psychologist—but he can be home in fifteen minutes."

"I don't think that's necessary, ma'am. You can if you like."

Mrs. Oppman left them in the living room and went to get her son. The room was pleasant and inviting—two taupe-colored velvet sofas facing each other across a cherrywood coffee table; a brown spinet piano against one wall; bookcases on the other; family photos on the mantel over the fireplace.

"Two sons," Phil said, pointing to one of the photos.

"She seemed to think we came to see Gene."

They were sitting on one of the couches when Mrs. Oppman returned. A few paces ahead of her was a tall, handsome teenager in jeans and a Lakers T-shirt. He had neatly groomed short blond hair and keen blue eyes that showed no sign of nervousness.

Phil made the introductions. When they were all seated, he said, "Gene, do you know Barry Lewis?"

"Lewis?" His brow was furrowed. "No, sir. Should I?"

"You might've seen his name in the papers recently," Phil said in a matter-of-fact tone. "He's the ACLU lawyer who helped the White Alliance have their parade. Does that ring a bell?"

"Oh, yeah." Gene nodded. "I read about that, but I didn't remember the lawyer's name." He was leaning against the sofa cushions, his fingers tapping a silent arpeggio on his thighs.

"Then how is it that you called his home four times within the past two days?" Phil asked in the same matter-of-fact tone.

"Why would I do that?"

The boy's fingers had stopped moving, but his face shone with sincere bewilderment—all the more troubling because Jessie knew he was lying. "That's what we'd like to know," she said.

"My husband's on the way," the mother said. "I want him here before Gene answers any more questions." She had mustered authority from somewhere and forced it into her voice, but it was an uneasy tenant.

"No problem." Phil smiled.

They sat in a silence disturbed only by the ticking of a clock on the mantel and the distant drone of the refrigerator. Jessie could see from their stiff, soldierlike posture that for Mrs. Oppman and her son, the silence was uncomfortable. As a detective, Jessie was used to waiting. Now she pondered several things: the fact that the all-American teenager sitting across from her would make harassing calls to the Jewish attorney who'd agreed to defend a neo-Nazi; the truthfulness of what Sheila Lewis had told them; her own anger with Frank over the mess he'd created with Espes and the unresolved issues between them; her sudden (and annoying) uncertainty about what she would wear to Matthew's party now that she knew Gary would be there; who killed Barry Lewis.

More than ten minutes passed before the front door opened and closed. Seconds later a tall, blond-haired man in his late thirties strode into the living room.

"I'm Robert Oppman. Can you tell me what's going on here?" His tone fell just short of belligerence.

"We're talking to your son about several calls he made to Barry Lewis on Wednesday and Thursday of this week," Phil said.

Oppman sat down next to his son and placed his hand on the boy's knee. "Gene, did you make these calls?"

"No."

Oppman looked at the detectives. "I believe my son."

Jessie said, "At our suggestion, Mr. Lewis recorded his calls over the past few days." She explained about the phone trap. "The voice on the calls coming from this phone was young. We assumed it was Gene's. Unless, of course, your other son made the calls?"

Mrs. Oppman opened her mouth and quickly closed it.

Robert Oppman looked at the boy. "Gene?" His tone and the expression in his blue eyes signaled defeat.

"It was just a prank," the boy said in a bored voice. "It wasn't a big deal."

"Whose idea was this?" Oppman demanded, now angry. "I can't believe it was yours."

"It was mine." A defiant thrust of the jaw. "Nobody told me to do it."

"Where'd you get Mr. Lewis's phone number?" Jessie asked.

He turned to her. "I called the operator."

"The number's unlisted," Phil said.

The boy retreated into silence.

"Gene, in the phone call you sounded very angry at Mr. Lewis," Jessie said. "Why is that?"

No response from Gene.

"Answer the detective." Oppman removed his hand from his son's knee.

"Did he do something wrong to you, Gene?" Jessie asked.

"He pissed me off, okay? They all piss me off."

"Gene," his mother protested sharply.

"Who pisses you off, Gene?" Jessie asked. When he didn't answer, she said, "Why did Mr. Lewis annoy you?"

" 'Cause he's making himself out to be some kind of hero, defending Roy Benning. And he's not. He's just another money-hungry Jew lawyer trying to make a name for himself. I wanted him to know that I knew."

"This is not what we taught our son." Mrs. Oppman's face was crimson. "This is not how we talk in this house. He's getting these ideas from those people he's been with."

Gene Oppman threw his mother a look of disgust.

"Peggy," Robert said, "I don't think—"

"Tell the detectives what these people are teaching you, Gene! Tell them the garbage they're putting in your head!"

"It's not garbage." Pride animated his blue eyes and his voice. "Mr. Benning talks to us about important things, like what's happening to this country and what we're gonna do about it. He told us the truth about the Jews and World War Two, not the *garbage* they teach us in school." Another glance at his mother.

"Was it his idea for you to call Mr. Lewis?" Phil asked.

The boy shook his head. "I told you, it was my idea."

"But you got Mr. Lewis's phone number from the group, right?" Jessie said. "Did you get his address, too?" Again, no answer. Was that courage or loyalty or fear of retaliation? "Gene, are you aware that making an annoying phone call is a misdemeanor?"

"So?" There was a flicker of unease in his eyes.

"Is Mr. Lewis pressing charges?" Robert Oppman asked.

"Mr. Lewis is in no position to press charges," Phil said. "Someone blew him up in his car this morning in his driveway."

"Oh, my God," Peggy Oppman whimpered.

Robert Oppman's face was frozen in shock. Gene had paled.

" 'You're a dead man. D-e-a-d,' " Jessie read from her pad.

"Those were your words to Mr. Lewis on Thursday night, Gene."

"Gene, don't say another word," Oppman ordered. "Detective, I won't allow my son to answer any more questions without an attorney present."

"You're certainly entitled to do that," Jessie said. "I don't think that's necessary, though, at this time."

"Dad—"

Oppman whirled toward his son. "Shut up!" He faced Jessie and Phil again. "Is my son under suspicion?"

"We're just beginning our investigation," Phil said. "We'd prefer to do this informally, but if not, well, given your son's activities, we may have to take him in for questioning. His attorney will be allowed to be there with him, of course."

"He's fifteen years old!" Mrs. Oppman cried. "He has the wrong friends, but he didn't kill anyone! He doesn't even drive, so how could he have been at Mr. Lewis's house?"

"Your son could've been an accessory. He made an anonymous harassing call to Mr. Lewis in which he threatened him He—"

"That was a joke! I didn't know Lewis would get killed!"

"Gene, I told you not to say anything!" Oppman snapped.

"They're thinking I killed the guy, and I didn't! Look, can I just say what happened?"

Oppman glanced at his wife, then at his son. "All right."

"We were talking about Roy Benning's case and—"

"Who is 'we'?" Jessie asked. "You and other members of the White Alliance?"

Gene nodded.

"When was this?"

"Sunday night, right after the old Jew—the old lady died. We were at Mr. Benning's, playing pool in his rec room. That's where we usually meet. Anyway, somebody said wouldn't it be a gas if Lewis got a couple of crank phone calls, so I said I'd do it." He shrugged. "That's it."

"Who's the 'somebody'?" Phil asked.

"I don't remember." The boy looked away.

"Yes, you do," Jessie said. He still wasn't looking at her, so she couldn't read his eyes. "Was it Benning?"

"I told you, no."

"You afraid they'll punish you for telling, is that it?" Phil said kindly. "Tough spot, but we can help you."

Gene whirled toward him. "They're not like that! You don't understand. We're a team. We do things together. We understand each other."

"You *hate* together, huh?"

"Detective—" Robert Oppman began.

"Yeah, we do!" Gene shouted. "We hate what's happening to this country! We hate that it's being taken over by all these foreigners! That they're getting all the jobs!" He slumped back against the sofa cushions like a rag doll.

"Blacks, you mean," Jessie said. "Hispanics, Asians. Jews like Barry Lewis. But you don't have to worry about Mr. Lewis anymore, do you?"

"I didn't kill him, all right? I didn't kill him, but I'm not sorry he's dead. That's not a crime, is it?"

Jessie felt suddenly weary. She suppressed a sigh. "We may have more questions for you, Gene." She took a card from her purse and held it out to him. "If you remember who told you to call Lewis, or anything else, let me know."

"I won't remember." He made no move to take the card.

"You never know." Jessie dropped the card onto the table.

Chapter Thirty-one

The answering machine in the den was blinking furiously. Jessie pressed playback and started undressing while she listened to her messages.

Manny had heard that she'd been on the scene when Lewis had been killed; was she okay? Ditto from Brenda and two other colleagues and from Frank, who wanted to know why she hadn't returned his call. Helen reminded her that Neil would pick her up at twenty to seven.

It was five after six now, and Neil was neurotically punctual, but Jessie was desperate for a shower. She dumped her jacket, slacks, and blouse on her bedroom floor. Everything reeked of smoke and would have to be dry-cleaned. Phil hadn't said, but her hair probably reeked, too. She showered quickly, allowing herself a minute to soap her body, two minutes to shampoo her hair. As she was rinsing off the lather, she let the warm water run down her face and winced when it touched her bruised cheek.

After blow-drying her hair, she examined her face in the bathroom mirror. Her cheek was puffy and streaked with red. Her father would be concerned. Helen would be frantic. Frances would make a comment about women who chose to be cops. Jessie applied Neosporin ointment, doctored the bruise with several coatings of cream concealer, then dusted with loose powder. Not too bad.

She decided on black silk pants and a white lace blouse, both of which she'd bought on sale at Saks for a special occasion. Matthew's turning nine was special, but she knew she wasn't dressing for him. When the doorbell rang, she was ready. She grabbed her purse from her dresser, hurried to the entry hall, picked up the wrapped gift for Matthew, and opened the door.

"Neil, thanks for—" She stopped.

"Helen had some last minute crisis and asked me to pick you up." Gary smiled. "You look great, by the way."

"Thanks." She handed him the gift and pulled the door shut behind her. "I appreciate your coming." He looked handsome, she thought, in gray slacks and a navy blue wool blazer. He smelled good, too. Hugo Boss.

"I offered before, remember? What happened to your loaner?"

"None available." She looked down and smoothed her pants.

"I love your hair like this. New style?"

"The not-quite-dry look," she said lightly, feeling uncomfortable because of the attention he was paying her but not disliking it. "I didn't want to keep Neil waiting."

"Smart woman." He grinned.

She knew he was remembering the numerous times they'd laughed about Neil's fastidiousness. It was a safe memory, and she allowed herself to smile. She walked ahead of him to the passenger side of the Audi and waited while he put the gift in the trunk and opened the door for her. As soon as the engine was on, she turned on the radio and settled back against the seat.

"So how's the investigation going?" Gary asked as he pulled away from the curb.

"How's the weather, Gary?"

Gary smiled. "I can take a hint."

"Smart man." She closed her eyes and listened to a Mozart

sonata and appreciated the fact that Gary didn't feel the need to talk during the ten-minute drive to Cheviot Hills.

It was an affluent neighborhood, just south of Beverly-wood, with deep, sprawling lawns and hilly streets occupied by expensive homes in a variety of architectural styles—Tudor, Spanish, colonial, Cape Cod, ranch. Helen had set her eye on a white colonial with a backyard overlooking the Hillcrest Country Club, but the price, even in the depressed Southern California market, had been two hundred thousand too steep. Instead she and Neil had bought a brick-faced two-story, four-bedroom on Forrester Drive—a duplicate of their Winnetka house—with twice the square footage of Jessie's home. And, Jessie was sure, a roof that didn't leak.

Their parents' metallic gray Cadillac Seville was in Helen's driveway.

"Helen *did* tell you our parents are going to be here, didn't she?" Jessie asked. Frances and Arthur hadn't seen Gary since before the divorce. "I hope it won't be awkward for you."

"I can always charm your mom. And I'm wearing a barb proof vest."

"You'll probably need it." She unbuckled her seat belt and reached for the door handle.

"Jess?"

Her stomach muscles suddenly tight, she turned toward him. "What?"

"The other day at the marina, I made you uncomfortable. I wanted to say I'm sorry."

"It's all right. Forget about it."

He put his hand on hers. "You were honest with me, and I needed that. I've accepted the fact that you're involved with Pruitt. I may not like it, but I've accepted it." He grinned. "Anyway, I decided it was time for me to get on with my life. I'm meeting people, going on dates. The whole thing."

"I'm glad, Gary." She felt awkward, hearing this.

"The point is, I'm okay with our being just friends. So you don't have to feel uncomfortable tonight, or any other time we happen to see each other. I figured you'd want to know."

"Absolutely," she said firmly, wondering why she didn't feel the relief she'd anticipated. "Thanks for telling me, Gary."

Frances let them in. She smiled and said, "How nice to see you, Gary," then lifted her face to Jessie for a kiss and frowned. "What on earth happened to your cheek? Did you hurt it on the job?" She reached her hand toward Jessie.

Jessie flinched instinctively. "I bumped into a wall in the house last night. I was half-asleep." She silenced Gary with her eyes. "It's no big deal, Mom."

"Let your father look at it. Arthur, come take a look," she called to her husband, who was at the other end of the wide entry hall, talking to Neil. "That's a lovely outfit, by the way, dear."

"Thanks." Jessie rarely earned her mother's approval. Frances was elegant as always, this time in a two-piece black wool crepe dress and a strand of pearls. Her blond hair was longer than Jessie remembered and softened the angular contours of her face.

"Put on Neosporin," Jessie's father, the doctor, prescribed after he hugged and kissed Jessie and shook hands with Gary. He was wearing a double-breasted navy suit and a beautiful silk tie that she knew her mother had picked out.

"I did. Where can we put these?" she asked Neil, who had walked over with Arthur. She pointed to the gifts Gary was holding.

"In the family room. I'll get Helen. She's upstairs, helping Matthew fix his tie. We'll let him open his gifts first or he'll be too excited to eat." Neil smiled.

It was nice to see her brother-in-law so relaxed. He was a dark-haired, handsome man, always pleasant, always caring, but his rigidness often made him seem older than his forty-four years. She had worried for the longest time that he was too old for Helen, but Frank was eleven years older than

Jessie, and age wasn't a problem, not if two people loved each other.

"Bumped into a wall, huh?" Gary whispered as he walked with Jessie down the hall. "You owe me."

She pinched his thigh and thought how nice it was to be friends again.

Matthew loved the Optimus Prime Transformer set Jessie had bought him and the compact billiards/multigame table from his grandparents (over two hundred dollars at Toys 'Я'Us—Jessie had eyed it), and he shouted "All *right!*" when he unwrapped Gary's gift—a baseball and mitt signed by Nolan Ryan.

"How nice." Frances smiled but wrinkled her nose, as if she could smell the sweat of the mitt's previous owner.

"The *Times'* sports editor got them for me," Gary said. "You also get two practice sessions with me at Rancho Park, to be arranged with you and me and your mom and dad. If you want."

"When can we start? Sunday?"

Gary was grinning at Matthew, and the boy was beaming, and Jessie knew that Helen had been right to invite Gary. Jessie had worried unnecessarily about Frances, too. Her mother was in an exceptionally good mood and spent most of the evening flirting with Gary, whom she'd adored before the divorce and about whom she'd said incredibly nasty things to Jessie the last time his name had come up. Gary, Jessie decided, could charm the rattles off a snake. Then again, his stock had risen when Frances had learned from Helen that Jessie was seeing a cop.

Helen and Neil were like newlyweds, continuously smiling at each other across the table; there was no gap—age or otherwise—between them tonight; every time Helen brought in a course and set it down in front of her husband, she touched his hand or arm or shoulder. The birthday boy was stealing glances at his parents, too, and Jessie silently blessed the Tucson vacation and Dr. Rossman's sessions and whatever magic the therapist had worked to bring the shy joy to a freckled face that, only months before, had been clouded with insecurity and fear.

They had birthday cake. (They would have another, larger cake tomorrow, when Matthew's classmates came to a second, no adults party.) Matthew made a wish and blew out the candles. Gary said he had to leave and would call Matthew to set up their first session. Frances said, "Don't be a stranger, dear," and kissed Gary's cheek, and Jessie wondered whether he had a date.

Frances went to unpack in the two-bedroom guest house over the garage—she and Arthur were spending the night and would drive back to La Jolla in the afternoon. Neil, Arthur, and Matthew played billiards in the family room while Jessie helped Helen clear the table and load the dishes into the dishwasher. The kitchen, like the rest of the house, was beautiful—large and recently remodeled—and Jessie thought about Sheila Lewis in her expensive new kitchen.

When the dishwasher was filled and the counters wiped, Jessie told Helen she was going to the guest house. "I forgot to ask Mom something," she added, seeing the question in Helen's eyes.

Frances had changed into a long pink robe and pink mules and was hanging up her dinner outfit. She was clearly surprised to see Jessie.

"I thought I'd keep you company, Mom." Given Jessie's relationship with her mother, the words sounded ridiculously false to her ears. She sat on one of the twin beds and wondered how to begin.

"That's thoughtful of you, dear." Frances slipped shoe trees into her black leather pumps. "I'm so glad Helen invited Gary. He's a sweetheart, and it's clear he's still crazy about you."

"We're just friends, Mom."

"You know best, of course." She placed the shoes on the bottom of the closet. "Are you still seeing that detective?"

Frances never referred to Frank by name; it helped her pretend he didn't exist. "Yes."

"Marsha Jessop told me about a wonderful attorney she knows who lives in Los Angeles. He's thirty-eight, never married."

"I appreciate it, Mom, but I'm not interested in meeting anyone right now."

"You don't have to marry the man, Jessica. Just go out with him once."

Jessie shook her head.

"God forbid you should give me or your father the satisfaction, is that it?" Frances shook out a royal blue silk dress and walked to the closet. With her back to Jessie, she said, "You didn't come up here to keep me company, Jessica. Obviously, something is troubling you. Are you going to tell me what it is?"

"You know this case I've been working on? The ACLU lawyer whose house was—"

"He was killed this morning, wasn't he?" Frances turned around. "Your father and I heard it on the radio when we were driving up. They said it was a bomb. Horrible." She shuddered.

"Mom, I keep thinking about your Jewish relatives."

Frances sighed. "Jessica, I've explained ad nauseam that I've told you all I know. Why do you persist in bringing this up?"

Jessie played with the button on the cuff of her sleeve. "Sometimes, I think you're ashamed."

"Ashamed of what? What are you saying, Jessica?"

"Sometimes . . . sometimes I think you don't want to admit you have Jewish relatives."

"That's ridiculous!" Frances hissed. "How dare you say that!"

Jessie looked up. Her mother's mouth was pinched, her eyes narrowed. "Why didn't you want a rabbi to marry Gary and me, Mom? Dad wouldn't have minded. It's not as if we're devout. Aside from Christmas and Easter, I don't remember going to church much."

"You're not being fair, Jessica. Gary's *parents* didn't care about having a rabbi. Neither did Gary. I thought having a judge would make things simpler for everyone."

"Easier for you, you mean."

"Did I ever say anything to make you think I don't like Jews? Did I ever criticize Gary or his parents or any of the Jewish friends you brought home?" With an angry motion, Frances zipped her garment bag shut and folded it.

I should stop now, Jessie thought. I should stop before it's too late. "You have this look of distaste whenever you see someone wearing a skullcap or Hasidic clothing, Mom. You say things like 'This is America' or 'Why can't they look like everybody else?' You don't say the same thing when you see Sikhs or Hare Krishnas or other people who dress differently."

"I don't have to explain myself to you! I am *not* one of the low-life criminals you deal with!" Frances's hands were clenching and unclenching. Her nostrils were flaring.

All the familiar warning signals. Jessie continued anyway. "You're annoyed whenever there's an article in the paper or a movie on the Holocaust, Mom. Why is that?"

"That's not true." Frances advanced toward Jessie. "I don't know what you're talking about." There were angry patches of red on her white face. Her lips were trembling.

"You *are*, Mom. When *Holocaust* came out on TV, you said, 'Enough is enough.' When *Schindler's List* came out, you said, 'Why do we need to hear this over and over?' Don't you think the story should be told? Or maybe you think the Holocaust never happened?" Jessie was amazed that the words had come out of her mouth. Someone else seemed to have said them.

Frances drew her hand back and smacked Jessie across her cheek, just below her bruise. The impact jarred Jessie's jaw and brought tears to her eyes.

Frances sat down on the bed facing Jessie. Mother and daughter stared at each other.

"You deserved that," Frances finally whispered. "Make

sure to tell your therapist I said that the next time you discuss your monster of a mother."

"You always think I deserve it."

Frances flinched and looked away. "Why don't you leave, Jessica."

"Why'd you hit me, Mom? Because I told the truth?"

Frances faced her daughter. "Can't you leave this alone?" Her voice and face were filled with weariness and a hint of desperation.

Jessie didn't answer.

Frances stood and walked to the dresser. She will stand there until I leave, Jessie thought, but a moment later her mother resumed her place on the bed. In her hand was her wallet. From behind her driver's license, she pulled out a sepia-tone photo with a crimped, off white border. It was a smaller size of the photo Jessie had seen.

Frances pointed to the bearded man standing in the center of the photo. "That's my father, Yaakov Kochinsky. He owned a textile factory and was quite well-to-do, even by today's standards. He was very well respected by everyone in Tchebin, even the Poles."

Jessie stared, openmouthed, at her mother. She didn't know what she'd expected—certainly not this. Never this.

"That's my mother, Yiska, next to him," Frances said. "When this picture was taken, she was forty-three, but her skin was as smooth as a twenty-year-old's. Next to her are my oldest brother, Chaim, and his wife, Sonia. Next to them, my brother Berish and his wife, Shaindl. Shaindl is five months pregnant, but you can't tell, can you?" Frances looked up at Jessie.

Jessie shook her head. The pressure in her chest was so intense that she could barely breathe, and she couldn't understand how Frances could be talking so calmly, as if she were identifying ordinary people in an ordinary snapshot.

Frances's finger moved. "Sitting in the middle are my father's parents, Mordechai and Rivka. That's my sister Bronca with her husband, Motl. That's my sister Chaya. That's my youngest brother, Shimon. He was eighteen. Next to my father is my oldest sister, Henia, and her husband, Berel. The twin girls on the floor are hers. The little boy is Chaim and Sonia's. He's so sweet looking, isn't he?"

"Very sweet," Jessie said, her words almost inaudible, because her throat was dry and she felt lightheaded and because she knew that Chaim and Sonia's sweet-looking little boy was dead. They were all dead. She could hear her heart pounding in her ears.

"That's me, on my grandfather's lap." Frances pointed to the center of the photo. "I was five years old. See my braids? My mother would do them every morning. 'Your hair is like silk, Fraideleh,' she would tell me, and even when the Germans came and there were shortages of everything—food, heating oil, gasoline—she'd find something to use as ribbons for my hair. My hair was very blond—white, almost—and my eyes are green, and my Polish was perfect, and that's why, a year later, when we heard that the Germans were planning another action and were rounding up all the Jews of Tchebin to transport them, my mother and father decided to leave me with a Polish family until after the war."

"But you were only six years old!" Jessie whispered. "Did you understand what was happening?"

"Of course I understood." Frances's smile was sober. "In Poland during the war, Jessica, six-year-olds were not children. Our bodies were young, but our souls were old." She paused, lost in thought, then said, "That was in November 1941. The Germans had taken over my father's factory, but my mother had hidden some wool fabric and made me two dresses and a coat. That evening she tied real ribbons on my braids and had me put on one of the new dresses. I cried. I wanted to stay with my parents and my brothers and sisters and grandparents, but my parents promised that they'd come back for me soon and we'd all be together again." Now Frances's smile was ironic.

"You must have been so frightened!" Jessie said, trying to imagine what her mother had felt, finding it impossible. She wanted to cry for the little girl abandoned by her family, but it was all so strange, so unreal.

"I was terrified," Frances said. "But my father assured me the Polish family was very nice. The husband had worked in his factory and was now working for the Germans. He and his wife had three children but were willing to take me in because my father had been good to them over the years and had given them money to keep me safe and promised to give them more when he returned."

Frances put the photo on the bed. Jessie picked it up. There were so many names to learn, so many faces to memorize, so many relatives she'd never known, would never know. Why had her mother kept them a secret?

"That night," Frances continued, "I kissed my mother and the others good-bye, and my father took me to the small house on the outskirts of the city. The husband and wife and their seven-year-old pudgy blond daughter and two older brown-haired sons were waiting for me. The husband's name was Janek. The wife was Sofia. 'What a beautiful child!' the wife said. 'Now you will have a playmate, Annushka,' she said to her daughter. Sofia stroked my hair and called me *moya kochana.* My sweetheart. 'We will take excellent care of your little girl, Pan Kochinsky,' Janek told my father. 'She will be one of our own.'

"Sofia showed me to the closet-size basement room I would be sharing with Anna. A second bed had been forced into the room, and there was barely any space to walk. I stored my small valise under the bed Sofia said was mine and changed into my nightgown. My father listened as I recited my evening prayers by heart—I couldn't bring my prayer book. If the Germans found it, my father had explained, I'd be exposed and the family would be in grave danger. The straw mattress was thin and prickly and the blanket worn, and I clung to my father's arms, but I waited until he left before I cried myself to sleep."

Jessie had never seen her mother cry. Even now she was dry-eyed, and it was difficult for Jessie to reconcile the sad, vulnerable little girl in her story with the strong-willed woman sitting across from her. When had the metamorphosis taken place? And at what cost? Jessie moved toward the edge of the bed until her knees were almost touching her mother's.

"In the morning," Frances said, "Sofia came into the room and gently shook me awake. 'Get dressed, sweetheart. Breakfast.' She was peeling potatoes when I came upstairs. Her husband was at the kitchen table with the children. They were staring at me as they ate. I asked Sofia to help me braid my hair. 'Of course, *moya kochana.*' She took the brush from my hand and fixed my hair and attached my ribbons. I sat down at the table and stared at the gruel she put in front of me. In it were pieces of sausage—I'd seen sausage in the windows of the Polish butcher shops when I'd gone to the market with my mother. My father had explained that God wouldn't be angry at me for eating nonkosher food to survive, but that first morning I left the meat. 'No appetite, poor thing,' Sofia said.

"Janek left for work and took the children to school. Sofia brought me into the front of the house and showed me a bucket and scrub brush. 'You must earn your keep,' she said. I told her that I didn't understand, that my father had given her husband a great deal of money to care for me. Her face became red with anger. 'Your father gave us a few zlotys, hardly enough to make us risk our lives by hiding a filthy damn Jew.' She threw the hot water from the bucket at me and warned that if I mentioned a word to her husband, she'd turn me over to the Germans."

Jessie winced at the image. She clasped her mother's hands and squeezed them gently.

Frances returned the pressure. "My dress was soaked and I was shivering, but she wouldn't let me change. The smell of wet wool was in my nose as I scrubbed the kitchen and the room where her two boys slept. I can still smell it now." She paused. "For lunch there was a piece of dry bread on a plate. And the sausage. 'In this house we don't waste food,' Sofia said. 'It's no wonder your parents didn't want a spoiled brat like you.' She watched me as I gagged on the first bite, and I knew from the hard smile in her eyes that she hoped I would vomit."

Jessie felt herself gag, too. Bile rose in her throat. "Did you?" she asked, wondering what difference it made now.

Frances looked at her daughter. "No." Pride flashed briefly in her eyes. She pulled her hands out of Jessie's, stood abruptly, and left the room. She can't finish, Jessie thought, but a moment later her mother returned.

Frances handed her a washcloth. "There's an ice cube in here. Hold it against your cheek so it won't swell."

Jessie positioned the cloth against the cheek her mother had smacked and thought, How bizarre. But then, this entire evening had a surreal quality. Any moment now, she was sure, she'd wake up and realize she'd been dreaming.

Frances sat down again. "Just before Janek came home, Sofia made me change. My skin was chafed. My knuckles were raw. Janek asked me if my appetite was better, and I told him yes, that everything was fine. 'A good thing your father brought you here last night,' he told me. 'The Germans took everyone this morning. But do not worry,' he said when I started crying 'We will take care of you until your parents return. I promised your father.'

"That night I prayed that a miracle would happen and that my father would wake me in the morning to take me home. But of course, it was Sofia who woke me. She was so pleasant that I thought her cruelty of the day before had been a nightmare. She braided my hair and called me sweetheart, and there was no sausage in my gruel. But as soon as Janek left, it was back to business. I kept quiet, but every once in a while she slapped me or shoved me or pinched me. 'Lazy Jewish bitch. You're doing half a job. The Germans would know what to do with a girl like you.' " Frances reached toward Jessie and adjusted the washcloth on her cheek.

Jessie placed her hand on her mother's. So this is where the rage was born, she thought. Pity for her mother flashed through her—it was a strange, unfamiliar sensation.

Frances slipped her hand out from under Jessie's. "When

Janek came home, he brought red satin ribbons for my braids. 'Something to cheer you up,' he said. I burst into tears and ran to my room. Toward morning I was dreaming about my mother, feeling her hands caressing my head, but when I opened my eyes to smile at her, I saw Sofia sitting next to me on my cot. 'Now you won't have to bother me anymore about your damn hair, will you, *moya kochana?*' In her hands were clouds of pale yellow. My hands flew to my hair and clutched air. I opened my mouth to scream. She clamped an iron hand over my mouth and kept it there until I stopped jerking."

"How could she be so cruel!" Jessie whispered. Hot tears smarted behind her lids. There were no tears in her mother's eyes—it was as if she were telling a different girl's story. Maybe that's the only way she can tell it, Jessie thought.

Frances continued as though Jessie hadn't spoken. "When I came upstairs for breakfast, Janek stared at me, and Sofia exclaimed, 'Your beautiful hair! What have you done with it?'

" 'I thank you for the beautiful ribbons, *Pan e Pani Ostrokowa,*' I said, 'but my hair was too difficult to manage.'

" 'See what a good child she is, Janek,' Sofia said. 'So mature.' I could see the hurt in his eyes. The next day Anna wore the ribbons."

As a child, Jessie suddenly remembered, she'd wanted braids, but Frances had said, "Braids are for peasants." "Is that why you didn't want me to have braids?" Jessie asked now, already knowing the answer. She had learned a great number of answers tonight.

Frances responded with a wistful smile. "And that's how it was for over four years. I learned later that there were many Christians who were wonderful to the Jewish children they took in. Sofia wasn't one of them. Some days were better, some worse, depending on her mood." She shrugged. "Janek was always kind. The boys were indifferent. Anna was happy to have my company and relieved that someone else was the object of her mother's anger. And sometime during those years I stopped saying my prayers and waiting for my father. I knew that he and my mother and the God I had believed in had abandoned me." Frances gently removed the photo from Jessie's hand and slipped it back behind her license.

Jessie started to protest. She needed to study the photo again, needed to find a connection between herself and the faces that belonged to the exotic names—"Yes, that's my nose, my chin, my eyes. My forehead. My smile." Maybe her mother would show her the photo another time. Why not, now that the secret was out?

"What happened after the war?" Jessie asked as if she were listening to a bedtime story. She wiped the tears from her eyes.

"When my father didn't come with the money he'd promised, Sofia convinced Janek that they couldn't afford to keep me." Frances's smile was bitter. "She took me to Krakow, a large city forty kilometers away, where a Jewish agency was trying to reunite children like me with their families or arrange for their adoption. She left me at the steps of the building with a sack containing my few possessions, things Janek had bought me."

Abandoned again. Jessie's heart ached again for the girl her mother had been and for the childhood she'd lost.

"I wasn't unhappy to leave Sofia," Frances said as if she'd heard Jessie's thoughts, "but I thought of myself as Christian and wasn't eager to be taken in by a Jewish agency. They couldn't locate any of my family. I was ten years old, but I was petite and thin and I said I was six. I sensed that families would prefer adopting younger children. My visa said I was born in 1940, not 1936. That's the date on my citizenship papers and all my legal documents, too. So I gained four years, Jessica. A small victory." A half-smile played around Frances's lips as she looked at her daughter.

Jessie smiled, too. For as long as she could remember, her mother had been self-conscious about aging. She'd certainly never joked about it. Until today. "So you came to the United States?"

Frances nodded. "I arrived in March, 1946, and lived in Brooklyn with Esther and Milton Holtz. They'd been childless for twelve years and were thrilled to have a six-year-old daughter."

Jessie frowned. "You didn't tell them your real age?"

She shook her head. "I thought they'd send me back. I was lucky—I didn't develop until I was sixteen. The Holtzes were wonderful. I could've opened a store with all the clothes and toys they bought me. I felt guilty, because they were trying so hard to make me happy, and I couldn't be what they wanted."

"What do you mean?"

"They were Orthodox, sincerely devout. I was angry with God. At first I followed their lifestyle—I was afraid they'd send me away if I didn't—but I observed less and less and did things I knew would upset them. I don't know why I was so mean." Frances shrugged. "They were relieved when I moved into my own apartment. I was seventeen—twenty-one, really. Then I met your father. He was at Columbia Med School. I was working in the registrar's office. We were married by a justice of the peace a year later."

There was so much to absorb, too much for one evening. Jessie's mind was reeling. "Did you convert?"

"I didn't think it was necessary." A defensive note had crept into Frances's voice. "Your father didn't mind. I told the Holtzes that we married. Your father told his parents. We came to Los Angeles for your father's residency at UCLA, and decided to stay. The Holtzes wrote constantly at first. I wrote back infrequently, then not at all. Eventually, their letters stopped. Years later, after Helen was born, I tried to get in touch with them and learned that they'd died. They were nice people." Frances stood and took her wallet to the dresser. With her back to Jessie, she said, "Well, now you know all my secrets. Are you happy?"

Are *you?* Jessie countered silently. "Do you think about your family often, Mom?"

"I try not to think about them *at all,*" she said pointedly, turning to Jessie. "It's a part of my life I'd rather forget."

Jessie searched through her memory for a clue to her

mother's Jewishness and found nothing. Frances had done a thorough job of erasing her past. "Does Dad know?"

"I'm not a liar, Jessica. He knows everything—my real age, too. I've never kept anything from your father."

That wasn't quite true, Jessie thought, remembering her own childhood. But now was not the time for that discussion. "You didn't tell me or Helen the truth."

"What truth?" Frances said with sudden anger. "That I lost my parents and all my relatives because I was born a Jew? That I was abused and lived with the threat of being handed over to the Germans for the same reason? That being a Jew brought me nothing but pain and misery? Why would I burden you or your sister with that truth?"

"I'm half-Jewish, Mom," Jessie said quietly. "I would've liked to know that."

"You are what you choose to be, Jessica. I'm perfectly happy with the life I've chosen. I have no regrets, no guilt."

Don't you? Jessie wondered. Or was there some regret, some guilt in Frances's own anger, the anger Jessie and Helen had been subjected to over the years? She stood and kissed her mother on her cheek and had an urge to hug her. "Thanks for telling me, Mom. I know this was painful for you."

"You didn't exactly give me a choice, did you?"

The phone was ringing when Jessie entered her house. She ran to answer it.

"I was worried about you, Jess," Frank said. "Where the hell have you been? Why haven't you returned my calls?"

"I'm sorry. I was late for Matthew's party and didn't have time to call you back. I just got home."

"Want me to come over? I miss you, Jess. I think we need to talk."

"I think we need to talk, too, Frank. But not tonight, okay?"

"It's this Jewish thing, isn't it? I don't want that to come between us, Jess."

"I don't either."

"Soon?"

"Soon."

She missed him, she really did. But she'd promised herself she'd be honest with him about her feelings the next time she saw him, and how could she be honest when she wasn't sure anymore who she was?

Chapter Thirty-two

Saturday morning the air was crisp and invigorating and the view from her roof spectacular, but the foul, pervasive smell of the mastic was making Jessie queasy. She worked quickly and within half an hour had finished patching the cracks in the tar paper, which she hoped was the cause of the living room leak. If not, she'd have to hire a professional roofer.

She decided to clean the windows. They were grimy from the rain, and she welcomed the manual labor—it freed her mind. She sprayed and wiped and thought about her mother and the terror and bewilderment and anger that had so violently shaped her from the time she was wrenched from her family—only six years old!—and about Barry Lewis, who had died a horrible death probably because he was defending a man who claimed that the Holocaust of which her mother had been a victim had never happened. Her thoughts flew to Frank. He was misinformed, not bigoted—he was a decent, caring man with wonderful qualities, it wasn't just the sex— so why was she reluctant to tell him she was half-Jewish? Gary would be surprised; she could picture his lopsided grin, and she wondered why she felt something that bordered on regret now that she and Gary had settled into friendship. Maybe it was just the letting go. When her mechanic called at one-thirty to tell her the Honda was ready, she had finished all the windows but resolved nothing.

She changed into a hunter green tunic and black leggings and walked to the car repair shop on Olympic Boulevard. The short Armenian owner pointed proudly to her new windshield and windows. She told him he'd done a beautiful job, but her enthusiasm waned when she saw the bill: $670! And he hadn't used Honda replacement parts. She paid with her charge card and told herself she'd be reimbursed by the LAPD—the damage had occurred while she was on the job. If Espes gave her trouble, she'd talk to someone higher up—she had no intention of claiming the money from her insurance company. Thinking about Espes reminded her of Frank's meddling, and she was angry again. Something else to resolve. With all the people occupying her mind, she could have mental group therapy.

She had a sudden urge to see her mother and drove to Helen's. She found the adults sitting on the bricked patio, a decent distance from Matthew and his friends, who were being entertained by a magician who seemed to be going through the motions.

"Well, *you* look casual," Frances said when she saw Jessie.

Translated, that meant "You're horribly underdressed." It wasn't the first time her mother had criticized her appearance, or even the hundredth, but Jessie realized with sharp disappointment that she'd expected Frances to be softer. Changed, somehow.

There was no change. Her mother was briskly affectionate, but it was as if she'd never revealed her painful past to Jessie. It was only when Frances and Arthur were ready to leave for La Jolla an hour later that Frances referred to last night's conversation.

"You didn't tell Helen, did you?" she said in an undertone to Jessie as they were walking to the Cadillac. "I can tell."

"No. She has a right to know. Don't ask me not to tell her."

"And if I *did* ask you?"

Jessie opened the passenger door for her mother.

"I don't think Helen will be quite as fascinated or pleased as you are to find out she's half-Jewish," Frances said.

"You may be underestimating her."

"I know my daughters." A faint smile flitted across her beautiful face. "I spent years trying to create a secure existence for myself and my family. You may not understand why I chose that existence, or approve of it, but don't throw it away because of a mistaken notion that there's something noble or romantic about being Jewish. Believe me, there isn't."

The phone was ringing when Jessie returned home. Probably Frank again. But the male voice on the phone was unfamiliar.

"Emery Kraft speaking, Detective Drake. You may have heard my name."

Of course she'd heard Kraft's name. He was the founder of HIT. She tensed, then frowned. "How did you get my phone number?"

"From Sheila Lewis. I wouldn't have bothered her at a time like this, but it was imperative that I reach you. I've received a death threat. So has Roy Benning."

"Where do you live?"

"Pasadena."

"That's way out of my jurisdiction. Did you call 911, Mr. Kraft? They'll send someone to your house."

"I know that Pasadena doesn't fall under your jurisdiction, but I understand that you were investigating the vandalizing of Mr. Lewis's home and are now investigating his murder. Clearly, you're more familiar with the case than anyone else."

"Mr. Kraft—"

"I also realize this is the weekend, but Mr. Benning is in grave danger, Detective Drake. I thought that after what happened to Mr. Lewis, you'd want to take quick personal action on this."

Was he implying that she'd been negligent? Or was she being sensitive? "What's your address, Mr. Kraft?"

* 　　 * 　　 *

Emery Kraft lived in an exclusive section of south Pasadena known for the wealth of its longtime residents and the historical value of their homes. Kraft's house—a two-story structure with a deep salmon stucco exterior, white trim, and a new Spanish tile roof—was set back several hundred feet from the gated entrance.

The filigreed white wrought-iron gate was locked. Jessie pressed the button near the intercom speaker on the side of the arch and announced herself. She heard a buzz and pressed against the gate. It opened, and she stepped inside onto the grounds.

A tall, large-framed man with thick, pewter-gray hair met Jessie halfway along a bricked walk leading to massive double doors. He wore dark brown wool slacks, a white shirt, a cream-colored cable-design cardigan, and a bow tie. At his side was a dog with a coarse black-and-tan coat. The squire at home.

"I'm Emery Kraft." He smiled at her somberly and shook her hand. "I appreciate immeasurably your coming here so quickly."

"No problem." He had a firm grip, and Jessie saw him studying her from behind his metal-framed glasses. "Your dog is beautiful."

"He is, isn't he?" Kraft leaned down and ran his hand along the animal's mane. "You can pet him if you like. He's quite friendly, and I can sense that he likes you."

Unlike Ben-Natan's beasts, this dog *did* look friendly. His tail was wagging briskly. She bent down and stroked his neck. He licked her hand, and she remembered why she'd wanted a dog when she was eight years old. Her mother, of course, had said no.

"He's pure German shepherd, by the way," Kraft said. "His name is Rolf. Shall we go inside?"

Not Adolf? Jessie followed Kraft up the walk.

The house was beautifully decorated, but she found it oppressive. The entry hall had black marble floor tiles and cranberry flocked wallpaper. Burgundy area rugs protected the polished wood floors. Around a rectangular ebony coffee table in the living room were two sofas and two tall armchairs upholstered in a burgundy brocade that was repeated in the heavily swagged drapes that darkened the three French windows. The walls were a gray moiré. So were the walls in the dining room, where the same burgundy brocade draped the windows and covered the seats of the twelve armchairs—large and thronelike with clawed feet—arranged around a mahogany table. The heavily carved china cabinet, tall and wide and imposing, stood sentry. The house had an essentially masculine aura. Jessie wondered if there was a Mrs. Kraft.

Kraft led Jessie to his study, Rolf at his heels. Here, too, the furnishings were dark—even the spines of all the books were somber—and the only bright spots in the room were the framed certificates and diplomas on the paneled walls.

Kraft and Jessie sat on a black leather couch. The dog lay down near his master. On a mahogany butler's tray in front of the couch were a silver urn, cups, saucers, cream, sugar, linen tea napkins, and a china plate with an assortment of pastries.

"Coffee, Detective? I use a mixture of fresh-ground French and Colombian roasted beans."

"No, thanks." Jessie counted two cups and two saucers. "Mr. Benning isn't coming?"

"He phoned after you and I spoke, and I told him you would be here, but he's terrified to go out in public."

"Is he at home?"

Kraft shook his head. "I have no idea where he is, nor do I have a phone number where I can reach him. Neither does his wife. In a sense, I think it would have been better if he weren't out on bail. In jail, at least, he'd be protected."

"You put up the bail, isn't that right?" Jessie had read in the papers that Benning had been charged with manslaughter and that Kraft posted the fifty-thousand-dollar bail.

Kraft nodded. He poured himself a cup of coffee, inhaled the aroma, then took a sip. "Roy Benning didn't kill anyone. I'm sorry Mrs. Hochburg died, but you and I both know that

Roy Benning was charged not because of what he did, but because of his beliefs. And that, Detective, is fundamentally unfair. Don't you agree?"

"Tell me about the death threats you and Mr. Benning received." She took her notepad and pen from her purse.

Kraft sighed and returned his cup and saucer to the butler's tray. "I sense that you disapprove of me, Detective Drake."

"Mr. Kraft—"

"Please, indulge me for a minute. Tell me, what do you know about me and History Is Truth?"

"I know that you head an organization that denies the existence of the Holocaust and the fact that six million Jews were murdered." She tried to keep her voice stripped of emotion.

"You are absolutely correct. I am a credentialed historian, Detective Drake. You can examine my diplomas, if you like. They are bona fide." He gestured to the frames on the walls. "I spent years researching the period referred to as the Holocaust. My goal was not to disprove it—I *believed* what I had heard about the six million Jews who had perished. But when questions arose as to the veracity of those facts, I felt obligated to establish the truth for myself. I spoke to witnesses. I read hundreds of documents. I viewed newsreels. And the truth I arrived at is that the Holocaust did not happen as was reported, and that the history our children are learning is a lie."

"World War Two didn't happen, either?"

Kraft smiled. "I'm prepared for sarcasm. Of *course* there was a world war. But Germany didn't instigate it." He lifted a cookie from the plate and took a bite. "My housekeeper made these, and they're absolutely wonderful. Won't you have one?"

Jessie shook her head. "I seem to recall that Germany invaded Poland, Mr. Kraft."

"Germany didn't want war, Detective. She was *forced* into war by the British and the Americans. In fact, she was the greatest victim of the war—her population decimated, her economy crushed." The dog was on all fours, panting lightly, eyeing the pastry in Kraft's hand. Kraft fed him the cookie and took another.

Jessie felt like Alice in Wonderland, having tea with the Queen of Hearts. "I was a political science major, Mr. Kraft. I minored in history. Germany *was* the aggressor, and she suffered defeat and all that goes with it. And she methodically executed six million Jews and several million other 'undesirables,' including Gypsies, homosexuals, and the mentally ill."

"It is true that Jews died. So did Poles, Germans, Czechs, Austrians, Hungarians, Russians. War claims many victims, Detective. But six million Jews deliberately exterminated?" Kraft shook his head and patted the cookie crumbs from his mouth with a napkin. "It is one of the most fascinating examples of political propaganda that I have ever studied, a Zionist conspiratorial fabrication whose aim is twofold: to bleed the German government of billions of dollars in reparation payments and to arouse the Western world's guilt and translate that guilt into astronomical financial aid to the state of Israel. Ultimately, the Zionists want to control the economy of the free world."

Essentially, it was the typical "the-Jews-are-out-to-control-the-world" line of anti-Semitism that Jessie had read about. Coming from Kraft, it sounded more respectable. She remembered what Manny had said—"HIT's message is anti-Semitism dressed up in a suit."

"Are you saying that the Germans didn't forcibly remove Jews from their homes and transport them to concentration camps?" she asked.

She wondered suddenly what the hell she was doing—she'd come here to question Kraft about the threats against him and Benning, not debate history with someone who was clearly off the wall. She admitted to herself that she was fascinated to hear his perversion of history. Particularly now that she knew that it was her history that he was perverting.

"Jewish people were *relocated* to protect them from the hostile native populations of Poland and Hungary. Really, this was no different from the Japanese internment camps." He fed a cookie with a jam-filled center to Rolf. The dog growled contentedly.

"The internment camps are a horrible indictment of American policy, Mr. Kraft, but six million Japanese didn't die there."

Kraft's fingers disappeared in the dog's coat. "Six million Jews didn't die, either. Approximately one and a half million died in the relocation camps of starvation—a result, by the way, of the Allies' preventing the Germans from delivering supplies to the camps—and from disease, primarily typhus. Others were killed by the Russians. The gas chambers are a myth. Zyklon B as a homicidal agent is a myth. Hitler's 'final solution'—a myth. The war memoirs of Churchill and Eisenhower are quite detailed, yet they make no mention of gas chambers or a genocide program."

"That's because British and American troops captured Germany, not eastern Poland, where the death camps were," she said, gratified that she remembered this part of her twentieth-century European history course. "But there *are* detailed reports about the atrocities Allied soldiers witnessed in other camps. Eisenhower wrote one, too."

"Nevertheless," Kraft said, as if he'd successfully refuted Jessie's objection. "The notorious crematoria of Auschwitz-Birkenau and the other alleged death camps were used to cremate victims of starvation and disease. Zyklon B was used to rid the inmates' clothing of lice."

Jessie had read a cursory examination of the Holocaust in her college studies. She'd watched *Holocaust* and *Shoah* and *Schindler's List* and knew that Kraft's "truth" was fallacious, but she wished she had the specifics to refute his statements.

She said, "The Germans left documents that referred to the extermination of the Jews, Mr. Kraft. They left photographic evidence. They testified at the Nuremberg trials and admitted to having committed atrocities, of wholesale murder."

"Under *coercion,* Detective. They may have hoped they would receive clemency if they said what the Allies wanted them to say. In any case, denial was pointless. The world believed them to be guilty. The media had already convicted them—a media which, by the way, is controlled by Jews. As to the documents, they were unquestionably forged or doctored, as were the photographs."

He stood abruptly. The dog moved aside. Kraft walked across the room to a bookcase, removed several volumes from the shelves, and placed them next to Jessie on the couch. "Read these if you want more information. They corroborate everything I've said."

She moved imperceptibly back from the books. "Hundreds of documents were forged? Including many signed by the war criminals who were on trial?" When Kraft didn't answer, she said, "Survivors described the gas chambers. They saw family members brutally killed in front of their eyes."

Another shake of the head. "Hardly impartial witnesses. Survivors exaggerate. I don't blame them, you know. War is a devastating experience. But as a historian, I cannot accept their testimony as valid. You are a homicide detective. Without finding corroboration, do you believe as fact what a witness tells you? Especially if that witness is biased or emotionally involved?" The dog had returned to its former spot. Kraft resumed stroking him.

"We're not talking about one witness. We're talking about thousands. And if thousands of people were to tell me the same thing, I'd believe them. What happened to the six million Jews of Europe if they weren't killed?"

"As I explained, a million and a half died of starvation or disease in the camps. The others?" He leaned forward. "Some believe that many of the missing Jews are in Russia. Others, myself included, believe that they are right here, in the United States. They were brought into this country and easily disappeared among the crowded populations of large cities like New York."

"Is that where my mother's family is?"

Kraft frowned. He blinked. "Pardon me?"

"My mother's entire family—parents, grandparents, sisters, brothers, nieces, nephews—were forcibly removed from their home in Tchebin, Poland, because they were Jews. She was left with a Catholic Polish family. Could you tell me where in New York her relatives are? I'm sure she'd love to be reunited with them." She took pleasure in the startled look in Kraft's eyes.

Kraft blinked again, and when he spoke he had recovered his composure. "I can understand your hostility, Detective. While I stand firmly behind what I've told you, my intention was not to upset you. I had no idea that your mother is a European Jew who survived the war."

Until last night, neither did I. Jessie thought it strange that the very first time she was identifying herself as a Jew was in front of this man. Telling Frank should be easy. "You mean I don't look Jewish? No horns?"

"You're trying to bait me, to tar me with the brush of anti-Semitism so that you can easily dismiss what I say as racist invective. I am not an anti-Semite. I abhor racism. I do not have a white sheet in my closet, nor do I burn crosses on people's lawns." He drew closer to her, his thigh pushing the books along the leather. "I find you to be an intelligent woman, as are many of your people. And exceptionally attractive." He smiled at her.

She was repulsed by his nearness and his clumsy attempt at flirtation. The corner of one of the books dug into her thigh. She tried to move back but found that she'd reached the arm of the sofa. "Your organization supported the parade celebrating Hitler's birthday."

"To be honest, I don't share your opinion of Adolf Hitler. To you, he was a maniac determined to rule the world and exterminate all the Jews. To me, he was a much maligned and misunderstood man who wanted the best for his country."

The dog yelped mildly, as if on cue. Kraft silenced him with another pastry and said, "No more, Rolf," with gruff affection.

"A Nobel Peace Prize candidate, Mr. Kraft?"

Kraft smiled thinly. "As for Mr. Benning and the parade, he is a free agent. I myself prefer a dignified debate in the halls of academe to a street confrontation, but I feel adamantly that Mr. Benning and the paraders were exercising their constitutional rights. Mr. Lewis shared my belief, which is why he defended the parade and was willing to defend Mr. Benning."

"And now Lewis is dead, and Benning is in hiding. What kinds of death threats did you and Benning receive?"

"I've been receiving harassing calls ever since Mrs. Hochburg died. So has Mr. Benning, but neither he nor I took them seriously until Friday, when Mr. Lewis was killed. Today a man called and said, 'Prepare for the Angel of Death.' Mr. Benning told me he received a letter with a similar message."

"Did you recognize the caller?"

"Regrettably, no."

"Did Mr. Benning identify any of the people who threatened him?"

"Again, no."

"Do you have any idea who killed Lewis?"

"I should think that's obvious, Detective. Joel Ben-Natan, or one of his minions. He's been vocal in his hatred of Lewis and Benning. I'm surprised the police haven't arrested him yet."

Was that the reason Kraft had asked her here? To point her in the direction of the Shield? "*I'm* surprised that someone of your background and sensitivity would suggest that a person should be arrested for voicing his opinions."

Impatience flickered across Kraft's face. "Very clever, Detective, but Ben-Natan has made threats."

"To you?" Jessie made a show of opening her notepad.

"Not directly. He's made angry statements directed against HIT, and I'm convinced that it was one of his men who called me today. Ben-Natan *has* called Mr. Benning's home several times and suggested in so many words that he look over his shoulder."

"But he hasn't made a specific threat?"

"No. He's too smart to do that."

"And you don't know where to reach Mr. Benning?"

"As I told you before, Detective, no."

"Mr. Kraft, I'm sure you'd be the first person to agree that as a detective, I can't accept as fact statements that I hear secondhand without first corroborating them." She smiled.

"You're playing games with me." Kraft returned her smile, but his voice was icy. "You may dislike me and my views, but you are sworn to serve and protect the citizens of this city, and that includes me and Mr. Benning." He picked up his cup and sipped. "That bothers you, doesn't it?"

"I'm a professional, Mr. Kraft. Like you, I'm committed to pursuing the truth. I'm certainly going to convey your concern to my superior. Where can I reach Mrs. Benning?"

Kraft gave Jessie the phone number and an address in Culver City. "But as I told you, Detective, Mrs. Benning has no idea where to reach her husband, either."

Jessie stood. "I'd still like to talk to her. When you speak to Mr. Benning again, ask him to call me. And if you get any more threatening communications—calls or letters—please notify me."

Kraft stood, too. Rolf moved to his side and nuzzled his leg. "What about police protection? I have an alarm, but aside from a housekeeper who comes in Monday through Friday, I'm alone here."

"Call your local station. To be honest, though, I don't think they have the manpower to spare." She walked across the Oriental rug, opened the door, then turned. "Of course, you *could* relocate to protect yourself from the hostile native population. Then again, if you did that, you might disappear forever. It's happened before, you know, to millions of people."

Kraft sighed loudly. "I'm afraid that my first impression of you was erroneous, Detective Drake, and it has nothing to do with the fact that you're Jewish."

"Well, then, I guess I'm a better judge of character. My first impression of you hasn't changed at all, Mr. Kraft, and it has nothing to do with the fact that you're *not* Jewish."

Chapter Thirty-three

Ezra Nathanson opened his front door. "You're up early, Detective Drake. How can I help you?"

Jessie tried not to stare. Nathanson had pushed up the left sleeve of his black-and-gray-striped shirt and wrapped leather bands around his forearm. Strapped below his elbow was a small, leather-covered square box. An identical box was strapped above his forehead.

"May I come in?"

"Do I have a choice?"

He sounded nervous, but who wouldn't be, finding a homicide detective on his doorstep on a Sunday morning? "I don't have a warrant. I can wait if you're in the middle of something."

"My question was rhetorical. And no, you're not interrupting. I've just finished my prayers. Usually, I go to morning services at *shul*—synagogue—but I wasn't feeling well this morning. Lucky for you, huh?" He smiled and stepped aside to let her enter, then shut the door behind her. "Aren't you off on weekends?"

They were standing in a small entry hall. "Usually." She certainly wasn't getting paid overtime—the department budget was tight, and Espes would never authorize it after the

241

fact. She wasn't quite sure why she'd decided to question Nathanson today.

"Can we sit down?" she asked.

"Of course. This way." He started walking to the right.

"Is today a Jewish holiday?" she asked, following him into a living room filled with bookcases. "I didn't mean to intrude."

"No holiday." He looked puzzled, then said, "Oh, you mean my phylacteries. Jewish males over the age of thirteen—bar mitzvah—put those on every morning, except for Saturdays and holidays, before saying their prayers."

"Why?"

"Is this part of your official investigation?"

She flushed. "I'm sorry. I was curious. I didn't mean to be rude."

"*I'm* sorry. *I* was rude." His smile was genuine. "We follow God's commandment—'Bind them'—meaning His teachings—'as a sign upon your arm and let them be frontlets'—phylacteries—'between your eyes.' We keep His teachings near our heart"—he pointed to the box on his upper arm—"and near our mind." He touched the box above his forehead. "It's a daily reminder that God took us out of Egypt and redeemed us from slavery."

"What's in the boxes?"

"Parchment with four segments of the Torah, our Bible. Two of them are from the *Shema,* the prayer we say twice a day. It attests to our belief in God's sovereignty. It commands us to love Him unconditionally—with our hearts, our souls, and our might—and to teach His precepts to our children."

Not a bad way to start the day. Jessie thought about the grandfather and uncles she'd never known. They had wrapped the leather straps of their phylacteries around their arms and foreheads, too; they, too, had loved God with their hearts, souls, and might. "Thank you," she said. "That's very interesting."

He gestured to the blue tweed sofa. "I'll be right back."

Jessie sat down and waited. When he returned two minutes

later, the boxes and straps had been removed and his shirt-sleeve buttoned, but there was a reddened square indentation above his forehead.

There was no smooth segue from religious ritual to a homicide investigation. "I assume that you know that Mr. Lewis was killed?"

Nathanson nodded. "I feel terrible for his family."

"When was the last time you spoke to him?"

"Wednesday night, I think." Nathanson leaned back against the sofa cushion. "I called and told him I wanted to meet with him, to try to dissuade him from defending Benning."

"What did Mr. Lewis say?"

"He hung up on me."

So far, Nathanson was telling the truth. Jessie opened her notebook. "During the call, you said, 'I don't think you've considered what an explosive situation you're creating by defending Benning.'" She looked up at Nathanson.

"You were testing me, huh? You taped Lewis's calls, is that it?" He shrugged. "I admitted I phoned Lewis. So what?"

"I'm curious about your choice of words. An 'explosive situation'?"

Nathanson frowned. "That was just a figure of speech."

"Where were you between the hours of nine o'clock Thursday evening and eight-thirty Friday morning?"

He stared at her. His face had reddened, camouflaging the indentation from the square box. "I can't believe you really suspect me of killing Lewis!"

Anger or fear? "Just answer the question, please."

"My sister and her husband had theater tickets. Their sitter canceled last minute, so I went to their house to watch the kids."

"What was the time frame?"

"I got there around seven, seven-fifteen. I left around one in the morning. My sister and brother-in-law and I were talking. There's nothing criminal in that, is there?"

"I'll need to contact your sister. Just routine." She smiled.

Nathanson didn't. "Her name is Dafna Abrams. She'll be at

her store today." In grudging syllables, he gave Jessie his sister's home and business phone numbers and addresses.

"Did anyone see you come home?"

"My neighbor across the street was on his porch. After I parked in my garage, I asked him if everything was all right. He was nervous because his teenage daughter was out with friends and should've been home by twelve-thirty. He'll remember the time." Nathanson gave Jessie the man's name and address.

Was Nathanson a concerned neighbor, or had he tried to establish when he'd come home? Jessie would check with the neighbor, but it wouldn't prove much. Nathanson could have left again and driven to Lewis's house.

"The last time we spoke, Mr. Nathanson, you said that on the night you went out with Miss Pasternak, you changed your flat tire yourself. I assume you had it repaired. Do you have a receipt?"

"Don't you believe me?"

"I'm not paid to believe you or not believe you. I'm paid to verify information and ascertain the truth." God, she sounded like Emery Kraft. "Can I see your receipt?"

"I don't know if I kept it." He stood up and reached into his pants pocket, took out his wallet, and rifled through its contents. "Here it is." He handed her a yellow paper.

She unfolded it. The receipt was from a gas station on Robertson and Olympic. It was dated April 5, the day after the court hearing. The flat had occurred on April 2.

She handed back the receipt. "You drove around on your spare for three days?"

"I didn't have a chance to take care of it before," he said, sitting down. "I wasn't worried. I don't drive that much."

"What kind of car do you drive?"

"A Nissan Maxima. Black."

"License plate number?"

He gave her the number. "Why do you need that?"

"Just for our records." She wrote down the information. "Mr. Nathanson, have you been calling Roy Benning?"

Nathanson stiffened. "Absolutely not."

"What about Emery Kraft?"

"The HIT leader? No. If they said I did, they're lying."

"Somebody called Mr. Kraft and told him to prepare for the Angel of Death. Somebody has threatened Mr. Benning, too."

"I can't say I'm surprised. And I'm not sympathetic."

"Are Kraft and Benning examples of Amalek, do you think? Evil personified—isn't that how you defined it metaphorically?"

Nathanson didn't smile. "I know Benning only from what I've seen on TV and read in the papers. As far as Kraft is concerned, he may not be Amalek, but he *is* evil. And so is his attempt to rewrite the past. He's an anti-Semite in historian's clothing. I heard that his father is Jewish, by the way. Which is interesting, because people say Hitler was part Jewish. So was Frank Collins, the guy who wanted to demonstrate in Skokie."

"I met with Kraft yesterday. He talked at length about historical revisionism."

"He's not a 'revisionist'! He's a denier. There's a major difference." Nathanson leaned forward and, in a calmer voice, said, "Erase the stigma of the gas chambers and the atrocities, and you've got your basic war. Hitler's not a monster, the Nazis don't look so bad, and it's okay to hate the Jews again." He ran his hands through his hair. "What did he tell you? That there was no German policy to liquidate the Jews? No gas chambers? That all the documentation is false and that the 'six million dead' is a Zionist conspiracy to milk the German cow for reparations?"

"Basically."

"Did he bring up Fred Leuchter?"

"No."

"They love to mention Leuchter. He's a self-proclaimed execution-chamber expert and engineer. They sent him to visit Auschwitz as an expert witness for the defense in a Canadian trial of a denier to prove there were no gas chambers. The judge threw out Leuchter's report because Leuchter

had no relevant engineering credentials." Nathanson paused.
"They don't mention Pressac, of course. He's a pharmacist—
a former Holocaust denier, in fact. Using documents the Sovi-
ets took from Auschwitz, he described the floor plans and
ventilation systems of the gas chambers. He even reproduced
order forms for the crematoria."

Jessie nodded.

"The problem is, when a lie is repeated enough, it sounds
like the truth. He sounded credible, didn't he? Kraft, I mean."

"Yes. But I studied enough history to see some of the flaws
in his arguments." She hesitated. "I wish I'd been better informed so that I could have refuted all of them." This was
why she'd come, she admitted to herself. Not to question
Nathanson the suspect, but to gain insight from Nathanson the
teacher of Jewish history.

Nathanson glanced at her with interest. "Too many people
don't know enough history. Twenty-five percent of the people in this country aren't sure the Holocaust happened. Fifty
percent of high school students don't know what the word
Holocaust means."

"Fifty percent of high school students don't know much ge-
ography, so I'm not surprised." She smiled lightly.

"Yes, but not knowing where Katmandu is won't have serious consequences. When a guy like Kraft comes along and
tells kids the Holocaust never happened, they believe him.
When college newspapers print ads by guys like Kraft and
label the message in the ads as 'another opinion,' they're le-
gitimizing garbage!"

She flinched at his anger.

"Sorry. If you were Jewish and faced with the specter of
anti-Semitism, you might understand how frightening this is."

"I *do* understand. And I *am* Jewish—at least, my mother is.
She was hidden during the war with a Polish family. Her own
family was killed." Was this, too, why she'd come here this
morning? To share her new knowledge with Nathanson, to
explore her identity? Why else was she telling a stranger her
personal history?

His eyebrows rose. "You never mentioned you were Jewish."

She couldn't bring herself to tell him she'd learned about her Jewish heritage less than two days ago. And why *was* she so quick to identify herself as Jewish, to abandon her identity of almost thirty-five years? Was she subconsciously attempting to get back at her mother for years of abuse? Frances would probably think so. Or was she searching for an anchor, a system of belief that would fill the void she'd felt during her traumatic childhood and adolescence? She'd have to ask Manny.

"I haven't been raised Jewish, so I don't really consider myself Jewish," she told Nathanson.

"Actually—" Nathanson was interrupted by the ringing of the phone. "Excuse me. I won't be long." He left the room.

Jessie walked over to one wall of bookcases. It was filled with tall, leather-bound volumes whose spines had gilt writing in Hebrew. In the bookcase on another wall were English language books arranged in no apparent order—a *Norton's Anthology*, *Huckleberry Finn*, Balzac's *Human Comedy*, *Catch-22*, *An American Tragedy*, *Native Son*. *The Collected Works of Shakespeare*. *Ulysses*. Nathanson was eclectic in his literary taste.

There was an entire shelf of books about the Holocaust. She lifted out *While Six Million Died* and *Denying the Holocaust* and saw farther back another book propped against the wall of the bookcase. The jacket had been removed. She pulled it forward and opened it to the title page and froze. *The Anarchist's Cookbook*. A do-it-yourself guide to manufacturing explosives. Shit, she thought. She was without a gun, alone in a house with a teacher of Judaism who may have blown up Barry Lewis.

"Anything special catch your eye?" Nathanson asked, coming back into the room.

Her heart skipped a beat. She pushed the book back where she'd found it and turned around, holding *While Six Million Died* and *Denying the Holocaust*. "These look interesting."

"They are." Nathanson tapped the spine of *Denying the Holocaust*. "Deborah Lipstadt's book will answer any questions you may have on the subject. You can borrow one or both if you like."

"Another time." She put the books on the light oak coffee table in front of the sofa and checked her watch. "I have to go. Thanks for being so cooperative."

"All done? Am I still a suspect?" He smiled.

"Everyone's a suspect until we find the guilty party." She forced a matching smile to her lips and headed for the door. Next time, she'd come with a search warrant. And Phil. And a gun.

"By the way," Nathanson said, "if your mother's Jewish, you're completely Jewish, not half-Jewish."

Jessie turned. "But my father isn't Jewish. And I was raised Episcopalian."

"No difference. Jewishness is passed on through matrilineal descent. Even if your mother converted, you'd still be considered Jewish. You don't look happy," he noted.

"I'm just surprised. I know next to nothing about Judaism."

"You could learn, if you're interested. You could take classes in Hebrew and Jewish history or whatever appeals to you. I'd be happy to help in any way. What's your first name?"

Was he a teacher or a murderer? "Jessie. Jessica."

" 'Yiska' is Hebrew for Jessica. It means 'princess.' You don't like the name?" he asked, seeing her startled expression.

"It's a beautiful name," she said quietly. "Thanks again." She passed through the entry and out the front door.

"Yiska," she said aloud, practicing the sound as she walked down the street.

Yiska was Frances's mother's name.

Chapter Thirty-four

Ezra Nathanson was putting the two books back when he spotted the other volume, pushed toward the back. He'd forgotten that it was there.

Had she seen it?

If she hadn't, he could dispose of it. But he knew she had; he realized now that there had been something changed about her after the phone call. And if she came back to search for it and it was missing, she would know he'd destroyed it.

He walked over to the front window and lifted the curtain. There she was, knocking on his neighbor's door. He watched her disappear into the man's house, wondered what she was thinking, where she was going next.

In the bedroom, he looked at the framed photo on his dresser for a long time, his face twisted with anger and pain. He sat on his bed, hesitated, then picked up the phone extension. He punched ten numbers. After three rings, someone answered.

"Joel?" he said. "Ezra."

Chapter Thirty-five

"One, please," Jessie said to the man behind the desk.

A minute later, holding her ticket, she passed through the security booth and waited while the uniformed guard, a scanner in his hand, examined the contents of her purse. She was glad now that she'd left her 9mm automatic at home. Sitting in Nathanson's apartment, she'd decided that she had to come here, to learn more about the heritage and past that had so recently become hers.

The lobby was filled with people—men, women, children. Jessie waited her turn, then handed the yellow copy of her ticket to the man standing at the turnstile and joined the others gathered around the guide, a brown-haired woman in her fifties wearing a black skirt and a rose-colored sweater. Jessie wondered if she was a survivor.

"Welcome to *Beit Hashoah,* the Museum of Tolerance," the woman said in a soft southern drawl. "Our tour consists of two parts. First, you'll visit the Tolerance Workshop, which examines all kinds of prejudices. Next, you'll learn about the Holocaust in an independent tour guided by sound and light. Afterward you can visit the archive collection and a multimedia computer research section on the second floor. Please follow me."

She led the way down a circular, carpeted ramp. In the center of the circle, attached to a gold-toned scaffolding, were enormous cubes whose sides bore black-and-white photos of people.

"The Tower of Witnesses," the tour guide explained. "These are family photographs Jews brought with them to the concentration camps. Over twenty-five hundred photos were discovered at Auschwitz when the camp was liberated."

Their faces and clothing made them resemble the people in her mother's photo, Jessie thought, studying the cubes. She wondered where the other photos of Frances and her family had gone.

They entered the Tolerance Workshop through a door labeled "Prejudiced" (the one labeled "Unprejudiced" was intentionally locked—an effective point). Multiple interactive video screens filled the room. Those on the walls dramatized the insidious, subtle reach of bias against Blacks, Asians, Jews, women, the handicapped, the overweight. Screens suspended from the ceiling showed film clips from the riots that had shaken Los Angeles in the aftermath of the Rodney King beating trial. Jessie watched the screens for a few moments, reliving the riots she'd witnessed firsthand, but she was impatient to pass through the wide doors that led to the Holocaust section of the museum.

Finally, the doors opened automatically. Inside a wide, darkened hall, Jessie and the others stood in front of an illuminated recessed minitheater and listened to a brief introductory lecture. The lights went out. They were instructed to turn around and take their "passports"—small oblong plastic cards bearing the photos of Jewish children who had actually been trapped by the Holocaust.

Jessie examined her "passport"—she was Pola Glicksman. Six years old. Born in Sosnowiecz, Poland. Blond hair. An innocent half-smile. Jessie held the passport and moved on.

One by one, different displays were lit and darkened. Oblivious of the people around her, Jessie walked and learned again of prewar Berlin, of Hitler's rise to power, of the escalation of violent, anti-Semitic acts. Of Kristallnacht. And although she had read about the war and viewed its dramatization in film, she was seeing it with different eyes now that she knew it was her mother's history. Her own history, too.

She "overheard" Jewish Berliners at a cafe dismiss the severity of the Nazi threat and learned of their tragic fates.

She learned that the native citizens of Poland, Lithuania, Hungary, and Russia collaborated eagerly in rounding up their Jewish neighbors and massacring them.

She scanned an enlargement of a German document that listed how many Jews remained in each of the occupied countries and how many countries were already *Judenrein*—free of Jews.

She listened to a re-creation of the infamous Wannsee conference and "heard" the Third Reich's leaders debate the most expedient way to kill the Jews—shooting would utilize too many bullets; filling trucks with carbon monoxide was not always effective. Zyklon B offered excellent possibilities.

Midway along her walk through history, she inserted her passport into a computer and learned that Pola Glicksman and her family had been taken to Auschwitz. Frances had escaped that destiny, but what about her parents and the rest of her family? Frances hadn't said; maybe she didn't know. Jessie would ask her mother another time.

She stood in front of a replica of the ruins of the Warsaw ghetto and inhaled the dust of the rubble.

She saw a map of Europe that showed, in brilliant, illuminated red, the arteries of the railway systems that efficiently transported Jews to the death camps. She wondered which route her family had taken.

She walked past life-size barbed-wire gates, replicas of those that had welcomed Jews arriving to Auschwitz, and faced two doorways:

"Children and others."

"Able-bodied."

She was Pola Glicksman, not Jessie Drake. Clutching her passport, she entered the first passageway, and when it ended she saw that the "able-bodied" visitors had joined up with her in a bunkerlike, stark gray, oblong room. Dirt covered the cold stone floor. She sat on a stone slab bench and watched one of the eight wall-mounted video monitors. She saw bins filled with survivors' jewelry and prosthetics and all their worldly possessions. One bin contained wigs and shorn hair and a long, blond plait that reminded her of a little girl who had once worn ribbons in her braids. She heard survivors tell their stories and had no difficulty imagining that she was in a gas chamber, not a room in a museum.

Except, of course, that she was able to leave.

When she exited the Hall of Testimony, she inserted her passport into a computer and learned that Pola Glicksman, along with one and a half million Jewish children, had died. Jessie's throat was thick with unshed tears for Pola and for the other children, for her mother's twin cousins, for Chaim and Sonia's sweet looking little boy, for Shaindl's infant, as yet unborn when Frances had left her home.

On the second floor of the museum, Jessie saw Anne Frank's diary and a canister of Zyklon B. A computer screen in the multimedia learning center offered her information on topics that included the rise of the Nazis, European Jewry, and the countries and cities affected by the Holocaust. She would come back another time to read about all those topics; today, she needed to know more about her origins. She tried accessing her mother's hometown but found no listing for "Tchebin" or "Tzebin" or "Chzcbin" or any alternate spelling she could think of.

A young woman came by. "Can I help you with anything?"

Jessie explained what she was looking for.

"Unfortunately, towns with populations under five thousand aren't in the computer files," the woman said. "The Simon Wiesenthal Museum next door may have more information in its archives. Are you searching for a specific family?"

She was suddenly overwhelmed with indecision and exhaustion, and needed more than anything to go home. "I'm not sure." Jessie thanked her and left.

Chapter Thirty-six

"Check the view," Phil said to Jessie, gesturing to his left as his Cutlass strained up the incline on Forest Lawn Drive past the green expanse of Forest Lawn Memorial Park, one of the most renowned mortuaries in L.A. County. "That's the back lot of Universal Studios down below."

"Uh-huh." And a wrong turn several minutes earlier off Barham Boulevard would have brought them to Universal's theme park, where life was exaggerated and death was staged, instead of to a mortuary in the Hollywood Hills where death was permanent.

Phil turned right and drove past the gates onto the grounds of Mount Sinai Mortuary. An attendant motioned him to a spot at the end of a long lane of parked cars. There were five other lanes, all equally long.

"Quite a crowd," Phil said, nodding at the parked vehicles as he and Jessie walked toward the chapel. "Kind of surprising for a guy as unpopular as Lewis."

"They'd be here for the parents, don't you think?" The morning air was brisk, and she was glad she'd worn her jacket. "And I imagine his law associates and some of his clients would come. Plus there are people who probably want to see the show."

"You're right. Maybe the killer's here, too."

"Wearing a sign?" That's why she and Phil were here this Monday morning—it was standard police procedure to attend the funeral of a homicide victim in the hopes of witnessing telltale behavior on the part of a suspect or suspects. Entering the chapel, Jessie wondered which suspects would be here today.

She sat in the last row next to four men in gray, pin-striped suits who she decided were from Lewis's law firm. The room was decorated in soft, comforting neutral shades except for the splash of color in the vinelike pattern on the leaded-glass windows that formed a continuous band at the top of the left, right, and front walls. The rabbi—a tall, thin clean-shaven man in his thirties with an earnest expression and resonant voice—was talking about Barry Lewis's love for his parents, wife, children, and sister, Janice, who had flown in from Chicago with her husband, Marvin.

". . . especially tragic for the parents, Morris and Rose Lewis, who lost their entire families in the Holocaust, rebuilt their lives, and have now suffered the tragic loss of their beloved son. Barry was known for his philanthropy to the state of Israel and other Jewish causes. He and his wife, Sheila . . ."

Not an easy eulogy to deliver, Jessie thought, given the circumstances preceding and surrounding Lewis's death, but she supposed rabbis were adept at handling sensitive situations. Five minutes later it was over. The rabbi announced the pallbearers and invited all the others to pass in front of the casket at the front of the chapel before they returned to their cars and drove to the burial grounds. Jessie and Phil exited the way they'd entered.

"See anyone?" Phil asked as they were returning to his car.

"I think I spotted Rita Warrens sitting toward the front." When Phil looked blank, she said, "The ACLU executive director?"

"Right." Phil nodded. "Did you check out the suits next to me? Probably from Lewis's law firm."

"That's my guess, too."

They were lucky—no one had parked behind them. Phil backed out of his spot and drove up a wide, serpentine road to the burial grounds. Not wanting to be conspicuous, he and Jessie waited in the car until both sides of the road were lined with parked cars.

A cavity had been prepared in the green lawn. Walking toward it were ten pallbearers, holding the casket. Jessie watched from a distance as the rabbi approached, escorting Sheila, her daughters, a woman and a man who Jessie decided must be the sister and brother-in-law, and Lewis's parents.

The casket was being lowered into the ground. Jessie scanned the crowd to her left and saw Rabbi Korbin. Mark Pell was there, too—that was a surprise, given the man's outspoken antipathy toward Lewis. She glanced to her right, prodded Phil, and pointed. "Ezra Nathanson."

"The guy with the how-to book? Is the twin brother here?"

"I don't see him."

Several men had approached the grave and, one by one, were lifting shovels full of dirt and dropping them onto the casket. The thumps echoed in her ears. She had the sudden sensation that someone was staring at her back. She turned around. Kraft was several feet behind her. He smiled at her and nodded.

"Emery Kraft is here!" she whispered, turning to Phil. "Can you believe the son of a bitch's nerve?" This morning she'd told Phil about her meeting with the HIT founder, but not about the personal exchange between them.

Phil frowned. "Why would he come?"

"To show how much he loves Jews, I guess." She grimaced. "And to have a little fun. Bastard."

Ten minutes later the grave was covered. A cantor sang a final prayer in Hebrew, and some of the crowd formed two lines through which the mourners passed. Jessie and Phil remained in the background with the others, including the four men they'd pegged as Barry Lewis's colleagues. Kraft had disappeared.

The double line broke up. Jessie spotted Rita Warrens

heading toward the parked cars. "Phil, I'm going to talk to Rita."

Phil nodded. "I'll watch the others."

Jessie hurried across the lawn and caught up with the ACLU director as she was opening the door to a white Saturn.

"Miss Warrens?"

Rita turned. Her eyes were red. "This is horrible, isn't it?" she said when she joined Jessie on the lawn. "Sheila told me you were there when it happened. You could've been killed, too." She touched Jessie's arm.

"I was very lucky," Jessie said quietly. Last night she'd awakened in a cold sweat after reliving the explosion in an all-too-real nightmare. "Have you received any more letters or phone calls?"

"No letters, but during the two days after Mrs. Hochburg died, our phones didn't stop ringing."

"Were the calls for you or Mr. Lewis?"

"Mostly for Barry. Some for the ACLU. People were angry with us for representing Benning. I explained that the ACLU wasn't involved with Benning's defense."

Emery Kraft approached the two women. "Miss Warrens, I wanted to convey my condolences. Barry Lewis was a brave man. Like your fine organization, he stood up for his principles. That doesn't diminish the tragedy of his violent death, but it may bring you a measure of comfort."

"Thank you." Rita's eyes welled with fresh tears.

Kraft squeezed her shoulder. "Call if I can be of service." He turned to Jessie. "Nice seeing you again, Detective."

Jessie nodded curtly. After he left she said, "Do you know him well?"

Rita shook her head. "He and Benning came to see me after Mrs. Hochburg was injured. They asked if the ACLU would handle Benning's defense. I told him no, not unless a constitutional issue was involved."

"Kraft says he and Benning have received death threats. I wondered if you had, too."

She shook her head again. "Benning phoned me a few

times. I don't know what he's more scared of, the death threats or going to jail. I almost feel sorry for him." A breeze ruffled her blond hair. "Am I in danger?"

Jessie detected an edge of panic in the petite woman's voice. "I don't know. I'd be extra careful, if I were you. And let me know immediately if you get any more calls. You have my card?"

Rita nodded. "I will. Thank you." She walked around the front of her car, opened the door, and got in.

Clusters of people were standing on either side of the road. Pell was talking with Korbin. Jessie approached the two men.

"How are you, Detective Drake?" Rabbi Korbin asked.

"Luckier than Mr. Lewis, Rabbi. I'm surprised to see you here today, given your feelings about the deceased."

Korbin frowned. "I was angry at Mr. Lewis. I didn't want him dead."

"My wife and I came for the parents," Pell said. "My wife knows Rose Lewis for years."

"Can I speak with you privately for a minute, Mr. Pell?"

"Anything you have to say to me, you can say in front of Rabbi Korbin."

Fine. "We know you called Mr. Lewis at his home on Wednesday night. We're talking to everyone who had contact with Mr. Lewis in the days before his death. It's just routine."

"I'm a suspect?" Pell's smile was grim. His face was flushed. He turned to Korbin. "You hear that, Sheldon? She thinks I killed Lewis." He faced Jessie and said, "Sure, I called Lewis Wednesday night. I was angry. But I called from Cleveland. Check, and you'll see. Call me at the OJA, and I'll give you the name of the hotel where my wife and I stayed."

"That would be great," Jessie said pleasantly. And it would be nice to be able to eliminate Pell from the list of suspects. "When can I reach you?"

"Any time today. I'll be in. Sheldon, I'll talk to you later." He nodded stiffly to Jessie and left.

Korbin watched Pell for a moment, then turned to Jessie.

"Should I be insulted that you're not asking me for my alibi? I contacted Barry Lewis, too."

"We have to investigate all possibilities, Rabbi. We can't pick and choose."

"Mark Pell's not a murderer."

"What about Samuel Hochburg? Or Joel Ben-Natan?" Or Ezra Nathanson?

Korbin shook his head. "I find this entire situation terribly troubling."

"By 'situation' you mean the possibility that a Jew killed another Jew?"

Korbin frowned and clasped his hands behind his back.

"Can I ask you something on another subject, Rabbi? I'm looking for information on a Polish town named Tchebin. There's nothing on it in the computers in the Museum of Tolerance."

"You visited *Beit Hashoah?*" He gazed at her intently. "I'm pleased that you made the time. What was your impression?"

"I was devastated," she said quietly.

Korbin nodded. "I hope you won't misunderstand if I tell you that I'm pleased about that, too. May I ask why you're interested in Tchebin?"

"My mother was born there."

"I see. Your family is Polish?"

"Jewish." She saw the surprise in Korbin's eyes and the slight lift of his brows and wondered again why she was identifying herself in this way. Visiting the museum had helped clarify her past, but she was still unsure of who she was. "My mother was hidden during the war," she added.

"Tchebin was known for a dynastic Hasidic rebbe. It was also the temporary residence for the rebbe of Bobov. The Simon Wiesenthal Museum has a book on it which you can borrow, if you like. Your mother doesn't remember much about her hometown?"

"My mother finds it difficult to discuss her life before and during the war."

"Most hidden children do." Korbin sighed. "There's a society of hidden children, you know. They have conventions where they share their experiences and their feelings of abandonment and lack of identity. One convention met in New York, another in Jerusalem. If you're interested, call me at the museum and I'll give you a contact number. Your mother might like to know about it."

"I'll tell her." That wasn't a lie. Jessie would tell Frances, though she wasn't sure when. And she wasn't sure whether her mother would appreciate the information or be annoyed by it. "Thank you, Rabbi Korbin."

"You're quite welcome, Detective Drake. I don't envy you."

"Excuse me?"

"A Jewish detective trying to find the Jewish killer of a fellow Jew. It has a Kaftkaesque quality to it, don't you think?"

"The killer may not be Jewish."

"I hope with all my heart that you're right."

"In any case, it's my job, Rabbi."

"I know," he said quietly. "That's why I don't envy you."

She said good-bye to the rabbi and walked back to where she'd left Phil. He wasn't there. She found him sitting in the Cutlass.

"Learn anything?" he asked when she was sitting next to him.

"Pell has an alibi." She explained what the OJA director had told her. "We'll check it out, of course. And I told Rita Warrens to be careful. What about you? See anything interesting?"

"Kind of. Your pal Nathanson spent some time in another section of the cemetery before he drove off."

"His parents died a while back. Maybe they're buried here." Jessie looked out the car window toward the cemetery. It was empty now, except for two mortuary employees who were removing the chairs and equipment from the burial site. She opened the car door. "Let's check it out."

Phil led the way. There were no tombstones, just plaques embedded in the lawn, and Jessie felt eerie, as if she were stepping on the dead.

"It's somewhere in this area," Phil said when they were about three hundred feet away from Barry Lewis's freshly dug grave. "It's hard to be exact, 'cause I was watching him from a distance."

He searched to the right. Jessie searched to the left, bending down to read the names on the plaques.

"Over here!" Phil called.

Jessie stood and joined him and, bending again, read the names on two adjoining plaques: Adele Nathanson; Beloved Wife and Mother. Herman Nathanson; Beloved Husband and Father. Someone had placed a smooth, round stone on each of the plaques.

Another plaque next to Adele's caught Jessie's eye:

Carol Nathanson
Beloved Wife and Daughter

"Coincidence?" Phil asked.

"I don't think so." Jessie pointed to the date of death. "That's the same day that Adele and Herman Nathanson died."

Chapter Thirty-seven

"So Ezra Nathanson's wife and his parents died on the same day," Phil said as he turned on the ignition.

"It could be Ben-Natan's wife." Jessie fastened her seat harness. "Joel changed his last name from Nathanson to Ben-Natan five years ago. That's when he formed the Shield."

"Should we pay him a visit?"

"We're practically in his neighborhood."

Ten minutes later Phil pulled up in front of the white house on Emelita. The rain stains had dried; the pink streaks from the roof tiles were still visible. There was no car in the driveway.

Standing in front of the wrought-iron gate, Jessie rang the bell. When no one answered, she rang it again, then shook the gate. No Ben-Natan. No dogs, either.

At the end of the empty driveway was a two-car garage with a solid wood door, painted white. A six-inch space separated the right exterior of the garage from the cinder-block wall that marked the neighboring property. Jessie glanced at the wall.

"There's a window," she said. "I'm going to take a look."

"Have fun. I'm wearing my best suit, or I'd do it."

She hoisted herself onto the top of the cinder-block fence, then carefully brought herself to a standing position and walked, one foot in front of the other, as she'd done on the balance beam when she was twelve years old. Of course, the balance beam was only inches off the padded mat. When she was in front of the window, she crouched and peered inside, tenting her eyes with her hand to block the sun's glare.

"What'd you find, a bomb gift-wrapped for Roy Benning?" Phil asked after she'd dropped to the ground.

"And one for Emery Kraft, with a pretty red bow." She smiled. "Hardly. Ben-Natan's got a nice workshop. A couple of saws. He's neat, too, not messy like some people I know."

"Look who's talking 'messy.'" Phil pointed to her jacket and slacks. "Your mother should see you now. No leftover pipe lying around, huh?"

She brushed off the sleeves of her jacket and her slacks. "Let's try the Shield's office. I have the address in my notes."

The office was in a three-story building on Chandler Boulevard near Ethel, a five-minute drive from Ben-Natan's house. Phil found a parking spot halfway down the block.

"Looks like someone else decided to go straight from the cemetery to Ben-Natan," Jessie said, pointing down the street.

The two brothers were in front of the building's entrance. Ben-Natan was gesticulating dramatically. Nathanson walked away. Ben-Natan hurried after his twin and put his hand on his shoulder. Nathanson threw off the arm but returned with Ben-Natan to the building and disappeared inside.

"Are the brothers close?" Phil asked.

"Not according to Nathanson, or Ben-Natan. I don't want to talk to them together, do you?"

Phil shook his head. "What're you thinking?"

"Same as you. Nathanson has the book. Ben-Natan has the nerve. An explosive combination?"

Phil took Laurel Canyon back to the city. It was more picturesque and a more direct route than the freeway to their next destination, but the road was a series of endless curves. When Jessie was behind the wheel, the curves didn't bother her, but by the time Laurel Canyon ended at Sunset and turned into Crescent Heights, she was queasy. It had to do with being in control, she knew. She tried telling that to her stomach.

Their first stop was on Santa Monica and Croft. Phil stayed in the car while Jessie picked up three videotapes from a television broadcasting station. It was a short drive from the station to the Cedars-Sinai Medical Towers, where Grace Benning worked. Phil parked at a loading only zone on Third Street in front of the courtyard between the east and west towers, which connected to the Cedars-Sinai Hospital complex.

"I hate hospitals and doctors' offices," he grumbled as he and Jessie walked from the car to the courtyard. Ahead of them was a nurse, pushing a man in a wheelchair, and a miniskirted young woman whose heels clacked on the brick and concrete floor.

Jessie's gynecologist was on the tenth floor of the east tower. She'd had her miscarriage on the hospital's third floor. "We're not going inside. We're meeting her right here."

Standing in the middle of the courtyard was a woman in her thirties with shoulder-length blond hair brushed back and held in place with a thick gray headband. She was wearing a straight gray wool skirt that ended well below her knees, a pale peach blouse with a lace-edged collar, and a gray sweater. She peered at Jessie and Phil questioningly as they approached. Aside from pale pink lipstick, she was wearing no makeup. She had a broad, almost square face with a short nose. Not pretty. Not unpretty.

"Mrs. Benning?" Jessie said. When the woman nodded, Jessie introduced herself and Phil. "Is there somewhere we can talk?"

"What about right here?" She pointed to one of the seating walls surrounding the flower beds in the courtyard. "I can't stay long. I've missed a lot of work because of what's happening with Roy, and I'm way behind with my insurance billings. So why don't you ask your questions, and I'll tell you what I can." She walked to the bench, carefully smoothed her skirt under her, and sat down.

Jessie couldn't decide whether she'd heard impatience or belligerence in the woman's voice. She sat down next to Grace. Phil sat on Jessie's left and folded his arms across his chest. Facing the street, Jessie saw a steady pilgrimage of men and women of all ages making its way to the twin shrines of healing.

"When did your husband go into hiding?" she asked.

"Friday. Roy heard on the news about Lewis. He packed a few things, waited for me to come home from work, and left. He was afraid he'd be next." Her lips trembled. She stilled them with her hand. She had short, stubby fingers filled with paper cuts. "I don't know where he's getting food, or anything. I don't know what'll happen to his job if his clients can't reach him."

"Where does he work?" Phil asked.

"He's an insurance agent with Premier Home."

Jessie remembered reading that in one of the newspaper articles after Denning's arrest. "You have no idea where he is?" She leaned closer. It was difficult to hear above the honking and other background noise.

Grace shook her head. "He won't say. He's afraid someone'll follow me if I come see him. He calls me at least twice a day at work. I'm not living at home right now. I'm too scared. When you called this morning, I'd just come home to pick up a few more things. I'd like to know what you're going to do about this." Her tone was definitely belligerent now.

"We're trying our best to help, ma'am," Phil drawled.

"Like you helped Barry Lewis?" Her blue eyes were hard and unflinching. "You find the person that killed him, and my Roy can come home." She blinked back tears and fingered the simple gold cross suspended on a thin gold chain around her neck.

"Who do you think killed Mr. Lewis?" Jessie asked.

"I'm not a detective," she said, pausing to let her sarcasm hit home, "but it's obvious to me it was one of his people."

"You mean a relative?" Jessie asked, knowing exactly what Grace Benning meant.

"I mean someone of the Jewish faith. I mean someone who thinks they can get away with everything, including keeping solid Americans from saying what's on their minds!" Her face was flushed with the passion of her hate.

A young, jeans-clad mother crossed from the east tower to the west, pushing a stroller with a sleeping infant and holding the hand of a whimpering little girl.

"I told you it won't hurt," the mother said. "I promised, didn't I? Why are you crying?"

"Did you have someone specific in mind, Mrs. Benning?"

"I brought you that letter you wanted, the one Roy got that said 'Prepare for the Angel of Death.'" She opened her purse, took out a white envelope, and handed it to Jessie. "Roy's been getting death threats on the phone, too. So has Mr. Kraft. I don't know about the ACLU woman." She frowned. "You should check with her. They could be after her, too. I wouldn't be surprised."

Handling the envelope as little as possible, Jessie slipped it into a plastic bag, which she put in her purse. "I alerted Miss Warrens. As of this morning, she hasn't received any threats."

"Well," Grace said, her tone implying that Rita Warrens's immunity from danger was temporary. "Has she heard from Roy? I know he went to see her with Mr. Kraft after the woman died."

"Apparently, your husband called her a few times. Miss Warrens seemed to think he was troubled."

"You'd be troubled, too, if someone was trying to kill you! I don't know why you don't arrest these people so we can all be safe in our homes."

"By 'people' you mean Mr. Ben-Natan? Mr. Kraft said your husband recognized one of his callers as Joel Ben-Natan."

Grace nodded. "And others, like that Hochburg person who started all this. He was parked across the street from our house last week. He was there again this morning, I'm sure of it. He said Roy should die, you know. He said that on live television. I have it on tape, if you want to hear it. Him and his mother brought all this on themselves, and now Roy's in hiding and

I'm all alone and in danger, and I'd just like to know, why? Why can they get away with this? Why can he threaten my husband and other God-fearing Christians?"

"People say things in the heat of emotion that they don't mean," Phil said. "Did Mr. Hochburg call your home and make threats?"

"Well, he didn't announce himself, if that's what you mean. But I'm pretty sure he was one of those who called." She paused. "There was another man who called. He had an accent."

"What kind of accent?" Jessie asked.

Grace flashed her a contemptuous look. "*Their* kind of accent. Jewish. From Europe. *You* know." She said this almost with a sneer.

Kraft told her I'm Jewish, Jessie decided. She'd never been the target of racism. It was a strange, unsettling experience, one she'd have to explore later. "There's nothing romantic about being Jewish," her mother had warned.

"Is there anyone who might know where your husband is?" she asked Grace.

"No."

"What about your family?" Phil asked.

"We have no family here. We're both from Milwaukee, born and bred. It's just Roy and me. The good Lord hasn't blessed us with children." Again she touched her cross and sighed.

"Where can we reach you?" Jessie asked.

"You can call me at work, or in the evenings, at my friend Doreen's. That's where I'm staying until you find the person that killed Barry Lewis." Grace gave both phone numbers, then stood.

Jessie and Phil stood, too. A visibly pregnant woman walked up the courtyard, her body swaying gently from side to side. Grace Benning followed her with her eyes as she turned left.

"I have to get back. I miss Roy, Detective Okum. I want him home, safe. Can you help us?" She avoided looking at Jessie.

"We'll try our best."

Grace Benning nodded and left.

"Something there," Phil said to Jessie, watching as the woman walked to the glass doors of the west tower and opened them.

"Uh-huh. Did she seem hostile to me or was it my imagination?"

"Definitely hostile. Why is that?"

Jessie hesitated, then said, "I told Kraft my mother is a Jewish Holocaust survivor. I think he told Grace Benning."

Phil grinned. "Goddamn, Jess! You pulled his leg, huh?"

"Actually, my mother *is* Jewish. She was hidden with a Polish family during the war. She just told me Friday night, after Matthew's party." Jessie watched her friend and partner carefully.

Phil stared at her. "No shit!" He was silent a moment, then said, "Why didn't she tell you before?"

"She didn't want to tell me now, but I kind of forced the issue. So how do you like your Jewish partner?" she asked lightly.

"Same's I liked the other one." He put his giant arm around her and walked her to the street.

A parking ticket was tucked under the windshield wipers of the Cutlass. Phil pulled it out and stuffed it into his pocket.

"I hate doctors," he said.

Samuel Hochburg sliced the air as he brought the cleaver down with sudden swiftness onto the slab of meat. *Thwack.*

Jessie and Phil approached the counter. Displayed on two shelves behind a glass front were steaks, lamb chops, and other cuts of meat and a tub filled with a mountain of pink-red beef still coiled from being pressed through the holes of a grinder.

"Mr. Hochburg? I'm Detective Drake. This is Detective Okum."

Hochburg looked up. "I'll be with you in one minute, please." He didn't seem to recognize her as the cop who had twisted his arm behind him and cuffed him and forced him to his knees.

Even to Jessie, the events of the parade seemed light-years away. She almost hadn't recognized him, either—he looked different, somehow. Older. Now she realized why—it was the gray-white beard stubble that sprouted unevenly on his face. She wondered if not shaving was a religious rite of mourning.

Hochburg lifted the cleaver again and severed the meat first into quarters, then eighths. *Thwack, Thwack.*

"Pow!"

Jessie turned toward the sound. At a small table in the bottom left corner of the long, narrow room, a young boy wearing a black velvet skullcap was playing with plastic soldiers and tanks.

"Pow!" the boy said, slamming two tanks together. "Pow! Pow!"

Hochburg rinsed the cleaver at the sink and placed it on the wooden counter. "More questions?" he asked, turning to Jessie as he wiped his hands on his red-stained apron. "I thought I was finished until the trial."

"Mr. Hochburg—"

"Pow!"

"Yankie, quiet, please," Hochburg admonished gently. "My six-year-old grandson," he explained to Jessie and Phil. "His mother works, and he's getting over a cold, so he's with me today. You were saying?" He spoke with just a trace of a European accent.

"First, we wanted to offer our condolences on your mother's death," Jessie said, wishing she could avoid the "second."

Hochburg nodded. "You put your jacket under her head. That was very nice of you." He saw her surprised look. "I remember you, Detective. After all, you arrested me." He smiled and moved his black velvet skullcap, a larger version of his grandson's, farther back. "I have no hard feelings. You were doing your job."

"We're here because we're investigating Barry Lewis's murder," Phil said. "We're talking to everyone who knew him."

Hochburg placed his heavily veined hands onto the glass top of the counter and leaned forward. "You know something? I hated Lewis for what he was doing. I even called to tell him, but when I heard he was killed . . ." He shrugged. "We ask God to give us *ad meah ve'esrim shana*—to a hundred and twenty years. My mother, may she rest in peace, was seventy-nine. I hoped she would live another fifteen, twenty years. I would have been happy with ten—less, even—but God had different plans. *Hamokom nosan, hamokom lokach.* God gives. God takes away. We can't question His ways."

"You don't blame Lewis for her death?" Jessie asked.

"Will it bring my mother back?" He selected a knife with a long, slim blade. "You think I'm happy that his wife is a widow, that his daughters are without a father? I know what it's like. I was eight years old when they shot my father in front of my eyes."

"I'm sorry," Jessie said, knowing the words were inadequate.

"Yah." Sighing, he lifted a section of beef, deftly pared off a layer of fat, and tossed the fat into a trash can under the back counter. "Lewis's father came to my house last week to pay a condolence call. He's a nice man. He sat in my house crying, like it was his mother who died. He offered to pay for the funeral, for everything. I said, 'Mr. Lewis, it's not your fault this happened.' So now he's crying for his son."

Jessie felt almost obscene continuing, but she had no choice. "Mr. Hochburg, this is a routine question we're asking everyone who was involved with Mr. Lewis. Where were you last night?"

"Home." He continued trimming the beef, turning it on all sides to examine it.

"Was anyone with you?"

"My wife, may she rest in peace, died two years ago. Cancer." His eyes misted. "My daughter-in-law brought me supper, but the rest of the night I was alone. So I have no alibi."

He sounded almost defiant, Jessie thought. "Have you been threatening Roy Benning?"

Hochburg turned and spat on the ground. "That's what I have to say to Nazis like Benning."

"His wife says you called him," Phil said.

Hochburg hesitated. "I called him once," he admitted.

"Did you threaten him?"

"You think I remember what I said? My mother was dead. I was in shock. I was angry."

"Are you angry now?" Jessie said.

He put down the knife. "Yes. With Benning and with the others, yes. Forever, yes. But I'll leave him to the courts. Why should I sit in jail for starting up with garbage like him?"

"His wife says your car was parked in front of their house last week and this morning."

"Last week I was sitting *shiva* for my mother. That's seven days of mourning," he explained. "I'm an Orthodox Jew. Orthodox Jews don't leave the house during *shiva*. This morning I got up from *shiva*. I had better things to do than sit in front of Benning's house."

"Did you call Emery Kraft and tell him to prepare for the Angel of Death?"

"Never." Hochburg shook his head vehemently. The ringing of the bell announced a customer. He glanced toward the front door.

A tall, slender, brown-haired woman approached the counter. "I'm so sorry about your mother, Mr. Hochburg. May you and your family have only happy occasions from now on."

He nodded his thanks. "Mrs. Bernstein, I have your order ready in the back. I'll get it." He left the room.

Hochburg's grandson came up to Phil. "Wanna play war with me?" He held out a GI Joe and a tank.

"Can't right now. Do you like playing war?"

Vigorous nods of the head. "My *zeidi* bought me a whole set for my *afikomen*."

"It's a gift kids get on Passover," Jessie whispered to Phil. "What's a *zeidi*?" she asked the boy.

He cast her a "doesn't-everybody-know?" look. "A grandfather."

"Nice set," Phil said.

Hochburg returned with a cardboard box filled with packages wrapped in pink paper. He put the box on the counter. "That's ninety-eight dollars and seventy-two cents," he told the woman. "Make it ninety-eight even." He smiled and handed her a bill.

"My *zeidi* was in a *real* war," the boy said, racing a tank across the face of the display case. "He and his mommy escaped from the Germans and helped people called parsons. Right, *Zeidi?*"

"Partisans, Yankie." He took the woman's check and deposited it in the cash register. "I'll help you to the car," he told her.

"Partisans," the six-year-old repeated. "My *zeidi* was only eleven years old, but he did all the stuff they did. Right, *Zeidi?* That's what Daddy says."

Jessie and Phil exchanged quick glances.

"Kids," Hochburg said, his face as red as the stains on his apron.

"Boom!" Yankie said. "Boom! Boom! Boom!"

Chapter Thirty-eight

Peggy Oppman stood in front of the open pantry and frowned. Then she walked down the hall to her son's room.

"Gene?" She knocked on the door and opened it.

He was sitting at his desk. "What?" He didn't turn around.

"Did you have a party in school today? We're missing a box of crackers and another box of cereal, some cans of soda, plus some fruit and cheese."

"I had some when I came home today."

"You don't like cheese, Gene. You never eat fruit."

"I did today."

"There's a bag of rolls missing, too. Gene, are you taking food for someone at school? If you are, tell me. I won't mind."

"Yeah, that's what I'm doing. There's this kid who has no food. I thought I'd help him out. Be a good boy."

"You're lying, aren't you? I can tell when you're lying."

"What're you going to do, Ma, call the police and report me for eating too much?"

Peggy sighed and left the room.

When he heard the door shut, he pushed his chair back and walked over to his closet. He took out the boots, buffed them with the sleeve of his T-shirt, put them on, then stared at himself in the full-length mirror on the back of the closet door.

"Heil Hitler!" He aligned his fingers and snapped them in a sharp, downward angle the way Roy had shown him. He clicked his heels together.

His mother was suspicious, but he could handle her and his father. They hadn't even grounded him for calling Barry Lewis.

"Let's talk this through," his father had said after the detectives had left. "Why do you think you called Mr. Lewis?"

"I'm confused," Gene had said. "I don't know why."

"That's a good start, son," his father had said.

Still wearing the boots, Gene sat back at his desk and tried to focus on the open textbook. The phone was to his right. He lifted the receiver and punched the numbers on the small card in front of him.

"West L.A., Detective Patterson speaking."

Gene returned the receiver to the cradle.

Chapter Thirty-nine

"I have a lead on my call girl," Phil told Jessie. "A friend who worked for the same madam remembered that the dead woman mentioned she was having trouble with one particular john. Seems he liked to play with knives." He checked his watch. "The friend lives in Woodland Hills. I don't know how long I'll be. You want to watch the tapes yourself, then leave them for me?"

"I may watch them at home. First I have to write up the notes from our talks with Grace Benning and Hochburg."

"Boom," Phil said.

"Yeah, boom." Jessie grinned. "You don't really think Hochburg blew up Barry Lewis, do you?"

"Grandpa was with the partisans. Partisans used explosives to blow up bridges and trains." Phil slipped his jacket back on.

"How come I'm the one who always writes up the notes?"

" 'Cause my handwriting's illegible." He fixed his tie and smoothed back his hair with his palms. "How do I look?"

"Like a handsome married devil about to see a call girl." She uncapped her pen. "Why don't you work on your handwriting?"

"So I won't have to write up notes." He blew Jessie a kiss and walked out of the room.

*   *   *

Dafna Abrams looked almost exactly like the twin brothers. Same hazel eyes. Same brown-black hair. Hers was cut short and framed her face. Standing ten feet away from Dafna, pretending to study the "marked down" Passover items on a cloth-covered table, Jessie watched her help a middle-aged woman select a silver tray.

The store was filled with Judaica: Hebrew and English books, some for adults, others (these were illustrated) for children. Silver and porcelain and pewter candelabra. An entire glass cabinet was filled with silver cups of varying sizes and ornamental motifs. An adjoining cabinet held a selection of other beautifully crafted silver items, including a miniature windmill, a tower with a turret and flag, and a small vessel attached to which was a tiny pitcher. Jessie couldn't imagine what religious ritual the tower or any of the other things were used for.

In a display counter against the left wall of the shop were long silver serrated knives with silver handles and slim, silver cases similar to the one Jessie had noticed on the doorposts of Ezra Nathanson's home and Ohr Torah.

"Are you looking for a gift or for yourself?"

Jessie turned and faced Dafna. "I was admiring this." She pointed to a hammered-silver case. "What's it for?"

"It's a *mezuzah* case. It's hollow. You insert the *mezuzah*, a handwritten parchment containing two sections of the Torah. The plural is *mezuzot*. They go on every doorpost in the house." She walked around the counter, unlocked the display case, removed the *mezuzah* case, and turned it over. "The parchment is extra."

Jessie took the case from her. "What's the significance?"

"It's a *mitzvah*, a commandment: 'And write them'— meaning God's teachings—'on the doorposts of your house and upon your gates.' It's a reminder to conduct a God-fearing life."

"Like the phylacteries?"

Dafna smiled. "Exactly. The *mezuzah* is also said to protect the home. Pious people have their *mezuzot* checked twice in seven years to make sure the letters inscribed on the parchment are in good condition. I know of several people who've had their *mezuzot* checked because they've suffered misfortune—and discovered that the parchments were imperfect."

"That's eerie." Jessie put down the case. There had been red paint on Barry Lewis's doorpost. Had there been a *mezuzah?* Then again, Lewis had been killed in his car, not in his home.

"*Life's* eerie, isn't it?" Dafna smiled again and replaced the case in the cabinet. "Would you like me to show you a few more *mezuzah* cases, or do you want to look around? We have a fine collection of Judaica and a wide range of prices."

"Actually, I'd like to talk to you. I'm Detective Drake with the LAPD. I—"

"Ezra told me you'd be calling." The smile had dimmed. "You want to know what time he came to our house Thursday night and what time he left."

Jessie nodded. Nathanson had wasted no time in contacting his sister—but then, why would he have?

"Ezra arrived after seven. He left at one in the morning. He and Avi—my husband—and I sat around talking after we returned from the theater." She relayed the information in the unemotional style of a soldier reciting his name, rank, and serial number.

Almost verbatim what Nathanson had told Jessie—it sounded too pat. But that didn't mean it wasn't true. And she wasn't here just to validate Nathanson's alibi. "It's terribly sad about your sister-in-law and your parents, dying like that. I was sorry to learn of it."

Dafna's eyes widened. "Ezra talked about that? He usually doesn't." She paused. "I guess it's because you're investigating Barry Lewis's murder."

"I guess," Jessie said, not understanding the connection. "Their deaths obviously had a strong impact on everyone. That's when your brother Joel formed the Shield of Jewish Protectors, isn't it?"

Dafna nodded. "I think it made him feel less vulnerable, more in control."

"And that's when he changed his surname to Yoel Ben-Natan? Ezra explained that's the Hebrew translation of Joel Nathanson."

Another nod. "Joel wants to move to Israel eventually. And my guess is, he thinks the name has a more military ring. Even as a kid, he identified with the heroes of Jewish history, like Moses and Joshua." She smiled, her earlier defensiveness forgotten.

"I don't know much Jewish history, even though my mother's Jewish. I assume Ezra told you that?"

"It came up," Dafna said, the sudden pink in her face belying her casual tone. "I hope you don't mind."

"Not at all." Nathanson and his sister must have had a good time speculating about the female Jewish homicide detective. Jessie smiled. "I noticed that unlike Ezra, Joel doesn't wear a skullcap. Why is that?"

Dafna neatened an arrangement of small silver pillboxes on a tray. "Basically, Joel felt he couldn't commit to a God who let the people he loved die because they were Jewish."

Jessie thought of her mother, who had totally abandoned Judaism and reinvented herself for a similar reason. "And Ezra?"

"He became more committed to Judaism. He told me later that it gave him the faith he needed to go on. Joel couldn't understand that. He wanted Ezra to be angry, not philosophical." She sighed.

"What about you? I hope you don't mind my asking," Jessie added quickly.

"I don't mind. At first I was bitter. Then, like Ezra, I came to the realization that you can't blame God for the evil men do."

What evil was she referring to? Jessie wondered.

A heavyset woman approached the counter, holding a small white box. "Someone bought this here for me. Can I exchange it?"

"Of course." Dafna opened the box, took out a footed silver cup, and examined the tiny white sticker on the underside of the base. "This was eighty-nine dollars, plus tax. I can show you some things in that price range, or you can look around."

"I'll look around." The woman walked toward the tall cabinets at the back of the shop.

"What happened to your parents and sister-in-law, exactly? I didn't want to press your brother for details. If it's too painful to discuss. . . ."

"No, that's all right," she said in a low voice. "Carol was at my parents' house in North Hollywood. She was in her ninth month, and my brother had to be away and didn't want her to be alone." Dafna ran her hand across the counter. "Someone burned a huge wooden swastika on their home late at night when they were all asleep. It was in September, and there were Santa Ana winds. The entire house caught fire. My parents and sister-in-law died. The baby, too—a girl." Dafna's eyes had filled with tears.

"Their *mezuzah* didn't save them," Jessie said softly. "I didn't mean that sarcastically," she said, blushing under the woman's suddenly fierce stare. "I just meant . . . I'm sorry."

After a long, uncomfortable moment, Dafna nodded. "Their *mezuzah* didn't save them." Her voice was heavy with sadness. "The police suspected a neo-Nazi group, but they could never prove it. They took all our fingerprints, for purposes of elimination. I remember how strange it felt, as if we were the criminals."

Had Ben-Natan symbolically "burned" Barry Lewis for defending the enemy who had killed his parents and wife and unborn child? "I don't blame your brother for being bitter," Jessie said.

"Ezra's better now. For the first few months, he wouldn't talk to anyone or go anywhere. It's only recently that he's started dating again. Avi and I are happy about that."

Ezra's wife had been killed? Jessie hoped her face didn't betray her surprise.

"Detective Drake, I know that you have to question everyone, but my brothers aren't violent people. Ezra's the most gentle person I know. My kids adore him. So do all his students."

Did Dafna know that her "gentle" brother had a copy of *The Anarchist's Cookbook* hidden behind his literary works? "Your brother Joel made angry statements about Barry Lewis. He's done the same about HIT and Roy Benning."

Dafna shook her head again. "With Joel, it's more talk than anything else."

"He's been arrested a number of times."

"For disturbing the peace. For failure to disperse." Dafna shook her head again. "He's vigilant about protecting Jews, but he's not a killer, Detective Drake. He—"

"Can you tell me the prices of these items, please?" the heavyset woman called.

"I'll be right with you." Dafna walked along the counter and joined the woman. A few minutes later she returned to Jessie. "I told you the truth about what time Ezra was at our house. I hope you believe me."

Jessie smiled in answer. "Thanks for your time, Mrs. Abrams, and your cooperation."

"You're welcome. But I haven't really told you anything you don't already know."

Yes, you have, Jessie thought. She started to leave, then turned back. "Do you have any basic books on Judaism?"

"We have several excellent ones."

From a row of bookcases on the right side of the room, Dafna selected several volumes and showed them to Jessie, explaining the philosophical focus and features of each. Jessie thumbed through five, then chose one.

"This one looks damaged." Dafna frowned. "Let me go in the back for another copy."

While she waited, Jessie walked to the display case and looked again at the *mezuzah* cases.

"Interested in a *mezuzah,* Detective Drake? I'm sure Dafna will give you a great price."

Jessie turned and faced Joel Ben-Natan. Yaffa wasn't with

him. Neither were the dogs. "My partner and I stopped at your house earlier today to speak to you. We were interested in knowing where you were Thursday night."

"At home, of course. Where'd you think I was—taping a bomb under Barry Lewis's car?"

"Smart-ass. "And I suppose Miss Aloni was with you?"

"All night." He grinned and leaned forward. "I'll tell you the details if you promise not to arrest me."

"Roy Benning says you've been harassing him."

"Roy Benning's lying." Ben-Natan's lips tightened. "I don't even know the son of a bitch's phone number."

"But you *did* harass Mr. Lewis with phone calls the night before he died."

"I was trying to enlighten him."

"We have the tape of your calls. Sounded more like you were trying to frighten, not enlighten. Who do *you* think killed him?"

"God works in mysterious ways." He picked up a pillbox and pried open its lid.

"God didn't put a pipe bomb under Barry Lewis's gas tank. You must have an opinion."

"Like you really care."

"Try me."

"The White Alliance. They hate Jews. Lewis is a Jew. They make it look like one of us killed him."

The possibility had occurred to her. "What about Samuel Hochburg?"

He shut the pillbox and put it on the tray. "I can't say."

"The Shield of Jewish Protectors doing its job, huh?"

He was saved from answering by Dafna, who returned holding another copy of the book. She raised questioning brows when she saw her brother standing with Jessie. She greeted him, then walked behind the register.

Ben-Natan followed Jessie to the register. "Detective Drake was admiring the *mezuzot,* Dafna. Did you tell her no Jewish home should be without one?"

So Ezra Nathanson had told him she was Jewish, too. "I'm thinking of getting one eventually," Jessie said.

"Why not now? I'm sure Dafna will give you a special price. You're practically a friend of the family."

"Stop it, Joel. You're embarrassing Detective Drake." Dafna rang up Jessie's purchase and slipped the book into a plastic bag.

"Did my sister mention that the *mezuzah* provides protection?"

"Are you saying I need protection, Mr. Ben-Natan?" Jessie handed Dafna her Visa card.

"Being a detective is dangerous. I heard you were almost blown up along with Lewis. Next time you might not be so lucky."

"Joel!" Dafna slammed the register drawer shut. "I apologize for my brother, Detective Drake. He's not usually this rude."

"I'm just concerned about the detective."

"I appreciate your concern." Jessie slipped her credit card into her wallet, took the book, and headed for the exit. At the door, she turned. "By the way, Mr. Ben-Natan, I didn't notice a *mezuzah* on your door, either." She smiled and left the shop.

"Hey," Frank Pruitt said.

"Hey, yourself." Jessie smiled, hearing the nervousness in his voice that matched hers. She shut the door behind him.

He kissed her, then handed her cellophane-wrapped roses. She was touched by the gesture and happy to see him—it had been too long—and glad that she'd called him. He followed her to the kitchen and watched while she filled a glass vase with tepid water and arranged the roses.

"They're beautiful, Frank." She turned to face him and kissed him, holding his face between her hands.

He touched her cheek gingerly. "Is this from the explosion?"

She nodded. "It's much better now." The pain was a faint

memory, and with makeup on, she barely noticed the bruise anymore. The fear was still vivid and visited her, mostly at night. Sometimes during the day.

"You could've been killed." He pulled her close and held her for a moment. "God, I've missed you, Jess," he whispered.

"I missed you, too, Frank."

He kissed her cheek, then the hollow of her throat. His hands slipped under her sweater. She felt herself responding, she'd missed his touch so intensely, but she drew away.

"I think we have to talk," she said.

"Okay." His voice said otherwise.

In the den, they sat on the black leather sofa. She said, "First of all, Espes told me you were asking around about him."

"So?" Pruitt leaned back against the sofa cushion.

"So I can handle my problems on my own, Frank. You embarrassed me, and Espes is furious with me."

"I'm sorry. I just wanted to help. Do you want me to call Espes and square things? Tell him you had no idea I was calling?"

She shook her head. "Just leave it alone, all right?"

"All right." He took her hand. "I won't interfere again. Am I forgiven?"

"Yes."

"What's 'second'?"

"That's more complicated."

"It's this Jewish thing, right?" He sat up straight but held on to her hand. "I've been thinking about it since the last time I saw you, and I still don't know why you got so upset."

"What you said sounded anti-Semitic, Frank. That's why."

He shook his head. "I'm not an anti-Semite. Look, I'm willing to admit that the Holocaust happened if you're willing to admit that maybe it didn't."

"Frank—" She tried to pull her hand away.

He held tight. "It's a difference of opinion, Jess. It has

nothing to do with the way we feel for each other, which is pretty damn special."

"It's not an *opinion*, Frank. That's like saying people have differing opinions about whether the Civil War happened. The Civil War happened, Frank. So did the Holocaust. Six million Jews died."

"It's not the same thing."

"Yes, it is."

"All I'm saying is, you can't know."

She moved closer to him. "I went to the Museum of Tolerance yesterday, Frank. I think you should go. It'll open your eyes to the truth." When he shook his head, she said, "I'll go with you, if you want." She touched his face.

"Maybe."

"When?"

"I don't know. Lemme think about it."

"How about this Sunday?"

He dropped her hand. "Don't push me, Jessie."

"This is important to me, Frank."

"Why? Why is it so goddamn important, huh? Why the hell do you care if I like Jews or not?"

"What if I told you I was Jewish, Frank?"

"What if I told you I was Buddhist? Shit, Jessie." He linked his hands behind his head and studied the ceiling.

"I *am* Jewish, through my mom."

He swiveled his head toward her. "You're testing me, right? I don't think that's funny, Jessie."

"I'm not testing you, Frank."

He stared at her, his dark brown eyes unfathomable. "Why didn't you tell me before? Were you ashamed of it?"

"I just found out Friday night. My mom told me the whole story." She repeated, in brief, what Frances had revealed, all the while studying his reaction.

"Jesus! That's some story," he said when she had finished. He was silent a moment, then said, "So you're only half-Jewish, right? Because your dad's not."

"Ezra Nathanson said I'm completely Jewish, because my mom is. Anyway, what difference does it make?"

"No difference. I was just curious. Makes no difference to me," he repeated.

"That's good," Jessie said softly. "So will you go with me to the museum on Sunday, Frank?"

"Yeah, sure." He nodded. "Unless some emergency comes up at work, of course. If that happens, we'll do it the next week."

"Of course." She put her arms around him and rubbed her lips against his, then pulled him to his feet and led him to the bedroom.

He unbuttoned his shirt. She pulled her sweater over her head and unhooked her bra and felt his eyes on her.

"You're staring at me," she said lightly.

"It's been a long time, sweetheart."

They finished undressing and joined under her down comforter. His hands were warm and knowing against her skin and touched all the right places, and she felt a pleasant aching begin to build. She knew it was going to be fine between them, and she opened her eyes to smile at him and found him staring at her. He shut his eyes quickly and said her name, Jessie, oh Jessie, and pretended to moan with pleasure as he moved against her.

She closed her eyes and pretended, too.

After Frank left, she watched the videotapes.

The one from the parade revealed nothing new.

Neither did the one taken at the scene of Lewis's murder.

On the videotape taken the night his front door was vandalized, Jessie saw a familiar figure as the camera panned around the crowd of lookers. She stopped the video and rewound it.

She watched until she saw the figure appear, then froze the frame. The figure, held captive on her television screen, jerked spasmodically as if anxious to escape her scrutiny.

It was Ezra Nathanson.

She unfroze the frame. Nathanson turned to avoid the camera.

She noticed that he wasn't wearing a skullcap.

Maybe it was Ben-Natan.

Maybe it was Nathanson, pretending to be Ben-Natan.

Pretending, she knew, wasn't all that difficult.

Chapter Forty

Jessie was showering when the phone rang. She stepped out of the shower, grabbed the bath sheet she'd slung over the door, and reached for the portable phone on the bathroom counter. "Yes?"

It was West L.A. "A kid called for you. Was upset when I wouldn't give him your home number. Wouldn't tell me his name."

"Did he leave a number?" She anchored the phone between her ear and shoulder and toweled herself dry.

"Negative."

Gene Oppman, she decided. She thanked dispatch, hung up, and walked into her bedroom. From her purse she took the list the phone company had faxed her, found Robert Oppman's number, and called. When Mrs. Oppman answered, Jessie asked to speak to Gene.

"What's wrong? Has he done something that—"

"Nothing's wrong, Mrs. Oppman. But I need to speak to him."

While Jessie waited, she took underwear from her dresser drawer. She was slipping on panties when Gene came on the line.

"What do you want?" he said in a sullen voice.

"You called *me*, Gene. Why don't you tell me what you want?"

"Who says?"

"Gene, it's seven in the morning. I have better things to do than play games. Call me at the station when you grow up."

"Wait!" In a whisper he said, "I want to change phones."

She hooked her bra, moved over to the closet, and pulled a forest green silk blouse off a hanger. A moment later she heard the boy tell his mother to hang up. Then she heard a click.

"Detective Drake?"

"Still here. So why'd you call me, Gene?"

"I'm worried about Mr. Benning. I saw him last night and—"

"You know where he is?" she asked sharply.

"I found him this empty store not far from me. Anyway, he told me he was meeting with this potential big client today, and I worried about it all night, 'cause I didn't think it was such a good idea, but this morning he was gone!"

"Where was he meeting the client?" She pulled on her slacks.

"At the man's house. It's under construction, and the man told Mr. Benning he was looking to switch insurance and wanted to meet with him and maybe buy a policy."

Or lure him out of hiding. "When is he meeting the client?"

"Seven-thirty. The man had to get to his office and wanted to wrap this up with Mr. Benning or find another insurance agent."

"How is Mr. Benning getting there?"

"His car. A brown Buick Skylark. He's been parking it in an underground space of an apartment house near me. I asked the landlady could a friend of mine park there for five dollars a day. She said seven dollars, so I said okay."

"Do you know the address of this client's house?"

"It's on a street in Beverly Hills that has the name of a tree, but I can't remember the name!"

Several Beverly Hills streets were named after trees. Jessie

could hear the hysteria building in the boy's voice. "We'll figure this out together, Gene. Was it Elm?"

"No. I should've called you yesterday. I know that now. I
tried, but I couldn't go through with it!"

"Don't worry about it. Maple?"

"No."

"Linden?" A silly question; the boy probably didn't realize
that was a type of tree.

"No!"

"Palm?"

Silence. "I think so. Yeah, it was Palm!" he said, excited.
"Can you go find him? Please?"

Palm was a long street, and there were quite a number of
houses under construction in Beverly Hills at any given time.

"What's Mr. Benning's license plate number?"

"I don't know."

"Think carefully, Gene. Did he mention whether the street
was south or north of Santa Monica Boulevard?"

"I don't remember!" he cried in an anguished whisper.
"You think he's in trouble, don't you?"

"I'm not sure, but it's a good thing you called. Did he say
anything else about the neighborhood?"

The boy thought for a moment. "He said something about
people paying mountains of money for something flat. He
laughed."

The Flats! That was the term given to the more expensive
lots on the four long blocks between Santa Monica and Sunset.

"Gene, you did well. I'll check this out."

"Will you call and let me know if you find Mr. Benning?"

"I won't have news before you leave for school."

"I'm not going to school. I can't, until I know. . . ."

Maureen told Jessie that Phil was on his way to the station.
Jessie left a message with the desk sergeant, asking Phil to
meet her on the five hundred block of Palm, just north of

Santa Monica. She would start there and work her way up toward Sunset.

There were three houses under various stages of construction on the five hundred block of North Palm, but no Skylark.
In the middle of the six hundred block, she found a taupe Skylark in front of a house that had a stucco exterior and tile roof
but was clearly under construction. The grounds were fenced
in by chain link. Scaffolding ran around the exterior. A huge
Dumpster squatted in the driveway. Debris littered the deep
expanse of gray-brown dirt that would be the lawn.

There was no other vehicle nearby. Either the "client"
hadn't arrived yet, or he'd been and gone. Jessie checked her
watch: 7:42. Where the hell was Phil? She called West L.A.
dispatch on her car phone and gave her location. She waited
another minute, got out of the Honda, and crossed the street.
She opened a gate in the chain-link fence and, careful not to
trip on the debris, picked her way toward the front entrance.

"Mr. Benning?"

Her voice echoed in the two-story entry. Ahead of her was
a framed staircase; to her right and left, framed rooms. Beyond the staircase, plasterboard had been nailed to the walls.

She stepped farther into the hallway, inhaling the clean
scent of new wood. Floury particles of dust rose to greet her
and swirled around her head like a spectral host.

"Mr. Benning?" she called again.

The thought occurred to her that she'd been set up by Benning and the kid, although she wasn't sure why. She reached
inside her jacket for her Smith & Wesson and debated
whether she should return to her car and wait for Phil.

A flat, explosive crack shattered the silence. She dropped
to the plywood flooring and felt a bullet whizz over her head.

The gunshot had come from the drywalled area behind the
staircase. The two-by-fours provided no cover. Her heart
thumping, she rolled to her left over discarded nails and fragments of lumber until she was out of the entry hall and in the
framed room.

Another shot rang out.

She rose to her knees. Pressing her gun against her side, she crouched and ran in a weaving path toward the framed doorway on the back wall. She passed through a square, midsize room into a larger one with exposed gas pipes and plumbing. The kitchen. The right wall was covered with plasterboard. So was the back wall. She scurried across the plywood to the doorway and found herself facing a narrow hall covered in plasterboard.

Gripping her gun with both hands, she quickly checked the space to her right, then to her left. Both were empty. She hugged the wall and, with noiseless steps, inched along its cold surface until she came to another wide doorway. If she was right, this was the back entry to the room where the shots had originated.

She listened to the silence and could hear only the rapid beating of her heart. She braced herself, then swiftly entered the enormous, two-story room, surveying its perimeters with sweeping motions of her trained weapon and eyes. The upper portion of the room, she noted, was still roughly framed.

The shooter wasn't there, but she wasn't alone. Lying prone on the floor under a tent formed of remnants of plasterboard and plywood was a person. Judging from the jeans-clad legs and boots, the only parts visible, it was a large male.

Benning?

Her gun extended firmly in front of her, her eyes darting everywhere, Jessie approached him. She identified the sickly-sweet smell of blood before she saw it trickling in a steady stream between his legs and along the periphery of his body and seeping into the white-coated plywood floor.

She heard a creak above her, then a scraping sound. Looking up, she saw a jagged spear of glass slice through the air. She stifled a scream and jumped back. The spear shattered in a tinkling of glass as it struck the spot where she'd been standing.

Jessie ran out the doorway and up the rough planks of the stairway. The shooter was nearing the end of the long, narrow hall. She fired as she ran. The bullet pierced a sheet of glass she hadn't realized was there, wedged between the sides of the hall. She stopped herself seconds before she crashed into the glass. The shooter turned right into a room.

To Jessie's right was a solid stretch of drywall. To her left was the open air above the room where she'd left the bleeding man. She decocked her gun and slipped it into her waistband. Holding on to a stud with her right hand, she swung her leg around the stud onto the sixteen-inch space between the two-by-fours and grabbed hold of the next stud. She repeated the process until she was past the glass barricade, then stepped back into the hall and cocked her gun.

When she reached the spot where the shooter had turned right, she found not a room, but a back staircase. Cursing, she ran down the stairs and out a doorway. She was pounding past a huge, rectangular cavity that would be a swimming pool when she heard a car drive away. She knew it was the shooter, but she didn't slow her pace until she reached the open gate in the chain-link fence across the back of the property and stepped into the alley and found nothing but four large trash cans.

With her gun holstered, she raced back to the house and made her way among the labyrinth of rooms to the two-story one where she had left the bleeding man she thought was Benning. She moved aside the larger fragments of glass, stepped closer, and, kneeling, lifted a square of plasterboard off his body.

She found his hand in a pool of blood. She raised his wrist and checked for a pulse. Nothing. She removed another section of plasterboard, then another. When she removed the last piece, she gagged and covered her mouth and turned quickly away. She stood on shaky feet and stumbled toward the doorway, leaning against the wood frame, and panted in short, even breaths with her mouth open to keep the bile from rising.

"Jessie? Jessie? Are you in here?"

A moment later Phil was next to her. "I saw your car outside. What the—!"

She pointed behind her, unable to talk. She heard her partner's heavy tread and knew from his whispered, "Jesus Christ!" and his retching exactly when he'd found Roy Benning's body and his severed head.

Chapter Forty-one

"He was knocked on the back of his head, then decapitated," Jessie told Phil, cringing at the image that flashed in front of her. "Reiser of the Beverly Hills PD thinks they found the two-by-four that was used to knock Benning out."

"Benning was a big guy." Phil leaned back in his chair and frowned. "That's what I don't get." He picked up his coffee mug.

Jessie sat on her desk. "The killer had the element of surprise. He parked in the alley. Benning probably thought he arrived before his 'client.' I thought so, too."

Phil nodded. "So the killer waits inside the drywalled room. Benning enters. The killer whacks him on the head, and . . ." He lifted the mug to his lips but put it down without drinking.

He was avoiding looking at her. He'd been embarrassed earlier because he'd vomited and she hadn't. Typical male pride. "Reiser says he'll keep us informed. He doesn't mind our asking questions as long as we keep him informed, too, and don't step on his toes."

"Is he going to talk to the kid?"

"I suggested we do it, 'cause we already talked to him. I told Reiser about the letter Benning received. I said I'd let him know if Latent Prints finds anything."

"So how did the killer know where Benning worked?"

"The *Times'* write-ups on Benning's arrest mentioned it."

Phil nodded. "What about the murder weapon?"

"The ME says a fine-toothed saw or a serrated knife." Again she pictured the grisly scene. She swallowed hard. "Reiser's men didn't find a weapon. Nothing in the Dumpster, either. He thinks the killer brought it with him. I agree."

"The guy carried it around in broad daylight?" Phil's raised brows expressed skepticism.

"The house was under construction, so a guy with tools wouldn't stand out. Reiser's men checked with the neighbors in front and in back. No one noticed the guy or his car."

"He wasn't worried about the construction crew arriving?"

"Beverly Hills is strict. No construction before eight A.M. That gave the killer forty minutes. Plenty of time."

Phil twirled the mug between his hands. "Jessie, you think the same guy did Lewis and Benning?"

She slid off the desk. "Maybe the kid'll have some answers."

Gone were the smirk and the cocky pose of indifference. Gene Oppman was a young boy sitting rigidly on the living room sofa wedged between his parents. His hands were clutching the cushions. His face was pale. His eyes were saucers of fear.

"We have to ask you some questions, Gene," Jessie said, making sure to keep her voice free of accusation.

The boy nodded.

"Why were you helping Mr. Benning hide?"

The boy looked at his father. Robert Oppman nodded.

Gene said, "We were buddies. I got to know him when he came to speak to the group. He didn't have any kids, so he liked to talk to me." He shrugged. "Anyway, when he told me he needed to disappear for a couple of days, I told him about this empty store. He wasn't doing anything wrong." The last statement held a hint of his earlier defiance.

"Of course not." Jessie smiled. "Gene, since you were good friends, you might know things about Mr. Benning that could help us find who killed him. You want to help us, don't you?"

He blinked rapidly. "Yes."

"Was he bothered by anything recently?"

"He was scared. He thought the same person who blew up Lewis would do him." The boys eyes flashed. "I know it was one of those Jews that killed Mr. Benning. Why couldn't they leave him alone?"

Jessie wondered how Gene would react if he knew she was "one of those Jews." It was obvious from the boy's tone that Benning hadn't told him. Maybe Grace hadn't told her husband, either.

"Was there anything else troubling him?" Phil asked.

The boy hesitated. "He wasn't selling enough policies. That's 'cause this Jew they hired was taking all his clients away." A quick glance at Jessie to see her reaction. "After the parade'n being arrested'n everything, the manager wanted to fire him, and Mr. Benning said he'd take him to court if he tried to do that."

"It must've been hard for him, being away from his wife." Jessie was rewarded with the flicker of unease in Gene's eyes.

"I guess."

"He didn't talk about his wife?"

"Not too much." The boy moved his hands to his knees.

"You probably feel disloyal betraying his secrets, Gene," Jessie said softly, "but if there were problems between him and his wife, we have to know about it." She waited.

After a moment Gene mumbled, "He was upset, 'cause she was always on him. Like about not doing better at work. And about the parade." Here, his voice grew stronger. "She was pissed 'cause he pushed the old woman and now he was going to be on trial and he could end up in jail and where would she be? But it wasn't his fault, 'cause the woman hit him first. Mr. Benning wouldn't be dead if the Jewish woman hadn't hit him!"

"What else was his wife upset about?"

"Lots of stuff. He said that the only thing she loved about him was the money she'd get from the insurance when he died. But he was joking," Gene added quickly. "He liked to joke a lot."

"Did he mention anyone specific threatening him?" Phil asked.

Gene shook his head. "But he knew they were after him. The Jews, I mean. They got him arrested, and he knew they'd bribe the jury and the judges and he wouldn't have a chance. That's what Jews do." He threw Jessie a challenging look. "But he said he wasn't going to sit in jail for the rest of his life. He had a plan. He was excited about it, and a little scared, it seemed to me, and—" The boy broke off, flustered.

"What plan?" Jessie asked. Had Benning intended to flee?

"He was working it out in his head. But then they killed him, so it didn't matter." Tears streamed down his face.

"Was it Mr. Benning who asked you to harass Mr. Lewis with the phone calls?"

A mumbled "Yes."

"Why?"

"He knew Lewis didn't want to defend him, that's why. He knew Lewis thought he was better'n him. That's what Jews think of non-Jews, you know."

The logic of racism. Jessie sighed and put away her notepad.

Gene led Jessie and Phil to the vacant store where Benning had made his home since Friday. The back door lock was broken. At the side of a small, worn brown sofa in the back office, she found a black nylon gym tote with underwear, two tan knit shirts, a pair of brown slacks, a pair of gray sweats, and socks. In the tiny bathroom were a toothbrush, electric shaver, and a toiletries bag.

"I brought him the blanket." Gene's eyes brimmed again.

Jessie and Phil found no papers or other items that had belonged to Benning. The dead man's wallet and briefcase had been found near his body. On the way back to the Oppman house, Gene pointed out the apartment garage where Benning had parked his car.

An enterprising kid. It was a shame he was being influenced by the wrong people. "Is there anything else we should know, Gene?" she asked when they were standing in front of his house.

"No."

"If you remember anything, call me."

Jessie saw from his ravaged face that she didn't have to remind him that this time, he'd called too late.

Jessie followed Shulamit Cohn to a paneled room lined with bookcases. There were four rectangular tables in the center of the room. Piled on top of the tables were more books.

"I'll tell Ezra you're here." Shulamit left the room.

Jessie sat and picked up a book written in English that dealt with the laws of the Sabbath. She thumbed through the pages.

"Dafna told me you stopped by to question her yesterday."

Jessie hadn't heard Nathanson enter the room. She turned to face him. "That's my job."

"You lied to her." His eyes flashed as he walked around the table and slammed his palms on it. "You implied that I'd told you all the tragic details of my past so that she'd supply them to you. Is lying part of your job, too?"

"Sometimes." She met his eyes coolly. "Why didn't you tell me your parents and wife and unborn child burned to death in a fire?"

"It wasn't relevant to your investigation. It wasn't, if you'll excuse me, any of your damn business!" His face was red.

"The police suspected a neo-Nazi group of burning the cross that caused the fire. I'd say that's pretty damn relevant."

"They'd have to talk to anyone who's been harassed by neo-Nazis, wouldn't they? You'd have quite a few suspects, I think."

"Where were you this morning between seven and nine o'clock?"

Nathanson yanked a chair away from the table and flopped down onto it. "Don't you ever get tired of asking the same questions?"

"Sometimes. So where were you?"

"Who's dead now?" When Jessie didn't answer, he sighed and said, "At seven I was asleep. I got up at seven forty-five, showered, dressed, and went to synagogue for an eight-thirty *minyan*, a quorum of ten adult males required for communal prayer. I went home for breakfast, then came here. Satisfied?"

Not quite. He could've killed Benning, gone home to change clothes (given the circumstances of the murder, they would've been splattered with blood), and had plenty of time to go to synagogue. But could the man sitting in front of her have brutally murdered Benning at seven-thirty, then prayed to his God an hour later?

"I have a video from the news station that filmed the vandalizing of the Lewises' door," Jessie said. "Guess who I saw in the crowd? Your brother."

"My brother wasn't there." His hands were clenched.

"Tell that to the camera."

They stared at each other across the table. Through the walls of the room, she could faintly hear Shulamit Cohn's voice.

Finally Nathanson said, "That was me, not Joel."

"The man in the video wasn't wearing a skullcap."

"I removed it. I didn't want to be conspicuous."

"So you painted the *Mogen Dovid* on Barry Lewis's door and came back later to see the reaction to your handiwork?"

"No! I told you I didn't."

"You also told me you weren't near the Lewis house on the night of April second."

"I was afraid you'd suspect me if I admitted I was there."

"Why *were* you there?" When he didn't answer, she said, "You're lying now, aren't you? You're protecting your brother. That's him in the video."

"I'm not lying. I'm—" He broke off. "I bought a police scanner after the fire. I don't know why. Anyway, I was listening to it after I dropped Eileen off. When I heard about the vandalism on Monte Mar Drive, I knew it was Lewis's house."

"You said you sent your letters to Lewis to the ACLU office."

"Practically everybody in the Jewish community knew Lewis's address, Detective. At one point they were planning a picket."

"So let's see. You're late for a blind date because you have a flat. You take your date home early and detour to Beverly-wood to see a *Mogen Dovid*. You take off your skullcap so you won't be conspicuous." Jessie paused. "Does your Torah teach you it's all right to lie when it's convenient?"

"I lied about being there because I was frightened. I don't know why I went there. It seemed important at the time."

She knew he was watching her, gauging her reaction. She kept him waiting while she pretended to ponder what he'd told her. "It's bullshit, Mr. Nathanson," she said in a quiet voice, taking a perverse pleasure as he winced at her language.

"That's what happened."

Jessie tapped her pen against her notepad. "You're in serious trouble. You lied to me on several points. You have no alibi for the vandalizing. No alibi for Mr. Lewis's death."

"I told you—"

She put up her hand to silence him. "You could have gone to Mr. Lewis's home after you returned from your sister's." She leaned forward. "And you have no alibi for the brutal death this morning of Roy Benning."

Nathanson stared at her, his mouth open. "Benning is dead?"

He could be telling the truth. He could have practiced his "shocked" reaction for hours. "Someone cut off his head," she said, deliberately making no effort to soften the description.

He blanched and gripped the table with both hands. "And you think I did that?" he whispered. "That I'm capable of . . ." He looked away.

"You hated Benning because he was a neo-Nazi, and neo-Nazis killed your parents and wife."

"I didn't kill him." Nathanson was still not looking at her.

"Lewis was defending Benning," Jessie continued. "It's too coincidental to think their deaths aren't connected. Unless, of course, God is exacting retribution on the enemies of the Jews and killing them in very dramatic ways—one burns to death, the other is decapitated. Sounds almost biblical to me."

Nathanson jerked his head toward her. He opened his mouth, then quickly shut it.

"What were you going to say?" Jessie asked.

He was looking beyond her head, as if he hadn't heard her. With an abrupt motion, he pushed himself away from the table, the chair legs screeching on the linoleum. He stood and crossed the room. When he returned, he was holding a book. He sat down again.

"We say a special prayer on Rosh Hashanah and on Yom Kippur during *musaf*, the afternoon service. The prayer was composed about a thousand years ago by Rav Amnon of Mainz, Germany."

"Mr. Nathanson, I'm not here to learn about Judaism."

"Rav Amnon was an adviser and friend to the bishop of Mainz," Nathanson continued as if she hadn't spoken. "When the bishop demanded that he convert to Christianity, Rav Amnon, attempting to delay, said, 'Give me three days to consider your request.'"

"I don't see—"

"Please, let me finish," he said with quiet authority. "When Rav Amnon returned home, he was appalled that he'd given the bishop even the impression that he'd consider converting and betraying his God. He spent the three days atoning for his sin. He fasted. He prayed. He did not return to the bishop.

"The bishop had Rav Amnon brought to him. 'Why did you not return as you promised?' he demanded. Rav Amnon said, 'For the sin I committed in saying I would consider convert- ing, my tongue should be cut out.' 'Your sin is not in your tongue,' the bishop raged, 'but in your legs that did not bring you to me as you had promised. For that sin, your legs will be amputated.'"

Jessie winced at the image and wondered where this was leading.

"They cut off Rav Amnon's legs, joint by joint. They did the same to his hands. After each amputation, the bishop asked, 'Now will you convert?' Each time, the answer was, 'No.' Finally, Rav Amnon was carried home with his amputated parts. On Rosh Hashanah, a few days later, he asked to be carried to the Ark to sanctify God's name and recited the prayer he'd composed, *unesaneh tokef*. Then he died. Three days later he appeared in a dream to Rav Klonimos ben Meshullam, a great Talmudic and kabbalistic scholar of Mainz. Rav Amnon taught Rav Klonimus the prayer and asked that it be made part of the universal Rosh Hashanah liturgy. Later on, it was included in the Yom Kippur liturgy as well."

"That's an amazing story," she said softly. She was horrified by the brutality of the mutilation, moved by the martyr's courage and selfless devotion to his God. "But how does it relate to Barry Lewis's and Roy Benning's murders?"

"It probably doesn't. But the coincidence startled me."

"What coincidence?"

"The prayer discusses the holy court on the annual days of judgment. The second section asks simple yet terrifying questions: 'Who will live and who will die?' 'Who will die at his predestined time and who before his time?'" Nathanson had recited them by heart. Now he looked at Jessie. "You talked about Lewis burning to death and Benning being decapitated. The prayer lists ten forms of unnatural death. The second is 'who by fire.' The third is 'who by the sword.' In Judaic law, if a person was sentenced to die by the sword, he was decapitated."

Jessie tensed. "So you think there's a pattern?"

"No." Nathanson sighed his relief. "'Who by fire' isn't the first type of death mentioned in the prayer. The first is 'who by water.' Still, I think you can see why I was startled."

Jessie nodded. "What are the other types of death?"

"'Who by beast, who by famine, who by thirst, who by storm, who by plague, who by strangulation, who by stoning.'"

"Pretty strong stuff. Sounds like nobody has a chance."

He leaned forward. "The point of the prayer is that *everybody* has a chance. The coda proclaims that 'repentance, prayer, and charity will remove the evil of the decree.'"

"Unfortunately, it's too late for Lewis and Benning, isn't it?"

Chapter Forty-two

The receptionist at Premier Home Insurance had written down the name and phone number of the client who'd called Benning.

"I told all this to the other detective," she said to Jessie.

The woman's annoyance crackled through the phone receiver. Jessie didn't blame her. "Would you remind repeating it to me?"

A sigh. "His name is Herev." She gave Jessie a phone number that began with a 310 area code.

Jessie noted the information. "Did you recognize the caller?"

"Nope. She didn't sound familiar."

Jessie frowned. "She?"

"Mr. Herev's secretary."

"Could the caller have been Mrs. Benning?"

"I don't know. I'm new here. I've never talked to her."

Figures. "How did you reach Mr. Benning to tell him about the client?"

"I didn't. He called late Friday to say he wouldn't be available for a couple of days. On Monday, he called every couple of hours to check for his messages. I told Mr. Herev's secretary Mr. Benning would have to call *him*. She said that was fine, that he could reach Mr. Herev between four and four-thirty that afternoon. When Mr. Benning called, I gave him the information. I can't believe he's dead," she added almost as an afterthought.

"Thanks for your time." Jessie gave her the station phone number. "If you think of anything else—"

"She had an accent. I just remembered."

"What kind of accent?"

"I'm not good with that. Just an accent, you know?"

Jessie thanked her again, depressed the hook switch on her phone, and tried the number the receptionist had given her. After five rings, someone answered.

"Yeah?" a male voice said.

"Who am I speaking to?"

"The pay phone in the Beverly Center. Who the hell are you?"

Jessie hung up. "Thanks for your courtesy," she said aloud.

"Talking to yourself again?" Phil asked.

She turned toward him and smiled. "Long day. What'd you learn from the Beverly Hills PD?"

"You first." He pulled out his chair, hung his jacket around the back, and sat down.

Jessie repeated her conversation with Nathanson.

"So Nathanson lied, huh?" Phil shook his head. "He *was* there the night Lewis's house was vandalized. Think he did the star?"

"I think he thinks his *brother* did. That's why he went there that night, to protect Ben-Natan."

"Makes sense." Phil swiveled his chair gently back and forth, then said, "Spooky coincidence, that stuff in the prayers, huh?"

"Nathanson thought so, too. But there's no pattern, because the first death is by water. I also spoke to the receptionist at Premier Home Insurance." Jessie told Phil what she'd learned.

"Clever, calling from a shopping mall." Phil frowned. "What women involved in the case have accents?"

"Yaffa Aloni, Ben-Natan's Israeli girlfriend." Jessie had

immediately thought of her. "But anyone could put on an accent."

"Like?"

"Sheila Lewis. Or Hochburg's daughter-in-law."

"Or Grace Benning."

"The receptionist never talked to Grace, so she wouldn't need an accent."

Phil nodded. "You didn't see the shooter's face?"

Jessie shook her head. "Could have been a man or a woman. What did Reiser tell you?"

"Lemme get some coffee first." He took his mug and walked across the room. A minute later he was back. "They still haven't found the murder weapon," he said, sitting down. "They spoke to the construction crew and the supervisor—no one saw anyone suspicious hanging around." He took a sip of the coffee. "Hot!"

"The killer picked a good location. The house was under construction, and the covered exterior gave him privacy. So nothing interesting, huh?"

"One thing."

The phone rang. Phil answered it. "Homicide. Detective Okum." He listened, then handed Jessie the receiver. "Kraft," he mouthed.

She rolled her eyes. "Detective Drake. Can I help you?"

"Obviously not. I warned you Roy Benning was in danger. I told you he was terrified. Now he's dead, and I fear for my life."

"I appreciate your concern, Mr. Kraft. We're doing everything possible to find Mr. Benning's killer as quickly as possible."

"And in the meantime, what am I supposed to do? Barricade myself in my house? Hire an armed guard?"

"I think you should take whatever precautions you can."

"I asked you to arrest Ben-Natan. Had you done that, Roy Benning would still be alive."

"I appreciate your advice, Mr. Kraft."

"I don't like your tone, Detective. Nor your attitude."

Jessie found herself listening to a dial tone. "Another satisfied customer," she said as she replaced the receiver.

"What did the hit man want?"

"Cute." She smiled at the appellation. "He wants us to arrest Ben-Natan for Benning's murder."

Phil smacked his forehead. "The man's a genius! What the hell are we waiting for?"

Jessie grinned. "So what interesting thing did you learn?"

"Guess who supplied the lumber for the Palm house construction?" He locked his hands behind his neck.

Jessie shook her head.

"Lewis Lumber and Hardware Supply." Phil smiled. "As in Morris Lewis, father of the deceased."

"Shit," Jessie said.

"Is everything all right, Jess?" Helen's brow was furrowed.

"Everything's fine. I had a rough day, and I needed some company." She sat on one of the peach leather bar stools under the speckled peach-and-gray granite kitchen counter.

"What about Frank?" Helen put a plate into the dishwasher.

"He's busy," Jessie lied. She chose an apple from the wooden bowl on the counter and took a bite.

"Did you have supper yet?"

"I had a tuna sandwich." She'd also showered and changed into a pair of jeans and a sweater. She'd felt grimy and exhausted.

"That's lunch, not supper." Helen wiped her hands on a towel. "We had lasagna. I'll warm some up in the microwave."

Helen made terrific lasagna. "If it's no bother. Where's Neil?" She bit into the apple.

"In San Francisco, at an engineering conference." She took a Pyrex dish from the refrigerator and put it on the counter. "He'll be home tomorrow at noon. I told you he was going, remember?"

"Right. Sorry. How's Matthew? Recovered from his parties?"

Helen smiled. "Matthew's great. He's with Gary at the park right now, practicing with his new mitt." She lifted a large portion of lasagna onto a plate and carried it to the microwave.

Jessie frowned. "Do you think that's a good idea, having Gary spend so much time with Matthew?"

"It's not 'so much time.' It's a couple of practice sessions—they were part of the birthday gift, remember? And Matthew adores Gary. He always has."

"That's what I mean. Gary's not part of the family anymore. I don't think you should encourage him to come around so much. Matthew could get confused."

"Gary and I are friends, Jess. And in my opinion, Matthew's not the one who's confused."

The microwave *ping*ed. The doorbell rang.

"Get the door, will you, Jess? That's them."

"Sure." She walked down the hall and opened the front door.

"Hi, Aunt Jessie!" Matthew leaped at her and hugged her. "Uncle Gary and I had the greatest time. I'm getting better, right?" he asked Gary.

"You're gonna be a killer." Gary grinned. "How are you, Jess?"

"Fine." His Dodgers cap was on backward, and he looked damn cute in jeans and a sweatshirt. "Helen's in the kitchen."

"I have to do homework," Matthew announced. He grimaced, kissed Jessie again, then bounded up the carpeted stairs.

"Great kid." Gary watched him, then turned to Jessie. "I heard about Benning. Brutal." He shook his head. "The Beverly Hills PD hasn't been forthcoming. You know anything?"

She hesitated, then decided she no longer had to shield Gary from the dangers of her job. "I was there."

He frowned. "When?"

"Probably a couple of minutes after Benning was killed.

The killer shot at me. I shot at him." Or her. "We both missed."

"Jesus!" Gary whispered. "Are you okay?" He lifted his hand to her cheek and quickly dropped it.

She wouldn't have minded feeling his hand on her cheek. "I don't want to talk about it. I'm sorry."

"Whatever you say."

"Don't tell Helen. She'll freak out."

The lasagna was on the counter. Helen offered Gary a portion and heated a small square for herself. Jessie set out placemats on the breakfast room table. The three sat down and ate.

"Mom's been acting strange lately," Helen said when she'd finished. "She called on Saturday night after they got back to La Jolla. She called again on Sunday and Monday. Each time she asked if you and I had talked lately. What's up, Jess?"

"She and I had a long conversation."

"About what?"

"It's complicated."

"I can leave if you want privacy," Gary offered.

Jessie shook her head. "Actually, I was going to tell you, too, Gary."

"Tell him what?" Helen said with a hint of annoyance. "You're making this sound very mysterious."

Jessie took a sip of water. "You know that picture I found a while back, the one with Mom's Jewish relatives?"

"Not that again." Helen groaned.

"Your mother has Jewish relatives?" Gary said. "You never told me."

"It wasn't a big deal. Anyway, I was talking to her after Matthew's party on Friday night, and she told me the whole story." She paused and addressed her sister. "Mom's Jewish, Helen. She was born in Poland. Her parents left her with a Christian family."

Gary stared, openmouthed.

"You're making this up!" Helen exclaimed. "Mom was born in New York. If this is a joke—"

"It's not a joke. She was born in Poland. Her entire family

was killed in the war. She was adopted by American Jews who brought her to the States." Jessie related what Frances had told her.

No one spoke for several minutes. Jessie listened to the hum of the refrigerator and waited.

Finally Helen said, "Why did she tell you all this Friday night? If it's true, why didn't she tell both of us, before?"

Was that a hint of jealousy in her sister's voice? "I more or less forced it out of her, Helen. Mom didn't tell us because she basically reinvented herself. She felt abandoned. She was terrified and angry and confused. Rabbi Korbin told me that a lot of hidden children have a difficult time with their identity." And so do the children of hidden children, she thought.

"You talked to a rabbi?" Helen asked. "When?"

"He's the dean of the Simon Wiesenthal Museum. I met him because of the case I'm on."

"I can't believe this," Gary said. "I mean, I *believe* it, but I can't fathom it, you know? Your mother's so strong, so confident, so . . ."

Jessie knew. She took another sip of water.

"Well, fine," Helen said after another long silence, although her tone said otherwise. "I can understand Mom. She went through a horrible experience. She wanted to forget all about it." She nodded. "I think she did the right thing, the sensible thing, don't you, Jessie?" When Jessie didn't answer, Helen asked, "Does Dad know?"

"Yes." She leaned forward and covered her sister's hand with her own. "I went to the Museum of Tolerance on Sunday, Helen. They have an entire section on the Holocaust. It's very moving. I think you should go, too. I'll go with you, if you want." She had made the same offer to Frank. She wondered if he'd ever go.

Helen drew her hand away. "Why would I do that?"

"Because it's our history." She spoke more impatiently than she'd intended, still thinking about Frank. "It's important for you to know what happened to Mom and her family and all the Jews who died."

Helen shook her head and frowned. "The Holocaust is horrible and tragic, but Mom didn't want to tell us about it. She must've had a good reason."

"But now we *know*, Helen. We can't deny what we know."

"This doesn't involve me! If you want to get into this, fine. *I* think you're obsessing. As far as I'm concerned, nothing's changed." She took Jessie's and Gary's plates and stacked them on her own.

"You're Jewish, Helen. Doesn't that change things?"

Helen shook her head. "I'm Episcopalian, like Dad. Mom's Episcopalian, too."

"She's not. She never converted. If Mom's Jewish, we're completely Jewish. So is Matthew, because you are."

"Who told you that, another rabbi?" Helen turned to Gary. "Gary, you're Jewish. What would you say if someone told you that you were Catholic because they found out your mother was Catholic? You'd say they were crazy, right?"

"Helen, this is between you and Jessie. I think I should go." He moved his chair back.

Helen faced Jessie. "It doesn't matter if Mom didn't convert. She raised us as Episcopalians. That's what we are. That's what Matthew is. This entire conversation is ridiculous." She lifted the dishes. "I want your promise that you're not going to say *one word* about this to Neil or Matthew."

"It's not my place to say anything, Helen. Eventually, Matthew has a right to know."

"There is nothing to know! Matthew is *not* Jewish."

"If he'd been living in a Nazi-occupied country, Hitler would have killed him, too."

Helen slammed the dishes onto the table. Her face was white. "That's a horrid, horrid thing to say! I can't believe you'd say something so vile! I thought you *loved* Matthew!" She shoved her chair away from the table and ran out of the room.

Jessie's eyes teared. She took the plates to the sink and turned on the faucet.

"You were rough on her," Gary said.

"I know." She rinsed the top plate and placed it on the drainboard. "The conversation didn't go the way I'd planned." She wiped her eyes with the back of her hand.

"It's a huge shock. She's right about that." He was standing beside Jessie now. He rested his hand on the nape of her neck. "Give her time to think things through."

Jessie nodded.

"Any time you want to talk, call me. Promise?"

She turned and leaned her head against his chest. His arms went around her. Strong, comforting. She lifted her face and kissed him on the mouth.

He pulled away. "Was that friendship or something more?"

He sounded a little angry. She didn't blame him if he was. "I don't know."

"What about your detective?"

"I don't know that, either."

"You can't go around changing the rules of the game all the time, Jess. You can't assume I'm going to be there, waiting."

"You're right. I'm sorry." She looked away.

He walked to the doorway and turned. "When you figure it all out, let me know."

On the evening news she watched camera shots of the exterior of the house on Palm and listened to the anchors reveal the grisly details of the murder. Images of Benning intruded on her mind long after she turned off the TV. When the phone rang after midnight, she was still awake. She brought the receiver to her ear.

"Hello?"

"It's me, Gary. Sorry if I woke you."

"I wasn't sleeping." She relaxed against her pillow, pleasantly surprised that he'd called, wondering what he was going to say.

"The paper faxed me some news I thought you'd want to hear."

"What is it?" She propped herself up on one elbow, instantly alert.

"Judge Phoebe Williams was found dead at her house in Palm Springs."

Jessie sat upright. "Jesus! When did it happen? Today?"

"Apparently she's been dead for five or six days. The gardener found her. He——"

"She drowned in her pool, didn't she?" Jessie's heart was pounding in her throat.

"How the hell did you know that? Are you psychic? Answer me, Jessie!"

Who by water. . . .

Chapter Forty-three

"You think I'm next, don't you, Detective Drake?" Rita Warrens asked, panic whistling through her veneer of calm.

"I don't know that at all. Given the connection between Lewis, Benning, and Judge Williams, it seems probable that we're dealing with one killer who targeted the people he or she holds directly responsible for the parade and Mrs. Hochburg's death."

"I'm the one who originally met with the White Alliance."

"Yes, but Barry Lewis is the name associated with the case, not yours. Your home wasn't vandalized. You didn't receive death threats."

"Then why are you calling me?"

"Because I can't second-guess the killer, and I felt you should be informed. And careful."

"Have you notified Emery Kraft? He could be a target, too."

"I plan to." She dreaded talking to the "hit man" again—maybe she'd have Phil call.

"Should I go to my ranch until this is over?"

Judge Williams had gone away, too—on a long-awaited vacation, according to her clerk. Now she was dead. The preliminary report was accidental drowning. The Palm Springs police were taking a closer look now that Jessie had told them about Lewis and Benning and the connection among the three.

"Does your ranch have a security system?" Jessie asked.

"No. Out there, you don't really need security systems."

Nowadays, you needed security systems everywhere. "Do people know where your ranch is?"

"Everybody in the office does. They tease me about it, call me Annie Oakley. They know I go every weekend. Why?"

"For now, I'd stay in the city. Make sure you set your alarm all the time. Be careful about opening your door. Have someone pick you up for work and drive you home. Stuff like that."

"You're scaring me, Detective Drake."

"That's my intention, Miss Warrens."

Jessie hung up and went to the restroom. She was returning to her desk when Espes motioned to her. Not again, she thought wearily as she joined him in his office.

"Have a seat," he ordered. "How's the investigation going?"

Was this the prelude to another tirade? "Detective Okum and I are pursuing all possible leads," she said, sitting down.

"So I gathered from your detailed report." Espes leaned back. "Emery Kraft just called. He doesn't like your attitude."

Jessie tensed.

"He says you've been rude, that you've minimized his concerns about his safety. He claims you ignored information he gave you that could've saved Benning's life. He believes that because you're Jewish, you're unable to conduct this investigation with any degree of objectivity—that you don't give a shit about who killed Benning or, for that matter, Barry Lewis. Any comments?"

She forced herself to speak calmly. "Kraft wanted me to arrest Ben-Natan. I told him we didn't have evidence to support that action. Kraft wants protection. I suggested that he contact the Pasadena PD. My being Jewish is in no way interfering with my professionalism or my determination to find the person who killed Lewis and Benning." She hesitated, then thought, What the hell; she was tired of Espes and his games. She said, "Emery Kraft is an arrogant, dangerous, anti-Semitic son of a bitch, and yes, I was rude. I intimated that I don't like anti-Semites. Sir." Her face was hot. She didn't care.

"More or less what I said. Except I didn't intimate." Espes smiled at her surprise. "And I told Kraft not to tell one of my detectives how to do her job."

She would never understand Espes, not in a million years.

"I read your memo about Judge Williams. Pretty wild, a killer using a different MO for each victim based on some Jewish prayer. You're sure her death is linked to Lewis and Benning?"

"Her ruling allowed the parade to take place. Her death fits the pattern—'death by water' is the first one in the prayer."

"Couldn't be a coincidence?"

"I don't think so. Why did the killer decapitate Benning? He could've just shot him. And why shoot at me? He could've run out the back way. Why risk getting caught? It only makes sense if he did it to buy time so he could decapitate Benning—to do it right, according to the prayer."

Espes nodded. "Any trouble with Beverly Hills PD?"

"They're being very cooperative. We're sharing information."

"Good. Let me know what's happening."

Phil was waiting when Jessie returned to her desk. "In with the dragon again?"

She told him about her conversation with the lieutenant.

"No shit! Espes to the defense?" He grinned and shook his head. Then he said, "SID just phoned. No prints on the bomb fragments or the gas tank or anything they recovered."

"Figures." Jessie sat down. "Anything on the Angel of Death letter Grace Benning gave me?"

"I just called Latent Prints. Not yet. You know it can take seventy-two hours. I spoke to Reiser. They got a call from one of Benning's neighbors who thinks she saw Hochburg watching the house Monday morning. She recognized him from the television news."

The butcher was an overnight celebrity. "Hochburg said he wasn't there."

"So maybe he lied. And if he lied about being there Monday . . . Did you see him with that cleaver?" Phil raised an imaginary knife and brought it down with a quick, slicing motion.

Thwack. Jessie nodded. "And Hochburg's an Orthodox Jew. He'd be familiar with the prayer and the order of the deaths it lists."

"That's one thing I don't get," Phil said, patting his mustache.

"Just one?" Jessie grinned. "I can name a dozen."

He smiled. "Why *did* Nathanson tell you about this stuff? He had to figure he'd be pointing the finger at someone Jewish. Like his brother, for instance. You said Ben-Natan isn't religious anymore, but he'd know all about this prayer."

She'd given this some thought. "Either Nathanson isn't the killer and didn't think there *was* a pattern and was so startled by the coincidence that he mentioned it to me without thinking. . . ."

Phil nodded. "Or?"

"Or he *is* the killer. In which case, he tells me about the pattern to divert suspicion from himself—the why-would-I-point-the-finger-at-myself? routine. He's playing games with us, showing how clever he is. 'Catch me if you can'—that kind of stuff."

"The question is, can we?"

"Can't you stay out of trouble, Jessie?" Manny shook his head. "I'm getting an ulcer listening to what's been happening to you in the past four days."

She'd phoned and told Manny she had to see him. Now she was sitting in the familiar room at Parker Center where she'd been at least a dozen times before.

"It's been grand." She smiled. "You sound like my mother."

"The last time we talked, you said you were going to discuss things with her. Did you?"

"As a matter of fact, yes." She spoke and watched shock, then pity, ripple across Manny's kind face as she narrated Frances's story.

"I'm speechless," he told her when she had finished. "Which for me, as you know, is not a typical condition." He was silent for a moment, drawing circles on the pad in front of him. "Hidden children are often forgotten victims of the Holocaust. They had to live in silence, in isolation. They had to pretend they didn't exist so they wouldn't be found and endanger the families who were sheltering them. Most of the Christians who took in Jewish children were kind and caring, by the way, unlike the woman your mother lived with."

Jessie nodded. "My mom said that, too."

"Many of the children came to love their new families, you know. Some refused to return to their Jewish parents. A heartbreak for the child and the parents. Some Christian families gave up the Jewish child only under duress." He drew a series of boxes. "I've talked to adults who were hidden. They still have feelings of uncertainty, a lack of identity. I know of one case where the child went to synagogue *and* to church for years." He paused and looked at Jessie. "You realize that your mother's history explains a lot about her pattern of abusive behavior with you and Helen?"

"It doesn't erase what happened, Manny, but at least I can understand it better. I feel so sorry for her."

He nodded. "Understanding is a step toward building a better relationship. Sympathy can't hurt." He smiled.

"You know what's strange? My mother insists she's not Jewish, yet I'm almost positive she named me for her mother. 'Jessica' in Hebrew is 'Yiska.' That was my grandmother's name."

"It's not strange. It's revealing. She couldn't quite give up her Jewish identity. How do you feel about it?"

"I like it," Jessie said quietly. "It makes me feel connected to these people I never knew. I told Frank I was Jewish," she added, "and Helen."

"Good for you!" Manny smiled. "And?"

"Frank said it doesn't matter to him, but I know it does." She could still see him staring at her, as if she were a stranger.

"I'm sorry." Manny tented his fingers. "You're sure?"

"Pretty sure. Helen doesn't want to be Jewish. It upsets her."

He nodded. "What about you?"

"It doesn't *upset* me, but I'm confused. All my life I thought I was Episcopalian. Suddenly I'm not. Is being Jewish genetic or spiritual, Manny?"

"I can't answer that, Jessie. You'll have to work it out for yourself."

"I'm trying to. I bought a beginner's book on Judaism. I started reading it and found it interesting. Then I wondered if I was doing it to get back at my mom. She wouldn't exactly be thrilled if she knew about my interest in Judaism."

"Is that why you're doing it?"

She thought for a moment, then said, "No. At least I don't think so. There's something about Judaism that appeals to me. I want to explore that feeling. My mom wants to go on as if nothing's changed. So does Helen. But everything *has* changed."

"Go easy on Helen, Jessie. Your mother's revelation must've come as a shock to her. *I'm* shocked. You've been thinking about this for a while and you *still* have questions. Give her time."

"That's what Gary said."

Manny's eyebrows rose. "Gary again?"

"Maybe." She felt herself blushing. "Enough personal stuff. I need your professional help. What you can tell me about the mind-set of a Holocaust survivor confronted with the parade, with Benning? All of it."

The psychologist frowned. "You think a survivor could be the killer?"

"It's possible. There's Samuel Hochburg, the son of the woman who died after the parade. He was with a group of partisans blowing up bridges when he was eleven years old. That was after his father was killed, right in front of him."

Freiberg sighed. "Who else?"

"Mark Pell of the OJA is a survivor, but his alibi will probably check out. There's Morris Lewis, Barry Lewis's father. Hochburg told me Lewis offered to pay for his mother's funeral."

"Atoning for the son." Freiberg removed his glasses and massaged the bridge of his nose. "Did I tell you I used to treat mostly survivors?"

Jessie shook her head.

"That was years ago, when I worked at the Jewish Federation. I still do it one afternoon a week." He put his glasses back on. "You know what's funny? I can help strangers, but I can't help my parents. They have the numbers tattooed on their arms, but they can't talk about the camps. My mother still has nightmares that they're coming to take her to the gas chambers. She won't take a shower to this day. Only baths."

Jessie didn't know to respond to the pain and frustration in the psychologist's voice.

"You know what I found most of my patients had in common?" Manny leaned forward. "Guilt. Tremendous, overwhelming guilt. They survived while others didn't. They didn't do enough. They didn't stop the genocide."

"But that isn't logical. How could they have stopped it?"

"Since when is guilt logical?" He smiled, then sat back. "You asked me how a survivor would react to neo-Nazis parading in his neighborhood? He'd see it as an encroachment on his protected turf. He'd feel abandoned by his government, just as Germany abandoned him then. And he'd feel the need to repay the debt of having survived while others didn't, to demonstrate that he won't be a victim again."

" 'Never again'?"

He nodded. "Exactly. The mantra of the JDL. And the Shield."

"Ben-Natan changed his name from Nathanson, did I tell you that?"

"'Ben-Natan' is an Israeli name. 'Nathanson' is European Jewish. Israel represents victory, assertiveness, independence. Europe represents the shtetl Jew, the victim."

Jessie thought that over. "I see what you're saying, about the survivors. Pell was very outspoken when I met with him. He wanted to take a physical stand against the paraders. Hochburg reviled Barry Lewis in court. He attacked one of the skinheads marching in the parade. So did his mother."

Freiberg nodded. "It made him feel he was a master of his situation, not a passive victim. Still, the fact that the neo-Nazis were allowed to parade must have terrified him and forced him to relive old traumas."

"What about Morris Lewis?"

Manny sighed. "Here the guilt must be crippling. He survived while others didn't, and now his son defends the enemy?" He shook his head. "I can't imagine what he's going through."

"But could he have killed his son?"

"If he thought he was redeeming himself and atoning for the lives of those who perished?" Manny shrugged. "Anything is possible. You've been a detective long enough to know that."

"How does what you've told me fit in with the list of deaths in the prayer Nathanson told me about?"

"*Unesaneh tokef.* 'Who will live, who will die.' In my synagogue, you can hear a pin drop when the cantor sings this prayer. It always gives me the chills, I can tell you." He stroked his chin. "Does it fit? It fits perfectly with the idea of repaying the debt for having survived, of being a master of one's situation. And it fits with the Angel of Death. Maybe the killer has convinced himself that he *is* the Angel of Death, God's messenger of retribution."

"Can I ask you something personal, Manny?" When he nodded, she said, "At the restaurant you wore a skullcap, which I guess means you're observant. Are your parents observant, too, or did they feel abandoned by God, like my mother?"

"My parents kept their Orthodox faith. But a lot of survivors didn't. I certainly can't judge them."

"I walked through the museum, Manny. I learned what happened to six million Jews. I asked myself, Where was God during the Holocaust? Where was He when the Germans took away my family?"

Manny sighed. "A lot of people have asked that question, Jessie. The real question is, where was *man* during the Holocaust?"

"You have no idea how Judge Williams was looking forward to this vacation," the black-haired clerk told Jessie. Her eyes were tearing. "I just can't believe she's dead."

"When did Judge Williams leave?"

"Friday afternoon, April twentieth. The day of that parade."

"Were you in touch with her?"

"Oh, yes." She nodded vigorously. "She called in on Monday to check her messages." The clerk hesitated. "To tell you the truth, I didn't give her all of them. A lot of people phoned, angry about what happened to Mrs. Hochburg at the parade, but I didn't see the point in bothering the judge on her vacation."

"Did any of the callers identify themselves?"

"Some did. I wrote down their names." She pulled over a spiral notebook and found the page she was looking for. "Councilman Perkins," she read. "Mark Pell of the Organization of Jewish Associations. Ms. Lesley Wittiger of the Anti-Defamation League. Mr. Ben-Natan of the Shield of Jewish Protectors. Rabbi Sheldon Korbin. Mr. Emery Kraft." The clerk glanced up. "Mr. Kraft called to say he supported the judge's decision." She turned the page. "On Monday, Samuel Hochburg called, three times."

"What did Mr. Hochburg say?"

"When I told him she was out of town and would be back in two weeks, he asked me where he could reach her. I told him he couldn't. I would *never* give out Judge Williams's home number or personal information." She looked at Jessie for confirmation.

Jessie nodded. "That was it?"

"No. He said, 'Please ask the judge how she feels knowing she's responsible for the death of an innocent woman.'" The clerk sighed. "I didn't blame him for being angry. Of course, I didn't give the judge his message."

"Was Judge Williams worried for her safety after the parade?"

"Not really. She told me she knew emotions would run high, but she figured they'd die down. They always do."

Not this time. "Did she get any specific threats?"

"Just the letter. I *did* tell her about that."

Jessie frowned. "What letter?"

The woman stood, walked to the file cabinet, and returned with a white envelope. "I asked did she want me to give it to the police, but she said she'd deal with it when she came back." She handed the envelope to Jessie.

Jessie opened it and, touching only the edges, unfolded the letter inside. A red Star of David had been drawn in the center. Below it was a simple message: "Prepare for the Angel of Death."

"When did this arrive?"

"Monday." The woman frowned. "Did I do wrong? Should I have given this to the police right away?"

"It probably wouldn't have made a difference," Jessie said, not knowing any such thing. "I'll take this. I'll need your fingerprints for purposes of identification."

She accompanied the clerk downstairs to have her prints rolled onto a card. Then she returned to Parker and took the Angel of Death letter and the clerk's prints to Latent Prints on the second floor.

"I sent over another letter on Monday," Jessie told a thin,

gangly, male technician named George. "Did you raise any prints?"

"What's the case number?"

She gave him the number allocated to the investigation of Barry Lewis's murder and waited while he checked.

A moment later he was back. "We tried the DFO, but—"

"What's DFO? I thought you used ninhydrin." It had a god-awful smell.

"We still do, after the DFO. The technical name is one-point-eight-diazafluoren-nine-one. Don't ask me to spell it." George smiled. "We can get pretty quick results with it, depending on the amino acid residue from the fingers. Anyway, the DFO didn't raise anything on your letter, so we did the ninhydrin. We might have something later today."

"What about *this* letter?" She pointed to the evidence envelope containing the letter mailed to Judge Williams. "Can you try the DFO on it now? It could be urgent." It could be nothing.

"Everything's always urgent. I've got tons of stuff to do before I get to yours. What case is this?"

"It's connected to the guy who was decapitated yesterday."

"Shit." He grimaced. "Okay. Let's do it."

She followed him to the lab. He put on gloves, took a Pyrex dish, and filled it with liquid from a large brown bottle. The liquid had a pale yellowish tinge and a chemical odor.

"The DFO crystals form a liquid when they're mixed with methanol alcohol," he explained. "We store it in brown bottles so it won't evaporate." Making sure the flap was unfolded, he dipped the envelope and letter into the liquid, then slid the Pyrex dish onto a shelf inside a glass-enclosed unit with a vent hood. "You don't want to inhale. The stuff's toxic, possibly carcinogenic."

Lovely, Jessie thought, listening to the vacuum as it sucked up the vapors.

A few seconds later he removed the Pyrex dish, lifted out the letter and envelope, which had turned light pink, and inserted both upright into holders.

"Now what?" she asked.

"We wait for them to dry. Then we examine them under a laser light—we don't want to overdevelop any prints that are there. Then we do the whole process again."

Several minutes later, he removed the twice dipped, twice dried letter and envelope and brought them to a table. He inserted the letter between two sheets of soft paper towels and applied an iron set to a low temperature.

"High-tech equipment," he said, noticing Jessie's skeptical glance at the iron. He smiled. "The heat penetrates the towel and reacts with the chemicals in the treated paper."

Under the laser light, yellow prints emerged on the front of the paper. "Looks like both thumbs. See how the ridges flow up and in toward the body?" He reversed the paper. "More prints here. Doesn't look like this person tried to avoid leaving any."

Probably the judge's clerk's prints, Jessie decided with a surge of disappointment. "That's it?"

"We'll try the ninhydrin, but we'll have to leave that overnight. Those'll show up purple under regular light. We can use zinc chloride afterward to enhance any prints we find. Then we look under the laser again."

The envelope, too, was covered with prints.

"I'll check these against the prints on the card you gave me. If I don't find a match, any suspects you want me to try?"

"Joel Ben-Natan and Samuel Hochburg." Jessie spelled the names. "Their prints are on file. I'll call you with their booking numbers." Ben-Natan had a record; Hochburg had been arrested and printed for assaulting the skinhead during the parade.

"That's it?"

"Also, Ezra Nathanson. His sister said North Hollywood printed everyone in the family in connection with a fire that killed his wife and parents. They'd still have the prints." Before coming downtown, Jessie had called the division. The detectives in charge of the Nathanson case were no longer there—

one had moved out of state; another had retired. The man Jessie spoke to had promised to locate the file and fax her a copy.

"Hochburg is pretty recent," she added. "His prints may not be in AFIS yet," she said, referring to the department's automated fingerprint identification system.

George nodded. "If we don't find anything in the local AFIS, we can try the county or the state. I'll call as soon as I know anything."

Jessie thanked him and left. Rush hour traffic to West L.A. was heavy on the Santa Monica Freeway, and she had plenty of time to think about the fingerprints and her conversation with Manny.

Back at the station, she called Latent Prints and gave George the booking numbers for Ben-Natan and Hochburg. She called Helen but the line was busy. Probably just as well. Then, after checking her notes, she called Rabbi Korbin.

"He's on another line," the receptionist told Jessie. "Would you like to wait or leave a message?"

"I'll wait." She kicked off her shoes, flexed her cramped toes, and ate a granola bar.

A few minutes later, Korbin came on the line. "Sorry I kept you waiting, Detective. How can I help you?"

"Hello, Rabbi. I had a question I thought you could answer. Does the word *herev* mean anything in Hebrew?"

"Yes. *Herev* or *cherev*, depending on the pronunciation, means sword. Does that help?"

"I think so. Thanks." It certainly explained "Mr. Herev," Benning's nonexistent client. Clever. "One more thing. What's the Hebrew name for Helen? This has nothing to do with my investigation. I'm just curious."

"Helen? There are a number of possibilities. Hindl is one. Chava is another. Chaya. Chana. If I knew more specifically what you were looking for, I could be of better help."

"Those names are fine." "Chaya" sounded familiar, but Frances had pointed to so many faces, said so many names. "Thank you."

"Speaking of names, Detective, I just spoke with Morris

Lewis. He's making a large donation to the Wiesenthal in memory of his relatives who died in the Holocaust. He also wants to list Lola Hochburg. He's going through a terrible time, poor man."

More atonement?

Jessie said good-bye, hung up, and wrote "MORRIS LEWIS?" on a piece of paper. In her mind she watched him again, effortlessly lifting the sheet of plywood, and wondered why he'd delivered a doll house to his granddaughters when he knew they weren't home.

She drew a large Star of David around his name.

Chapter Forty-four

Frank called on Wednesday night. He was coming down with a cold, he told Jessie, and wanted to take a rain check on the Museum of Tolerance.

She was disappointed, but not really surprised. She told him she hoped he felt better and recommended vitamin C, and wished there were a tablet that would heal their ailing relationship.

"Talk to you soon, sweetheart," he said, and she realized with a sense of loss that she wasn't sure she wanted to.

Thursday morning, George from Latent Prints informed Jessie that they'd matched prints on the letter sent to Benning.

She felt a rush of excitement. "Whose are they?"

"Samuel Hochburg."

"*Hochburg?* What about the letter I gave you yesterday?"

"Nothing yet. It hasn't even been twenty-four hours."

She thanked George, hung up, phoned Reiser, and told him about the letter. "Any confirmation about the neighbor who saw Hochburg across the street from Benning's house Monday morning?"

"I was about to call you. Yeah, we have confirmation. Another neighbor noticed a man in a car parked across the street from Benning's place Monday morning. She thought it was strange, so she noted the license plate number. Just in case."

"Hochburg's?"

"Yeah. By the way, this is West L.A.'s case now. Have fun."

"He's got motive," Jessie told Espes. "He knows about explosives. He could've used any knife from his shop to decapitate Benning." He could be using the murder weapon this very minute to prepare meat orders for some unsuspecting customer. Gruesome.

Phil said, "I say we get a search warrant. If we tell Hochburg we want to bring him in and he says no, by the time we get back to him, he could be gone. With the murder weapon. The killer's done three so far. What if he's got others in mind?"

"Who else would he be after?" Espes asked.

"Emery Kraft," Jessie said. "Rita Warrens."

Espes rolled a pencil between his fingers for a moment, then put it down. "Do it."

"You brought reinforcements?" Samuel Hochburg asked Jessie. His smile was pinched, his eyes wary.

"This is Detective Reiser from the Beverly Hills Police Department. He's assisting us in our investigation." Thank God there were no customers in the store. The grandson and his toys were nowhere in sight.

"I told you what I know." Hochburg spooned ground beef from a tub onto a sheet of white wax paper on a scale, checked the weight, and added more beef.

"We have some more questions," Phil said in a mild tone. "We'd like you to come down to the station to answer them."

"We can't talk here? I have an order to fill for a customer who's coming in half an hour."

"The station would be better."

Hochburg stared at him, then turned to Jessie. "This is official, yes?"

Jessie nodded. She noticed several knives on the wooden block behind the butcher. Was one of them the murder weapon?

"And if I don't want to answer more questions?" His hands shook as he slid the wax paper off the scale onto the counter and wrapped the package of meat.

"We're arresting you for the murders of Barry Lewis and Roy Benning," she said.

Hochburg licked his lips. "Can I see the arrest warrant?"

"We don't need an arrest warrant. We—"

"Why not? I don't have rights anymore?"

"Come on, Mr. Hochburg," Reiser said. "Let's go."

"I asked a question." Again, he turned to Jessie. "I'm entitled to an answer."

"The law states that if there's probable cause, we can arrest a person on the street or in public, which includes a place of business," she explained patiently. "We *do* have a search warrant for this shop and your residence." Obtaining the warrant had taken two hours. Jessie had filled out the form, typed up the affidavit listing the circumstances justifying the warrant, and driven downtown to have it signed by a municipal judge.

"I didn't kill Benning! I didn't kill Lewis!" Hochburg's face was pale. "What's my crime, that I'm upset because my mother died? That I'm a Jew who didn't want Nazis parading in my neighborhood? That's against the law now in this country?"

"Mr. Hochburg, we'd like you to come with us now, please. We can talk at the station. You can explain everything."

Hochburg nodded. "Sure. Fine. Can I call a lawyer?"

"You can do that at the station." Phil took a small card from his wallet and read, "You have the right to remain silent. If you waive the right—"

"I know, I know. Fancy words." Hochburg wiped his hands on his stained apron. "I'll lock up the back and get my jacket."

"I'll have to accompany you," Jessie said.

Hochburg nodded again. "No problem." As he walked the length of the counter, he untied his apron and slipped it over his head.

With her hand on the gun in her holster, Jessie followed the butcher into a dank-smelling room with a row of large sinks. Above the plastic cutting boards lay a bloody, partially cut side of beef. Next to the beef were two large knives. Jessie tightened her grip on her gun.

Hochburg hung his apron on a wall hook. "This will spoil." He pointed to the beef. "I'll be out hundreds of dollars. Can I put it in the freezer?" He gestured to a metal door to the right.

Before she could say no, he hoisted the carcass off the board. He took two steps toward the door, then pivoted.

She whipped her gun out.

He hurled the carcass at her.

She fired. The bullet embedded itself in the carcass as it knocked her backward to the wet, slippery floor and landed on top of her, a hundred pounds of dead steer forcing her to the ground in a macabre embrace.

Her head struck the concrete. She heard Phil's yell, then two sets of running footsteps. Her nose and mouth were in the cavity of the carcass. Trying not to inhale, she grunted and pushed against the dead weight. Suddenly it lifted.

"You okay?" Phil exclaimed after he tossed aside the carcass.

She scrambled to her feet, ignoring her partner's offered hand. Her head was smarting. So was her pride. "Where's Hochburg?" She glanced at the wooden board. One large knife was missing.

"Reiser ran into the alley after him. I'll check the street."

"*I'll* check the street. You help Reiser. Hochburg has a knife." She ran into the front room of the butcher shop and out the door onto Fairfax Avenue.

To her left were a bank and an open parking lot, to her right a row of stores. The street was crowded with pedestrians— young women in skirts, some pushing strollers, others holding on to toddlers; several young men with no apparent destination; older men and women carrying plastic grocery bags.

"Police!" Jessie yelled, turning right, holding her gun downward at a forty-five degree angle.

The crowd parted for her. An obese homeless man sitting in front of a bakery watched as she raced by. She darted into a shoe store and swiftly surveyed the people inside. Frightened stares, but no Hochburg. She checked the neighboring stationery shop, then a pizza shop. At a produce store she fought her way past wide, clear plastic strips that slapped at her as she entered.

No sign of the knife-wielding butcher.

She was exiting a luggage shop when she sighted Hochburg down the block, sprinting from underneath a store awning toward a bus with open doors. She aimed, then lowered her gun as he shoved his way ahead of the queue of boarding passengers.

She was two hundred feet away. Her heart was pounding against her chest wall and her head was throbbing as she charged down the block toward the bus.

She was eighty feet away. She couldn't see the knife.

"Hochburg!"

He was on the second to the bottom step of the bus. He swiveled toward her, then tried to elbow his way around the two women in front of him.

She was forty feet away.

Hochburg jumped off the bus step onto the sidewalk, barreling into the people in his way, the knife clutched in his right hand. He ran to the end of the block and turned the corner.

Jessie rounded the corner seconds later. The street was empty. "Stop or I'll shoot!" she yelled.

He continued running.

Jessie fired into the air.

Hochburg came to an abrupt halt.

"Drop the knife!"

His hands shot up. His knife clattered to the sidewalk.

Jessie approached him warily. "Don't turn around. Lower your hands slowly onto your head."

Hochburg obeyed. "Don't shoot. Please."

Fifty feet ahead of Hochburg, Reiser and Phil entered the street from the alley. They stood with their feet apart, their guns aimed at the butcher.

"Don't shoot! Don't shoot!"

"Get down on your knees," she ordered. "Place your hands behind your back."

She walked up to him and held her gun to his head. With her other hand, she took the cuffs from her pants pocket and snapped them onto his wrists just as she'd done on April 20.

For Samuel Hochburg, the parade was over.

Chapter Forty-five

"What the hell happened to you?" Espes stared at Jessie's blood-streaked, camel-colored sweater and slacks.

She was tired of the question—everyone in the station had asked her the same thing. A reporter who happened to be nearby while Hochburg was being booked had snapped her picture. She could imagine Frances's reaction if the photo made the La Jolla papers.

Jessie told the lieutenant about the side of beef.

"Good thing you're okay." He coughed and covered his mouth.

The others had tried to hide their smiles, too. She supposed there was something funny about having a bloody carcass thrown at her, but she wasn't ready to laugh about it. Yet.

In the restroom, she washed the blood off her face and hands, then changed into a pair of jeans and a red sweater that she kept in her locker. When she brushed her hair, she yelped. Touching the back of her head, she felt a tender swelling.

"Rita Warrens phoned while we were picking up Hochburg," Phil told Jessie when she returned to her desk. "Hochburg's attorney is on the way, and Hochburg wants to talk to you."

The phone rang. "He'll have to wait, won't he?" Jessie sat

down and picked up the receiver. "Homicide. Detective Drake."

"This is Emery Kraft, Detective. I just received a letter from the so-called Angel of Death. I want someone to pick it up and check it for fingerprints. And I want police protection!"

Jessie sighed and rolled her eyes at Phil. "Mr. Kraft, you'll be happy to know we've just made an arrest in the case."

"You arrested Joel Ben-Natan! It's about time!"

The information would soon be on the news, if it wasn't already. "Not Ben-Natan. Samuel Hochburg."

Kraft was silent for a moment. "I assume you have proof?"

"I can't discuss the case at this time. You understand."

Phil was making funny faces. Jessie almost laughed aloud.

"Well, I must admit I'm surprised. I was so sure . . ." Kraft paused again. "I was no doubt swayed by Roy's conviction that Ben-Natan was carrying an earlier grudge."

Jessie frowned. "What grudge?"

"Roy didn't say. I assumed he meant an earlier altercation with the Shield. But it doesn't matter now. Roy is dead, and Hochburg is in custody. My congratulations. I underestimated you, and I was wrong. Shall I dispose of the letter, then?"

"Hold on to it, please. I'll have someone pick it up." If Hochburg's prints showed up, the case would be tighter.

"Any time today would be satisfactory, Detective. Tomorrow, I shall be occupied with a planning session for our History Is Truth annual conference. Shall I send you a brochure?"

Jessie wanted to tell him where to stick his brochure. She said good-bye, depressed the hook switch, and punched the numbers for the ACLU office. When the receptionist answered, Jessie asked for Rita Warrens. A moment later the director came on the line.

"Detective Drake? A woman in my office just heard on the radio that you arrested someone for Barry's murder. Is it true?"

"That's why I'm calling. I promised I'd keep you informed."

"Just today, I received a letter like the one Barry got—you know, 'Prepare for the Angel of Death'? That's why I phoned you."

Hochburg had been prolific. "Hold on to it. We'll want to check it for prints." They'd have a collection soon—the Angel of Death letters. Jessie could visualize the headlines. The letters would probably make the best-seller list.

"I tried not to handle the letter or the envelope," Rita said. "God, I can't believe it's over! Who was arrested?"

"Samuel Hochburg. I can't give you details now. Maybe later."

"I don't really care. All I want to do is get out of the city and ride into the foothills. I wish it were Friday."

That sounded pretty damn good to Jessie. "I don't blame you."

"Why don't you join me sometime? I have two horses."

"My riding is rusty, but I may take you up on that."

"I hope you will. Thanks for calling. I appreciate it."

After Jessie hung up, she went to see Hochburg. He was sitting on the bunk bed in his cell. He rose when he saw her.

"You wanted to see me?" she said through the bright orange metal grillwork.

"I just want to say I'm sorry. I hope I didn't hurt you."

"I'll survive." The back of her head throbbed in protest.

"I did what I had to do. I know you can't understand."

She didn't want Hochburg talking, not after he'd already asked to see a lawyer. A confession made now could be thrown out in court. "Mr. Hochburg, your attorney's on the way. When he arrives, we'll talk to you."

Hochburg nodded and returned to the bunk bed.

Jessie was soaking in a jasmine-scented bubble bath when the phone rang. She debated letting the answering machine take the call, but after three rings she reached for the cordless receiver on the bath mat.

It was Gary. "Just wanted to make sure you're all right," he told her. "I saw you on the tube on the six o'clock news. Is it true the butcher threw a side of beef at you?"

"Yes."

"What were you doing, filming *Dancing with Steers*?"

"Ha, ha. Brenda saw me, too." She'd also teased Jessie about the carcass. Everybody, apparently, found the episode funny, except her mother and sister. Frances had said, "Thank goodness you're all right!" and then, "Why a person with your talents insists on keeping such a dangerous job, your father and I will never know." Helen had been predictably hysterical, her anger at Jessie forgotten—at least for the moment.

"Aside from a bump on my head, I'm fine," Jessie told Gary.

"The bump knock some sense into you?"

"Not yet." She smiled and blew a triangle of bubbles.

"So what can you tell me about Samuel Hochburg?"

"Is that why you called?" She felt a flash of disappointment.

"It's my job. So?"

"Nothing you didn't hear on TV."

"Hochburg say anything?"

"He isn't talking, per his lawyer's advice."

"Smart lawyer. Is it true Hochburg was running with the knife he used to decapitate Benning and tried to stab you with it?"

God, the rumors that got started! "Hochburg never tried to stab me. We're running tests on the knives in the butcher shop, including the one he grabbed. The lab tests can take days."

"What about the judge? Any evidence linking Hochburg to her?"

"Not yet. I'll be working on that tomorrow."

"What about the bomb that killed Lewis?"

"No comment." She had no intention of telling Gary that Hochburg was experienced with explosives.

"How about getting together Saturday night?"

"I told you, Gary. I can't talk about it." If her ex-husband was anything, he was persistent.

"Dinner and a movie?"

"Is this a bribe?"

"It's whatever you want it to be," he said, his tone suddenly different.

Her heart beat faster. "You said you wanted me to figure it all out first."

"I decided you might need a little help."

She heard a beep on the phone. "Hold on, okay?" She depressed the Flash button. "Hello?"

"Are you all right?" Frank asked. "I left a message on your machine. Didn't you get it?" The concern in his voice was tinged with irritation.

"I'm fine, thanks. I was going to phone you back, but everybody's been calling. My mom, Helen." Gary.

"How about getting together Saturday night?"

"What happened to your cold?"

"It cleared up."

"What about Sunday and the museum, then?"

He was silent for a moment, then said, "The truth? I'm not comfortable going yet. Maybe in a few weeks. . . . So how about Saturday night, Jess?"

"I can't, Frank. I have other plans."

"You're mad, aren't you? I thought you'd appreciate my honesty."

"I'm not mad, and I *do* appreciate your honesty. And I really *do* have other plans."

The static crackled on the phone. "Okay. Give me a call?"

She started to say, "I will"—it was easier than telling him what she'd admitted to herself before falling asleep last night—that there was little more to their relationship than a shared interest in police work and sex. That although he was a tender lover who had eased her loneliness, it wasn't enough for her. That he had no soul.

"I don't think so, Frank," she said.

"We have a lot going for us, Jess. We can work this out."

"I'm sorry, Frank. Take care of yourself," she added, not knowing how else to say good-bye. She pressed Flash again, relieved to break off the phone connection. "Are you still there, Gary?"

They agreed that he would pick her up at seven on Saturday night. She hung up, put the receiver on the mat, and sank into the bubbles.

Friday morning, while Phil pursued another lead on the call girl murder, Jessie faxed a mug shot of Hochburg to the Palm Springs PD; a detective would show it to Judge Williams's neighbors. She'd finished transmitting the facsimile when she saw her name on the cover sheet of an incoming message.

It was from North Hollywood Division. Eleven pages. She skimmed the top one as she walked to her desk, then read through the report. It provided more details and grim photos and added two facts that Dafna and Ezra had neglected to mention:

The neo-Nazi group suspected of starting the deadly fire had called themselves the White Warriors. The group had subsequently disbanded. One of the members questioned by detectives on the case was Roy Benning. Another person questioned—not a member, but a friend who gave Benning an alibi—was Emery Kraft.

Kraft had mentioned "an earlier grudge"; naturally, he hadn't revealed how he'd known about it—being associated with cross burnings would tarnish his nonracist image. It was clear, too, why he suspected Ben-Natan of writing the Angel of Death letters.

It was possible, of course, that this was coincidence, that Nathanson and Ben-Natan weren't aware that Benning had belonged to the neo-Nazi group and that Kraft had given him an alibi. Detectives, as a rule, don't share information with citizens. Even if the brothers *did* know about Benning and Kraft, that didn't prove anything. They were hardly about to volunteer the information to Jessie and draw suspicion to themselves.

Jessie pulled the blue book for Lewis's investigation and thumbed through it until she found Ben-Natan's rap sheet. She scanned it but found no reference to Benning in any of Ben-Natan's arrests.

What if the brothers *did* know? Had Benning's involvement with the parade and Mrs. Hochburg's death revived old wounds? Who bore the grudge, Ben-Natan or Nathanson?

Or both? Had the twins, so different in ideology, been united by revenge?

She reminded herself that Hochburg had a more recent motive. He was experienced with explosives. He'd tried to escape arrest.

On a blank sheet of paper, Jessie wrote, "Ben-Natan, black Explorer" and the license plate number she'd accessed earlier from the DMV. From her notepad, she copied the license number Nathanson had given her for his Nissan Maxima. She could fax the Palm Springs police the descriptions and license numbers of the brothers' cars and have them ask the judge's neighbors whether they'd seen either vehicle.

She decided to verify Nathanson's number. At the computer she accessed Driver's License Files in the DMV system, then typed Nathanson's name. Seconds later the screen showed a replica of his driver's license.

She scanned the screen and was startled by the last entry: on Wednesday, April 25, Nathanson had received a traffic citation issued by a Riverside County Court.

April 25 was nine days ago. Two days before Barry Lewis was killed. According to the Palm Springs police, Judge Williams had probably died on Wednesday.

Palm Springs was in Riverside County.

Another coincidence?

Her palms tingling, she returned to her desk. She phoned the Riverside County Court, gave the clerk the citation number, and learned that a California Highway Patrol officer had stopped Ezra Nathanson for speeding on the westbound Interstate 10 near Banning at 5:38 P.M. Banning was just west of Palm Springs.

She phoned Rabbi Korbin at the Wiesenthal.

"More names, Detective Drake?" he asked in a jovial tone.

"No. Why didn't you tell me that Ezra Nathanson was Joel Ben-Natan's twin brother? And that Adele, Herman, and Carol Nathanson were killed by a fire allegedly started by a neo-Nazi group? You must have known. The ADL would've known, too."

"I told you I didn't know Ezra Nathanson because it's true. We've never met. I—we—assumed you'd find out for yourself that he and Joel Ben-Natan were twins, just as we assumed you'd find out about the tragic deaths of their family. We didn't want to point the finger at Ben-Natan."

"*Lashon hara?*"

"Yes. 'The evil tongue.' It would have made him more suspect—unfairly, as you see, now that Mr. Hochburg has been arrested." He sighed. "This is a terrible tragedy for the entire community."

"One other thing, Rabbi. If I give you an English date, can you give me the Hebrew calendar equivalent?"

"I have a book that tabulates exactly that. But I'd need the year as well as the month and day. The Jewish calendar is based on a lunar cycle, unlike the Gregorian, which is solar."

"It's September twelfth, five years ago."

"Is that the date of the Nathanson tragedy?"

"Yes, it is."

A pause. Then, "Hold on, please." A few minutes later Korbin was back on the line. "Five years ago, September twelfth came out on the ninth day of the Hebrew month of Tishrei. After sundown, that would be the tenth day."

"Oh." Not exactly what she'd expected. She had no idea what Tishrei was or whether it had any significance.

"The tenth day of Tishrei is the first day of Yom Kippur."

That was what she'd expected. Judgment Day.

Who shall live, who shall die?

Espes was with the watch commander. Jessie picked up the phone to call Kraft, then remembered he was busy with a HIT meeting. She phoned the ACLU office.

"Miss Warrens is at her ranch, Detective," the receptionist said. "Honestly, I'm glad. She needs a break from all the calls she's been getting about the arrest in the Lewis murder."

"Do you have her phone number at the ranch? It's urgent that I speak with her." *Was* it urgent? Or was it a strange coincidence? "If you want to verify who I am, call me back at the station."

"No, that's all right." She gave Jessie the information.

"Thank you." When she finished writing in her notepad, she said, "You mentioned that a lot of people have been calling since the arrest. What did you tell them?"

"That Miss Warrens has left for the weekend."

And according to Rita, almost everyone knew that she went to the ranch whenever she could. Jessie thanked the woman, hung up, and phoned the ranch. No one answered.

She phoned Ohr Torah. Shulamit Cohn told her that Ezra Nathanson had canceled his classes for personal reasons.

"He's distraught about Mr. Hochburg's arrest," Shulamit told Jessie. "We all are."

Nathanson wasn't at home. Jessie listened to twelve rings before she gave up.

She phoned Ben-Natan's residence.

"Yoel is not here, Detective Drake," Yaffa Aloni told Jessie in a surly tone. No, she had no idea where he was or how to reach him. "Do you want to leave a message?"

"I'll call back. Is that his dogs' barking I hear in the background?"

"No. Yoel took the dogs with him. He usually does. What barking? I don't hear anything."

"Sorry. It must be on my line."

Who by beast?

Chapter Forty-six

Espes was still meeting with the watch commander. Phil was in the field. Jessie told another detective and the desk sergeant where she was going and left a note on Phil's desk.

Rita Warrens's ranch was about an hour's drive in light traffic. Jessie could cut the time considerably if she used her siren, but she had no justification for doing so. In fact, as she drove north along the San Diego Freeway, she wondered what she was doing. The alleged Angel of Death—Hochburg—was in a jail cell; the proof against him, cemented by his attempt to flee, was convincing—far more convincing than Jessie's suspicions about the twin brothers. The traffic citation *could* be coincidence.

She merged with the traffic onto the Golden State, then five minutes later turned right onto the rebuilt Antelope Valley Freeway. She hadn't been here since a major section of the highway had collapsed during the Northridge quake, and she flashed briefly to the grim newspaper photo of the motorcycle cop who had been riding to work at four o'clock on that fateful morning and plummeted to his death. Unconsciously, she accelerated and didn't release the pedal until she had passed the reconstructed section.

Another time she would have paid attention to the stark beauty of the San Gabriel Mountains rising on either side of the multilane highway. Now she was intent on reaching Rita Warrens. She'd tried Rita's number several times, but no one had answered.

She exited at Santiago Road, south of Palmdale. Palmdale, she knew, abutted the Angeles National Forest and lay directly over the San Andreas Fault. Nature's beauty, nature's seismic beast. All around Jessie were brush and chaparral and sculpted rocks that looked as if they'd been tossed down haphazardly by God to dot the landscape.

Santiago Road became Old Miner Road as it passed under the freeway, then Santiago again. She turned left onto a paved street that soon became a winding, bumpy dirt path. She passed two shacks, no doubt abandoned years ago by prospectors who had given up their dream. The earth was brown and ungiving. The air was hot and dry and dusty; Jessie raised the windows and turned on the air-conditioning and tried not to think about what the road was doing to the Honda's shocks.

Five hundred feet ahead of her was the ranch. The main building was a modest one-story with white-painted wood siding. To the left was a corral. Behind it was a smaller structure, probably the stable. About half a mile away were the foothills where Rita Warrens had told Jessie she loved to ride.

There were two cars in the circular driveway. One of them was a black Ford Explorer. Jessie parked up the road, out of sight of anyone in the house. She decided to check out the house before radioing for local reinforcements and walked back to the ranch. As she approached the Explorer, she was assaulted by the furious barking of the Dobermans in the back seat.

They saw her, too. Their intensified barking terrified her as she peered inside the car. No sign of Ben-Natan. The dogs slammed against the rear window, then the side windows, their frenzy so intense that Jessie was certain the glass would shatter any second. She moved quickly to the hood of the car. It was warm to her touch, but not hot; she estimated that the engine had been off for about twenty minutes. She told herself the Dobermans couldn't escape—Ben-Natan had left only an inch of open space between the top of each side window and the car's roof to give them air—but she glanced over her shoulder every five seconds, and her heart was pumping madly when she reached the house.

Hugging the walls, her gun held downward, she made her way around the perimeter of the house, looking through windows. She strained to hear whether anyone was inside, but the insistent howling of the dogs drowned out all sound.

She broke the lock on a back door and entered through a bedroom. Moving with practiced caution, crouching as she approached doorways, she swept the house, room by room. She called Rita's name several times. She found no one inside, no signs of a violent confrontation.

Where was Rita?

And where were Ben-Natan and Nathanson?

The corral was empty. Her gun still cocked, Jessie hurried to the stable and entered. A dappled horse in the right stall neighed, then whinnied and paced in the confined space. In the distance, she heard the dogs yelp. Then silence.

The stall to the left was vacant. Had Rita gone riding into the foothills? Had the brothers followed her?

Jessie was about to leave the stable when she heard moaning. Glancing down, she spotted a pair of legs on the straw-covered floor of the empty stall. She crossed quickly to the stall's half door and yanked it open.

Ben-Natan—or Nathanson—was lying on his side, his knees bent to his chest. Jessie crouched near him.

"Ben-Natan?"

His eyes flickered open. He groaned. "The cavalry arrives."

It *was* Ben-Natan. His hair was a little darker than his brother's, his eyes more intense. "What happened?" she asked.

"Hit from behind." He lifted his hand, touched the back of his head, and winced. It was bloody. "I guess I'll live."

"Where's Miss Warrens?"

"Don't know." He raised his head, groaned again, and rested it on the ground. "She called this morning, asked me to meet her here at eleven. Something about a connection Benning hinted at between the fire that killed my parents and Carol and Lewis's and Benning's murders. She wanted to talk to me before she went to the police. When I got here, she wasn't in the house."

Was that connection Nathanson? "So you came to the stable?"

He nodded. "The door was open. I heard horse sounds. When I walked in, someone hit me. That's the last I remember."

"Where's your brother?"

"Teaching, I guess. Why?"

"Did you tell him you were coming here?" She hadn't seen a black Nissan Maxima. He must have turned onto a side road and left the car there, then walked to the ranch.

Ben-Natan didn't answer. His eyes spoke for him. "That's crazy," he finally said. "Ezra wouldn't hit me. And he had nothing to do with the murders. Where are my dogs?" he asked suddenly.

"In your car. They're fine." Ben-Natan was bruised but not in critical danger, she decided. "Stay here and don't move around. You may have a concussion. I'll be back soon."

"Where are you going?" he called, but she was out the door.

She knew she should radio for assistance, but in going back to her car, she would lose precious time. She ran at a steady clip, ignoring the cacophony of Ben-Natan's howling dogs, trying not to inhale the dust that rose like a cloud as her feet pounded the ground. Five minutes later the flat road ended, and she was on an incline on a narrow path that entered the foothills. Canyon country.

To her left was a hillock that soon became a hill, then a reddish brown mountain. Brush sprang up here and there in its crevices. The path twisted left, then right, then left again.

"Miss Warrens?" she yelled. "Rita?"

Her voice was swallowed by the silence.

She continued running, her legs tiring from the uphill exertion, and forced herself not to look to her right, where there was no mountain, only empty space beyond a drop that was becoming longer and more sheer with every turn.

She heard what sounded like a crack, and a horse's neighing, muffled by distance. Then a scream.

She ran faster, hugging the left side of the path, her pants scraping against the brush. Her throat was parched. Her ears were pounding.

Another crack.

The horse neighed again. Another crack, but it wasn't a crack, it was a bark, and she knew what she should have known all along, knew even before she twisted with the path and saw him standing on a mountain ledge that it wasn't Ezra Nathanson.

The German shepherd was at the foot of the mountain, barking at a chestnut roan whose flank was toward Jessie. Rita was clinging to the horse, her arms around his neck. The roan neighed again, panic emerging from his throat, and reared wildly, his back almost vertical as he tossed her to the ground.

The dog scampered to the ledge. Rita lay immobile in the middle of the path. The horse, forelegs still in midair, pivoted until he was facing Jessie. The legs came down a foot away from Rita's head. The horse reared again.

"Run, Detective, run!" Emery Kraft sneered.

Rolf growled at Jessie and strained against his leash.

"I'll shoot!" With her gun in her left hand and her eyes on Kraft and the dog, she ran to Rita, groped for her arm, and dragged her away just before the enormous forelegs stomped the ground.

The roan reared again and advanced toward Rita. Jessie pulled the unconscious woman farther out of the horse's way. The horse's legs came down. With an abrupt motion, he reversed direction and, with his tail, knocked Jessie to the ground and galloped up the path. The gun skittered ten feet away.

Kraft released Rolf's leash and drew a gun from his jacket. The dog growled and bounded off the ledge toward Jessie. Her blood rushing in her head, she scrambled for her weapon. The dog was nearing. She could feel his heat, see the lust in his eyes. Her hand touched metal.

A Doberman flew past her and tackled the German shepherd. The other Doberman dove at Kraft, knocked him down onto the ledge, and sank his teeth into the man's wrist. The gun fell from his hand.

"Rolf!" Kraft's scream was part agony, part command.

Jessie's hands closed around her gun.

The German shepherd broke away and charged his master's attacker. The other Doberman chased after his prey. The three were locked in loud, ferocious combat that ended when the German shepherd fell to the ground. The Dobermans straddled him. Kraft raised himself to his elbow and reached for his gun.

"Don't!" Jessie stood with her feet apart and aimed at him.

One of the Dobermans barked and raced toward Kraft as Ben-Natan staggered into view, holding his hand to his chest.

"It's Kraft!" Jessie told him. "Call off your dog!"

"Why?" His breath was ragged. His chest was heaving.

The dog lunged at Kraft's throat. Kraft shrieked.

"Ometz, lishmor!" Ben-Natan shouted.

The Doberman froze on top of Kraft. "Please!" the man whispered. "Please!" Ten feet away, Rolf was whimpering.

Twin dogs avenging twin brothers. "What command did you give him?" she asked Ben-Natan, her heart still pounding furiously.

" 'Guard.' I'll probably regret it," he said, his eyes on Kraft. He turned to Jessie. "I guess I'm not the beast you thought I was."

Chapter Forty-seven

"So why'd they do it?" Espes asked, leaning across his desk.

"Benning was going to implicate Kraft in murder," Jessie said. "In exchange for having charges dropped against him in the death of Lola Hochburg, he was going to provide us with evidence that Kraft was involved with setting the fire that killed the Nathansons. Benning told his wife. Grace told Kraft."

Jessie had conjectured most of it on the long drive from Palmdale to Long Beach, where she'd stopped before returning to West L.A. Gene Oppman had provided corroboration—reluctantly—and given her the manila envelope he'd taken from Roy Benning's tote bag after Jessie had informed him that Benning had been killed.

At the West L.A. station, Jessie had read the handwritten pages in which Benning accused Kraft of burning the cross five years ago and of blowing up Lewis with the pipe bomb. Benning denied involvement with the fire or the bomb. The envelope had also contained a tape of a conversation in which Kraft discussed having set the fire and promised to protect Benning if the police arrested him. Clearly, Benning hadn't trusted Kraft even then.

"Kraft didn't alibi Benning," Jessie added when she finished. "Benning alibied Kraft."

"So the kid knew it was Kraft." Phil drummed his fingers on his knee, then reached for the coffee mug he'd placed near the edge of Espes's desk.

"He won't admit that. He says Benning just told him that he had a plan to stay out of jail and that he'd made a mistake in telling his wife about it. My guess is Gene knew, but he was torn between his friendship with Benning, who was dead, and his hatred of Jews and admiration for Kraft." A mixed-up kid, Gene Oppman.

"So Benning was hiding from Kraft?" Espes stood, walked around his desk, and leaned against it.

Jessie nodded. "And from Grace. Benning tells her he's turning Kraft in—the next thing he knows, Barry Lewis is killed. Benning panicked."

"Why did Kraft kill Lewis?"

"My guess?" She recrossed her legs, still stiff from running. More than anything, she wanted to take a hot shower. "Kraft wasn't sure who Benning talked to. Probably to Lewis—he was Benning's attorney, after all. Also to Rita Warrens—Grace knew that Benning had called her a couple of times. Grace even tried to sound me out about it."

"Did Benning tell Rita about Kraft?"

Jessie shook her head. "Rita told me he was worried about something, wanted to know if he could trust Lewis to represent him fairly, because he was Jewish and Benning was involved with HIT and the White Alliance."

Espes nodded, then frowned. "Why kill the judge? Benning had no contact with her."

"Smoke screen. Kraft could blame all the deaths on Ben-Natan. That's why he chose the 'who-shall-live?' pattern from the Jewish prayer."

"How would Kraft know about that?" Phil asked.

Jessie turned to her partner. "Nathanson told me Kraft's father is rumored to be Jewish." She faced Espes again. "Or he could've done research."

"So who vandalized the Lewis house?" Espes asked. "Hochburg?"

Jessie shook her head. "We know he wrote the letter to Benning. And he may have written the second one to Lewis, the one Sheila gave me. I think Morris Lewis was the original Angel of Death. He was trying to scare his son, to get him to drop the White Alliance case."

"Too bad it didn't work," Phil said quietly, and took a sip of coffee.

"Too bad," she agreed. She felt terribly sad for the seventy-year-old Holocaust survivor. He would probably forever blame himself in some measure for his son's death. She still wasn't sure why he'd taken the doll house to his son at ten o'clock at night, knowing that his granddaughters weren't there, and sat in his car in the driveway. A gesture of reconciliation?

"Morris Lewis writes a letter," Phil said. "Hochburg writes one or two. Who wrote the others?"

"Kraft. He sent one to Judge Williams and to Rita Warrens. And to himself, of course."

"I understand Kraft's motivation," Espes said. "But why did Grace Benning help him?"

"According to Gene, she hated Benning. She hated Jews. Maybe she and Kraft had something going on." Jessie shrugged. "Also, she stood to inherit a lot of money as Benning's beneficiary."

"I'll bet Miss Grace was surprised to see you show up instead of Kraft, huh?" Phil smiled broadly.

"Kind of." Jessie grinned.

She and a uniformed policeman had found Grace in Kraft's Mercedes on a street off Santiago Road. The policeman had arrested Grace. She and Emery Kraft, whose hand had been treated and bandaged, were now in jail cells in Acton, the town closest to Rita's ranch, pending their transfer to West L.A. Kraft had refused to say anything to Jessie or to the two police who had driven him and a muzzled Rolf away.

The ACLU director was in a Palmdale hospital for observation. She'd regained consciousness by the time the paramedics had arrived with a stretcher, and though she'd suffered a minor concussion, the doctors had told Jessie they were confident Rita would be all right. Jessie had talked to her before returning to L.A. That had been over four hours ago. Now Jessie was in Espes's office, tired but exhilarated.

"Kraft phoned Rita late yesterday afternoon and told her he had to speak with her about something confidential," Jessie said. "She told him she'd be at the ranch from Friday through the weekend—she didn't suspect him, remember, because Hochburg had been arrested for the murders—and that she'd be riding all morning. He said he loved riding, too, and asked her what kind of trails she rode."

"Clever son of a bitch," Phil said.

"Definitely. Anyway, Rita said she'd be back around eleven-thirty. This morning Grace Benning, posing as Rita, told Ben-Natan to meet her at the ranch at eleven."

"Ben-Natan didn't recognize her voice?" Espes asked.

"Ben-Natan had never spoken to Grace, and he wasn't familiar with Rita's voice—he called her office enough times, but he did the talking. She basically listened. Ben-Natan arrived at the ranch. Kraft knocked him out."

"I still don't see how Kraft was going to pin this on Ben-Natan. What if the guy came to and just drove away?"

"The Acton police received a call at ten-thirty from a woman who identified herself as Rita Warrens. She reported a black Ford Explorer that seemed to be loitering in front of her house, and gave the police the license plate number. A few minutes later she called again and said the car was gone. I found a paper in the Mercedes with Ben-Natan's license plate number," Jessie added.

"They had it all figured out." Phil shook his head. "Hey! What happened to the horse?"

Jessie smiled. "He returned to his stable before the ambulance arrived. Ben-Natan calmed him down. On the way back from Palmdale, I stopped by the ranch next to Rita's and spoke to the owner—he takes care of her horses when she's in the city. He noticed the Explorer, too, by the way."

"And Nathanson's traffic citation was just coincidence." Phil shook his head. "Go figure."

"So that's it, huh?" Espes resumed his seat behind the desk. "Write it all up."

"What about the kid?" Phil frowned. "We just let it go?"

Jessie had given Gene Oppman a great deal of thought, too. "I told him we could charge him with tampering with evidence and withholding information. Scared the hell out of him."

"You mean thing, you." Phil smiled and shook his head.

"I think we should offer him a choice—we arrest him, or he agrees to get an education."

"What kind of education?" Espes squinted in puzzlement.

"He goes to the Museum of Tolerance. He talks to survivors. I'll call Rabbi Korbin—I'm sure he'd be happy to set up a program. And I'll walk Gene through the museum myself." Frank, she'd decided, would probably never want to go. And Helen? Gary had said to give her time; Manny had said the same thing.

"Think it'll make a difference?" Phil asked.

"I don't know. I sure as hell hope so."

There was a knock on the door.

"Come in," Espes said.

Another detective poked his head in. "Call for you, Phil."

"Coming." Phil stood and left the room.

"I'll have a report on your desk before I leave." Jessie stood and walked to the door. Damn, she was tired.

"Hey, Drake."

She turned to face Espes.

"It's late," he said. "Have your report ready Monday morning."

"Thanks. I appreciate it."

He nodded. "You think I'm a hard son of a bitch, don't you?"

Did he want truth or flattery? "Sometimes."

"Sometimes I am. Nice work."

"Thanks again." She smiled.

"Don't let it go to your head." Espes was smiling, too.

Samuel Hochburg was twenty feet ahead of Jessie as she walked out of the station. Accompanying him was a brown-haired woman. The daughter-in-law?

"Mr. Hochburg!" Jessie called.

The butcher and the woman stopped and turned around.

"They said I was free," Hochburg said when Jessie was standing next to him. He sounded anxious. "They said this Kraft was the killer."

"You *are* free. I just wanted to say . . ." What the hell *did* she want to say? "I'm sorry for everything you've gone through. I'm glad it's over for you."

Hochburg nodded.

"Can I ask you something? Why did you take the knife and run?"

"The knife was there, so I took it. I wasn't thinking. Why did I run?" he repeated softly. "Fifty years ago, German police came to our house. They had questions for my father. They had papers, too. They took him from the house. My mother and I followed. My mother was crying, begging them to let my father go. One of the men took a gun and calmly shot my father in the head. 'Now you can stop crying, Jewish dog,' he said.

"So *you* tell *me*, Detective, why did I run?"

On Saturday night, as Jessie opened the front door, she felt a flutter of nervousness and wondered whether this was a mistake after all, whether it wasn't safer to stay friends. But her nervousness disappeared the moment she saw him slouching against the doorpost, his hands in his pants pockets. A grin on his face.

You look beautiful, he said.

You look nice, she said.

He kissed her lightly on the mouth, then pulled her close and kissed her again. "Ready to go?" he asked.

"I want to show you something first." She took his hand and led him down the hall. "It's in the bedroom."

"Aren't we rushing things? It's our first date."

She wasn't looking at him, but she could imagine his smile. When they were in the room, she pointed to the wall over her desk.

"It came today. My mom sent it. She had it enlarged."

He leaned closer. "This is the photo you told me about?"

She nodded and pointed to the center. "That's my grandfather. His name was Yaakov Kochinsky." Her finger moved to the woman standing next to him. "That's my grandmother, Yiska. And that's my mom." Jessie pointed to the little girl with the golden braids.

"This is beautiful, Jessie. It says a lot that Frances sent it to you." His arm went around her.

"I know. I called and thanked her and told her how much it meant to me. She said something like 'I know you'd be pestering me about it, Jessica.' " She smiled. "But I swear I heard a catch in her voice. I told her I didn't remember the names of all the people in the photo, and she said she'd tell me about them sometime." She also intended to borrow the book about Tchebin from the Wiesenthal, the one Rabbi Korbin had mentioned. Maybe her mother would be willing to look at it, someday. "I asked her if she named me for my grandmother. 'Jessica' is 'Yiska' in Hebrew."

"Did she?"

"She didn't answer right away. Then she said yes."

Gary studied the photo a moment longer, then looked down at the desk. "What's that?" He pointed to a box next to a sheet of torn wrapping paper. "More gifts?"

Jessie opened the box and held up an oblong hammered-silver cylinder.

"It's a *mezuzah.*" Gary sounded puzzled.

"Ezra Nathanson dropped it off yesterday at the station while I was in Long Beach. There was a note thanking me for saving his brother." The note had added, ". . . and for helping defeat Amalek."

She turned the *mezuzah* case over. "The parchment's inside. Ezra included a copy of the blessing you say when you put the *mezuzah* on the door. The Hebrew's transliterated into English." She turned the case over again. "It's beautiful, isn't it?"

Gary nodded. "Why do you think he gave it to you?"

"I was admiring the *mezuzot* in his sister's store. And Joel Ben-Natan told me every Jewish home should have one." She smiled.

"Is this a Jewish home?" His tone was light. His eyes were gazing at her intently.

"I'm interested in learning about Judaism. I'm thinking about taking some classes in Jewish history, maybe a beginner's Hebrew class." She glanced at him to see his reaction.

Gary took the mezuzah case from her hand. He held it a moment, then said, "Want me to help you put it up?"

She smiled. "I'd like that very much."